THE TIGER AND THE DOVE
A TRILOGY

BOOK ONE

THE GRIP OF GOD

by
Rebecca Hazell

IM • PRESS

ACKNOWLEDGEMENTS

I would like to thank every historian, alive or deceased, who traced the culture and history of Kyivan Rus', of the Mongols, of Iran and China and even of Tibet. Without their thoughtful research, this trilogy would be no more than a haunting dream stuck in my imagination. In the present day, I would like to thank my first editor, Iris Bass, for insisting I think big; Professors Trudy Sable, Ruth Whitehead, and Peter Conradi for their encouragement and advice; linguist Vlad Zhurba, who helped me with ancient Ukrainian names and spellings; my many manuscript readers; and my husband Mark, who tirelessly read and re-read my seemingly endless revisions.

Book Cover Image Credit: Wikimedia User Shakko
Book Cover Design by Elisabeth Hazell

DEDICATION

This trilogy is dedicated to Sakyong Mipham Rinpoche

This novel is dedicated to my beloved husband Mark

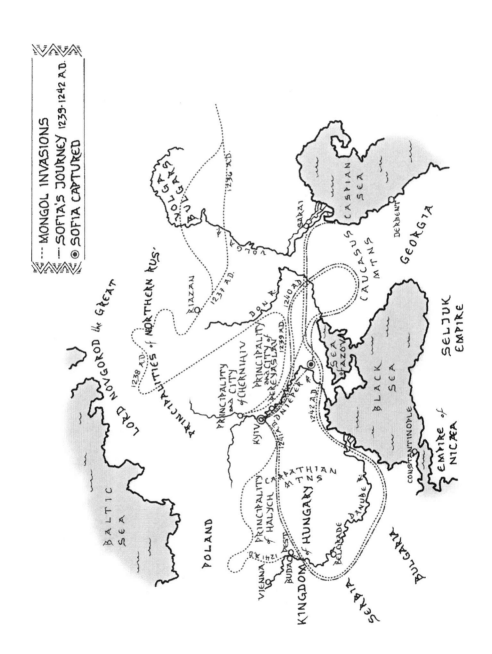

If you had not committed great sins,
God would not have sent punishment like me upon you.
—Chinggis Khan

"No eye remained open to weep for the dead."
—a Rus' chronicle of the Mongol invasions

When I was a child, I spoke as a child, I understood as a child, I
thought as a child ..."
—I Cor. xiii. 11

June 14, Anno Domini 1263

Beloved Daughter,

How could I ever forget telling you about my childhood in Rus'? It was as much a delight to me as to you. And yes, miraculously, I still have the book that you saw when you were small, and I did indeed say I would give it to you when you turned twelve.

What I did not say then was that it was not intended for you at first: I was both translating my first journal from the tongue of Rus' and adding to it. I didn't know why, perhaps to make sense of my life. When I was a child, I used to tell my Papa stories about little things, and I had begun that journal at just your age, thinking to use it one day to tell him about a journey I had made without him.

But after disaster befell me and then my homeland, I made life bearable by turning woe into story. The book you ask for is only the first of three, a long account of a long journey, not only of miles and years but of the heart. After all that has befallen us recently, you have a right to know how we got where we are, so far from home and everything familiar. Like me, you had to become a woman almost overnight.

And since time passes so swiftly and life is so fragile, I send all three journals to you now and pray to be at your wedding in Paris next year.

My love is always with you.
Mother

OCTOBER TO NOVEMBER, Anno Domini 1239

The night before I set my fate in motion, the wind blew a foretaste of winter through cracks in the palace walls and I lost sleep trying to elude it under my quilts. I finally drifted into uneasy dreams—Domovik's hairy hand was brushing across mine, a sign of trouble coming—when shouts and spears pounding at our gates startled me awake.

Old Baba Liubyna sat up from her pallet with a snort and cried, "We are under attack!"

I rushed to the terem window to see. Dawn's handmaidens were just parting the curtains of the sky and turning the world red and gold. Below, our sentries had admitted a handful of horsemen into the courtyard, though the isinglass windowpanes transformed them into filmy specters. I turned to my nursemaid. "There is no attack!"

But of course she had to see for herself, and then to order me to dress in all possible haste. "Something is up, and your father may need you." What she really meant was that she, not I, should have the upper hand.

Well, we would see who was the princess and who was the servant. I would decide what to do for myself! But all I could think of was to call for Kateryna. I flung open my door only to find my slave already standing there, trembling as usual like a dark mouse.

"Go downstairs and see what is happening," I ordered.

Before Liubyna had finished dressing me, Kateryna was back. "Their banner belongs to the city of Chernihiv, Princess. The envoy spoke to the Prince and left."

I sighed. Slave girls just didn't know the right questions to ask. Impatient to hear more, I hurried down to see for myself, Baba Liubyna calling after me, "Sofia, you must act with proper dignity!"

In the Great Hall, tinted blood red by the rising sun streaming through the windows, Papa was sending out his own messengers. "Daughter, there you are! Guests arrive soon for a most important meeting, and you must greet them. Speak to Cook about food and drink; we may need to slaughter extra meat for the midday meal. Have the Great Hall readied and see to all the stoves." One of his stewards claimed him, and he was gone.

"Most important" and "guests" must mean Prince Mikhail of Chernihiv, the Grand Prince of Kyivan Rus', since those messengers had been from his city and he was the most important guest I could imagine. Satisfied with my own answers and feeling most important myself, I ordered slaves to fetch more wood for the stoves, lay fresh straw on the Great Hall floor, and sprinkle it with rosemary before hastening to the kitchen to tell Cook and the staff to bring out our best wine and mead and special delicacies.

That done, I rushed upstairs to change into my blue silk gown and gold brocade tunic trimmed with sable. This much Baba Liubyna allowed. But when I told Kateryna to bring out my bejeweled koruna and my Mama's pearl and ruby collar, Liubyna said, "Don't be a silly. You needn't dress that finely," which led to the usual quarrel about why she still treated me like a child. Though I won, it was at the expense of my good humor and too much time.

When I finally returned to the Great Hall, Papa was gone. Not knowing when his guests would arrive, I had to stand alone at its entrance, waiting. He returned only when the sun was past her zenith, dressed in his state robes of gold and red brocade, his heavy cross hanging from his neck, his belt glittering with jewels, and his wolfhound Swiftwind trotting by his side. But he merely glanced at me, strode to the fire, and stared into it while my stomach growled and my feet ached.

The first two men to arrive were petty boyars, one a broad-faced buffoon called Witty Boris. After exchanging bows and greetings and receiving the cross from me to kiss, Boris openly leered at me. As he passed on, he said to his friend, "What a luscious morsel. She used to be a skinny little stick—now I'd gladly stick it into her! I'd offer for her today if our mighty prince would accept me." His friend laughed knowingly.

How my cheeks burned. I was barely twelve, beginning to blossom into womanhood, and proud of the way my Viking, Slav, and Turkish blood had produced "hair the color of flames, eyes as green as moss, and cheekbones curved like eagle's wings." That praise came from a mysterious love poem I had found recently. I could not imagine who had written it to me. Not Witty Boris! That lecherous old cock was unfit to touch my shoes. At least when he and his companion saw Papa standing by the fire, rigid as a spear, their laughter died on their lips—the last of that afternoon for us all.

Papa's cousins by marriage arrived soon thereafter, and on their boot heels came more boyars as well as Papa's senior warriors. I welcomed them and led them to their places, hiding my impatience to greet Grand Prince Mikhail, who surely must ride up with his retinue soon. And then Papa signed to me that everyone had arrived!

Worse, instead of speaking with them in the Great Hall where I could listen in as usual, he said, "Come," and led the men toward his quarters.

"Sofia, once you are done here, find your tutor," he added as he swept by, Swiftwind at his heels. "Or el se your nursemaid. She'll set you some task." I bowed obediently as the men filed out after him, faces grim as war axes, voices rumbling like falling stones. The Hall's heavy door thudded shut, leaving me alone while the tread of men filing up the stone stairs echoed down mockingly.

Servants began entering the Hall to set up for supper; too late now for dinner. I should have overseen them, but I burned with such fury that I forgot. Instead, I marched over and glared at the closed door. Why could a dog go with Papa and I could not? I wanted to shout and stamp my feet, but I remembered in time how unseemly that would be.

Taking a deep breath to calm myself, I had to ask the hard question: why, with no Grand Prince Mikhail, had Papa dressed so finely for this ill-assorted gathering? I imagined him seated on his great carven chair, his ruby earring glinting in the light from the tiled stove and the men clustered around him like leaves clinging to the strong branch. What could the hasty messenger's news be? It could not be good.

I dragged myself out to the small room set aside for my studies. Happily it was empty, and hope briefly flared. Alexander might be in Papa's book room. Perhaps, if I went quietly through Papa's chambers instead of the terem to look for him, I might hear something.... But I dared not intrude on the meeting. I must wait for supper. With a tongue loosened by wine, someone would surely spill the news into my ears—

Oh dear, I should be directing the servants in the Great Hall! What kind of mistress of the household was I? I rushed back into the Hall, ready to issue commands, but the long tables and benches already sat in place, the carved armchairs waited at the head table on the dais. Well, at least I could get some bread and cheese from the kitchen.

That done, I wandered back to the Great Hall. I knew I should join Baba Liubyna and the other women in domestic tasks, but after the day's disappointments I had no heart for anything useful. And I loved the Hall with its massive stone walls, its pillars carved with sacred symbols, its ceiling of polished tree trunks. They were my loyal protectors, while the dais confirmed my rank and the tables and chairs were solid friends. Stirring up the fire in the great stove, I asked Dolya for her blessings. No one wants to slight the goddess of luck who lives behind the stove. I saw her as a sort of Baba, but with a fiery, flickering look to her because, as the saying goes, fortune is as fickle as flames.

From nowhere an evil vision flashed before me: the room ablaze, steel clashing on steel, screams and shouts. I leapt up and crossed myself. Alexander always insisted that my visions were not real, and though I wasn't sure about that, I shook my head to clear it of mischief.

So what to do now? I could slip into Papa's study from the terem and find a book to read. It boasted over twenty. One, studded with jewels, held the Holy Scriptures, saintly stories, and homilies drier than stale bread. I knew I should study them, but I favored the tales of Barlaam and Joasaph, or Akir the Wise, or Alexander the Great.

What was I thinking? If I found *my* Alexander there, I'd have to endure lessons. Well, I could visit the kittens in the barn—no, Liubyna would find me there. Or I could hide in the nice-smelling herb room or take old Shchap for a ride to—

"Sofia, what are you doing standing there staring at nothing?" Baba Liubyna's voice grating in my ear made me start in surprise. "You should be in the weaving room."

Why did she always appear when I least wanted her? I tried to look innocent. "Oh, not so, Baba." She was not really my grandmother, of course. All my grandparents were long dead. "My father told me to find Alexander, but he must be upstairs at the meeting. The servants just left, and I was feeding the fire." Not quite the truth, but not a complete lie. To mollify her further, I added, "And I was asking Dolya's blessings."

"Well, you may yet turn into a proper princess. Now, you go change out of your finery and get to the weaving room. Just because men are full of their great plots doesn't mean work should stop. I'll be there shortly."

How I hated the weaving room; some meddlesome old servant woman would surely pinch my cheeks and tease me about marriage. But Papa would hear of it if I disobeyed. So I glided across the floor in proper swan-like fashion with only Liubyna's eyes on my back keeping me from bolting for the Hall's entrance and out to the courtyard. But beyond her sight, I raced up the terem's spiral stone stairs and into my room. Having donned an old gown with mousy Kateryna's help, I hastened out and almost crashed into one of our servants. He bowed and moved aside.

As I was about to sweep past, an imp of disobedience seized me and I stopped. "Volodya," I whispered, "go see if Baba Liubyna is still in the Great Hall."

He smiled down at me. "Yes, Princess," and stealthily descended the stairs. He was soon back. "It's safe for you to go down," he whispered in turn.

"Very well, then," I said, trying to sound grand. Running down the stairs and through the Great Hall, I nearly collided with a slave woman who backed away and bowed. I seized my cloak and cap, ran to the entrance, and pulled open the heavy door. A gust of chill wind tried to force its way in back, but the sun brushed aside a cloud and beckoned me outside. Pulling the door shut behind me, I raced down the stairs and into the courtyard, avoiding servants, dogs, chickens, geese, tethered goats, and mud puddles. I glanced back to see if anyone was following me, and Papa's palace, alive with graceful patterns carved in stone and with bright painted flowers and beasts dancing across shutters, trim, and banisters, cheered me on.

Where to now? The palace was lost to me. Baba would find me in the terem or in the khoromy's jumble of rooms: Great Hall, sweet herb room, dreaded weaving room, any storage room—she knew me too well. What about the tiny wooden church or the bathhouse, waiting like attendants for soul and body? No, the church was sacred. And though Laznik was my friend, no one wanted to be alone in the bathhouse since Mama and my baby brother had died there during the birthing. Their ghosts might return and fasten on you. Perhaps one of our retainers' houses, grouped like courtiers behind the palace, or the smithy or the dairy or granary—no, not with servants coming and going. Well, I would not hide in a cowshed or a chicken coop. Only Shchap could carry me beyond reach. I would return just before supper, armed with a likely excuse for disappearing.

Dashing through the courtyard past sheds bursting with goods destined for Constantinople, I felt such pride. Two years' worth of treasures lay inside them from Papa's estates and from trade or tribute: amber, lush furs, ivory from the great northern seas; and casks of mead, some varieties sweet and soft on the tongue, some as sharp as pepper. I knew from having secretly sampled every kind. In a few days, we'd be sailing gloriously down the Dnieper, Papa and me, his polianitsa—his adventuress of the steppes! At last I would see Constantinople, which he called the most beautiful city in the world, although how could it outshine Kyiv? But he said that even ravished and shamed, it was like Heaven brought down onto earth. My much-missed Uncle Vasily would show us all her wonders, and we would meet people from all corners of the world and sell everything for huge profits before returning home next summer.

I passed from sunlight into the dark stable, dense with the aroma of horse and hay. "Vsevolod, Ilya," I called. "Bring me Shchap." Several stablemen, lost in chat with our visitors' grooms, jumped to attention. Soon I was riding out of our gates, with my grooms armed to protect me against the vagrants who grew in number every year.

We rode by the smerdi's cluster of hovels, leaking smoke, and the nearest field, black and rich. The trees were going as bald as an old boyar's head, the meadows were turning into graybeards, and the skies were no longer dark with flocks of birds heading south for the winter. The wind teased the maiden sun, draping her with clouds and then stealing them away. In the distance, axes rang on wood, usually a homey, comforting sound.

But anger struck me again, as sharp as any axe blow. Why had Papa dismissed me like that? And why had no one truly important come to this oh-so-private meeting? Mighty princes of other cities often visited us, and Papa included me. Like our distant cousin, Prince Danylo of Halych, who had been a frequent guest until the last civil war. His deputy, Commander Dmytri, whom I called "Uncle", would carve me tiny wooden horses or bears while I watched in delight. And just last year when Papa had invited all the great princes to come make peace, I had often mingled with our guests. Several said I was a charming hostess, and one even offered for me, though Papa gracefully turned the proposal aside. When the meeting had settled who was to rule Kyiv, I was sure I had played a role.

Those politics matter little now, but they were paramount then. Kyiv's glory might be tarnished, but she was still the Mother of all Rus'. So, seeking to revive her greatness, Prince Mikhail had plunged Rus' into civil war and the Golden Throne had passed from hand to hand like a child's ball until he prevailed. These days we often hosted Grand Prince Mikhail, for we now lived under his great arm. Though he was a proud aurochs of a man, I was not awed in the least. Once he gave me an amber necklace for virtue and good fortune. Papa praised me for—

"Princess!" Jackdaws screamed from a tangle of weeds, a wedge of geese trumpeted above me, and my men had stopped. Shchap was wandering onto a field sown with spelt for next spring. Blushing, I turned her away from the black furrows. I had dishonored the labor of our smerdi, our "stinkers", whose toil in our fields and woods brought bread to our table and wood to our hearth. Free they might be, but they seemed more beast than human to me, sharing their huts with their animals and reeking of swine and cattle and sweat, even after bathing. Papa protected them just like farm animals, too.

But I also might have offended Polevoi, whose consent we needed for our crops to thrive. Although our peasants had brought him into the barn inside the last sheaf of the harvest, his children might be the very birds that had called out that warning. I whispered a charm and promised to leave two eggs on the field to appease them.

Our trail wound through a stand of bony birches, and we passed a landowning peasant who stood aside and bowed low. I saw little difference between "black men" like him and smerdi; the dark soil of Rus' was so embedded in both that they were almost one with it. I was often at Papa's side when they came to him to judge their fights over scraps of land or who had cheated the other over a calf. What would they do without him to shepherd them, just as King David had shepherded Israel?

I suddenly heard myself. Shame on me, looking down at all my inferiors when they treated me with respect and even affection. Then my other misdeeds arose in my mind to accuse me: dishonest to Baba Liubyna, careless with my servitors, disobedient to my father. In one breath, I asked forgiveness from both Mother Mary and the meadow spirit. Someday I too would shield my people. I'd be as brave as David, kind as Mary, and wise as Solomon.

I felt no better, though. My hot rage had merely been a thin barrier against chill unease, and now I had to ask: what did this secret meeting portend? Another civil war, a plague? Would it prevent our trip to Constantinople? It was already almost too late, and if the snows came, that might be that.

Or was it about the Tatars? Although nomads, friend or foe, had always been a fact of life, these were a terrifying mystery. They had appeared from nowhere two years ago and used fire-breathing dragons to overpower one city of northern Rus' after another, massacring, pillaging, and burning everything down. And then they had simply vanished.

Or so we had hoped. But last spring a shadow fell over the sun for an afternoon, coloring the world blood red, and soon after that a great bonfire of a comet appeared in the night sky, with five long tails streaming from the east. It grew brighter for several days before slowly shrinking and vanishing. And then Tatars sprang up from nowhere and attacked to our south, sacking Pereyaslav and its territories. Nomads had never behaved like this before, for you cannot destroy a city and get anything more from it after that. Ever since then, invisible leeches of dread seemed to suck at every mind, even mine sometimes.

I set my dark thoughts aside when we stopped in a little stream-threaded glade, my favorite spot on Papa's land. The shimmering leaves were mostly gone, and leaf mold and mushroom scented the air. After dismounting and leading Shchap to drink, I crossed myself and paid homage to the rusalki and the vodianii,

> *I come before you, little Water Mothers,*
> *Penitent, with head held low.*
>
> *Have mercy on me, forgive me,*
> *You and all our ancestors,*
> *Grandfathers of the streams!*

I also added charms against any fickle leshii or nasty besyonoki that might be lurking about. What a bond I felt with Mother Rus' and her spirits, even the untrustworthy ones. Papa's severe old priest could never make me give them up. Father Kliment had clearly lost touch with his mother soil after his pilgrimage to a Mount Athos far, far away.

I knew he was wrong to deny her spirits because I had met two of them right here when I was three. Jolly Uncle Vasily had moved far away, and I missed him terribly. Mama had grown frail before the birth of her new baby, and I was made to be very quiet around her. She often sent me with Baba Liubyna to gather mushrooms. I was sitting under this very tree when Sheep and Blade appeared by my side, small like me. Sheep resembled a baba, from gown to headscarf, but her mouth was a bird bill. Blade was a bald old man with a beard so long that it touched the ground, but it was gray, not green like a leshi's. No one but me could see them, which was part of their charm, that and how they vied with each other for my favor after Mama's death.

Mama and the baby died during her labor. She was not yet seventeen. I was with Papa when the news came, but he covered his eyes and turned to stone; I rushed to the bath house, but Mama's women were wailing over the bloody bodies; heartbroken, frightened, and forgotten in that melee of misery, I fled.

When Baba Liubyna found me huddled under the stairs, she took me into her arms and said, "This world is always in balance, little one. Love and loss go together. But I will care for you now." And she did, though it was Sheep and Blade who comforted me most.

After the funeral, with Mama gone to Heaven never to return and me with a hole in my heart, Sheep and Blade often visited me. Through them I met their relatives: hairy old Domovik, who dwelt in the very timbers of our palace; his wife Kikimora, who with her hen-beak and motherly ways was clearly Sheep's cousin; stern, damp Laznik, whose domain was the bath-house; self-important Khozyain, who guarded the entire compound; and, of course, hay-haired Polevoi. Baba Liubyna and our village shaman, who sometimes secretly visited her, had always warned me to respect them, and grown people set out offerings to appease their possible malice, but the spirits were my friends and protectors.

Alas, as I grew older, they slowly withdrew from my sight. I went for months without seeing any of them, then a year, then two, and I sadly decided that I had grown too old to see them anymore. How I wished I could call them all to my side again, to protect me from civil war, from the Tatars, from—

"Princess, the shadows grow long. Perhaps we should go back now." It was my groom Vsevolod, only a few years older than I was. I liked him and his protective ways. He was good looking, too, with blond hair, a long nose, and a downy first beard on his cheeks.

I sighed. If I must marry, why could it not be to a young nobleman as handsome and gallant as Vsevolod? All the nobles and boyars I knew were ugly and old and arrogant like Witty Boris. It wasn't fair.

Only when we left the woods and I saw our blue shadows stretching in front of us did I realize how late it was. I kicked Shchap into a gallop. Papa would be so angry! As we rode through the palace gates, the evening goddess was spreading a mantle of bright-edged clouds across the setting sun. With my eyes so dazzled, it took a moment to realize that the courtyard was too quiet. And in the stables, not only our guests' but most of our own horses were gone, including my father's. My heart dropped into my stomach.

As I hurried up to the khoromy stairs, Alexander came outside. How gray his hair had become since Papa had brought him to me. I never thought of him as a slave; he was family. And he never seemed to mind my mercurial nature. His face seemed drawn with worry, not a good sign. Dreading what I would hear, I called, "Where is Papa?"

But he only shook his head and beckoned to me. Inside the Great Hall, he spoke for my ears alone. "He and his men left for Kyiv. He was most displeased, Princess. He wanted you with him, but his business was urgent so he had to go without you."

"Papa left this late in the day? He wanted me with him?" Only deep trouble could explain this. And where had I been? Hiding in the woods, dreaming about spirit friends!

At breakfast the next morning, Baba Liubyna announced, "A jug of milk went sour overnight. Some spirit is angry because the kitchen boy forgot to put it back into the cold room."

I said nothing, though I went down to the kitchen to see. It looked like he might get a beating, so I had to confess that it was I who had offended Polevoi. I got no thanks, either. There was much grumbling about having to leave so many offerings on the field to appease him.

Then I had to count eleven unbearable days without hearing from Papa. I must abase myself when he returned. I never dared go riding for fear of missing his homecoming, and every new sound outdoors drew me running to see if he had come back. When sleet turned our road into a river of icy mud, more worry assailed me. What would happen to our journey to Constantinople now? Though Alexander and Liubyna both insisted I continue my lessons and tasks, my mind would often wander into painful reverie and my hands fall idle. I still marvel at their patience: Baba only gave me a few sharp raps on the ear. How little I knew. I was sure they were as painful as any beating. No one had ever been allowed to beat me, unlike my girl cousins and aunts, who all complained with pride of the misery they endured from their fathers or husbands.

The weather finally cleared. We three were sitting together by the fire in the Great Hall because I had refused to be cooped up in the weaving room. Alexander and I were reviewing Latin verbs while Liubyna and I knitted socks, and servants were pulling out tables and benches for another lonely dinner with our stewards and men-at-arms. Swiftwind sat up, ears alert to the clatter of horses outside.

I rushed to the window, but I could hear Papa better than I could see him, even through the thick walls. He and his men had dismounted as grooms ran up to the horses, Vsevolod among them, his hair glowing in the pale sunlight. "Where is Princess Sofia? Find her and bring her to me! Now!" Chickens, ducks, and geese scattered shrieking as servants fled the courtyard to look for me, who might be anywhere.

Hastily taking up the cross of greeting, I heaved the entrance door open and hurried down the steps to meet him; Swiftwind bounded down them and jumped up in greeting, but Papa almost knocked him aside. How, then, would he punish me?

"Here I am, Papa."

New, deep creases were carved into my father's features, but he smiled when he saw me. A great load of fear slipped from my heart. He had already forgiven me. I was so happy that I almost flung myself into his arms, only just remembering my dignity. Blushing, I bowed to him and timidly offered him the cross.

After kissing it he said mildly, "Greetings, Daughter. I rejoice to see you well."

"And I you, Father." I felt shaky with relief.

"Come inside, little dove." Papa led me up into the Great Hall, his men behind us. Baba Liubyna and Alexander greeted him with bows as one servant hurried up to take his fur-lined cloak and cap and another offered him a washbowl of steaming water and a towel.

"Alexander, you will go to Constantinople with Sofia. After supper, pack what you need." My heart lifted even further. Alexander looked both surprised and pleased as he bowed respectfully. "And Liubyna, after you eat, finish packing her things."

Papa's men were already taking their places at supper, but instead of leading me to the dais, my father ordered that our meal be sent upstairs to his chamber. A private supper with him! I trotted behind him in triumph—just like Swiftwind, I think now. Inside his room, he cast aside his commanding attitude and scooped me into his arms.

I hugged him back with all my strength. "Welcome home, Papa. I missed you so."

"And I you, my little flower."

"I am so sorry I wasn't here when you left. It was entirely my fault—"

"Never mind. What's done is done," he said, releasing me.

Servants removed a book of sermons and some writing materials from Papa's table and set it with a lace cloth, dishes, spoons and knives while others appeared with spicy soup, roast goose, venison, bread, and honey cake. My mouth began to water. One servant pulled out Papa's ornate chair for him; another brought in a stool for me. I happily added wood to the fire stove.

But when I looked up, Papa was staring at me yet not seeing me.

Vaguely alarmed, I tried to charm him with a story I had been saving for him. "Oh, Papa, I must tell you. Elizaveta Dairymaid told Baba Liubyna that a two-headed calf was born in one of the villages. And so late in the year! Can you imagine? Baba Liubyna says it's a portent!" My words swam feebly against the current of his silence, unusual since he loved my storytelling. And when a maid brought him a goblet, instead of letting her fill and water it, he took the wine bottle, poured and drank, and filled his cup again. He must just be weary. Best to wait and say no more.

Once we were alone, he sat heavily into his chair, muttering, "All these years … guarding my own 'flock of sheep,' never coveting what wasn't mine, ever offering a helping hand to others." He shook his head. "What a fool I was. We princes may 'share the same grandfather' but we have written our history in each other's blood! And now…."

"Well, if God's wrath fells the innocent, it will be because Prince Mikhail failed to protect them." At last he truly looked at me, who had been listening with growing alarm.

"Sofia, your journey to Constantinople begins tomorrow."

"Oh, Papa, this is such good news!" I leapt up and put my arms around his neck, feeling his red beard tickle my cheek, but he stared straight ahead.

"Sit down, Daughter. I must speak with you about dark matters. But first, we break bread. I've eaten nothing since last night." I sat back down, my stomach in a knot. He asked for blessings, ate in silence. I pushed my food around my plate until he was finished.

"Come sit by the fire with me," he finally said. I pulled my stool next to his chair. The low rays of the sun poured a honey-like glaze into the room, gilding his beard and illuminating his grim-set mouth. "I won't be going with you tomorrow."

"What? That cannot be! What is it? A plague, another civil war?"

He took a deep breath and said, "No, Sofia, it's the Tatars ... again."

"Again? After Pereyaslav?"

"No, even before that. Over sixteen years ago—long enough for a babe to grow into a man and for some men's memories to grow cold. Not mine! They first routed our enemies the Polovtsy. We Rus' should have welcomed that, but their khan persuaded us that if the Tatars wiped out his people, they might turn on us next. It seemed best to stand beside the enemy we knew. Yet when our armies went to battle, the Tatars destroyed them at River Kalka, while the wily khan and *his* army fled!

"The Tatars released a few captives to bring back word to Rus'. I'll never forget when one of Papa's warriors stumbled into the Great Hall, gasping and weeping. Not only had my elder brothers been slain in battle, but Father and his fellow captured princes had been thrown down in the mud and buried alive under a great platform. Those monsters held a feast on it, laughing at their victims' cries beneath them while they were slowly crushed to death! Nor would there be ransom for anyone else who had been captured: all were dead. Our man claimed that they had vowed to wipe Rus' from the face of the earth! Mother fainted into my arms, my little brother and the servants wept in terror. We believed Tatar armies were at our doors.

"Instead, they simply disappeared. Every family in Rus' forfeited a father, a brother, a son. Yet after the funerals, those princes who had stayed behind returned to their customary conflicts as if nothing had happened."

I was aghast. I had known that most of Papa's cousins and uncles had died with his father and older brothers, but it had seemed so long ago. Once I had asked him about them, but he'd only said, "They rode to war seeking glory. Instead, they lost their lives and nearly destroyed us all." That had put a stop to my questions.

Now I saw. Papa had been my age when this disaster had struck, and he had been forced into manhood on the spot. He and Uncle Vasily had inherited a vast mosaic of holdings equally, but Papa had become head of the entire extended family. He had rebuilt trade links, avoided civil war when he could, and allied himself with stronger princes when he could not. But first, he had faced such loss, and he at least had never forgotten.

Papa broke into my thoughts. "Well, the fiends left Rus', but only to turn elsewhere. For years, merchants from afar have warned us of demons laying waste to great empires, spreading terror like a plague, killing without mercy!" He shoved his chair back and began to pace. "Worse, when the Tatars attacked northern Rus' two years ago, our princes refused to unite and their cities fell, one at a time! And when they vanished, men believed they had gone for good. Hah! They were merely preparing another assault. Pereyaslav was their first victim. Chernihiv was their next." My eyes widened.

"Yes, the day I left here, it had just been destroyed, and we southern princes were all summoned to Kyiv for a great council. Two Tatar armies are on the march. One moves north against Novgorod and the other marches on Kyiv."

"Kyiv? They wouldn't dare. She's the greatest city in the world!"

Papa didn't hear. "Some khan named Mongke has spied her out across the Dnieper and claims he admires her. When I arrived, his envoys were there offering to spare us if we submit totally and surrender a tenth of our wealth and people as slaves."

"But that would be as bad as war!" I cried.

"It would be better than for *all* to die. Other cities were spared when their princes submitted; cousin Danylo of Halych already has. Yet Grand Prince Mikhail wants to defy the Tatars, may even have killed their envoys by now. He expects aid from King Bela of Hungary, but how can he trust Catholics? They use us to their own ends and despise us behind our backs!

"In the end, Mikhail called me coward when I argued for submission, and I left."

Everyone knew you could not rely on Catholic kingdoms. And if you killed envoys, how could enemies parley with each other?

But a promising thought came to me. "Papa, don't despair. Father Kliment told me about Prester John's Christian kingdom in Asia. He is already on the march to destroy the Tatars before they attack again."

"Sofia, Prester John's kingdom is a false hope." He returned to his grim recital. "Half of the Polovtsy have fled into Hungary. What an irony. Our troubles began when they called on us to defend *them*, and now they are gone."

He snorted, drained his wine cup, and turned to me. "Kyiv may suffer for her prince's folly, but you must not. The Tatars won't attack yet, and with the Polovtsy gone, it's safe for me to send you to your Uncle Vasily."

"By myself? But Papa, surely there is some other way—"

"Where else can I send you? To Prince Mikhail? He must flee to Hungary if he kills the envoys, but Tatar wrath will follow him wherever he goes. Nor can I entrust you to Catholics or even to cousin Danylo. When I joined Prince Mikhail, he broke with me. I must send you to my brother."

"But why can't you come with me? Or let me stay until you can leave, too. I don't want to run away. After all, as the saying goes, it is best to die in one's own land."

"No, little dove, that is true for warriors, not for women. I cannot turn from the Tatar threat—that *would* be cowardly. But I must send you to safety; I know the kind of harm they delight in, especially against those of high rank. If Prince Mikhail defies them, war will follow and I must lend my sword arm to Kyiv. And if he submits, I want you far away before the Tatars seize their spoils from us. Your journey to Constantinople will still be a grand adventure. And who knows? Perhaps God will send these wild men somewhere else, since beyond violating all rules of warfare, they follow no reasonable battle plan. If so, I will join you when I can."

"Oh, Papa!" I threw myself into his arms. He stroked my hair while my tears rained onto his chest. How dare those Tatar fiends menace my home, tear him from me!

"We are all in God's hands. Now, dry your eyes and be my fearless polianitsa." I swallowed my sobs. I had so wanted Papa's confidences; now I could scarcely bear them.

That evening, sometimes blinded by tears, Baba Liubyna and I packed my clothing and jewelry and even the linens for my dowry that I had embroidered with ancient symbols: Great Mother, Tree of Life, Bird of Renewal. I gave her all my favorite ribbons, poor thanks to one I loved so much and might never see again. And I told her I was sorry for ever being disagreeable to her, a gift that probably meant more to her.

We also tried to see into the future with my steel mirror, a lit candle, and the old foretelling chant. We thought it had failed because the mirror showed nothing but blurred red shifting images. So we gave up and just sat on my bed, holding hands in silence.

The night seemed endless yet too short, marred by shattered sleep and dire dreams. Before dawn, we arose and prayed together before the ikon of the Holy Mother and Son sitting high in the sacred corner. After crossing myself and removing the ikon, I kissed it and placed it in my casket along with Mama's bejeweled collar and my ruby-adorned koruna. It always reminded me of a quarter-moon bent in a curve. When I wore it, it felt like a halo on my head. It brought out my best conduct.

Liubyna bustled out. I glanced outside the window to see servants hurrying with torches or bundles, grooms bringing sleepy horses from the stables. Those of Papa's warriors who would go with me were gathered around their captain, Oleg the Fearless. Gray-haired and scarred, sword at his side, leather cuirass on his chest, and helmet under his arm, he looked equal to any threat. He had once been my father's guardian.

Were he and his men sorry to miss the glory of fighting Tatars? Papa's warriors seemed to value valor even above God. Seeing no glory in a war that arose from killing envoys, I begged the Holy Mother to stay Grand Prince Mikhail's hand.

I wished my cousins were coming, but though Papa had sent out word that they might join me, his messenger had returned to report that everyone had refused his offer. The women and girls were afraid to leave home, and the men and boys wanted to fight. I would stay, too, if only Papa would let me.

But free peasant families were streaming into the yard, laden with packs and carrying hens or leading pigs. Word of my departure had spread quickly, and several men had come to him requesting to leave with me out of fear of the Tatars. Papa had reluctantly agreed, and now there were so many! Were they as sorry to leave home as I was? How strange that they might share my lings.

Liubyna returned. "Here, my darling, I've brought you some kasha for breakfast. You don't want to be caught in all that commotion downstairs. Now, do you have everything?" She rambled on, poking into various bundles and rearranging their contents.

The sun had risen when Papa appeared at the door of my room with a sable-lined deerskin cloak and beaver mittens. He slipped it over my shoulders, saying, "It's a little long, but you're still growing. Gems are sewn into the seams where they cannot be felt. You never know when you might need them. Wear it in good health, little dove."

"Oh, Papa." Despite myself, I burst into tears.

"Be brave, Sofia. My men cut their teeth on war; they'll guard you. And I sent for some warriors of the Black Mask tribe to take you part of the way. Now we must go."

I looked around my room. The brick stove, my carved and painted chest and bed, the washstand with its copper basin and ewer, the embroidered coverings for windows and bed, even Baba's rolled-up pallet seemed cheerfully unaware that I was leaving, perhaps forever.

Suddenly the room withdrew, became strange, as if it had fallen under a spell from which it would never awaken. I shuddered and crossed myself.

Outside, the rising sun was banishing the mist to reveal a fine cold morning. Liubyna and I followed Papa into the courtyard. It was full of empty motion and meaningless noise. Alexander joined me; at least he would be by my side. Had Baba Liubyna not been so old, she could have come, but Papa was sending Kateryna the mouse instead. She was hardly older than I was, and besides, she was a slave. I could expect no comfort or guidance from her.

The house servants and slaves were assembled, some of the women sobbing loudly. I bade goodbye to everyone in turn, even the slaves, and decided to pray for them all daily. Father Kliment began blessing us travelers, beginning with me. After I had kissed the cross, he held up a small ikon of Saint Anthony strung on a cord. "This is to protect you and give you courage on your journey, Princess." The old priest solemnly hung it around my neck. Our quarrels forgotten, my eyes filled with tears and I kissed his hand.

Liubyna and I embraced, our tears mingling on our cheeks. She had already given me several amulets to wear at neck and waist for protection against the evil eye and malign spirits, but now she pressed her most precious treasure upon me: a tiny faceless woman carved from ancient bone and marked with sacred symbols. "Great Mother," she whispered. "For protection." I hugged her for the last time and mounted Shchap, praying to the Holy Family, the saints, and all the spirits of Rus' to bless us all.

Jangling gear, snorting horses, and weeping women. We filed out of the courtyard, past our wild-haired smerdi standing agape before their small jumble of log cabins and wattle huts. Even they seemed precious, and I vowed to pray for them, too. As we rode by the orchard, I said goodbye to sweet summer pears that I would never taste. We passed dark fields patiently awaiting spring, but would anyone be left to plow them by then? A chill breeze tore the last leaves of autumn off poplar and birch, maple and oak, while the larches stood as bare as souls awaiting God's judgment. With me gone, who would come to my stream to honor the spirits of wood and water, or witness the woodpeckers tapping rhythms on the trees, or rejoice in the song of the lark or the races of the swallows?

I was sure I heard Moist Mother Earth call out, 'Never forget the sweet soil of Rus' or the spirits of house, forest, and field that watched over you.' And I never have.

Even delayed by the peasants, who were mostly on foot, reaching Kyiv took too little time. Her whitewashed walls were glowing in the lowering sun as we reached the bridge leading to the oldest and loveliest of her four entrances, the Golden Gate, which was opened only for princes and state occasions. Atop it, like a crown, sat the little Church of the Virgin of the Tower, its copper-clad roof gleaming in the setting sun. To me, Kyiv was indeed a queen, enthroned on hills and girdled with pearly battlements. Her skirt hem was beribboned by the wide, slow-flowing Dnieper River, and on the opposite bank, her loyal subjects, the steppes, rolled away to the horizon.

Our group separated into two, Oleg leading the peasants and minor servitors down the hill to Podil, the area outside Kyiv's walls where craftsmen and the Jews lived, and where merchants landed wares. They would all stay somewhere down there overnight.

The rest of us passed over the bridge above the dry moat, me atremble because I hated heights. Papa expected to enter as usual, but there was trouble. The guards did not want to allow him through the Golden Gate, as was his God-given right. It seemed that Prince Mikhail had given orders to bar his entry. I had rarely seen Papa's temper, but it came out now, and after a few shouts and threats, he frightened those soldiers into letting us through. I secretly thanked Mother Mary. Once across that bridge was enough for me.

Inside the thick walls, we passed several churches, some of them golden-domed, just a few of Kyiv's four hundred. Beyond them stood compounds guarding rosy marble palaces or brightly painted wooden mansions. And, squeezed between them, were gray log huts with tiny gardens. But many churches were damaged, and ruined palaces sprawled inside their wrecked enclosures like drunkards, their outbuildings burned, their grounds lost to weeds, their princes lost in battle and replaced by vagrants and rats. We also passed fire-blackened timbers that had once been rows of homes. Kyiv had been plundered three times in the past eighty years, once by a rival prince and twice by Polovtsy.

As always, church bells filled the chill air with beauty, but tonight they seemed to call out, 'Repent before the Tatars throw open death's gates!' Yet no one seemed worried, just carried on with their burdens, their carts, their horses. A shout made me jump, but it was just someone hailing his friend. Was anyone here even aware of the Tatar threat?

We reached Papa's compound at dusk. His city palace seemed as aloof as ever, as if it held secrets about him that I would never know. Servants hurried about with torches and bundles, his men conferred with him in murmurs, and I was sent early to bed. Kateryna wrapped herself in an old but new-to-her traveling cloak and went to sleep on the floor, but when I could not do the same, I lit a candle, found my sewing basket, and embroidered a keepsake for my Papa.

Early the next morning, Kateryna helped me dress in a green silk gown trimmed with fur at wrist and hem. Over it went a brown wool tunic with velvet edging, gaily embroidered with flowers, vines, pearls, and spangles to keep evil from entering anywhere. I pulled on my soft red leather boots and, along with Baba's amulets, put on my best necklace, its rubies twinkling in the candlelight. Before plaiting my long hair, Kateryna combed it until it shone as red as the sun. She bound my brow with a gold-embroidered fillet that had been Mama's when she was a maiden and attached gold hoops at my temples to ward off evil. Last, I donned my beaver skin cap.

Papa smiled approvingly when he saw me coming down the stairs. My finery would represent him properly and give heart to my retinue.

Before leaving the city, he led us all to seek blessings at the Cathedral of Hagia Sofia, Kyiv's great palace for our Lord and His Holy Mother. It naturally held a special place in my heart. Inside, pillars of stone and precious marble still soared toward Heaven despite the ruin that had befallen this holy site. What a long journey those pillars had made over land and sea to adorn this sacred space, some of them from Constantinople herself, and now I was to make the same journey in reverse, away from all that I loved. The air, thick with incense, echoed with invisible voices: "Kyrie Elieson, Christos Elieson." "Lord have mercy, Christ have mercy," indeed. High above on the dome floated the mosaic of the risen Christ and his archangels. Flickering candles and suspended oil lamps made the gilded tiles around Him glitter like tiny angels.

After praying before Mother Mary raising her hands in blessing, I went up to the ikons lining the ikonostasis before the altar, all windows into Heaven. Every ikon held a saint ready to comfort any humble heart and to plead its cause with God. I crossed myself thrice, bowed, and kissed each ikon, praying for everyone I had left behind, for the people of Kyiv, for my traveling companions, and for Papa most of all. The saints radiated comfort, the Holy Mother smiled down on me, and I felt them all throw a veil of protection over me and gently loosen the band of dread squeezing my heart.

We left through a back gate today, descended into Podil village, passed along streets that in summer would boast markets offering filigreed jewelry, silk brocades, Persian carpets, lively steeds, heady spices, Frankish swords, and fascinating foreign faces. Now just a few local stalls stood open. Foreign merchants would not wait to be trapped in a doomed city, but then they never stayed for winter, either. I had to say goodbye to it all, wondering when I would get to go there again with Papa to see how his merchandise was selling. Trade was in my blood; the two great pursuits of a prince were war and trade.

At the docks, where the peasants awaited us, I tried to picture thousands of Tatar troops sweeping across the water, but how could they when high bluffs guarded the city? The wharf was almost empty but for our people and a small troop of Black Mask warriors that had just arrived: crafty scouts, powerful bowmen, superb horsemen. I had only seen them at peace in their camps and once knocking at our palace gates, but never dressed for war with their terrifying black-masked helmets and leather armor.

When I saw our boats, I could scarcely believe my eyes. I had expected Papa's customary lodyas; with bases hewn from giant tree trunks and sides twice a man's height, they could carry a hundred men with all their goods. Instead, only two such vessels awaited us, but half the usual size and incapable of holding much of anything. The rest of Papa's boats were decrepit disasters, though his peasants were already fighting over them.

Pavel Snub-Nose and Freckled Hlib, servants I had secretly played with as a small child, were storing goods and supplies under a canvas tent that covered the mid-deck of my boat, while the other one was being filled with trade goods, slaves, and the pack animals. Bright-haired Vsevolod was calming the horses. Oddly, they were steppe ponies, as undersized as the lodyas. The peasants, having settled their quarrels with shouts and sometimes fists, filled the remaining craft with themselves, their animals, their belongings.

I stood and watched, bitterly wishing for the good times to return—not that they had seemed so at the time. Twice in the past five years, I had said goodbye to Papa from this very dock before he sailed away on the high spring waters, his massive lodyas packed with his warriors, slaves and goods. I would return home, empty-hearted, uneasy, and hemmed in by servants and guards, to await his return. Even then I knew how dangerous and rare these ventures were, for the vast trade route stretching between the Orient, Norse lands, and Eastern Christendom was breaking up. But in the early fall I had joyously greeted him, eager to see what he had brought me. Alexander had been a gift from Papa's first voyage after Mama died, when I had been too young to go even as far as Kyiv.

Papa startled me from my reverie. "Sofia, Oleg says we are ready."

The old warrior came up and bowed. "My men and I braved many dangers on Dnieper before this. We take good care of you." I tried to smile.

A Black Mask warrior came up and saluted me, too, and I nodded politely. "You know Khan Alp," said Papa. "He and his men will lead you past the Dnieper rapids."

Alp's head was shaven but for his braided forelock. Thin mustaches drooped down past his stern mouth, and a golden ring in one ear flashed in the sunlight. His black helmet with its iron facemask hung at his shoulder over a beaver skin cape. "We meet again, Princess," he said. "You give us grain last year in our need. I glad can pay of your gift."

This was a surprise. I did know him. Once when Papa had been in Kyiv, a ragged band of these warriors had knocked at our gates, wanting to "trade". With the women screaming about murder and pillage, I had felt it my duty to speak with them. Only Oleg at my side, along with two of our stewards and a handful of men-at-arms, kept my courage up. Oleg assured me they were allies, but rather than let them in, I decided to just give them some grain and cloth. This Oleg agreed to, and they left peaceably. Alp had been their leader.

Afterward, with their heads cooled, a few women muttered about wasting our stores, but when Papa returned, he called me his brave little peacemaker. And now Alp was repaying my gift indeed.

The nomad chief motioned his men into their boats. Oleg shouted final orders. "It is time, Sofia," Papa said throatily.

From the purse at my belt, I drew out my bit of embroidery. "Here, Papa, to carry with you: the Holy Cross and a trident for our noble blood."

"I will keep it near my heart always," he said, tears welling from his eyes. "And I have a gift for you." He handed me a small book with wooden covers. I opened it, but the pages were blank. "Fill this book with stories of your journey. I hope to read it someday."

I threw myself into his arms and wept. He whispered, "Now all my dependents are under your care. They will need your strength and fearlessness. You can do it. Never forget, you are descended from Prince Rurik, the father of all Rus'." His words were a longed-for sign of his trust in me; I vowed to live up to them. I nodded, wiping my eyes. He kissed me goodbye, and Oleg helped me onto our lodya. The last men boarded, the ramp was removed, the boat pushed from the dock, and Oleg's men began rowing.

"God be with you, little dove," Papa called. "My love follows you everywhere. I will send for you when this is all over, or someday greet you in Constantinople."

"God be with you, too, Papa. And my love always follows you. Kyiv has a true warrior prince to protect her, and I am the luckiest daughter on the sweet soil of Rus'." It came to me that we might never see each other again, a thought I thrust away.

I waved goodbye to him until the curve of the river separated us.

I was staring dully at lily pads and rushes along the shores of an island we were passing when Oleg came up beside me. "We must reach Black Sea before ice comes. I tell my Prince not to send peasants, but he closes his ears. Bad already, but others hear about us and join us in Kyiv—more bleating sheep to slow us down. They better keep out of my way!" He shook his head and turned away.

I had never heard anyone censure my father before! "But leaving them behind would be cowardly," I retorted. "We of noble blood must shield the weak."

He just snorted. "Monkish ideals, Princess," and he walked off, ordering someone to do something that meant nothing to me. I spent the rest of the afternoon gloomily watching forests and meadows and villages glide past as if they and not the boat were moving. Finally, I dismissed Oleg's words. After all, he was merely a warrior with a limited viewpoint. Travel was never safe, and its season was long past, so of course he was worried. It was November, and soon Grandfather Frost would tuck sleeping Mother Earth under his snow blanket.

In ordinary times Papa would never leave so late in the year, though until now I had not known that his decision to go traveling and to take me with him was because of the Tatars. Had we left when he originally planned, it would have been challenge enough, but we had lost two weeks. If the weather turned against us and the river froze, our small band would have to struggle through a land haunted by bandits, wolves, and evil spirits. It was a measure of his desperation that Papa was sending me at all.

But I was certain that his love, like God's, would guard me against all danger. He had given me purpose, too: to be both polianitsa and protectress. And now that I thought more clearly, Prince Mikhail would surely submit and Papa would be able to join me in Constantinople, perhaps even catch up with us soon. Meanwhile, I must be a good leader. I would write down my experiences, too, so that I could amuse him with stories of my trip. The journey suddenly felt like an adventure again. Even the Tatars seemed less real.

That night we encamped on the west side of the river along a narrow shore. With dark bluffs looming over us, the opposite shore seemed flatter and more inviting, but when I asked about it over a cold supper, Oleg said, "They say Tatars hate water, never go near it. So we camp this side of river wherever banks give cover. And no fires and all speech must be short and soft." A baby began wailing. He frowned. "I tell peasants to keep quiet, but only so much I can do."

That reminded me of my role, so after supper I toured the camp to see to my peasants' welfare and to remind them of the danger. Alexander let me go once I had found one of Oleg's men to guard me. Kateryna hovered behind me protectively, too. But every family leapt up to bow and smile, even the newcomers who had attached themselves to our company.

That night, I slept soundly in my brightly painted tent under my warm cloak and furs. Oleg slept just outside its entrance and Alexander's tent was pitched nearby, but most of the party had only makeshift affairs or the stars for a canopy, neither of which protected them from the biting autumn air.

I awoke before dawn, the world clothed in dark mists as thick as a garment. After hastily dressing with Kateryna's help, I went out to seek the sunrise. By climbing up the riverbank, my slave struggling after me, I reached a point above the fog. The air was as crisp as fresh apples, the morning goddess was tinting the whole sky rosy gold, and as the sun rose, frost burst into sparkling diamonds around me. The whole world seemed new and bright, and my heart leapt up in gratitude. I turned to Kateryna and we shared a smile.

Neither the bustle of breaking camp nor the cry of a water bird could disturb the morning's deep stillness. Gliding out onto the mist-veiled river felt like a dream.

A mysterious rustling: something was skimming ahead of the boat, just out of reach. "Look, Alexander! Did you see? A vodianik," I whispered and pointed.

Alexander peered into the mists. "Princess, that was only a duck. You must not give in to these imaginings." I was not convinced. Under my breath, I whispered a protective charm in case he had offended the spirits.

The sun rose higher, and the mists whirled off like vanishing vodianii to reveal tree-lined banks or gently rolling hills to my left. To my right, often on high cliffs, deep forest sometimes made way for half a dozen crude huts and tiny fields. People paused in their tasks to stare, and occasionally a child or two ran to the embankment and gaped at us.

By midmorning, though, the peasants' boats were falling behind, so I ordered Oleg to slow our pace. He just shook his head. "But we must," I insisted. "It is my special duty to care for the peasants. My father told me so when we parted. I must lead them, just as you lead your men. Soon they will gain the strength to row faster."

Oleg frowned and shook his head. "Princess Sofia, my prince never spoke this to me. I decide. They keep up or row in dark until they catch up. In Kyiv when we first hear news about Tatars, I tell him, get you away. You could be halfway to Black Sea by now. But he wavers. And then Christian ideals blind him and he sends peasants. Nothing but trouble."

A roar of outrage deafened me. I turned my back on him and strode as far away as I could get, which was not very far on that little lodya. How dare he judge his own prince! I knew what Papa had told me! It was well after midday before I cheered up again, mostly because of the wondrous sights we passed. I took out my little book and began to write down impressions. They would make good stories when I was ready to sort them out.

By the time we stopped for the night across from a marsh, the evening goddess had arrayed the setting sun in a gilded cloud-mantle. After she sank behind the hills, the sky faded to deep cobalt and the river turned dark. Delicate drifts of mist began rising from it. Above us, until the mist hid them, golden stars clustered so thick that the air glowed.

As I was about to enter my tent, I turned and looked across the river. In the marsh across from us, green globes glowed faintly through the fog: rusalki, the spirits of maidens who had died just before their weddings. Doomed to wander the wastelands, they lure young men to their deaths. At this safe distance they merely seemed beautiful and sad.

While Kateryna combed and braided my hair for the night, I thanked God for the fine weather. It would be easy for Papa to follow us. Then when we reached Constantinople, he would find a great prince to marry me. He might already know the right man, handsome and not too old, who would see my worth, love me, and even bring me home to live near Papa!

But as if in mockery, two days later we awoke to bitter weather. By the afternoon, a relentless sleet had driven ice into every crease of my cloak, even though I was tucked under the canvas shelter, while the lodya's creaking sounded like some moaning lost spirit. The frozen rain tapered away at sundown, but dreary mist took its place.

Touring the camp that evening, I came upon a peasant boy burning with fever and a sore throat. He looked so wretched huddled in his mother's lap. She was bathing his brow with a wet rag, for he had choked on the bitter willow bark she'd tried to get him to chew. I decided to give him some of the cordial that Liubyna had sent with me, which always soothed my throat. I ordered Kateryna to go find it. And when she returned, I poured out a dose with my own hands, basking in the bright effect of my generosity upon the peasants gathered worshipfully around me.

But when I returned to boast of what I had done, Oleg shouted at my guard, while Alexander scolded me. "You should never risk yourself like that for a peasant, Princess. The child's fever could spread to you, God forbid, and to others. Illness endangers us all!"

Turning to my poor slave, he added, "And you should have stopped her!"

Kateryna looked as if she might weep, and we both fled into my tent. I could hardly tell a slave that I was sorry, nor could I blame her for obeying me, so we just sat in miserable silence, avoiding each other's eyes until bedtime.

Worse, the next morning, Oleg wanted to leave the sick boy's family behind. His mother came to me, weeping and wild-eyed, and begged me to speak with him. When Oleg refused me as well, I argued, "They can keep the boy apart from the others on the boat and camp away from us all. Papa would allow it." He just walked away. Outraged, I cried, "It is our duty! I will not leave without them!"

Oleg turned around, flushed with anger. I glared back at him, and he started forward as if to seize me and force me aboard. Luckily Alexander interceded before things got worse.

"It is no use arguing with Sofia. She's as stubborn as an aurochs. You either have to carry her aboard struggling or let her have her way this *one* time."

He held Oleg's gaze until the old warrior shrugged, nodded, and said, "This wastes time. They can come and camp apart—if anyone wants sickness in their boat."

Now I was angry with both Oleg and Alexander. Aurochs indeed! Papa had taught me to stand my ground like a man when I knew I was right.

Alexander followed me onto our lodya, clearly intending to lecture me further, but when I turned my back on him, he took my arm and spoke softly into my ear. "Princess, you were wrong to offend Oleg. If I hadn't spoken, he *would* have carried you aboard against your will. He knows it would have undermined your position and his, and luckily he has a soft spot for you, but it is best not to press on it. You must defer to him from now on. Prince Volodymyr always followed his lead. I once heard him say that without Oleg's guidance he might never have survived his early years as prince."

I blushed. "I never knew." So, although I could not tell Oleg outright that I was sorry, for the rest of the morning my modesty and humility toward him spoke for me. And a good thing: even Oleg's beard seemed stiff with rage.

That afternoon he finally relented enough to say as we passed a bend in the river, "Up that way: burned bones of Pereyaslav." I crossed myself and prayed for those who had perished. A few hovels were hunched together near the banks, and a man came out from one as our little flotilla glided by. When he saw us he began shouting. More people came out and began calling and waving desperately. My heart went out to them. They must be survivors from that destroyed city, hoping for refuge or at least aid.

I was about to ask to stop when Oleg held up a hand and said, "No!" As we sailed past, I looked back. Two boats were turning toward the shore, rowed by men who had joined us at Kyiv's docks.

I sighed. "Your prince would have offered help, and those men back there are acting with true Christian charity."

"My prince is ruled by his priest." He promptly ordered his men to row faster. I looked back in helpless outrage. Most of the boats were slipping farther and farther behind.

Alexander touched my shoulder and spoke softly. "Remember, he is doing what he thinks is best." He was right, of course. I had forgotten too easily, and now it was harder going for all the others. I spent the rest of the day avoiding Oleg.

That night in my tent while Kateryna was settling my furs around me, I could just hear Pavel speaking to Hlib, "... heard the princess say ... so when they begged to join us, I said ... keeps out of Oleg's sight ... says Tatars are still ..."

"If they ... should we tell Oleg?"

"... just snarl at us ... ignorant serv ..." Their words dissolved like smoke as they moved away. And I was asleep. The next morning I had forgotten.

From then on I resolutely obeyed Oleg, behaved graciously toward the peasants, treated Kateryna kindly, wrote notes in my wooden book, and worked hard at my lessons with Alexander—especially language lessons, which I actually enjoyed.

There was little else to enjoy. The land was mostly flat and uninteresting, and slowly the grasses shrank and the trees thinned until solitary trees dotted the riverbanks like suitors bidding sad farewell to their beloved. Now I learned how dreary travel could be. I could only write so much about nothing happening, and even Alexander's lessons only kept me busy part of the time. Besides, every time I saw something interesting and called out, "Look, Alexander!" he would give a dry lecture on it that killed my joy.

At least in the evenings the peasants would request small things like a length of rope or ask me to judge disputes that flared up. I tried to follow Papa's example. They were rough folk, but good. There were the usual wife and child beatings and drunken quarrels, but families also laughed and sang together until Oleg put a stop to it.

Alas, my hopes for a swift reunion with Papa dwindled day by day, while my family and friends moved farther away with every stroke of the oars. Or they were dead like Mama and my worldly-wise Cousin Irina. After her marriage at twelve, my age now, she had often hinted mysteriously about the joys of the marriage bed. She had died during childbirth when she was only fourteen. I still missed her.

Still, there were moments of utter magic. Mostly the Dnieper was narrow enough that I could see both banks clearly, but at other times it widened until they seemed to disappear into haze. Knowing no better, I thought the river was as wide as a sea. And once, when the earth stretched into endless grassland on either side of the silver river, a peasant defiantly began to sing. Others joined him, and it felt as if their voices rose straight from the river's heart. Oleg went rigid and his warriors rowed on, stonily silent, but I saw no problem with song right then, since no one was around to hear it but us.

I glanced dreamily over the edge of the boat and glimpsed a green maiden swimming under my reflection, combing her weed-like hair, perhaps waiting to drag me to a watery grave. I blinked and she was gone. Whispering a charm and crossing myself, I sat back in the boat, half-thrilled and half-afraid.

But that day marked the beginning of an undeclared civil war. When nightfall arrived, Oleg found the peasant who had led the singing and beat him senseless. Had I not begged him to show mercy, he might have killed the man. It was a tense group that broke camp the next day. From then on, no matter what Oleg told them to do, the peasants either obeyed unwillingly, as in not to light campfires or shout, or they ignored him, especially those who had joined us from Kyiv and Pereyaslav.

Nor could the sights that we passed lift our company's dark mood. Once when the river narrowed again, we passed a village on the east bank, its cottages charred and collapsed, the orchards chopped down, the crops gone rotten. I was certain Tatars had done it and spent the rest of the afternoon in dutiful prayer. Another day, we glimpsed an abandoned fort, its timber walls tumbled and haunted-looking.

"In good times such outposts were barriers to your nomad enemies," Alexander said, "but in bad times they were useless. Do you remember your lessons?"

Yes, no one could blame this on the Tatars. That fort had fallen long ago. It brought home the truth that Rus' was now as frayed and ripped as an old sheet, and that malign spirits ruled her borderlands. The steppes had always been like a great grassy sea whose waves of wild tribes had swept over Rus' before flooding Western Christendom. Some had settled down and become peaceful trading partners, but most had simply raided us before moving on—although never like the Tatars. With the Polovtsy gone, would the Tatars take their place, or were they truly demons from hell that would destroy all Rus'?

No, I must not imagine such a thing! I crossed myself and took out my book.

Once we passed a low hill rising from the plains like a flattened bubble. Alexander was ready with a lecture. "That is a burial mound of an ancient warrior king, probably Scythian. Do you remember? They ruled here long before Rus' was founded. Herodotus tells us that they overran the Cimmerians until they were overrun in turn by the Sarmatians, the ancestors of the Alani." Despite Alexander's genius for turning exciting events into drab dust, the thought of some forgotten chieftain buried under that mound gave history a human face. Fearsome warriors, long gone: most unsettling.

Trees became a rarity along the banks; stiff gray wormwood replaced them. In some places it grew as far as the eye could see. One night, I overheard a disquieting conversation among Oleg's men about wormwood. "Perhaps the Tatars are the tribes of Gog from Magog that herald the Apocalypse."

"Yes, Revelation! They bring hails of arrows and fire mixed with blood, too, and they burn the earth and kill people beyond number."

"The fiery star Wormwood raining poison must be their poisoned arrows raining death from the sky, or it could be their fire-breathing dragons …"

I shuddered, but then wondered how wormwood could rain poison when it was such good medicine? When I fell out of that walnut tree, Liubyna had made a poultice of wormwood and wine….

I fell asleep and dreamt of falling stars.

Shallow rapids began forcing our party ashore to carry the boats and baggage for some distance—now small boats and horses made sense. Khan Alp's warriors always kept a keen lookout when we did this, but there was never any sign of bandits.

As well, the banks narrowed more and more, and dark cliffs reared up on both sides, squeezing the river ever tighter. "We near biggest rapids," Oleg told me one day. "This late in year, water is too low to drag boats in shallows. We carry them along cliffs above."

Craning over the side of the boat to witness the breathtaking rush of water, I asked, "How long will it take?"

"Take care, Sofia!" Alexander seized my arm as the boat rocked violently.

"God willing, we pass them all in one or two days," said Oleg. "In summer, bandits lie in wait above them." He fell silent for a moment, a hard look passing over his face. "I send out scouts first, but bandits not likely now."

Alexander moaned. "Bandits? Dear God, please spare us this time."

"What could you possibly know about bandits, Alexander?"

He turned to me, his face a pale green. "I know far too much."

Oleg smiled grimly. "They want bribes, not to kill. Still, so many people ... without my men, they are lost." Looking at my fear-marked face, he added, "Not to worry, Princess. Remember, *we* use cliffs this time. If you wish, I tell you names of rapids." While I saw through his ruse, I nodded eagerly. Such wonderful names they were, too, like 'Do Not Sleep', 'Ringing Din Falls', 'Insatiable', and 'Seething'.

Alexander suddenly stumbled to the side of the boat, leaned over the edge, and made disgusting noises. Kateryna, huddled like a brown lump, sighed and closed her eyes.

The rest of the afternoon passed in near-silence. While Oleg's men battled the rushing waters and Alexander was mostly bent over the side of the boat, I pondered bandits. Once when I was on the way to Kyiv with Papa, an ill-assorted band of brigands had attacked us in the woods with staffs, a few swords, and shouts that terrified only me. Their greater numbers were no match for real warriors, and Papa and his men had slain several before the others fled. Papa was proud of me for not screaming or fainting like most women, but he never knew that my horse had reared and forced me to bring it and my spinning head under control. That battle was as splendid as stable muck. I wanted no more adventures like that! Weary of rocking, cold spray, and dark thoughts, I wedged myself between some bundles of furs to take a nap.

But as my eyes were closing, I glimpsed, atop the bluff on the western side of the river, an armed horseman staring down at us, as unmoving as rock. I sat up and shouted, "Oleg!"

Just then the boat pitched, and a bundle broke loose and spilled onto me.

Pavel and Hlib unburied me, and Oleg rushed to stop more goods from shifting amidst snorts of laughter from his men. When he finally got to me, looking annoyed, I cried, "I saw an armed horseman back there!"

Oleg called to the lookouts, but one answered for all, "Captain, we were looking at eastern shore. We see nothing. We hear Princess shout, see furs fall, and ..." Someone smothered another laugh.

"*Anyone* see this horseman?" Oleg scanned the faces turned toward him: curious, amused, indifferent. No one answered.

"I know what I saw! They should be watching better, not laughing at their princess!"

He shrugged and turned away. Everyone else went back to work in silence.

As the afternoon passed, my anger shriveled into uncertainty. Perhaps I had imagined the man. Or perhaps he was not a warrior but just some lonely traveler. Or he might be an apparition— I stopped myself.

Toward evening, we landed on a narrow stretch of shore. While Oleg carried me out of the lodya, Alexander and Kateryna struggled ashore. My tutor still looked sick, poor man. I basked in secret pride that I had not felt even fleetingly ill.

The banks were too high and the shoreline too narrow for more than a few boats to land beside us. Most men had to continue farther down the river to stop for the night, and soon people were spread out along both sides of the river. After we had set up camp, Oleg came up to me. "I must go warn peasants about cataracts. And if someone *is* watching, we must be prepared. Khan Alp sends men out now to see." He set off, mumbling curses as he went. At least he took me seriously, small comfort now that I doubted myself.

By the time he and his men returned, it was dark and little campfires dotted both riverbanks like fallen stars. He was wet, weary, rigid with rage, and ready with his fists.

In the morning, those who had spent the night downstream joined our train as we sailed past. They seemed not to care that beatings probably awaited them.

The river's roar grew so loud that Oleg had to shout to me, "We haul boats out soon. Peasants are witless rabbits, may hit rapids. And those who followed us from Kyiv are worst of all, defying me and not caring about danger they bring to all. They deserve bad end after those fires! After we land, I send out scouts to hack path, look for danger—and for stranger you *think* you saw."

I blushed with shame.

As we neared the first falls, Oleg's men swung our two lodyas into the shallows beyond a cluster of boulders and landed on a strip of shore. Above us lay a little meadow that rose into low, almost treeless hills. After emptying the boats, Oleg's men heaved them onto their shoulders and carried them up the bank.

When my peasants saw us land, some kept going downstream, but others tried to outrace each other for our spot. Boats collided; curses filled the air; a woman screamed as her small craft nearly overturned and her bundles slid into the current along with her pig, which swam ashore squealing; Oleg's men bellowed advice or leapt into the frigid river to help; and I rushed to the bank to watch, thinking it a miracle that no one drowned. In case we had angered the rusalki, I whispered a pacifying charm.

When the chaos died down, I began to worry and pace, knowing Oleg wouldn't care about the peasants who had sailed on. Worse, the ones who had landed with us promptly set up camps and started smoky fires. Of course Oleg's warriors kicked out the flames and struck the men who had started them. One of them, not one of my peasants, actually pulled a knife and tried to fight back, but one blow and he was felled like a tree.

Alp, meanwhile, had sent scouts to explore the track and the countryside leading to the cataracts, while Oleg's men got ponies and people into a rough line, a small miracle because everyone, whether warrior, peasant, or newcomer, seemed quietly at war with someone. I went up and down the line trying to encourage my people, but they merely bowed and returned to their dark mutterings with each other as soon as I had passed.

Finally I sat down facing the river, shivering and discouraged, Alexander and Kateryna beside me. "You did the best you could, Sofia," he said quietly. That was little comfort.

We sat listening to the rush of rapids and Oleg endlessly cursing and striking people back into line. Midday came and went, but the scouts had not returned. Gusts of wind cut through us all like one sharp knife after another as we watched the sun sag lower and lower.

"Too late to move now. We must wait for morning," he finally said. "We make camp, but no fires!" People scattered over the meadow, brought out food, sorted through wet stores, and hung soaked clothing to dry.

After Hlib and Pavel had pitched my tent, Pavel approached me. "Please, Princess, speak to Captain Oleg. People will soon rebel. They say he is too harsh, no better than a Tatar. They want a new life, not more anger and beatings."

"I wish I could. Oleg won't listen to me." He sighed, bowed, and left.

I retreated just inside my tent both for warmth and to get out of Oleg's way, but there was nothing to do but watch him pace endlessly, looking angrier every time he passed by.

I only came out when two scouts appeared near sunset to report that fallen trees blocked the trail in several places and that their fellows had been clearing it and cutting logs for rollers under the boats. There was no sign of recent travelers.

"Unused trails at least means no bandits," said Oleg.

From the look he gave me, he clearly thought that they also meant no stranger. Worse, he added, "I see little point in taking peasants farther. They can stop here and ready themselves for winter and be out of my way. They have no future in Constantinople."

I had nothing to say to that, though I felt like it would be abandoning these people to unknown dangers. But Oleg also might be right: I at least had not thought realistically about what the peasants would do once away from Rus'.

I was heading back to my tent feeling doubly dejected when someone shouted. I looked around. Cresting the nearest hill and outlined by the setting sun was a warrior on a steppe pony.

Silence fell but for the snorting and shuffling of our horses, the cry of a child. The man rode down the hill, pausing to remove his pointed helmet and drop it onto the ground, along with a sword, an axe, a pair of double-curved bows, and a quiver full of arrows. Then he nudged his pony forward with his knees, his arms spread wide as if crucified. Oleg and Alp strode toward him, a dozen of their warriors behind them with bows drawn.

I had seen truly, then, but fear vied with triumph. I started forward, spell-bound, but Alexander's hands fell on my shoulders. "No, Sofia. You must not meddle in *this* matter."

Khan Alp strode up to the horseman, and they spoke at length with much motioning of hands. Finally the stranger wheeled his horse around toward his weapons. Alp stood expectantly with his hands on his hips.

But just as the man reached his gear, an arrow sped from nowhere and with a sickening smack pierced his neck! A strangled cry; he tumbled from his horse.

Alp stood rooted like a tree for an endless instant, then ran to the man and tried to pull the arrow out, but the fellow was already gripped by death throes, his legs digging into the earth, his back painfully arching. The arrow snapped in Alp's hands. The stranger gave a horrible rasping cry and lay still. The pony, meanwhile, had bolted back toward the hills.

Blackness stole me away.

When I returned to this world, I had slumped against Alexander. Oleg and Alp were looking back at the camp, frowning and speaking together, while their men stood gaping around the corpse. Finally at a gesture from Oleg, one grim-faced warrior slung it over his shoulder and started toward the camp while another picked up the weapons. Others fanned out among the peasants to question them.

I slipped from Alexander's arms. "Sofia, no!" he called, but I was already running to Oleg, passing the man carrying the corpse. It smelled foul.

When I reached Oleg and Alp, I cried, "Who was he? Who shot him? Why?" Alexander caught up with me, breathless from his little race.

"A lone scout, Princess, seek his troop. This I take from him," said Alp. "He speak bad Turkish, we talk much with arms and faces. But this I know: he come in peace."

Oleg added, "We seek his killer now. Coward! He dies for this!"

"What troop? Are they Tatars?" Alexander intruded with his own questions.

"No, how could that be?" growled Oleg.

Alp added, "And not Polovtsy. Maybe Alani. I hear 'Alani'. I ask him break bread of us." He shook his head regretfully.

All the time we were speaking, men had been inching closer to stare at the corpse lying at the edge of the camp. Now an ominous hush fell. Two men were dragging a third between them, a stranger. They dumped him at

Oleg's feet. "The killer. Came to us at Pereyaslav." The man, dressed in filthy hunting garb, looked shriveled in the fading light. I tried to back away, but the peasants crowded around, walling us in.

"Why you do this?" The man wouldn't look up until Oleg kicked him. "Answer!"

"He was Tatar! They killed everyone! I was out hunting when they— I came back to death everywhere—my wife, my children, my friends, my city —" His voice broke, and he wept. "All around me, smoking ruins, butchered corpses. I found a dented helmet like his. I saw him, I knew—I went blind with hatred. No help for it!" Oleg kicked him hard.

"Tatar? Do Tatars put down weapons, come in peace?" he snarled. The man hung his head and slowly shook it. He pointed to a few of his men. "Send him to Hell, bury dead man. You others, go!" The peasants scattered like frightened ducks.

Alp added, "Tomorrow I send scouts, seek man's troop."

Oleg gripped my arm and marched me to my tent. "Stay inside." I sat down in the gloom. Moments later came a single scream. Kateryna looked in, but I motioned her away and let misery swirl over me like swamp gas. That poor scout, mistaken for a Tatar. What cruel ends for him and that fellow from Pereyaslav. How could anyone be that twisted by vengefulness? If only my servant boys hadn't overheard me! Finally, I called Kateryna in, prayed for everyone, and fell into troubled sleep.

At dawn Alp sent a pair of scouts to look for the dead man's people. Soon thereafter the stray families straggled into camp looking lost, only to meet with threats, curses and blows from Oleg. At least, after last night's tragedy he was not ready to abandon them yet.

Once again, people glumly loaded horses, picked up burdens, and formed a rough line. We set off, stumbling over the uneven trail the scouts had reclaimed. On our right lay sparsely wooded hills, to our left stood tangled brush and occasional stands of leafless trees, their bony branches supplicating the sky. I whispered a charm against any ill-willed besyonoki that might be lurking about. With only short rests, we walked up and down hills all day. The noise from the cataracts below drowned out everything but my somber thoughts. At least weariness would give me better sleep that night. As the sun sank lower in the sky, the roar settled into a growl behind us and the trail led down to a small, level meadow by the river. Oleg ordered a halt.

While their parents set up camp, several children chased each other down to the shore and, to Oleg's outrage, straightaway clambered back up, calling excitedly. A dozen or more men took to the river with fishing lines in hand. It was not long before the first were back with the fattest prizes I had ever seen. And of course fires were soon alight all over the camp! The promise of fresh-cooked fish seemed to outweigh the threat of Oleg's fists.

Oleg and his men kicked out a few, but the peasants defiantly relit them after they moved on. Finally he seized one fellow and held a knife at his throat. "I kill you first, then others who make fires. You want that?" Everyone stopped. We all stood like statues for several heartbeats until one man after another sullenly smothered his fire. I looked from Oleg to the peasants in despair. Why must he be so harsh and they be so foolish?

At another cold supper of dried meat and way-bread, Oleg came scowling to sit with us. "Well, fools got this far," he said. "Seems safe, no one here since last rains. Past rapids, we can row again, but I leave them behind for sure. They can fish all they want then! But tonight I add extra guards. Maybe horseman's people seek him." He rose and stretched.

"Oleg, I beg you to be less hard on my peasants. We are all tired."

He frowned. "Too bad!" He stood and scowled into the dark. "Where are dead man's people? Where are Alp's scouts? At least Tatars are far away." He strode off into the darkness.

I forced myself up and briefly toured the camp to encourage my people. No one was happy, and there were grumblings among small groups of men that sounded ominous to me. The last thing we needed was outright rebellion against Oleg.

After bidding Alexander goodnight, I looked up at the star-strewn sky, wishing that the Tatar wolves had now seen that Kyiv was the queen of cities, too mighty for them, and slunk back to their dens, and that Papa was already following us. Father Moon was beginning to rise, and I offered a prayer to him as well, for blessings on us all.

When I entered my tent, Kateryna was waiting. For once I looked at her properly. She was trembling as always, but I suddenly realized it was not with fear. She was cold! How thin her cloak was, how tangled her hair. I must be kinder to her. She combed out my hair and began to braid it again for sleep, but I stopped her. "We can do it after prayers, Kateryna. I am too tired to stand, and we are both cold. Here, take this bear pelt."

"Thank you, Princess Sofia." She smiled and ducked her head shyly. After running her hands over the supple, dense fur, she wrapped herself tightly and gave a happy sigh.

I stripped down to my linen shift, nestled under my pile of furs, and took out my two ikons. While Kateryna knelt properly, I crossed myself and began to pray, but before I had gotten much past Papa and Baba Liubyna, I was asleep.

DECEMBER? Anno Domini 1239

An evil dream: weird whistling demons were chasing me. I woke into darkness. It took several moments to realize that the whistling was real. A harsh medley of thuds, cries, groans, shouts, clashing metal, and screams of fear and pain brought me fully awake. Our horses, tethered on the far side of the clearing, were whinnying and jostling each other. The dead stranger's terrible smell was back.

"Kateryna?" I called softly. There was no answer. I crawled out of my furs to waken her. She was gone. Thinking to crawl to my tent flap, I threw my cloak over my shoulders and shakily drew my eating knife from its sheath, but another unearthly shriek threw me flat as something tore through the tent. When I dared to look up, small holes on either wall gleamed like little gray stars. I inched forward to lift the bottom of the flap a little, but at first all I could see was a boot sole. I lifted the flap a little higher.

A corpse lay on its back, open eyes glittering in the moonlight, knees bent and boots before my face, its beard obscuring its features. A stick jutted out of its throat—no, an arrow. I dropped the tent flap back down, gulped air, stared at those holes. Where was Oleg? He shouldn't leave me alone— Good God, this must be a bandit attack and he must be with his warriors fighting it off! But then Kateryna should not be out there. More shouts, screams cut short. Why didn't Alexander come for me? Should I go or stay?

It suddenly grew quiet. Oleg's warriors must be chasing the attackers from our camp. Nonetheless, I hesitated for an eternity, afraid to pass that corpse in case its angry ghost fastened on me. I began to feel both foolish and cowardly. By now Alexander should have come to make sure I was safe—

Dear God, had something happened to him? I awkwardly pulled on my boots, fastened my cloak, and slowly drew aside the tent flap.

At first the light from the half-moon transformed the meadow into glowing silver and deep black shapes, lending an eerie beauty to the camp. But then I truly saw. It was as if a tempest had struck: bodies scattered everywhere with arrows thrusting up from most of them, tents askew, goods spilled. Strange men with torches were moving among the fallen, bending over each in turn. A terrible stench struck my nose, a mixture of that dead man's bad smell, loosed bowels, sweat, and blood. I looked down at the corpse.

It was Oleg.

Just beyond him lay Kateryna, her arms flung out, a knife in her hand, blood still oozing from a slash across her breast onto the pelt that lay under her like a funeral bed.

"No!" I cried. The world went black.

An iron hand gripped my arm, twisted me around, and pulled me upright. My head cleared, and a stranger stood before me, so like yesterday's dead man that for a moment I thought it was his ghost. But this man was very much alive. His slanting eyes glinted down at me, his high cheekbones seemed carved of stone. A pointed, plumed helmet covered his head, animal tails dangling absurdly from its sides; metal-plated leather armor covered his clothing. Worst, though, was that foul odor of stale sweat, dirt, and of blood, old and fresh. Not even a peasant stank like that. He grinned at me.

I swung my little knife, but the man-beast knocked it out of my hand with a humorless laugh. Others like him came up, and they all began barking in some hideous dog speech. One of them squatted by Oleg and Kateryna, slit their throats, cut an ear off each as if carving meat for supper, and stowed his bloody relics in a bulging bag.

I'd have fainted again, but the man-beast wrenched me upright into painful clarity as he lifted his sword, smirking. With cunning born of terror, I twisted from his grip and fled. He shouted; within moments a pack of those dogs was so close behind me that I could almost feel their breath on my neck. Rabbit-like, I bounded one way and another, jumping over corpses and dodging felled tents, slipping right past one man, to his dismay and the hoots of his companions, but they rapidly encircled and then closed in on me until I had nowhere to go. I was panting with fear and frustration, and they were laughing!

The circle parted. The warrior who had first found me stepped into it, followed by another with a torch. He glared at me as he marched up, wicked sword in hand, reached out and gripped my arm so hard it nearly broke off, shook me like a little rag, forced me onto my knees, yanked my hair up, and raised his sword once again. I closed my eyes, waiting for the sword to strike.

The blow never came.

Finally, I opened my eyes. He had lowered his sword and was sheathing it, taking the torch from his man and holding it toward my hair, which must have been reflecting red-gold in its flickering light. Almost worshipfully, he touched a lock. He barked something, and two men marched back across the clearing to my tent and disappeared inside it while he followed them, silently dragging me over the terrible ruination as if it was not there. The others trailed behind.

He thrust me inside my tent, and I stumbled back onto my furs, rubbing my hurt arm. They were dumping out my chests and rifling through my things. None of this could be happening. Why had he not just killed me? One man pulled out my koruna and handed it to my captor; it gleamed dully even in the dark. They all stared at it, then at me.

He started shouting at me excitedly, "Jabber-jabber-Kyiv … jabber-Kyiv."

"What about Kyiv, you fiend? Go away and leave me alone!" I waved my hands at him as if I could shoo him away like some barnyard animal. He caressed my koruna with his filthy hands and barked something to someone. The tent flap lifted, and an older, taller man-beast with legs as bowed as a round shield, strode in. He took my koruna and studied it. They growled together at length, while I sat dazed, raging, and terrified.

Then it hit me: Alexander must be dead. In utter despair I cried, "Holy Mother of God, pity us in our time of need!"

Their talk stopped. Their eyes turned on me. The young man-beast leered in a way that could only mean more trouble. Throwing off his fur cape, he fell on me, threw me onto my stomach, and began ripping at my shift. I thought he wanted to strangle me with it. Later I wished he had.

I remember all too well what he did do, but to write it down is too painful.

After he left the tent with the others, I lay there with senses shattered. I grasped only one thing: that I had become a woman.

The cold finally penetrated my mind. I burrowed beneath my furs and lay as unmoving as the corpses littered outside, while my mind repeated endlessly, "I am ruined, ruined, no prince will marry me now."

Nothing in my life had prepared me for rape.

Of course, living on a farm, I had seen animals mate, overheard the rough talk of men and the gossip of women, and a few times I had happened upon servants coupling furtively in the stable. Yet enclosed by a charmed circle of loving family, loyal servitors, guardian saints, and spirit friends, I had never dreamt such an assault was possible.

But I did know that from the moment that beast had invaded my body, I might as well be dead. Now I was of no value even to myself. Papa had worked so hard to raise me to be a strong helpmeet for my future husband, had trained me to preside at table with princes and learned men, had taught me to estimate the value of a bundle of furs on sight and to know the different qualities of amber.

Thanks to his gift of Alexander, I had been able to saturate myself in the sweetness of learning, as the saying goes. I knew the entire history of the world from Genesis to the present, could quote the Scriptures with ease, and spoke four other languages. Since I had turned eleven, three princes had offered for me, but Papa had wanted to wait, always looking for the ideal man for my husband. We had both wanted more than rank or fortune from my marriage. He sought alliances, while I dreamt of a husband who would love me and never beat me, who would give me sons, God willing, and respect my opinions just as Papa did when he asked what I would do in such-and-such circumstances. I had never expected merely to manage our home but to be at my husband's side at all times just as my Mama had been with Papa. But now all my hopes and dreams were destroyed forever.

*M*y misery ran in circles for an eternity. Yet at the last, I had to set my woes aside and face larger truths, beginning with Oleg and Kateryna lying outside: arrow-pierced, heart-stabbed, throat-slit, ear-severed. Why had she run outside? Was I alive because our attackers had thought she was alone in my tent? What about Pavel and Hlib, my blond Vsevolod, and all the peasants? Had those brutes killed them all and violated the women? And most fearful of all, what had happened to Alexander? I moaned and sobbed and tried to pray, but for what? Mercy for the souls of the dead, forgiveness for such evil?

And who were these terrible men? Could they be Alani or Polovtsy?

Faint light began to seep into the tent. Outside, I heard movement and that snarling speech, but what reason was there to move? The sun had risen when I finally crawled over to peek out of the tent. A helmeted guard, the big one with the bowed legs, stood with his back to me, spear in hand and curved sword at his side. Oleg's and Kateryna's remains were gone. Nearby bundles lay ripped open, their contents scattered like body parts. Pools of half-frozen blood gleamed in the rising sun like sinister jewels. I looked to where Alexander's tent had stood. It was a trampled mess, and there was no sign of him or any of Papa's warriors.

Corpses, some headless or missing limbs, lay strewn about. Some of the marauders were stripping them of anything useful, even wrenching arrows from unfeeling flesh. A handful of women wept softly while they gathered scattered goods into piles or packed them back into chests, watched by ice-eyed guards. A few men under guard, mostly Black Mask warriors and Papa's slaves, were dragging the stripped bodies to a growing pile of human remains. There were the bodies of the feverish boy and a young girl, both sprawled like dropped dolls.

And then they threw Alexander onto the pile, stiff, naked, and caked with blood. His belly had been carved open. A great flap of skin sagged below it, ragged remnants of his entrails dangling out.

When my head cleared, I was on the ground. I lay there sick and sobbing until the cold penetrated my awareness. I burrowed back into my furs, too terrified to move, but I could not hide from the grim reality outside forever. I had to honor Alexander's training and try to think straight. I sat up and pondered.

First, our attackers were not bandits or Polovtsy or Alani. They were Tatars. And the horror stories about them were all true. It was said that in

Riazan, every single woman, even the nuns, had been raped—a word no one would explain to me—while the men had been forced to watch before the Tatars had killed them all, even the children, but for a handful released to warn other cities to surrender. In Kozelsk, it was said, they had even killed the cats and dogs. My women were full of such terrifying tales, but I had tried to ignore them.

Next, how could these Tatars have overcome us so easily? Were they in league with the Devil? Had they called on demons to bewitch us, to make the peasants foolish and Oleg too gruff? Was that murdered man their spy; were that vodianik in the mist and the rusalka beneath my lodya their familiars? There was no way to know.

Last, why had that fiend sheathed his sword and looked at my hair with such awe? Surely he had seen red hair before. Well, perhaps not.

Papa's farewell suddenly echoed inside me: "Now all my dependents are under your care. They will need your strength and fearlessness. You can do it." My duty was clear. I must set aside my own fall; these few survivors still needed me, God help them and their shattered dreams, and I had made a vow.

Stifling my sobs, I decided to try to overawe these monsters, which should be simple if red hair amazed them so. I found my blue silk gown and ermine-trimmed gold tunic, dirty with boot marks, and my Mama's bejeweled collar. Having never dressed myself before, I did as well as a bruised arm and shaking hands could manage. I combed out my tangled hair, braided it with trembling fingers, and draped my cloak around my shoulders. But when I touched the tent flap, it took several ragged breaths before I could move. Finally, I stood straight and strode out of the tent, head held high, though my knees were almost knocking together with fright. The guard jumped around in surprise.

Glaring at him scornfully and pointing toward the camp, I cried, "Find your captain, you stinking butcher!" He gaped at me but did shout something that brought over several man-beasts with slanted eyes, too-large heads, and flat faces as hard as rock. Only desperation kept my haughty pose from falling apart.

A youth strutted forward, the one who had violated me. He looked so young in the morning light, but the men moved aside respectfully. If he was their leader, it made my task harder: such a young buck might be most touchy in front of his men.

"What do you plan to do with us?" I demanded in my sternest voice. Gesturing at the chaos in the clearing, "Was that disgraceful slaughter last night not enough? These poor people will do you no good weary and starving." Had he understood me, he'd have laughed. As I was to learn, his people care less than nothing about their slaves.

After looking at me curiously, he gripped my sore arm and thrust me back into the tent. I cowered back, expecting another assault, but he merely crouched down beside me and mimed that I should stay inside. I slowly nodded, and he nodded back and, oddly, touched my hair again. Shaking his head and grinning, he left.

I was dejectedly removing my finery when the bow-legged guard poked his head in and handed me dried meat and way-bread pillaged from our stores. Before the flap fell back, I saw that work had stopped and that my fellow prisoners were huddled together under guard, eating. Had I made a difference? Who knew? I sank into dumb misery.

Later I learned that we were undone by a hundred men. Perhaps thirty of us were spared—a few women and girls, a handful of older boys and slaves, some Black Mask warriors, and Hlib. Khan Alp was dead, as were all of Oleg's men.

Snatches of memory remain: a homing pigeon released toward the rising sun, our boats set ablaze, that pile of naked corpses left to rot. So much for their new life.

We captives were thrust onto ponies and, guards gripping our reins, borne back north along the river, a handful of swift horsemen soon leaving us behind. Hlib was by my side for a moment, asking in a whisper what I thought would happen to us, but a guard shouted and struck him. No one else dared speak after that, and one of my peasants, a handsome woman named Myroslava, hastily hushed her sole surviving daughter's sobs. The cataracts' roar faded behind us.

At one point we veered far from the path, circling around something. Someone gasped and stared, as did we all. The headless corpses of Khan Alp's scouts were hanging from a tree branch like meat set out to cure. Shortly thereafter we neared the fatal campsite where the scout had died and again circled around the meadow. I had no spirit to wonder why.

We reached more level ground, the young captain called out an order, and we broke into a gallop. He sounded like a fierce puppy barking at its shadow, but he set such a cruel pace that many of us were soon in tears from our captors' cruel saddles. They had clearly been devised by Satan: not only were they absurdly small, but studs were embedded in the seats and the stirrups were too short. Sitting became an agony, and stretching out of my saddle for relief made my legs cramp.

Not that either form of misery could dull my sorrow for long, though I would briefly lose myself in some trifle like the knotted tails of our captors' ponies. Then I would startle back to the present, memories of the dead seared across my eyes. Poor Kateryna, brave Oleg, Khan Alp …

Worst was losing Alexander, who had taught me so much more than letters. As a small girl I would sneak up behind him as he happily pored over some scroll and pull one of his tight dark curls to watch it spring back. He always looked around at me with such sad eyes and smiled so sweetly. All his caring and gentleness, all his *knowledge* cut off by mindless savages!

When we finally stopped, the setting sun was weeping blood-red rays. Hlib, the lone friendly face in that wasteland of loss, set up my tent—through signing to our captors, he had gotten permission—while the youthful captain led his men in growling chants and genuflections toward the south. We ate my company's hard bread for supper, but they forced us to drink a sour, whitish liquid of theirs, surely some evil potion meant to enchant and subdue us.

I stumbled into my tent and had just lain down when the young captain entered it as if he owned it. Of course now he did, just as he owned me. He stripped off his helmet and armor and tossed them aside. Trembling almost as much from the sight of his strangely cut and braided hair as from fear of another assault, I turned away as he flung himself down beside me. He seized my sore arm and forced me around to face him. I steeled myself for another violation, but it never came. He simply gripped me to his chest and threw a leg over my body. I spent the night in a trance of misery, afraid even to weep, pinned to that foul-smelling boy while *he* slept deeply under what had been *my* furs.

He awoke before dawn, leapt from the tangle of pelts, thrust on his armor, and was out of the tent almost in one motion, already exhorting his warriors in his dog speech. When I looked out, the sun was rising and all of them were genuflecting to her, defiling the new day with their satanic rituals. I turned away, wishing I had not lost my other ikon, and knelt to pray properly.

But I had scarcely begun before my captor was pulling me up, dragging me outside, and thrusting me amongst my fellow prisoners, who were huddled forlornly together under guard. We stood there shivering while our kidnappers ignored us and broke their fast. Their boy leader even glanced over as if to say, 'See how much power I have over you?' I retaliated by thinking up insulting names to call him.

Yet when he finished, he motioned to me to join him and pushed his bowl into my hands. One of his men filled it with thin, gray millet gruel. Several others were forcing their bowls onto my fellow prisoners. It was tasteless; worse, there was a thick crust at the bottom of the bowl. After that mockery of a meal, our captors rinsed their bowls with water and drank it, and that was their washing up.

We broke camp, heading north along the river. Today I noticed more. Each of our captors was a living arsenal: an ax or curved sword stuck in his belt, a spear, at least one bow, and several quivers of different-sized arrows, many of them retrieved from the corpses of my people. Our only halts were to switch to fresh horses; they already had many extra, and now they had ours.

Late that afternoon, a peasant gasped, clutched her hands to her chest, and fell from her horse. The young captain called a halt, led us back, and dismounted along with his bow-legged lieutenant. Bow-legs strode to the woman and kicked her several times, but she did not move. One of the peasants near me muttered, "Her heart must have shattered from such hard riding, God rest her soul." I had never heard of such a thing before! Almost as one, we crossed ourselves, bowed, and silently prayed for her.

When I straightened up, the boy captain was glaring over at me. I glared back before he turned away and snarled something to his men. Some of them dug in their saddlebags, forced us off our horses, and moved quickly among us to wrap our chests tightly with lengths of cloth. Others padded our saddles with felt blankets before prodding us back onto our horses and starting off again. The rest of the day passed in somber silence. I often thought of that lost heap of a woman and prayed for her soul. Ironically, she had benefited us, since riding was now less painful.

When we finally halted at sunset, we prisoners almost fell off our ponies. Right away, my peasants formed a respectful ring around me, their eyes begging me for strength. And I must give it to them, as well as defend them from these Tatars as best I could. But all I could think to do was to treat their young captain as coldly as I could. I named him, too: Smerd, though he stank far worse than Papa's lowly smerdi.

That night, I turned my back on him when he came strutting into the tent, but he simply seized me and pulled me down beside him, wrapped his arms around me, threw the furs over us, and fell asleep.

I lay as stiff as a corpse, wishing for death. How I missed Mama's gentle embrace and Baba Liubyna's soft old lap. After Mama's death, it was Baba who sang me lullabies to chase away bad dreams, disciplined me when I got into mischief, taught me decorum, steeped me in ancient lore, and always called me back to the balance of things. That balance was gone for me, perhaps forever!

And how I missed Papa: his quiet authority, his endless energy, his wisdom and love. Yet now that I had been brought so low, it was best that we never meet again. I tried to stifle my sobs for fear of waking Smerd the Tatar.

After a few days, my mind cleared enough to wonder about our plight, beginning with why we had not all been slain. And given that we were alive, where were we being taken, and to what end? And since he never violated me again, what could Smerd want of me? Were they truly Tatars? If Papa was right, they took no ransom for captives of high rank and always killed them, so was Smerd planning some special torture for me later on? But why was I not forced to work like the others: the women made to cook and serve our captors, both at meals and in bed, and the men made to gather brush to make fires or to help groom and feed the horses. One false move brought down hails of shouts and blows on them all.

We had nothing to eat but millet slop and leathery strips of dried meat. I was always thirsty, but we drank only that magic potion, made from white rocks soaked all day in water-filled skin pouches. By nighttime, after being slapped against saddles while we rode, the rock water was turned white and sour.

Each day the Dnieper broadened until it became wider, shallower, and so slow-moving that a skin of ice formed on its surface. On a morning that smelled of snow, Smerd called a halt along a wide strip of shore. Our captors dragged us off our horses and herded us together to shiver in the wind while they reverently prayed and Smerd poured a flask of liquid into the river, they all shouted something like 'hurree hurree hurree,' and they briskly set to work performing a multitude of meaningless tasks.

At the end of all this hurry hurry hurry, we found ourselves remounted, our saddles sitting high on packed clothing and foodstuffs, and our horses lined up end to end in several rows along with the reserve ponies. I felt like a shackled bird atop my unsteady perch. Meanwhile, several men had blown up large sacks into giant misshapen balls, stored their coats and shirts, and rubbed grease on their bare skin, possibly to perform some satanic ritual. I could scarcely believe my eyes when they actually entered the freezing water and floated alongside the lines of horses, grasping onto the tail of the nearest pony and singing softly. They were, of course, guiding their horses across, but we captives all gaped in amazement.

When my mount entered the river, shards of ice collected like broken glass against its side. Even with my knees tucked as high as I could get them, my lovely red boots were soon soaked, and an edge of my cloak slipped into the stream before I could catch it. As ice stole into my bones, I was sure I could endure no more misery. And then the snow began to fall so fast that you could not see through it. I resigned myself to freezing or drowning. But after an eternity, the far shore did loom up and we reached solid ground. With only a pause to rub down the horses and repack the baggage, and no way for us shivering prisoners to dry off, we headed away from the river.

That night I almost welcomed Smerd's iron embrace because he was warm. I kept startling awake from nightmares, and once I saw his cat's eyes gleaming in the dark. He fell back to sleep, while I lay until dawn beset by terrible memories.

The snow stopped sometime during the night, and the weather turned bright and bitter. My peasant Myroslava awoke to find her little girl frozen stiff in her arms. She wept all through breakfast. Afterward, her guard dragged her wailing from her daughter's body and tried to force her onto a pony. Myroslava struggled and sobbed until at a word from Smerd, the man simply drew his sword, seized her by her braid, shoved her down, and struck off her head.

The world would have gone black but for Smerd seizing my arm as I fell. When my sight cleared, he was gaping down at me. Something in me snapped. Myroslava was *my* mother, her frozen daughter *my* child!

I shoved him and he stumbled back. Pointing at her sad, bloody remains, I shouted, "What kind of monsters are you? Do your mothers not weep for their dead children? She needed to pray for her since she could not bury her!" The tears I had held back for days spilled out. I shook a fist at him. "You savage! Have some pity!"

Smerd stared at me with narrowed eyes before turning his back on me and snarling something. A guard seized me, flung me onto my saddle, and bound my wrists tightly to the pommel. They began aching, not only from being tied but from cold leaking past my mangled mittens, while I was forced into a hunch that would nearly cripple me by nighttime.

I was thunderstruck. When I had first stood up to Smerd after the massacre, he had seemed to submit to my will, which I had taken to mean that I could protect my peasants. Now I saw the bitter truth.

More was to come. Although snow blanketed the earth, making the terrain look smoother than it was, Smerd still pushed our pace. At one point, a horse stumbled on an invisible hole and threw a captive boy. The boy was only bruised, but the beast's leg was broken. Smerd had to call a halt. A few of our captors gathered around the heaving animal, presumably to kill it and ride on. Instead, they forced it to lie down. It whinnied in alarm, its eyes rolling, while they squatted around it, crooning gently, and tied its legs together. One man slit its belly just enough to reach inside its body and knelt with his arm plunged inside it for several heartbeats while it tried to kick, then quivered, then died.

I squeezed my eyes shut in mute protest. When I opened them, the killers were draining the blood and sharing it out among their fellows to drink before skinning the corpse and cutting it into chunks. They even kept the bones and innards and packed everything onto an extra horse, including the bloody hide. It made sense to eat the meat, but drinking the blood? And why keep parts unfit for human use?

That evening even we prisoners ate portions of roast pony. Our captors happily gobbled great chunks, wiping their greasy hands on their boots. One of them even sang afterward, in a monotonous whine that brought tears to their eyes and mine, but for different reasons. I sat by Smerd, rubbing my wrists and trying to ease the pain in my back while he ate and barked with his bow-legged man, bits of chewed horse spilling from his mouth.

After he had shoved a plate of meat at me, he pointedly ignored me until he saw that I wasn't eating and tried to force some of it into my mouth. I pushed his hands away and ate daintily as a princess should. But juice dripped down my hands, and when I tried to wipe them on the frozen grass, the grease and blood hardened onto them. I had to copy his custom. My boots were ruined, anyway.

After the meal, the men showed the women how to cut the remaining meat into thin strips and set it out to freeze. Several men stuffed chewed bones into their food bags. I sniffed. We Rus' would feed such garbage to the dogs!

I stood aimlessly watching as Hlib set up what had been my tent in the gloom. He whispered to me, "Princess, the peasants ask me to thank you for your words about Myroslava this morning. You risked your life for us. You give us courage to go on." His words first chilled and then cheered me. I had not thought about endangering myself. I suddenly felt very brave.

Inside the tent, I steeled myself for another night imprisoned in Smerd's arms. I was combing out my hair when he stalked in, seized my bruised arm, swung me around, and struck my face so hard that sparks shot across my eyes. Only his grip kept me from falling. I was blinded by pain and surprise. When I regained sight and sense and outrage—no one had ever struck me before—he was shouting and pointing outside the tent.

At first I didn't understand what he wanted, but whatever *he* had in mind, he had just achieved something else: my life took on meaning again. Someday, somehow, he would pay for this and for all his crimes! Instead of quailing before him, I glared back. He gripped me ever tighter, but though tears started to my eyes from the pain, I held my ground. For several breaths, we tried to out-stare each other. Finally he spoke softly but with force, jerking his head toward the camp.

Now I understood. When I had attacked him that morning, I had dishonored him in front of his men. I nodded slowly. He grunted, nodded back, and released me. Neither of us moved for several heartbeats. Finally he spun around, strode out of the tent, and began snapping orders at someone, his bruised pride plainly restored.

I touched my swelling face. My cheek and eye felt crushed, but no bone was truly broken. I supposed he could have hurt me much worse or even had me killed. There was nothing to do but crawl under my furs and huddle into a tight ball. Fatigue and shock plunged me into sleep. I started to dream.

I was back at the cataracts, floating out of my tent into cold moonlight, where Oleg and Kateryna stood guard. Slowly they turned toward me, the arrow sticking out of his throat and blood pouring from a wound over her heart. Their dead gaze locked onto mine. Alexander appeared before me, blood streaming from his eyes like tears and that horrible apron of skin hanging from his gory belly. His mouth moved, shaping my name. Behind them stood Myroslava cradling her own head. They all dissolved, and Smerd stood in their place, leering down at me. I was back in the tent, suffocating under his weight. I awoke with a start; this last part of my dream was true. Smerd's face loomed over mine, a hand's breadth away.

Expecting another assault I cried out, "Oh no, stop, I beg you!" Briefly, I wished I could just die then and there. No, first I must make him suffer horribly and then kill him!

Smerd sat back and looked at me queerly, almost fearfully, while I prayed that he could not read my thoughts. He picked something off the ground and placed a cold, slimy thing on my bruised face before lying down as usual and falling asleep, his arms crushing me like a vise. I felt the thing on my face: a piece of raw pony liver. Did he have human feelings like pity? Or had he simply damaged his property and now must repair it?

The next morning my fellow prisoners gasped when they saw me. The left half of my face was one swollen, throbbing bruise. Smerd, meanwhile, either out of pride or remorse, ignored me while he strode about and barked orders with even more self-importance than usual. Straightaway some of the guards moved among us, smearing our faces, chests, and hands with stinking grease. I cried out when one of them roughly daubed my bruise, though the stuff cut out the cold surprisingly well. But why would Smerd bother to ease our misery?

That morning many a pitying glance was sent my way. At first I tried to stare straight ahead, ashamed of receiving sympathy from such lowly folk. But I so needed that fellow feeling … and after all, were they not God's creatures, too? So when we stopped, and they clustered around me protectively, I nodded and tried to smile bravely. I looked around at my wretched companions and wondered how they could bear the cold, for I had a fine cloak and mittens and I was freezing. What else they had borne without my seeing it?

For seemingly endless days, we crossed lands that grew ever more alien. Now and then heavy veils of snow shrouded the landscape only to be shredded by the relentless wind. When the wind ripped the snow away, the soil looked sickly, as though it had fallen under some curse. The frozen grasses were stunted, too, as if Mother Earth refused to suckle them. Threat seemed to lurk everywhere.

We reached a river, perhaps the Don where Prince Igor's poliane, his great warriors, had clashed with the Polovtsy so long ago—to think I had ever imagined myself a polianitsa! Tall reeds scratched at my sides, as if a rusalka on one side and a vodianik on the other sought to ensnare me. At least the river was frozen and easy to cross, though it moaned like a wounded animal under our weight. I glimpsed another laughing green maiden flitting beneath the translucent surface but had no energy to whisper an appeasing charm.

Sometimes we passed burial mounds or rings of stones surrounding worn, stiffly shaped statues—often of women, for they had breasts—that emerged from the horizon, glided by us, and vanished behind us. Once I'd have gaped in awe, but now I felt only fear. One time, our band passed an elaborate circle of stones, marked in quarters by four tall poles, upon each of which was impaled a rotted horse carcass. We captives crossed ourselves and whispered charms, but our guards ignored it.

And then came a night when I startled awake to wolves howling in the distance—they can snap a man's neck in one bite—and all my childhood fears attacked me. Since I was small, Liubyna had terrorized me with tales of wolf packs carrying off children. Worse, the men on guard began howling, too! Now *all* of our captors awoke and joined in, including Smerd. When he saw me cringing in fright, he laughed and bayed even louder. Some of the women prisoners raised their voices in terrified prayer, but I was struck dumb. Sorcerers can take wolf shape and travel hundreds of versts in one night—were these nameless marauders werewolves, too? Probably some had already changed shape and were loping off to visit their wild cousins on the steppes. After the howling faded away, I fell into nightmares about demon wolf warriors.

The bitter weather finally relented, and I awoke to an empty predawn sky as hard and luminous as marble. While our captors performed their morning rituals, I clutched my one remaining ikon on its cord. If only I could feel God's love again … but I could not remember what love felt like, to give *or* receive.

Then the rising sun thrust her rays through a stand of frosty grass, outlining each blade in brilliance and casting long purple shadows across the snow. The moment's immovable beauty pierced my soul, and joy briefly lit my heart. In that moment, I felt an answer: this world is alive and speaking to me always.

The land gradually began to swell into soft gray billows. Frozen streams sheltered in the shallow troughs of hills, leafless, stunted trees clinging to their banks. One day, cresting a rise, the lead scout gave a shout and pointed to a black dot in the far distance. Behind it I made out a jagged white line on the horizon. We turned south, putting the cutting wind at our backs. With every verst, the line grew until I realized what it was: snow-crowned mountain peaks. Had I been there under happier circumstances, I'd have been agog at my first sight of real mountains. Such sights were what adventure had meant to me, not this miserable journey to nowhere!

Meanwhile, the dot disappeared behind swells and reappeared, grew into a horseman, then into a warrior like our captors. Smerd had for some time been making strange arm signals. Now I could see that the warrior was answering in kind. At last he rode straight up to Smerd, jabbering and pointing, and the company set off behind him the way he had come. How had they known where to find each other?

Low gray patches were scattered across the rippling plain, ragged plumes of smoke drifting from the center of each. Smerd barked commands, and several men galloped ahead toward a particular patch. Only when we got closer did I see that each one was a huge encampment surrounded by vast herds of animals, more than I had ever seen anywhere. Yet they were dwarfed by those mountain ranges rearing above their foothills like great walls of stone and snow. We passed seas of horses, kept in bounds by mounted men using long flexible poles with a noose of rope on one end. Elsewhere, immense herds of lowing cattle or bleating sheep grazed under their herdsmen's watchful gaze.

We passed several huge camps, each divided into a central camp surrounded by four smaller ones that were set well apart from it. Most seemed to hold hundreds of black rectangular tents pitched in neat rows, with clusters of large round yurts lording over them here and there. These were just like the yurts of our Black Mask allies and the Polovtsy: gray or black, some decorated with colorful patterns of birds, vines, and animals. Their roofs swooped up to central chimney pipes belching smoke, while rows of wagons made pathways before them. At first we seemed to be heading for a particularly large camp, and we even passed by its northernmost section, where I saw many people moving about.

We had just gone by a huge, heavily guarded area—rows of covered wagons, square wheeled platforms as big as threshing floors, strange tower-like structures, and giant mechanical bows—when Smerd suddenly called his men to a halt and summoned his bow-legged man to his side. They whispered together for awhile, once glancing back at me. The wind knifed our backs even worse when we were not moving. At last, on Smerd's signal the company swung right and headed for the western camp instead.

When we arrived, stinks, smoke, roasting meat, clangs, animal noises, and cheerful shouting—much of the latter directed at Smerd, who shouted back—assailed us from all sides. Most of the people we passed were dressed like our kidnappers, and they looked so alike that at first I didn't realize that many were women. And others were children! Here was surely proof that our mysterious kidnappers were not part of a Tatar army, or any army. If they were Polovtsy, might I still be held for ransom? After all, it was a vast tribal union. Although some tribes had lighter skin and hair—our name for them in Rus' is the pale ones—this might be a dark-haired tribe. I might be reunited with Papa after all.

We wound past people, animals, tents, yurts, and carts and finally entered a pathway between lines of brightly painted wagons, four or five to each side. Some were like chests on wheels; others had dark, oily-looking felt roofs. Several were two-wheeled, their shafts tilting down to the ground. I had seen Black Mask families crossing shallow rivers in such wagons. A goat and a fat-tailed sheep were tethered to one of them, and a sturdy pony was picketed near a large yurt standing at the end of the wagon alley.

All of our party stopped except for Smerd and my guard, who led my horse up to his. After dismounting before the yurt and dragging me off my pony, Smerd turned to a four-wheeled wagon and cupped his hands before an altar that sat there, laden with filthy, greasy idols. Their dark force seemed to suck at my soul. I averted my eyes and whispered a protective charm.

A huge mongrel dog leapt out of nowhere, yelping with delight, and Smerd bent down to tussle with it—then it saw me, growled, and bared its teeth. I froze, but my captor spoke to it quietly, and the beast relaxed and began wagging its tail and sniffing at me. Still, I was sure its great teeth would sink into my flesh at any moment. Smerd shoved me toward the yurt's brightly patterned wooden door. It swung open to reveal a bony little witch with a net of gray braids strung across her forehead and trailing down her shoulders, perhaps Baba Yaga herself, grandmother of the Devil! But when I looked closer, she was only a wrinkled old woman with high cheekbones and, to my surprise, deep-set eyes as green as my own. Behind her stood a flat-faced youth about Smerd's age, grinning broadly. His head seemed far too large for his thin frame.

Crying shrilly, the crone ran up to Smerd, the boy trailing behind. A happy smile slid across my captor's greasy face. But instead of embracing one another, he and his people sniffed around each other's faces and hair, something I had seen before among nomads and not understood then, either.

Smerd pulled me forward to face the old woman. She looked me up and down, head cocked to one side, before reaching out and poking me in the chest and laughing when I stumbled backwards. For an instant I thought she was Baba Yaga after all and was going to eat me, but Smerd laughingly steadied me. One of our captors approached and gave the crone a bundle wrapped in one of my linens. Following Smerd and the other youth, she took my wrist and led me into the yurt, miming to me to avoid the raised threshold. Before entering, I glanced below the yurt, and of course it was not sitting on giant chicken legs.

Inside, the tent was warmed by a central hearth and decorated with colorful silk hangings and beautiful carpets, much like a Black Mask khan's yurt I had once visited with Papa. It stank of dirt and sweat, animals and blood, but the space was also surprisingly tidy. And no human bones littered the floor, no giant mortar and pestle lay ready for the witch to fly in—well, what would Baba Yaga be doing in a nomad camp, anyway? Two other women, quite young, were bowing to Smerd with their hands cupped. The younger one was swelling with child.

The hag pulled me onto the right side of the tent, while Smerd and his companion moved to its left. After cheerfully slapping each other on the back and removing Smerd's armor, the two youths vanished outside, leaving me alone with the women. They began pawing through my bundle and found my garments, my ruby-chain necklace, my golden fillet and temple rings, my Mama's collar, and even my koruna. And there were the ikon of Mother and Son from my bedroom and my little mother goddess and my Papa's book! I almost wept, I was so happy to see them. Chattering like a crow, the crone pushed the girls aside. Finding my blue silk gown and gold embroidered tunic, she thrust them into my arms along with the collar and koruna.

The other two women stared stupidly at me. I'd been wearing the same garments since leaving the rapids, and I stank almost as much as Smerd—I had been unable even to wash my face. Though I hated the idea of undressing in front of enemies, I peeled off my filthy clothing and awkwardly donned my finery. But when I picked up a veil, the old woman stopped me, miming that I should shake my braids loose.

"That is most unseemly," I started to protest, but she snatched the veil from me. The older girl seized my braid and rapidly undid it, while the crone waited to press my koruna into my hands. When I shook my head, she tried to place it on my head herself. Argument would serve nothing, so with a grimace I tied the crown on my head. It was a mockery of how a princess should dress.

The hag stepped back and looked me over before going to a nearby chest placed against the curving tent wall. She pulled out a gaudy gold and pearl necklace and signed for me to put it on over my collar and ruby necklace. Its glittering pendants reminded me of spear points and almost hid the collar. After adding several gold bangles to my wrists, heavy as shackles, the old woman grinned, threw my travel-stained cloak around me, and pushed me outside where Smerd was waiting with his thin friend. He nodded approvingly before almost tossing me onto my pony. My peasants were gaping at my koruna and loosed hair; even they knew it was improper.

Smerd and his friend led us all out of the camp toward the central tent city. He still seemed uneasy. Why? Foreboding flowed over me. Was I to be ransomed? Given away to some khan or shaman? Be sacrificed to a pagan god? I tried to pray, but no words came.

What a crush of people when we reached the great encampment! My surroundings shattered into meaningless mayhem: a roil of roasting meat, animal stench, bitter smoke, unwashed bodies; people entering and leaving tents with pots or tools or weapons, stirring kettles over fires, working on unrecognizable objects, searching through colorful chest-wagons, riding by on ponies; tethered goats, sheep, horses, even an occasional two-humped camel looking both sinister and stupid. And bleats, whinnies, barks, shouts, laughter, song, mingled with the constant clang of metal.

I had to force myself to pay heed to this strange world and its inhabitants. Most people resembled our captors: large heads, bowed legs, broad greasy faces, slanting eyes, thick lips, and dark brown or black hair. But some had dark red hair, so mine meant nothing after all. They wore belted robes of felt or hide, with long tapering sleeves that covered their hands. I'd seen that before, but these robes were different, with one front flap curving far over the other to fasten on one side. Some men wore skin vests or jackets, familiar enough, as were their almost helmet-shaped rimmed hats. But many others wore strange, peaked fur caps with flaring side flaps. At least I supposed they were men, since some had thin drooping mustaches and little beards on their chins—nothing like a full-bearded man of Rus'—but most had no facial hair. Everyone wore tapered leggings tucked into their boots. As few wore armor, they must not all be warriors.

But some people who seemed to be women were armed like men, though it took awhile to set the sexes apart aside from the unlikelihood of a man tending a child or cooking. Everyone wore embroidered boots with curled-up toes, but surely only women wore high heeled boots or veils or tall headdresses. And the women's robes seemed to be longer and closer fitting, sometimes with sleeves that were puffed at the shoulders. Their vests were longer and more colorful, too.

A pair of richly dressed men on brightly bedecked ponies stopped to greet Smerd, and several well-dressed men and women passed by who looked like they were from Rus'. When they saw me, they averted their eyes. There were so many others, too: men perhaps from Persia or Araby, with wrapped heads and loose attire; or Cathay, with padded silk coats, high cheekbones, and slanting eyes; but also Black Mask warriors and Polovtsy and black-skinned men and others who were utter mysteries; and many sorry-looking slaves, too, gray-faced, eyes downcast, toiling away at some task. Some were clearly from Rus' and of noble blood, their fine clothes now filthy and ragged.

We passed an open-air smithy where fires leapt and danced like demons, shedding a hellish light on greasy, half-clad men who sang in rhythm with their hammers' rise and fall, sparks snapping from their anvils. One pale-haired fellow looked up and called out to Smerd. My captor shouted back and pointed at me. The man stared at me, laughed, and yelled out, "Hey, little red fox. Looks like the wolf caught you by your bush!" We prisoners gaped at him in amazement, and he grinned back at us defiantly. How could a Rus' betray his motherland? Live at ease in such an alien world? And be so rude to me, his better? I did not understand until much later how truly rude he was.

We finally reached the southern end of the camp. Foremost, like a general leading his army, stood the largest yurt I had ever seen, attended by slightly smaller ones. All were decorated with gaudy flags and layers of tapestries and guarded by rows of felt windbreaks. What lay in it? My body boiled and froze at the same time.

Smerd led us around the fences toward its front and dragged me off my pony, while several of his men dumped plunder onto the ground and pulled my fellow captives off their horses. Two boys wandered up. One of them tried to kick a Black Mask prisoner before Smerd shooed them away. We all stood huddled together, staring stupidly.

Another camp lay to the east, mirroring the one we had just left, and one before us stood in the distant south. As well, perhaps a stone's throw in front of the main camp, a solitary yurt, darkly decorated, sat squat and brooding. A few black chest wagons ringed it, a white horse stood picketed nearby, and a boy and a woman, both dressed in white, stared at me across the frozen grasses.

Smerd seized my arm and dragged me into a wide alley of carts leading toward the great yurt's canopied entrance. My companions were herded behind us. A few gaudily dressed men standing outside the colorful door, their breath steaming, stared at us before hastening inside. Close to the entrance stood a tall shaft topped by a trident and black animal tails. I did bridle at that—after all, the trident *is* the royal symbol of Rus'. Between the alley of wagons and the yurt was an open space where twin fires burned, set a few feet apart.

Silence fell. Our captors were staring at me. Suddenly Smerd thrust me toward the fires, gesturing for me to walk between them. Unsure whether I was awake or dreaming, I stumbled toward them. Flames leapt on either side of me, heat shot at my cheeks. Everything was lit with such strange clarity: a white horse tethered nearby; the yurt's bright banners heaving and snapping in the wind or billowing up to unveil felt decorations hidden underneath like secret messages; lush carpets spread on the snowy ground before a colorful door; to either side of it, impassive guards in metal-plated leather armor, holding curved swords. Smerd and his friend were already awaiting me on the other side with such intense expectancy … his men … my fellow captives … the plunder. He was removing his silver-studded belt, throwing it across his shoulder, and signing to me not to touch the threshold.

From bright to dark: I was inside. Warmth, air filled with the stench of animals, sweat, smoke. Smerd's hard hands thrust me down and forced my head almost to the floor. Brilliant carpet filled my sight, a woven leaf less than a hand's breadth from my nose. The carpet stank. I felt more than saw Smerd in front of me, genuflecting to someone.

From the back of the circular room a deep, strong voice called out. Smerd pulled me up, shoved me before him. Time slowed to a crawl, every detail so precise, so hollow. We passed two central tent poles and a square hearth where a low fire burned. Smoke floated up lazily and vanished through a chimney set in the center of a great wheel, its red spokes bracing the ceiling like the ribs of a parasol. Smoking braziers stood here and there, adding as much haze as light or warmth. The colorful brocade hangings along the curving walls seemed to breathe and sigh, while thick carpets overlapped underfoot like waves.

An altar to one side was crammed with greasy idols. 'We have more power than your god, who has failed you,' they seemed to gloat.

I felt like a puppet, the stone-faced audience some thirty men and boys to my left and a few women to my right, all gaudily dressed and draped in thick furs. Smerd pushed me past two old men standing side by side, one a stern-faced, white-skinned, white-haired ghost dressed in dirty white and holding a white staff topped with a carved horse head. He nodded at me slowly as if confirming some inner thought.

The other, dressed in a saffron-yellow shirt and reddish purple robes, had twinkling black eyes and a face that was a landscape of wrinkles. He seemed surprised for a moment, and then he gave me a broad, gap-toothed smile. He was steadily moving beads along a loop. It reminded me of the times Papa had taken me to the Monastery of the Caves outside Kyiv to give offerings to the monks. They used beads like this man's for counting their prayers, and Papa had one, too.

Oh, to be back with him!

From a throne-like seat came that commanding voice again. Its owner was half-hidden in the shadows, but there were women beside him. One, bejeweled and clearly of high rank, sat to his left. Another, also grandly clad, stood next to her. To me both seemed old, well over thirty and perhaps even forty, yet still strikingly beautiful. The seated woman was dressed in pale blue, with black hair coiled atop her head, secured with long pins from which dangled strands of jade flowers, gold beads, and pearls. Her face, with its slanted eyes and dainty mouth, was perfect and as still as a cloudless sky. She radiated a deep calm; I felt it when she looked into my eyes.

The woman beside her, however, although her face betrayed nothing, seemed to crackle like lightning in a storm. Her gown was fiery red and she wore one of the elongated headdresses I had just seen in the camp. It sat atop a short veil, narrowed as it swooped up, and then flared into a square shape topped with feathers. Her features were also perfect, although broader and flatter. She had full red lips and the blackest eyes I had ever seen. She looked at me, too, and through me.

I could not bring myself to look at the man seated before me, though I could feel him staring at me. Instead I noted a broad-shouldered young man standing to his right. Vitality flowed from him, but his features were marred by an angry frown. His large head was shaven but for a braided lock on one side, a common nomad style. His bright green and silver figured robe was half-hidden by a heavy fur cape, and though he wore no armor, he was gripping the hilt of a sword hanging at his hip. He must be the chieftain's guard.

Finally there was nowhere else to look but at the important man, doubtless the khan of this great encampment, whom Smerd wished to please and who must be my new master. I sagged in terror. My worst fears had not even come close. His fierce expression seemed carved into a face marked by age and hardship. Of his many scars, the deepest ran over his left brow and across his right cheek, leaving his left eye a bulge of dirty white streaked with red, the lid but a remnant. Clearly the Devil had marked him for his own. Though he would have been dwarfed by any warrior of Rus', he was broadly built and wore armor with ease: black, including a black pointed helmet embossed with gold and topped with a stiff pennant. On his cuirass lay a circular pectoral of decorated metal. A sable cloak lay across his shoulders as if carelessly pushed out of his way. No wonder Smerd feared him.

Yet the khan stood up with arms open wide. Smerd stepped forward with cupped hands and received both a thorough smelling and a hearty embrace. As the chieftain sat down again, the young man with the sword caught my eye and smiled. I felt like a bird about to be leapt upon by a cat. I had seen that look before, where I could not think then, but it came to me later. It was how Smerd had looked at me before violating me.

Behind me Smerd's men were dragging in the other captives and the plundered goods. Prodded by their guards, they fell onto their faces around me. In grand fashion, Smerd's men brought forward my chests, my furs, my leather goods. Smerd snapped his fingers, and one of his men broke open a barrel of Papa's mead, poured some into one of my goblets, and handed it to Smerd. He handed it to the khan, who downed it in one gulp and grinned approvingly. Two more men offered my casket of gold. Last, a man came forward and emptied two bags full of withered-looking flat things in front of the khan. It took me a moment to realize what they were: severed ears.

Smerd pulled me forward. Snatching my koruna off my head, he bowed and offered it to his chieftain. Now I was no longer a princess; I was no one. If only one of *my* ears lay on that carpet. Smerd was jabbering again, pointing at the captives and the plunder, then at me. He kept repeating a word that sounded familiar: begi, the Turkish word for princess.

When he finished, at a nod from the khan he seized my arm and made me face the ghostlike man in white. Did this mean I was to be given to *him*? Numbness spread over me while the ghost-man looked me up and down. Our eyes finally met. His held mine and looked right into me. Silence stretched as taut as a bowstring. Finally, as if freed from a spell, I shivered and look down. The man spoke in a high-pitched, warbling voice, almost like a bird. Whatever this apparition said, it pleased Smerd, for he released me, crossed his arms, nodded cockily, and began to speak again in boastful tones.

But the khan's guard cut in, snarling something that stopped Smerd short. The scarred chieftain glanced up at him before turning back to Smerd and, it seemed, questioning him. My captor seemed torn between anger and guilt. A movement from the younger woman: a sly smile crept onto her lips. And the older woman's serene features stiffened into a mask.

Finally, the khan nodded as if satisfied. But the older youth shouted, pointing at Smerd and then himself, the insult in his voice almost visible. My captor's face darkened; he growled a retort. The proud young man spat something back, and Smerd raised both his voice and his fist. Their rage filled the entire yurt like thick dark smoke. The others in the tent broke into rumbles of alarm as the young guard lunged toward Smerd, his sword already half-drawn.

I thought, 'Dear God, he'll kill him and I'll be utterly lost!'

The chieftain had already dropped my koruna and seized the older youth's arm when I saw my hands stretched out before me and realized I had cried aloud. Surely now I was dead. I lowered my hands to my sides, trying not to clench them, trying to await my death with dignity. But the quarrel between the two youths seemed forgotten. I heard murmurs behind me, felt eyes boring into my back, heard those beads rattling endlessly.

Smerd gripped my wrist, dragged me up to the seated khan, and thrust me onto my knees. The man beckoned to me to crawl right to his feet. His stench almost made me sick. It took an eternity to find the courage to look up at him. He was leaning to one side in his chair, stroking his scarred chin, and looking at me in a way I had seen merchants look at a horse they might want to buy. He spoke and motioned someone forward.

The bead noise stopped, and the old man in yellow and purple appeared by my side and looked down at me kindly. He began to talk to me in a lisp. The dialect he spoke sounded somewhat like the Turkish I knew, repeating similar words with slight changes and looking at me intently. I felt stupid with fright. All I recognized for sure was "Kyiv."

Finally I barely whispered, "Do you ask where I am from? Kyiv is my city."

Hearing this, the chieftain cut off the other man's words and looked hard at me. Finally he nodded, waved a dismissal. Smerd pulled me up, motioned me back. I retreated to what seemed a respectful distance while Smerd talked on and on. Perhaps I was not to be given away after all. I begged the Holy Family and all the saints to show me they still loved me, to please grant me this! At one point, the scarred khan spoke, pointing at the bruise on my face. My captor must have made a clever reply, since the crowd burst into laughter.

The other youth did not laugh, however. He looked as if he would like to kill him, and then Smerd glanced at him with equal loathing. Their mutual hatred felt like plague on the wing. And then I felt it dig its claws into me as if it had found its prey. I tried to shake off the feeling. After all, it seemed I was not to be given away to the vicious-looking khan, which was clearly an answer to my prayer. While he and Smerd jabbered on endlessly, I decided that I must learn their language, either to ask to be ransomed or to find revenge, or both.

At last the audience drew to an end. Smerd cupped his hands and backed away respectfully while his men gathered up the plunder, shifting some to one side and removing the rest, along with the other captives. Me he seized by the arm, almost dragging me outside, although he took care that I not touch the threshold. His face seemed lighter, though, as if he had passed some test. Little enough to be grateful for, but I thanked God again and again that I at least belonged to him, not to that ugly son of Satan. Most of Smerd's men disappeared in different directions with the other prisoners.

Hlib and I looked back at each other helplessly. He was my last connection with my home.

On our way back to Smerd's camp, my new master—I must accept that fact—babbled happily with his bow-legged lieutenant, while his lean friend listened intently. For the moment, I was more grateful than afraid; better him than the frightening khan. When we reached his yurt, the hag was there, squinting and smiling in the lowering sun. How benign she seemed now. Even the huge dog, which came up to sniff me again, seemed less threatening. I remembered not to touch the threshold as we all reentered the yurt. The old woman—Crone seemed an apt name for her—beamed and nodded at me.

Inside, Smerd almost took wing, flapping his arms and squawking away at the thin fellow and Crone. He, the Bow Legs, and his thin friend sat down on furs beside a carved, red-lacquered table sitting next to the hearth. The two other women brought out a jar and cups, one of chased silver. I stood waiting for Smerd to put me to work. When Crone motioned for me to sit, too, I was too astounded to move until my master laughed and pulled me down beside him. The fire in its square hearth began to melt away the cold that had burrowed into me. But I was still in the hands of enemies and knew better than to be fooled by warmth and smiles of approval. I sat up straight and tried to keep my wits about me.

Crone laughed and chattered with the three men as she poured a clear liquid into each cup, pausing to touch Smerd's shoulder with affection. She must be his grandmother or nursemaid, which would explain her love for him. He took it as his due, almost seemed impatient. Then I recalled treating Baba Liubyna in just the same way. I swallowed the lump of sorrow that tried to fill my throat. No tears would betray me to my enemies!

Smerd dipped a finger into his silver cup and flicked a few drops of liquid around the room before gulping the rest down at once, not waiting for his companions to be served. No one but me seemed to think it rude. Indeed, triumph seemed to set everyone's spirits aglow. Yet even while they drank and laughed, Smerd and the other fellows sat so formally, with their right knees up and their left crossed under them, each facing the entrance as if expecting someone. At least he seemed more at ease, not haughty as with his men.

For the first time, I was able to look at him directly, too. It had always been dark before, or he had been dressed in armor, or I had been too hurt and angry and afraid. He was surely no more than three or four years older than I was. A shadow of a moustache and surprisingly smooth skin under the grease on his face added to his boyishness. The hair on his forehead had been tonsured, making his hairline look strangely high underneath the long fringes that hung over it. The rest of it was coiled behind his ears in two tight braids. He was wiry, but his shoulders were broad and his arms, as I knew, were muscled with iron. Had he not been such a brute to me, I might have thought him handsome in a wolfish way.

Smerd noticed me staring. He waved a hand toward me and spoke, and one of the girls brought another goblet, which Crone filled and gave me. I was so thirsty that I gulped it down, gasping in surprise when it burned my mouth and chest. Smerd laughed and reached out to touch me, but I shrank away. He frowned and turned back to his friends.

While they jabbered on, my eyes drifted around the dwelling, brushing lightly over surfaces. Bright appliquéd banners covered parts of the lattice that formed the ribs of the yurt. Between them, bulging sacks, knives, spoons, cords, snowshoes, and oddments hung from animal horns lashed to the lattice. Curtains, drawn aside, hung from a long rope that stretched taut across the middle of the tent. It seemed an odd place for them. On one side at the back of the yurt, a low divan, also carved and lacquered red, faced the entrance. And gaudy lacquer chests lined the walls like fat nursemaids hiding treats in their aprons.

I was beginning to feel strangely light-headed, almost peaceful. I sighed and leaned back, following the sweep of the ceiling from the low sides up to the high center. As in that ugly khan's tent, two pillars supported the wheel-like ribs, their bright red spokes radiating out from a beautifully carved blue hub. Smoke from the hearth curled around it before escaping up the chimney.

Smerd's quiet friend brought out a long-necked fiddle topped with a carving of a horse's head. As he played, my master sang. Although the music sounded like a cross between a war cry and a lament, he had a beautiful voice, and it was oddly soothing. I wished I could lie down, I felt so drowsy.

Just then, I noticed two black eyes staring at me.

There was something else in the room. Crammed into every available space, grotesque felt idols pulsed with dark energy. An altar to one side was laden with figures so smeared with lumps of fat and clots of dried blood that they all looked alike. More hung on either side of the entrance, and above it hung a dried hedgehog skin. Felt idols hung over the bed and stood at its feet and sides. In the flickering firelight, they seemed alive and ominously aware of me. My easy mood vanished like a wisp of smoke, and I wished I could melt away into some corner. But there were none. Suddenly the colorful hangings and chests, the silks and furs seemed watchful and malign. The ceiling lowered over me, ready to fall on me.

"No," I whispered, "no." I squeezed my eyes shut.

Someone was shaking me, shattering the spell those idols had tried to cast on me. I opened my eyes. Smerd was staring down at me. I seemed to have fallen over. He mimed to me to remove his borrowed jewelry. Then Crone was putting them into a chest across the room, but I did not remember taking them off. And she seemed so far away and small.

Smerd and his friends were gone, too. I blinked uncertainly at Crone, who was suddenly looming large over me, pulling on my arm. Even sitting up was too much. The room spun around my head, and I toppled back onto the furs. The three women burst into laughter, and Crone pointed at the clear drink.

To my surprise, the young women helped me up and led me to lie on the ornately carved divan while the old one pulled a bright, silk-covered bedroll out of a chest and draped a beautiful blue quilted brocade coverlet over me. She produced a little pot of oily salve, which she smoothed on my bruised face. It felt so lovely to be taken care of, to be warm again, to be treated kindly. "Thank you, thank you," I murmured, as tears welled up in my eyes. Perhaps I had landed in one of Matvei the Bard's fairy tales after all, and all I needed to do was sleep. Surely I would awaken freed from the evil spell that had entrapped me....

I woke with a start, still in the same strange world. Smerd and Crone were entering the tent followed by Bow Legs and the lean youth. It seemed that the sun had set, so I must have been asleep for a while. How my head hurt! Smerd, seeing my eyes open, spoke and beckoned to me. When I did not sit up fast enough to suit him, he threw aside my quilt and forced me up. It hurt, and I cried out and struggled to pull away from him, but he just thrust my cloak and cap at me before almost dragging me outside. He threw me on a waiting pony and mounted his, Crone and the other men joining us.

We seemed to sail through the icy blue dusk, perhaps right off the edge of the world—but that had already happened—no, we were returning to the main camp. Dear God, not back to the scar-faced khan!

Instead, we stopped in front of a large yurt that sat directly behind the khan's. A woman sitting outside was roasting meat on a spit, her face lit from below by the cooking fire's flames. Bow Legs opened the tent door, and soft golden light spilled out. Smerd shoved me inside.

To my great relief, the older of the khan's wives stood before me, as regal as any queen. The idea of a nomad queen had always sounded wondrous to me, and this woman was a indeed a wonder. Her skin was still firm, her high cheekbones, gracefully arched eyebrows, and slanted eyes still elegant, her body still slender. Smerd cupped his hands to her, and she to him. They were alike in face and as slender as birches, while the other nomads in this camp were like thick oaks, so she must be his mother.

He looked both pleased and discomfited until he turned to me and, frowning as if to say, 'You should know how to behave!' gripped my poor arm again and tried to force me down before her. But she put her hand on his, spoke softly, and he released me. She gracefully gestured to me to shed my cloak and hat.

As I looked around the yurt, my mood lifted a little more. Oddly, Crone had begun directing the servants just as if she lived there. One smiling, full-cheeked woman set out chased silver dishes on the low table by the hearth, another tended a pot of soup set on a large trivet over the fire, and others knelt shadow-like, waiting in the dimness beyond the circle of firelight until called on to do something. Except for the pungent smoke from the fire and braziers, this yurt smelled far less rank than the other two tents had. Beyond the cooking aromas, a faint scent of incense softened the air. However, the rest of the tent seemed much like Smerd's, idols and all, although this ceiling's hub was red and its shrine held idols of wood as well as felt. One of them might have been a winged angel.

Smerd approached the shrine and made offerings to the felt effigies, smearing a little food and drink on their lips, raising his cupped hands to them, and uttering some prayer. Bow Legs opened the tent door and threw a cup of liquid outside, barking something before sitting down at the table beside Smerd and the thin fellow. Again all three faced the entrance in that formal knee-up position. The woman—I would call her the Lady—and Crone seated themselves on the opposite side of the table. A tiny, tawny, longhaired dog that had been hidden on the far side of the fire climbed into the Lady's lap, clearly expecting to receive tidbits. And I stood there, head throbbing, not knowing what to do.

Smerd made no move to direct me. Worse, when the Lady turned to me as if to invite me to join them, he shook his head and said something. Instead, a servant showed me a place to sit in the shadows. Smerd and his companions wolfed down their food, while his mother picked out choice chunks of roasted meat for Crone to serve him. I thought he had forgotten I was there until he flicked a scowl like a dagger at me. I scowled back. The men having finished, servants served the Lady and Crone. Before she began to eat, however, the Lady looked over at me and said something to a servant. Smerd frowned but said nothing. To my surprise, the girl brought me a bowl of soup, a chunk of meat, and some bread.

I had not eaten since early morning, and I bowed my gratitude to the Lady. There was nothing in the oily broth but bits of boiled dried meat, onion, and a few grains of millet. No salt on the roast meat, either, and the bread was tasteless. I was too hungry to care.

While the women ate, Smerd and his friends downed cup after cup of some kind of liquor. Soon his speech grew thick, and his thin friend soon could hardly sit straight. Then the Lady spoke, and the tone changed. Her servants and his men vanished. She and Smerd began speaking in low voices, sometimes glancing over at me. He sat up straighter at something she said. Perhaps they were discussing the uproar that afternoon in the ugly khan's tent. Yes, Ugly Khan—that was a fitting name for him….

I awoke. I had fallen sideways. Mother and son were embracing in farewell. Smerd motioned to me, and I reeled up, bowed to the Lady, who nodded back to me graciously, and followed him into the ink-thick dark. Outside, Crone and Smerd's two men leapt up from beside the cooking fire and followed us to the horses. Without his guiding hand on my arm, much gentler this time, I might have stumbled and fallen, but Smerd seemed to know where dogs lay underfoot and where the farthest chest-wagons stood. Firelight gleamed in front of other tents, and laughter cracked the quiet into frozen shards, while beyond the camp lay a vast wilderness, implacable, dark, and empty. Our ponies' hoof beats and jingling bridles seemed an intrusion on the limitless silence. I looked up at the sky encrusted with glittering stars and felt dizzy, as if I could fall up into them. On the edge of the northern horizon, the mysterious Northern Lights, blue and green and pink, arced and shifted like the veils of some invisible sky goddess.

Or portents of danger. Who knew what they meant?

Back in Smerd's tent, Bow Legs disappeared. Crone and the other two women set out bedding on the divan and pulled the curtains closed, slicing the tent in two and leaving me alone with Smerd and his companion. The lean youth settled onto a pallet at the foot of the divan, facing away from it. And Smerd smiled at me like a wolf might smile at its prey. I looked from one boy to the other, shame creeping over my entire body as I realized what was to come next. Smerd motioned to me to remove my clothes. I had no choice but to obey. I began to weep, but he simply stood and watched, that smile on his face never wavering. After disrobing himself, he pushed me down onto his divan.

Now I learned what it truly meant to be a slave, to be shamed, to be forced to do things I hated. I wanted to die—even menial labor would be better. Afterward, sobbing, I wondered if I could find the courage to kill Smerd. How? Steal a knife? Poison his food or drink? Suffocate him while he was drunk? I could do none of those things.

A terrible thought struck me. One day I would be able to bear children. A child by that cross between a slavering wolf and a puffed-up cock? Never! I *would* die first!

Smerd rolled off me and raised himself onto one elbow. His breath reeked of liquor. Pointing to himself, he said, "Argamon."

"What do I care, you stinking monster," I cried.

Striking his chest, he repeated, "Argamon, Argamon!"

"All right, Argamon, you swine!" He beamed and pointed to me expectantly.

I did not want to tell him my name, as if possessing it would give him further power over me. I shook my head at him, and his delight vanished. He barked something at me and gripped my jaw so hard, I feared it might break. "Sofia," I gasped.

"Sofia?" He sat up and spoke excitedly to the youth at the foot of his bed, repeating my name. The fellow left and I felt a cold draft as the door to the yurt opened and closed. 'Good, I hope he freezes out there,' I thought. Argamon, as I must thenceforth call him, smiled and spoke my name once more, stroked my hair and wiped my tears with his filthy fingers. He threw himself half across my body, pulled the bedclothes over us both, and fell asleep in the dim red glow from the hearth.

I lay for an eternity, rubbing my jaw and hating him. Who was he? Who were his people? The Ugly Khan must be his father—why else would his mother be sitting beside him—which explained why he led warriors older and likely more experienced than he was. Why did he and that angry young man with the sword hate each other? Angry One—yes, a fitting name. He must not be a guard but another of the Ugly Khan's sons and therefore Argamon's older brother; clearly they were rivals. Well, Rus' was built by men who shed their brothers' blood. Who was the younger beauty? Why had she smiled and the Lady stiffened? What was my place in all this? Clearly, I meant something special to all of them. And what had become of the rest of the captives? Would I ever see them again? How I missed Papa, how I cursed the day he had sent me away!

At dawn blaring horns, thudding drums, and deep rumblings startled me awake to a headache, sore jaw and arm, and itches everywhere from fresh bug bites. And Smerd—no, Argamon—was gone. The noise faded, and when I peered around the edge of the curtain to see what was happening, Crone was overseeing the two women and several others as they rolled up carpets and packed pots, bowls, utensils, and oddments into chests. These Argamon's thin companion and some other men were quickly removing. The old woman looked over at me and smiled knowingly. My cheeks flushed. They all knew what Argamon had done to me the night before.

Finding my bundle at the foot of his divan, I dressed hastily under the bedcovers, clumsily braided my hair, repacked my bundle, took a deep breath, and stood. Clearly they had been waiting for me to rise, since they swarmed like bees into Argamon's side of the yurt and began to pack and remove the rest of the furniture. Crone handed me a wooden bowl of gruel and a cup of a drink that Papa's nomads called koumiss. There was nowhere to sit, and it was bitterly cold in the tent. I hastily downed my breakfast. The pregnant girl took and rinsed my cup and bowl and poured the rinse water from the dishes into a cooking pot, but I was already resigned to drinking dirty water as part of my next meal.

Not knowing what else to do, I picked up my bundle and tried to stand aside, but no matter which way I moved, it was always into someone's path.

Finally, Crone said, "Sofia!" and pointed to my cap and cloak and mittens lying by the door. She knew my name! Of course, she'd have heard that last night as well. Before I could put them on, Argamon's quiet friend seized me by the shoulder and smeared grease all over my face, hurting it again. Crone snatched my bundle from me and handed it to a passing woman, patted my shoulder, and herded me toward the door. The youth followed me like a shadow. I turned around and stared at him. How could such a thin body hold up such a large head? Or perhaps his fur cap made it seem bigger.

Outside, I took a deep breath. Clouds had blown in overnight, and the air smelled of snow. The fresh wind blew away my headache. And, forgetting to be unhappy, I gaped in disbelief. Argamon's camp was disappearing—all the camps were! Women were collapsing yurts and packing everything onto ponies or into wagons, while men lined up strings of laden animals and hitched them together. Someone began a song and others chimed in, filling the air with high-pitched trills and long wavering notes as heartrending as the endless steppes. The low black tents were gone, and only the largest yurts remained, many now sitting on the square wheeled platforms I had passed the day before. Up close I saw that each had a railing and poles to which men were harnessing double lines of oxen.

Argamon's yurt was now piles of felt, stacks of collapsed lattices, and spokes being handed into a wagon; all his wagons and oxen were already attached together in a long chain. One woman trotted to the front and mounted the lead ox. It was a clever way to use few people for many tasks, for now she alone could lead all those wagons and beasts at once. I did not like the thought of my captors being clever.

And where had all those people from the black tents gone, along with my enemy? I felt rather empty without him there to hate.

"Sofia!" called an old, cracked voice. Crone appeared beside me on a little gaily-bedecked pony, another on a lead. She beckoned to me to mount, and I unwillingly joined her. She spoke to my silent guard, and he ambled toward a knot of men on ponies, whistling in a peculiar low tone as he went. Nearby, a ready-saddled pony lifted its head and trotted up to him, and in one fluid motion he mounted it and rode off with the others. A blast of horns; I almost fell off my pony. Several horsemen galloped by, the blare of their bugles fading after they passed. With the screech of thousands of wheels, the great mobile camp began to move.

Had I arrived here only to be taken elsewhere?

Even with so people many gone, there were so many left astride horses, on foot, in wagons. Smoke drifted out of the chimneys of the mobile yurts; women moved in and out of them, stepping on and off their platforms as if they were sitting still. Old men loped beside the wagons, slapping grease on their shafts, perhaps to dull the wheels' painful shrieking. Beyond the caravans, men on ponies goaded vast herds of cattle and sheep before them, whooping and containing strays with their pole nooses. The animals shuffled and protested like weary grandfathers forced to hurry. In the distance, mounted guards kept pace with the procession. People, horses, goats, sheep, dogs, camels, laughter, song, sky, wind, racing clouds, and endless steppes walled me in with vast indifference.

Two great pillars of smoke billowed up from the center of the Ugly Khan's great camp. They seemed to be beacons, since all the smaller camps around it, including the one I was in, edged toward it to form a single enormous procession. Once our wing of the camp was in place, Crone tugged on my pony's reins, and we trotted up to the head of the caravan to join the Lady's retinue. There was no sign of the khan or his tent, I was glad to see, though the Lady's yurt remained intact on its platform. She nodded to me briefly, her tiny dog perched before the pommel as if everything had been arranged for its amusement, but someone rode up to ask her something. Riding, and on a nail-free saddle, was clearly a privilege, for the many hundreds of menials had to walk.

I was staring around in all directions when, not far behind us, the door to a gaudy yurt on a platform opened and out came the black-eyed beauty who had stood near the Ugly Khan—was it just yesterday? She turned to speak to someone: the old man in white. She seemed angry with him, and he with her. He offered her no farewells, swung onto a white horse tethered to the railing, and disappeared into the throng, while she mounted a gaily decorated pony and trotted to the head of her own baggage train, quite near us.

Her eyes met mine for a moment before sliding past as though I was beneath her notice. Why would she think ill of me? Or was she merely haughty? In contrast, other well-dressed women were moving about, forming friendly clusters. A few trotted up on their ponies to chat with Argamon's mother; children shouted gaily and played games of chase. Someone began a song and others joined in. But the dark-eyed woman and her retinue behaved as if they alone existed, so I decided she would be Haughty Woman.

Losing interest in her, I began watching the children, remembering sadly how I too had laughed and played not long ago. They were picking odd lumps off the ground or ripping up patches of frozen wormwood and stuffing them into leather bags. Even a few old people were playing this strange game. I turned in my saddle to see people scattered throughout the procession and among the herd animals, all stuffing bags. A child swooped behind the closest wagon, bent down, and raced on. Now I saw what they were all doing: scooping up steaming dung dropped by the animals. I forgot my envy. With no fields to tend, why would they want it, anyway?

The convoy crawled over the frozen wastes, a northeasterly wind whipping at our backs. Once again, chill crept into my bones and settled there like an old habit. No one else seemed to mind. Even the slaves walking beside the wagons seemed heedless of the cold, though several were missing fingertips or noses from frostbite. Crone at my side seemed to have forgotten me, just stared ahead at nothing.

After an eternity, I turned to her and, pointing at myself, timidly spoke. "Sofia."

Crone looked over at me, smiled, and nodded. "Sofia Beki."

She did not seem to understand. I tried again and said, pointing first to myself, then to her, "I am Sofia. What is your name?"

This time she understood and cackled, "Kamileh."

"Kamileh!" I exclaimed, happy that someone understood me. I rather liked this old woman who so loved that beastly Argamon, until with a jolt I remembered who she was—another cruel enemy—and had to forbid myself to cry. If Kamileh was kind to me, it was only because she was old and accustomed to serving, not because she really cared. I gave up trying to speak with her and rode with my head down as the ground passed slowly beneath my pony's hooves. Time rolled on as measureless as the grasslands. Powdery veils of snow began falling. I began to yearn for a chance to run with the children even if they were only picking up dung, or at least to stretch my stiff limbs, but our only brief stop at midmorning was to let the animals rest and graze. I stood like a lump until Kamileh tapped me on the shoulder and led me inside the Lady's yurt.

The Lady and a few other women were already there. The carpets and chests were still in place, and a low brazier served as a temporary hearth for a simmering pot of stew. The room almost felt welcoming, especially with the wind rising outside. We stayed inside for the rest of the day grouped around the brazier, which a menial fed with stalks of dried wormwood and large, dry patties from a leather bag like the ones the children had been stuffing. Now

I saw what the bags of animal dung were for. No wonder the tents smelled so. It also meant that they baked their bread right over dung embers. Any civilized person knew that was a good way to get sick!

Later in the day, we shared small portions of thin stew and cups of koumiss. Men and women often came in, hands cupped in homage, apparently seeking advice or orders. Women sewed, and sometimes a few sang over the screech of the wheels, but though the Lady smiled at me kindly now and then, it was both deadly dull and frighteningly strange. Afternoon slowly stretched its hands toward evening.

The light had faded to murky gray before the Lady sent one of her women outside; soon after came a blare of horns, and the screeching cavalcade halted. Silence had never been so welcome. Once camp had been set up, we ate strips of dried meat and chewy sour white lumps, and drank more koumiss. At least the liquor warmed me. Most people had set up small lean-to style tents, but I was given a place to sleep in the Lady's yurt. I bowed thanks to her; after all, I needn't behave like a barbarian myself. She patted my hand and returned to directing her servants and slaves. That gesture made me want to trust her.

Given my bundle and some felt bedding, quilts, and furs, I went to bed clutching my ikons and Baba Liubyna's mother effigy. I shivered under my covers all night, the wind and snow trying to burrow into the yurt from below while fleas and lice attacked from within. Of course, bug bites were nothing new, but this was winter.

Just before sunrise with the camp stirring, I stepped outside into a colorless world where the tents had turned into frosty hillocks and people flitted about like ghosts. The sun, when she finally appeared, was only a pale white disk imprisoned behind clouds; the sky never lightened beyond a drab gray that day. When people began their morning worship, Kamileh tried to get me to join, but I defiantly knelt in the snow to pray to Mother Mary. Soon everyone but me was busy.

After another tasteless breakfast, we broke camp. Again I stood in the way, and the Lady must have noticed how dispirited I looked, for she spoke to Kamileh, who motioned me to help her with a few minor tasks. I was surprised by how grateful I felt to be given something to do. The Lady also spoke to a servitor, and soon from somewhere in the center of her caravan those two columns of smoke swelled up into the wind. As if in answer, all around us nine other lines of smoke rose and moved in pace with us. I had not even noticed that yesterday. They must be from those other camps we had passed, and this must be how these nomads—I still prayed they were Polovtsy—signaled each other. The Lady must be their leader, odd as that seemed.

I expected the morning to drag on endlessly, but Kamileh had a surprise for me: speech. She swept her arms around to include the entire caravan and said, "Ordu."

I eagerly repeated, "Ordu."

Pointing at a yurt, she said, "Ger." That was a surprise. I had thought all nomads called their round tents yurts. We went through several other words, like "qoni," for sheep, "ukor," for ox, "nokhoi," for dog, and so forth. As for pony, there were more words than I could follow. But eventually Crone ran out of things she could point to. I was already feeling discouraged, because "ger" or "ukor" were not going to explain what was happening to me.

That night the dead invaded my dreams again, the sides of their heads leaking gore, their bloody throats gaping like extra mouths whose ghastly crimson lips moaned my name. They called to me with wails of pain and rage, shocking me awake, weeping. That woke everyone else. The Lady called to Kamileh, who moved her bedding next to mine and whispered in a soothing voice. It did comfort me somewhat, but most of the night, afraid of sleep, I tried to pray. I must have drifted off, though, for I awoke before dawn to see the Lady kneeling, hands cupped and head bowed, in front of her altar. Yesterday she had performed the same rituals as everyone else, but this seemed more intimate. Supposing she had her own idols to worship, I turned over, seeking a few more moments' respite.

DECEMBER? JANUARY? Anno Domini 1239 or 1240

amileh's attempts to teach me more of her speech only discouraged us both, so for numberless days I lived without words, benumbed by cold and lack of sleep, like an invisible ghost mimicking the living. I dully wondered if I had died and fallen into some cold Hell. Father Kliment had often threatened me with Hellfire, but lack of love, warmth, cleanliness, even sunshine, seemed just as brutal. Things did change, though. The sun finally came out, each day the other lines of smoke grew larger, more and more new ropes of smoke appeared on the horizon, and the distant line of mountains reared up ever higher and clearer.

One day men on horseback appeared from the south. Stopping before Argamon's mother, they cupped their hands, spoke with her, and charged off again. By midday nine more ordus had converged on ours. Each was another large wheeled city with vast herds and countless people. Other lines of smoke in the distance, many of them, must come from other ordus.

There could only be one reason for such huge numbers: we were following *Tatar soldiers*.

And each of these ordus held thousands of people to serve them!

I fended off despair with hatred. Sliding off my pony, I stumped along with my fellow slaves. Kamileh snatched at me and called out, but I was lost in bitterness: no ransom, no miraculous escape. And I had almost let down my guard just because these women had shown me a little kindness. After a few versts, though, all I wanted was just to lie down and rest somewhere warm. I tried to will myself onward, but finally I stumbled and nearly fell. Kamileh, who had trotted patiently by my side the whole time, pressed the reins of my pony into my hands in a gesture of trust. I could not resist her offer.

That afternoon we began passing ordus that had already settled in. So many fires burning, people bustling about, herds of animals pawing at the snow, so many empty spaces for black tents. The sun was near the horizon when we crested a hill overlooking a wide, empty valley, in its midst a narrow river flanked by trees. Beyond it ever-higher lines of hills swelled upward as if paying homage to the astounding snow-crowned mountains that now loomed above us. The Lady sent out buglers, and her ordus spilled into the valley and spread out on one side of the river.

Ours split into separate wings again, gers were set in place, the oxen and platform taken away, wagons unloaded and drawn up in rows on each side of the ger's entrance door, smaller gers rising behind the larger ones. I noticed that Haughty Woman's now sat slightly behind and to the left of the Lady's. Kamileh mimed for me to help her smooth carpets and furs over the floor while others hung bags on animal horns along the walls, set up curtains, put chests in place, rebuilt the hearth, and relit braziers. It felt good to have something to do; it kept me from thinking about all those other ordus around us. When all was in place, the Lady moved to each brazier in turn and sprinkled incense into it. Spicy fragrance filled the air, along with the aroma of boiling meat and baking bread. Happily, no one seemed to expect me to return to Argamon's wing.

The next morning, shouts woke me. Everyone was rushing outside, so I joined them. Darkness was eating the sun yet again! As the sky slowly turned into twilight, that strange white man with the white hair appeared from his ger and motioned to the Lady and her retinue to join him. By the time we arrived, he, a weird, witchy looking woman, and a youth had stacked firewood into a cone shape and set it alight. All three were holding flat, colorfully decorated drums, and his was enormous. Now I understood: he was a shaman. More and more people poured out of their gers and crowded around us, talking eagerly. Well, *I* at least had the sense to be afraid!

The white man looked around sternly, and silence fell. He began to drum and sway, to circle around the fire, to chant tunelessly while the other two beat their drums. They pounded on and on like an endless headache, but slowly the weird half-light faded and the world grew bright and clean again. When the shaman finally finished his dance, the fire had died down and he looked used and haggard, but he broke into a smile as he turned to the Lady and spoke words that seemed to make everyone happy. They bowed to each other, and the gathering broke apart. I was left with the mystery of how shamans could chase away the dark, but then I had no idea why such portents happened in the first place....

A day for mysteries: thick bands of smoke arose soon thereafter somewhere beyond the foothills. It did not seem like any signal, and no one paid attention to it; but as the day waned, whenever anyone opened the door, that thick pall of smoke rose higher, lit from beneath by a bloody glow.

That night I dreamt I was back at home, running through Papa's palace, desperately calling to him, while flame-eyed wolves howled all around it. Empty corridors stretched before me, I passed through rooms I had never seen before, and then the rooms grew round and small and fickle winds swept through them, tearing off curtains and tablecloths from window and table. At last there was no place to run. I was trapped in an empty ger. Its door started to open, and I tried desperately to close it, but I was not strong enough, and the door slowly forced me back. I awoke with a cry.

The next day, no one even had time to put me to work. I was fed in the morning and forgotten until supper time, when Kamileh collected me where I was standing staring at nothing. I went to bed as weary as if I had actually worked hard. I fell asleep with a lump of misery in my throat.

Shortly before dawn, Kamileh poked me awake and thrust my blue gown, gold tunic, and Mama's collar and fillet into my arms. I knew: the soldiers were returning, and with them that pig Argamon and the Ugly Khan. I crossed myself and whispered a brief prayer. While I groped and slipped with my own clothing, Argamon's mother was dressing in a brocade gown the color of a robin's egg and binding it with a heavy gold sash. Her main servant, the plump-cheeked woman whose name seemed to be Temulun, twisted the Lady's hair up into elegant coils and fastened them with those bejeweled pins. But the gown was stained and wrinkled, and my gown had boot marks on it. Our eyes met. The Lady seemed sad today.

Outside, the sun shone hard and bright, the wind blew bitterness. After their dawn prayers and a hasty breakfast, the menial women led me to the area in front of the Ugly Khan's huge ger. His wagons had been set in a rough semi-circle, leaving a large open space before it, and the shaman's ger had moved to one side. A crowd was already assembling in the space, but more and more people arrived, pushing to get the best view, until I was pressed against a wagon. I glimpsed the old man in white and, and there were the Lady and Haughty Woman standing side by side under the ger's canopy, their retinues behind them. Neither looked at the other.

A hush fell. From somewhere came a distant noise that at first sounded like constant thunder but grew ever louder, became deafening. Now the noise became horns, drums, scores of hooves. With everyone jostling to get the best view, I could see little, but a vast army must be pouring into the valley. The staff bedecked with black animal tails stood tall in front of the soldiers, so that would be where the Ugly Khan and his retainers were. I climbed up on a wagon wheel, and there they were: seemingly endless battalions of mounted warriors. Their bright standards flapping in the wind, they marched in strict formation and spread out before the camp. Drummers were perched on two-humped camels, pounding on drums the size of huge kettles; buglers blared out triumph. A mighty drum roll, and utter silence fell as the troops all dismounted in unison. From each troop a leading man rode forward toward the khan, prisoners and plunder-laden animals trudging behind them. I glimpsed Argamon and the angry young man leading the parade, so both must be important.

The Ugly Khan shouted some nasty-sounding speech to his soldiers and gestured toward the plunder and prisoners cowering near him. His army cheered as a finely dressed man and woman, each in chains, were dragged before him and shoved to their knees. The khan dismounted and shouted orders; a pair of men came forward with a carpet and thrust the man down on it. It seemed so strange, especially when they rolled him up in it.

A deathly quiet fell, and a terrible mystery unfolded before me. Several horsemen galloped forward, but instead of dragging the carpet away, they rode over it again and again, while muffled shrieks rose and faded from inside it. The only other sound was a long, pitiful wail coming from the woman.

I froze, could not think beyond wanting to flee. But I was stuck on my perch. It seemed as if this ritual might never end, but when it finally did, the khan marched forward and drew his sword, and the woman screamed one last time as he grasped her braid and yanked her head forward. The blade rose, it dropped. I tried to fend off the dark roaring in my eyes and ears, or perhaps it was the troops cheering like endless thunder and shaking their spears.

The Ugly Khan remounted his horse and moved toward his ger, his sons and attendants behind him, including the old man with saffron and wine robes, bundled in a dirty sheepskin coat. Everyone around me began clapping, singing, shouting, and surging forward. I lost my balance and almost fell to the ground; only gripping my wagon wheel kept me upright. Kamileh looked around and tried to beckon me forward, but I could not move and we were separated. The Ugly Khan entered his ger, followed by the white man, the ladies, Argamon and the Angry One, and many others. Suddenly there was room to move. I looked around for Kamileh, but she had vanished. Most troops dispersed toward their wings of the ordu. Women rushed among the ones who stayed, eagerly calling greetings.

Still reeling from those sacrifices, or perhaps executions, I leapt down and wandered aimlessly about. Soldiers were unloading horses and unpacking goods—silks, furs, rugs, gold cups, even cooking pots and such—or dragging forward captives tethered in lines like ponies, until there was scarcely room in the open area for all the loot and prisoners. The soldiers lined up, some with an arm around some happy woman—or women—and waited patiently while their captains shared it all out.

I wandered on, was somehow out of the camp and past the lone ger in front of it when lines of camels and oxen laden with dismantled siege engines began passing me. One of the soldiers leading them shouted at me, so I turned another way, and suddenly I was among the dead: spare ponies laden with wrapped corpses, brown bloodstains marking their shrouds. Wailing women were desperately searching among them. I retreated.

Threading my way through the crowd, I almost stumbled over the headless corpse of the woman, flooded in blood. The carpet near her was blotched in an eerie red pattern left by horse hooves. Everyone else acted as if the two weren't there. Breathing deeply to fend off faintness, I reeled away looking for some safe haven from the chaos. If only I could escape.

That was when I realized: with all the confusion, surely I could! The nearby river must lead to some small village or at least some ruins where I could find supplies or at least shelter. There were bound to be other refugees from this battle, and we could head north together. No one here would bother looking for one slave girl, at least not for long.

The crowd was thinning, and it was a simple matter to slip unnoticed back into the Lady's ger. Snatching a leather sack from the wall, I stuffed it with dried meat, white lumps, and a flask of koumiss. Not daring to wear my own cloak and mittens again until I reached the river, I found a thin quilted silk coat and felt cap that would have to do. I wrapped my little bundle of belongings in my cloak along with the flask and the food.

After peering out the door to make sure no one was watching, I strode toward Argamon's camp, which lay between me and the river. An eternal walk, but I got there without drawing undue attention. Luckily his wing was mostly empty, though beyond it a huge flock of sheep blocked the way to the river; in the distance two girls were tossing fodder to them. Two young men, fellow slaves or perhaps returned soldiers, took most of their attention. I edged around the flock and trotted toward the trees, trailed by their laughter.

I looked back before ducking into a grove of bare-boned trees by the river bank. The four had their backs to me. There were people from other ordus in the distance, too, but no one seemed aware of me. I decided to go northwest. After donning my cloak, cap, and mittens, I took stock. My supplies might last three days. How far could I travel in that time? And what if I found nothing to shelter me? Well, I might be a fool to run away without a better plan, but I wouldn't turn back. I tried walking along the bank, but snow drifts and bushes and ice-covered grasses made that impossible. I must walk on the ice river.

When I reached it, the wind sliced right through me. After a few halting steps, I admitted defeat and turned south, walking at the very edge of the river and clinging to overhanging branches and grasses. I began praying for help, both to the Holy Family and to my old spirit friends. After stumbling along until the sun was at her zenith, my legs threatened to go no further. I crawled up the bank through the thick underbrush and stiff grasses and huddled under a large leafless bush for protection. At least now that I was free, I could eat when I wanted. I dug out a strip of dried meat from my bundle and set to gnawing at it. But then it was gone. How cold I felt, how drowsy … but if I lay down, I could sleep for a short while and then feel strong enough to go on.

I swept away the snow, made a sort of nest, laid my head on my bundle, and curled up at the foot of the bush. It stood over me indifferently. The wind whistling through the trees sounded like the groans and sighs of dying people. Had the ghosts of my lost companions followed me here? If they were going to pursue me everywhere, day *and* night, my life would be damned wherever I fled. No, I couldn't worry about that now. I needed to sleep for a little while, to forget the cold.

Just as I was closing my eyes, my breath froze in my throat. Back there among the trees, something was slinking toward me. In case it was a vodianik or a leshi, I whispered an appeasing charm. But it didn't disappear. It flitted through the vegetation, ever nearer. Perhaps it was a wolf! I tried to think of everything I knew about wolves, but nothing came to mind, only that they usually hunted in packs. Might a scout act alone? Should I climb a tree? How absurd to think I could outrun a wolf through snow banks and then scale a tree before it reached me! I almost felt its teeth sinking into my leg. Chills assaulted me. My only hope was that since I was downwind, it might pass on if I lay stock-still. I shut my eyes and tried to shrink into invisibility, praying for protection against whatever the thing was. Oh well, best for it just to kill me. I never wanted to return to that fiend Argamon. What a fool I was to think I could escape.

The cold seemed to be fading. In fact I felt quite warm now, and almost glad that the end was near. I felt so drowsy....

A voice spoke above me, and my eyes sprang open in terror. A kind-faced old man was kneeling down beside me. An angel? It took several heartbeats to recognize him by his gap teeth: the Ugly Khan's interpreter. So there was no beast or harmful spirit after all. I sighed and closed my eyes again, but he was jabbering at me insistently, though the words came from too far away to make sense. A hand firmly shook my shoulder, but not with roughness like Argamon's. The voice sounded kind, too. He even seemed to be using Polovtsy speech, or perhaps I was just dreaming. But the dream would not go away.

"Please, wake up," he lisped. "Do you understand me?" I unwillingly nodded, hoping he would let me go back to sleep. "Ah, I knew you would speak Kipchak Turkish. Qacha cut me off once you spoke in your language, so I never got to use it." He shook my shoulder again. "Please get up. You can't freeze to death now, even if you want to. Argamon's men are searching for you, some of them close behind me. You are lucky I found you first."

"Better to die," I moaned, "rather than return to that stinking beast." Oddly, my teeth were chattering like tiny faraway birds.

"But Qacha will put Kamileh to death if you do; he'll blame her for losing you."

That opened my eyes! "So now I *must* go back or have Kamileh's blood on my hands? God spare me."

"You have lost everything, and you think you have nothing to live for." He looked up, shook his as if arguing with himself. "No, it won't help to tell her that many have suffered as she has, yet we keep going. She's too wretched to think about that right now." The words flowed over me, meant nothing.

To me he only said, "Let me help you sit up." How had he found me? As though reading my mind, the old man added, "I went looking for you. I met a few people who said they had seen a mysterious summer maiden wandering through Argamon's camp, and then a shepherd girl told me she saw the maiden heading for the river. And of course you would go south rather than north in a wind this cold. But now we must be going back, and into that very wind, I fear. And look what you brought! Here, drink up." He put my stolen flask to my lips. The liquor was like a river of heat flowing through me. "Yes, good. Drink it all down. Now, let me help you stand."

My lips felt like blocks of wood. "Who are you? Why did you come for me?"

He slowly helped me up the riverbank. "Me? I am just an old monk, passing through this life on my way to the next. My name is Dorje, and I was looking for you partly for Kamileh's sake. But also I have wanted to meet Argamon's princess ever since I heard about her. And when I first saw you, I felt as if I already knew you.

"It must have been terrible not knowing anyone understood you that day. But Qacha could not see why a princess of Rus' would be so far from home in winter, and he wanted to see if you betrayed knowledge of some unlikely steppe language. He wanted to be sure Argamon was not cheating just to best his rival. Had you recognized one, you would be dead and Argamon would be in disgrace. Although he almost disgraced himself anyway. Alas that I got no chance to speak with you before he took me off on campaign.

"So when I was in Noyan Qacha's ger this afternoon and Argamon wanted you brought there for the feast, I offered to fetch you. But all I found was Kamileh frantically searching for you and terrified for you and for herself. She begged me for help. I told her to wait to sound the alarm so I could start looking for you, or you would soon be in the hands of soldiers, possibly the wrong ones. When Argamon first brought you before Qacha and he and Qabul fought, I knew you'd be in danger despite your power—or because of it!"

"My power?" Had the cold benumbed my brain? Was this magpie of a man mad?

"Yes, your power over Argamon's fate—and Qabul's, as well. But many other conflicting and perilous forces surround you, too."

Suddenly he added, "Now, what I want to ask, if I may, is why were you out in the wilds with such an odd collection of people when you were captured?"

I could only answer in short bursts as I struggled through the under-brush, with many pauses between sentences. "My father thought Tatars were going north, not south … He was sending me to Constantinople to safety … and peasants came, too … Argamon's men killed almost all of…." Such despair and misery swept over me that I nearly sank to the ground.

"Please, I cannot go back there, not even for Kamileh."

The old man stumbled and almost fell back under my weight. "Do not give in to despair. It will not help. As to Argamon, you have no choice. And we must not upset him, or he may hit you again. Your fleeing shames him, but he also probably fears your falling into Qabul's hands—he has surely sent out his own men. I must restore you to him quickly before more damage is done."

He helped me stand back up, and we lurched along like a pair of drunkards.

"Hmm," he mused, "I will tell him that you didn't know you were expected to join the feast, which is true, and you got lost when you wandered away from the ordu in the general confusion of the army's return, which is mostly true. And you thought you should return to his camp, but when no one was there, you wandered down to the river to look around and got too chilled to come back. Yes, and Kamileh's quick thinking saved you when she learned you were missing! That should spare you both a beating.

"Tomorrow I will begin helping you master Mongol speech. You can help me learn the speech of Rus', too, if you agree. I love learning new lan-guages, but I have found no one to teach me yours yet. We are almost there now. You are missing a huge victory feast. There will be no more like it until the end of the next campaign."

"Mongol" speech? The thought of mastering anything made my head ache.

In a cluster of trees above the river, two ponies stood tethered, tails to the wind. I wondered distantly what kind of monk looked like a Tatar and wore robes of yellow and wine color. As he helped me mount, I saw more horsemen riding along the riverbank, searching among the brush. One saw us and pointed. We were barely astride Dorje's little mounts when at least a dozen hard-faced soldiers surrounded us. I must have been mad to think no one would come after me.

On the way back to the ordu, the old monk never once stopped talking, sometimes to me in the dialect that I thought of as Polovtsy, and sometimes to them in their snarling speech. He seemed to be draining off their anger and even won a few snorts of laughter from them after a while.

Despite my numbness, this much sank in: Argamon had indeed brought me to his war camp, which had been at rest for several weeks to prepare fresh supplies for the soldiery, and then he had left with his father's army. They were on a campaign to subdue the Alani and those Polovtsy that had not fled to Hungary. Dorje called them Kipchaks, though, and Tatars evidently called themselves Mongols. Many Kipchaks—since that is what I learned to call them—had submitted to the Mongols but rebelled as soon as their new masters moved north. Now they and the Alani had paid the price of their uprising: almost total ruin. The Alan capital and only great city, Maghas, had been destroyed and almost all of its citizens slaughtered—that was where the smoke had come from the day before. Tonight was a great victory celebration. Names like Batu Khan, Noyan Subodai, Berke Khan, Mongke Khan floated in and out of my ears. I had heard that last name somewhere.

By the time we reached the great encampment, the day was almost spent. All the low tents had blossomed back into place like malign black flowers. Fiddles, tambourines, drums, and high-pitched songs filled the camp with such noise that the old monk had to shout to be heard. Crowds of giddy merrymakers swarmed around us, swilling from leather bags or wooden cups, calling happily to each other, singing at the tops of their voices. A drunken man stumbled across our path and was almost ridden over. My escorts shouted after him as he tottered on, unaware of his brush with death. Smoke rose voluptuously where women turned roasting meat on spits; people stuffed their mouths with great chunks of meat while trading jests with their companions. We approached the area beyond the Ugly Khan's ger, overflowing with revelers. A group of musicians was playing drums, horns, cymbals, and horse-headed fiddles while around them men danced to the trilling music, their arms held wide as they moved in intricate patterns. And around them women sang and clapped their hands, and children chased each other through the crowd, shouting and posing in mock battle.

At some point, the guards left us. Dorje led me to a ger pitched near the Lady's. While he helped me off my horse, Kamileh and Argamon's lean friend hurried up, relief and worry mixed on their faces. They hurried us both inside, all the while jabbering with the monk. I fell onto the carpets and let their talk flow past me. I had failed.

I think I fell asleep because when I opened my eyes I was resting in the old woman's arms. A goblet of some spicy steaming liquid appeared at my lips. She gave me small sips, and it burned all the way into my body like a hot summer's day. I slowly stopped shivering, and my sorry mind began to sway and dance to the music. The ger became a bright meaningless dream, but I had found a new place of peace, warmth, and safety.

The door swung open. Argamon and his friend blew in with a gust of cold, the last rays of the sun briefly gilding them both and highlighting the scowl on his face. The two old people looked up. He barked something and everyone disappeared. I looked up at him, secure in my newfound peace, and smiled at his anger; it could not touch me. Surprisingly, Argamon smiled back and knelt down beside me, sniffed at me, and stroked my hair.

His arms were around me, carrying me and laying me down on a divan. I watched him distantly as he stripped off his clothing and eased mine off. He was touching and kissing me, but he did not know my new secret. Even when he took me, I still smiled. He could do as he pleased with my body; my mind was sealed off forever. Argamon beamed back at me. The fool must think I liked him now! That I could deceive him so easily made me laugh. When I laughed, so did he. His foolish laughter made me laugh even harder, and he did the same. I was laughing so hard that I began to choke and sob. Tears spilled out of my eyes like sad strings of pearls. Argamon rolled off me and stared, first in surprise, then in anger. Finally he got up, dressed, and stalked out. Laughter and song echoed across the steppes.

I awoke just before dawn. Something invisible was trying to crush my head. The fire had died down, and a single star gleamed through the ger's chimney hole, encircled by deep sapphire. Argamon had returned and lay sleeping peacefully beside me. Guilt struck, painful as a burn. I should never have submitted to that murderer, no matter what!

My sobs woke him. I felt a soft stroke on my back and whispered words as he drew me into his arms. When he tried to kiss me I turned my face from him; he tried to nuzzle and stroke me, but I pushed away. We struggled silently, his anger rising, until he began hurting me. I went limp and let him have his way.

Though Argamon turned his back to me and fell back to sleep, my pounding head kept me awake. I must have gone mad, thinking I could escape. And who was that old man, Dorje? He seemed kind but also a little crazy. I must somehow find him again. He had offered to teach me Mongol speech. And how did he know I was a princess of Rus'?

What was this power he said I possessed over Argamon and someone else: Qubil or Qabul? If I had any power over Argamon's fate, an absurdity, that must be why he had not been a total brute to me, if you didn't count forcing himself on me and striking me. Still, he had let me keep some of my own things—and had poor Myroslava murdered—and yet relieved some of my fellow prisoners' sufferings. Even when he had hit me, he had held back from maiming me. And he had treated my black eye …

No, I must remember my only reason to live: to avenge all those deaths. And if Dorje could teach me more about these Mongol beasts, I might find Argamon's weakness. Dorje had hinted that he had lost everything but kept going. Perhaps he too was planning revenge, and we could help each other. I glared at Argamon and solemnly vowed that I would find out what my power was, and since I could not bring myself to kill him, I would use it to ruin his life just as he had ruined mine.

When I awoke the next morning to a massive headache, a smiling Kamileh was drawing back the dividing curtain, but Argamon frowned and pointed at my clothing. I had barely dressed before he was forcing me outside and onto a pony. Followed by the old woman, his silent friend, and a few others, we left the central camp and rode back to his.

His men were clustered before their tents, already hard at work repairing weapons and singing, and heedless of the cold. Clangs and hisses filled the air as blacksmiths plunged red-hot sword blades into tubs of steaming water; others were repairing weapons and armor. Some were even sewing shirts!

Once at his ger, Argamon shoved me inside. His two slave girls leapt up and hastily bowed, but he only barked something and was gone. The pregnant girl gave me a bowl of gruel before returning to work, while I wished in vain for some nice soothing beet leaves for my aching forehead. The singing, whinnying, bleating, mysterious clashes, creaks, and bangs outside felt like an assault. And how would I ever find Dorje?

To my surprise, the odd old monk found me. I was sitting by the fire feeling forlorn when he and Kamileh appeared at the tent entrance, sharing the same smile. My spirit lifted instantly. I saw Argamon outside, planted in the brilliant sunshine with Bow Legs and the thin one and some others, singing while they repaired armor and weapons, too. Argamon's dog was asleep at his master's side—two curs, just alike.

Dorje knelt beside me. "Hello, child. How is your head? Hurts, does it? Between spiced wine and opium, no wonder. You feel fine at first, but later you pay. Come walk with me. I told Argamon I want to give you a tour of the camp."

So I had been both drunk and *drugged* the night before! Well, now I could feel less guilty, though I vowed to avoid opium in the future.

As we left the ger, Argamon signaled to his thin friend—I would call him Shadow—to join us, clearly as a guard. I soon felt better breathing the crisp air, and Dorje radiated more warmth and good cheer than a July sun. But what a magpie!

"You likely have many questions, so we will wander while you ask me about the ordu and I answer. No need to be shy, either. I am as trustworthy as salt."

His toothless grin looked so absurd that I had to smile back despite my unhappiness. "I do not know why I believe you, but I do. And I have so many questions that I hardly know where to begin. Since I was captured by these Tatars—"

"No, not Tatars, Mongols. The Mongols overran the Tatars years ago and forced them to join their armies. I am sorry. I broke in on your question. Do start again."

"Mongols, then. I do not know who anyone is, not even that beastly Argamon. The Ugly Khan must be a war chieftain, and the Lady must be Argamon's mother, but who are the Haughty Woman with the black eyes and the Angry One who wears the sword, and Kamileh—and for that matter, who are you?"

"I see. Well then, I can show you the camp another time and just tell you who everyone is. Let me think how to begin …

"Perhaps I should start with your 'ugly khan', Noyan Qacha. You were partly right: he is a great noyan—a royal general—and he commands a tuman, a battalion of ten thousand warriors. This is his main ordu, one of ten under his control. The other nine are spread out around us. But he is not a khan or even a Mongol. He and all the men of his tribe were forced into Chinggis Khan's armies, but he was brave and cunning in battle, and such qualities are rewarded, amply in his case. He became an anda—a bosom friend—to Chinggis Khan's eldest son, Jochi Khan, who is dead now. Jochi's son, Batu Khan, commands this western campaign, and Qacha now serves under him.

"Your 'beastly' Argamon is Qacha's second main heir and captain of a troop in this ordu. And you are quite right about Argamon's mother: a true lady! She is Qacha's first and main wife, and her name is Lady Q'ing-ling. She is not Mongol, either. She is from the kingdom of the Chin—some call it Cathay. Have you seen such people before?" I nodded. "She was one of many hostages sent to the Khakan when the Mongols first overran the Chin. Great Khan Chinggis gave her to Qacha.

"Now, the dark-eyed 'haughty woman' is Lady Har Nuteng, whose name actually *means* Black Eyes. She is Qacha's second wife. Jochi Khan was her father, and her mother was both Jochi's concubine and Chinggis Khan's daughter by one of *his* concubines. Jochi gave her to Qacha to reward him for loyal service."

"Wait. Who is Chinggis Khan?" I felt overwhelmed by names, ranks, relationships.

He lifted his eyebrows. "You do not know who Khakan Chinggis was? Well, that *would* be a long story. I will just say this: he became the greatest khan of all time. He united all the tribes of Mongolia and threw their armies against one settled kingdom after another, defeating them all. He had a vision of one great empire that would stretch across what I believe you call Asia. With success came ambition: to include the entire earth in his empire, from Cathay to Christendom and Africa. He believed that Great Sky Tengri—the supreme Mongol deity—sent him to bring about universal peace, odd as it sounds. His sons and grandsons now fulfill that vision as they move west."

Trying to understand so much at once, I asked, "And what is a concubine?"

Dorje looked startled, but he explained. "A concubine serves a man for his pleasure in bed, but he does not marry her. She might be a slave or she might be free."

I flushed with shame, remembering how I had once entered the weaving room and heard a servant gossiping about some "wicked harlot" who lived "happily outside the sacred bonds of marriage, parading her finery and strutting about his palace like it's hers. Bent for hell, she is." On seeing me, she had stopped and turned beet red. So she had been talking about some nobleman's concubine. Was I one? And bent for hell, too? I thrust the thought aside, not wanting to lose the thread of what Dorje was saying.

"Back to your list. Because Har Nuteng is descended from Great Khan Chinggis through both parents and is half-sister to our commander, Batu Khan, she is a member of a very privileged family, the 'Golden Family,' or the 'Children of Light,' as they style themselves. She prizes her lineage, which may be why she has always despised her husband and Lady Q'ing-ling. In return, once she gave Qacha a son, *he* spurned *her*. Indeed, he once told me he would have divorced her, but he knew Batu Khan would be offended. I have often wondered why she never divorced Qacha and went her own way. Perhaps she wants to stay near her son. Alas, I hear whispers among the slaves that she is a witch who consults with black shamans. At any rate, you had best avoid her."

It took a while to think through all these family lines, but finally it dawned on me. "So if Har Nuteng was Chinggis Khan's granddaughter on both sides, then Jochi Khan took his half-sister as a—concubine. That was incest! No wonder their daughter is a witch."

Dorje lifted his eyebrows. "I suppose I got carried away by my story. I did not say that Har Nuteng is a witch. I only told you what I heard. That does not mean it is true, only that you must be wary. As to incest, a Mongol man may take a half-sister as a concubine, but he cannot marry her or any woman from his clan, which satisfies that ban."

"Well, are not those black shamans she consults with practicing witch-craft?"

"Not exactly. They claim that dark spirits speak through them, which thrills people with fright, but if they were caught casting spells on a fellow Mongol, they would be put to death. Most just use tricks that anyone with wits can see through, and when they go into trances, they predict what people want to hear. On the other hand, some shamans are true seers like Qacha's shaman—Yulta Beki, the white old man you saw the other day. He mostly travels to the heavenly realms. He is trustworthy."

"May I ask this, then? Kamileh called me Sofia Beki or Begi. What does that mean?"

"Hmm … In Mongol, it usually means high priest or priestess, and 'begi' means princess. But royalty who are also shamans are called 'beki,' like

Yulta Beki or his wife, who is a shamanka. What with your powers, perhaps Kamileh thinks you are a royal shamanka, too. I must ask her."

Now I had more than one power? What were they? I was about to ask, but he held up his hand and said, "let us finish the others on your list. Ah, next is the 'angry one with the sword.' You mean the one who can wear his sword in Noyan Qacha's presence: Qabul. He is the noyan's eldest son, by Har Nuteng. Qacha treasures him because he was his first son to survive childhood. Qabul is Qacha's senior heir. Qabul was three by the time Argamon was born, and alas, Har Nuteng has pitted him against his younger brother ever since, claiming Argamon will steal his entire birthright from him.

"You see, as the younger heir, ordinarily Argamon would inherit Qacha's original pasturelands and dependents: his hearth. And as the elder, higher ranking son, Qabul should receive most of Qacha's spoils of war. But Qacha has no lands, and Argamon is also his only surviving son—indeed, his only surviving child—by Lady Q'ing-ling. She bore others before Argamon, but they all died. And more than once, *he* nearly died in accidents while he was growing up, so Qacha doubly treasures him. He will surely allot him part of Qabul's portion.

"So Qabul feels both slighted and threatened. Now that both young men lead jaghuns—oh, troops of a hundred men—the contest between the two is in bitter earnest. Before this, Qabul held the advantage: he has led his jaghun since he was sixteen, three years now. He also serves the battlefield commander in this ordu, and though he prefers to sleep in the eastern camp with his men, he sees his father almost daily. But this is Argamon's first campaign, and he sees much less of Qacha.

"Oh, and when you were brought to the noyan you may have seen Qacha's other concubines and their elder sons. Their youngest sons are back in his yurt deep in Asia, training for war along with other boys who will join the armies when they reach manhood." I shrugged. Why care about all Qacha's other relatives? And why did Dorje say "yurt"?

"Oh, dear, I have wandered from your list. I believe Kamileh was next. She is Lady Q'ing-ling's slave, but she is more like family. Qacha gave her to Q'ing-ling as a wedding gift, and Kamileh served her and nursed her children. I think she grieved almost as much as the Lady did when each died. She is devoted to Q'ing-ling and Argamon, and when he is in camp she often oversees his household. She and I are good friends as well.

"And last of all, who am I? I am Noyan Qacha's translator and one of his advisors, which is why I was there when Argamon brought you to him. Besides, I knew the prophecy and wanted to be there. I knew you would need help."

I stopped so suddenly that the Shadow nearly ran into me. "Enough! I will go no further until you explain! What prophecy? And what are all these powers you say I have?"

Dorje's eyes twinkled. "That is the most interesting part of my story, and I will get to it now that I have answered your first long list of questions. Luckily, I have a good memory! Come over here and sit down out of the wind. You are getting chilled.

"Oh, and this is Asetai." Hearing his name, Shadow smiled and nodded. I didn't nod back, merely followed Dorje to a nearby ger. He spoke to a woman coming out of it, and she ducked back inside and brought out a milking stool.

"Sit here, child," Dorje said, placing it next to the entrance. I hardly felt like a child anymore, but why argue the point? I sat down while he and Asetai the Shadow settled on their haunches, him facing me and my guard facing the endless steppes, as still as rock. The morning sun laid a mild hand on my cheeks, but I was fretting with impatience.

"First," he said, "the Mongols always pay heed to the unseen forces of the world, just as you Rus' do, yes? No one acts without the favor of the gods, and a Mongol army will even withdraw from certain victory if the omens are bad. True shamans like Yulta Beki take trance journeys to unseen realms, where their spirit guides reveal favorable days for victory. His white spirit horse carries him between all three realms: the celestial, where the North Star nails the sky in place; this world of day and night; and the underworld of dark spirits. And he has other powers. I have seen him strike birds from the sky with a spell." Demonic! I crossed myself.

"More important, I believe," he added pensively, "he sees into people's hearts." Did that mean this demon shaman could spy on our thoughts, too?

"So. Before the Mongol armies took the city of Chernihiv, all the noyans' shamans consulted their guardian spirits. Yulta Beki met his and, besides foreseeing victory, he had a mysterious vision that he later confirmed by fire-and-bone divination."

Seeing my blank look, Dorje added, "You throw the shoulder blade of a sheep into a fire and ask the gods a question. When heat cracks appear on it, if the lines are straight, the gods say yes; but if it shatters into crazed lines, they say no. Both the Mongols and the Chin do this, and it probably tells them as much as your divinations tell you."

"Well," I retorted, "I have often used a mirror and a candle to see into the future, but that is merely a harmless and useful custom; it's not the same at all. These Mongols, with their trances and bones, are in league with the Devil!"

Dorje raised his eyebrows but only said, "In his trance he saw a great city of Rus'. Within it, like jewels in a casket, were countless palaces for the Christ god, and one in particular would be named for a wise goddess. And he saw a princess with hair like red flames. She was on a river, floating away from the city. The wise goddess would carry special meaning for her, even share her name. And the sheep bones confirmed Yulta Beki's singular prophecy." I shivered. How could that dirty white shaman know about me?

"There is more. Whichever of the Noyan's sons captured this princess and made her his would become a mighty warrior who would bring power and wealth to the line of Qacha. But other lives would be blown about by fate like stray leaves blown by the wind."

I shuddered. This prophecy had already turned me into a stray leaf!

"Finally, Yulta Beki shouted that this princess would draw, or perhaps be, lightning from the sky, illuminating secrets of the living and the dead—his speech was growing more and more disjointed. It was clearly important, but no one understands its meaning. But they all understood the part about becoming a mighty warrior. Qacha and his sons seemed lightning-struck already, as well as terrified that only he who captured this princess would be both safe and rewarded, while everyone else must beware their fate.

"What is strangest is that mutual loyalty is a central Mongol value, yet this prophecy flew in its face. But in truth, this family has been divided by hatred and rivalries for years, and now the rivalries are simply out in the open. Since that night, all Qacha's sons have been eager as hawks to swoop down on this princess, especially Qabul and Argamon. Both would have invaded Kyiv singlehandedly to capture her! Here is the irony. I told you yesterday that the Kipchaks and Alani rebelled against Mongol rule—oh, do you know who the Alani are?"

"Of course. They are semi-nomads, although they are Orthodox Christian like us Rus'. They control trade over the Caucasus Mountains into Persia," I recited, thinking sadly of Alexander's geography lessons, "—or they did until now." I had been so enthralled by his tales about faraway lands, where Monopods walk on a single foot or where people have no heads and their faces sit in their bodies.

I pointed. "So are those the Caucasus Mountains?"

"Yes, they are." Dorje seemed impressed. "As I was saying, when rebellion broke out here, the conquest of Kyiv was delayed. Noyan Subodai—the great general who directs Batu Khan's campaign—sent several tumans, including Qacha's, to quell the uprising and destroy all the southern tribes up to the Caucasus. They want no one attacking their backs when they invade Rus'. Several of Chinggis Khan's grandsons led the campaign, including Kuyuk Khan and his cousin Mongke Khan." Now I remembered! Mongke khan's envoys had offered to spare Kyiv if we submitted. Papa had thought his army was heading north. He couldn't predict that a Kipchak revolt would divert the armies south.

"Now the red-haired princess seemed entirely out of reach. However, despite the delay, that old fox Subodai was still planning ahead. The generals always gather news about their enemies long before they attack, so he decided that since Qacha's troops would be so far south already, he was to send out scouts to explore the lands between Rus' and the Crimea to find allies or enemies of Rus' to subdue or court, since he wants to ensure that when his armies take Kyiv, no one aids it. He wants vengeance for—"

"Vengeance?" I cried. "Kyiv has done nothing against the Tat—the Mongols!"

Dorje sighed. "You know that Mongke Khan demanded your city's submission?" I nodded. "But you may not know that your Prince replied by killing Mongke's envoys and throwing their bodies off the city walls. That foul act sealed its fate. The Mongols will utterly destroy it unless Mongke can sway Batu Khan otherwise; I hear that he was so struck by its beauty that he wishes to spare it, if not its people."

"If even this Mongke Khan can see how wonderful Kyiv is, it makes no sense to destroy her," I cried. "And she will never fall!" But she had before, and not so long ago.

Dorje's voice softened. "It cannot be helped. The Mongols respect enemy envoys, and they expect the same from other nations. Your prince doomed his people when he killed those men. Your father likely foresaw that and tried to send you away to safety, yes?"

Dead envoys. And Papa's being right about Prince Mikhail hadn't even helped. My flight, with all its mishaps, had only led me into the hands of the very enemies I was fleeing. Now I was trapped in a brutal world and at the mercy of satanic forces. The busy camp, and even the wilds beyond seemed in league against Rus'. My safe, loving home was doomed. Tears sprang to my eyes.

Dorje sat quietly while I stared at a dismal future. "Do you want me to continue?"

"Yes, I suppose you should."

"When Qabul first heard of this plan, he rushed to volunteer his jaghun. Knowing him, he probably wanted to head back toward Kyiv to find the princess. But Noyan Qacha refused, saying he needed his more experienced captains to lead troops in battle. He assigned newer captains like Argamon to lead the scouting parties. He expected Yulta Beki's prophecy to be fulfilled next year when they attack Kyiv, but nonetheless he sent Argamon's party far south of the city and west of its river in order to be fair to Qabul. They were actually returning to report to him when one of Argamon's scouts crossed paths with your company. He must have approached you thinking they might tell him something helpful, just as other merchants have done in the past.

"Instead, your leader killed Argamon's envoy and Argamon raided your camp in reprisal. Little did they expect to find a flame-haired princess from Kyiv—

"What is the matter, child? You look ill."

"Dorje, it matters little now, but we did not kill Argamon's scout. Not knowing who he was, the leader of our company invited him to join us for a meal. Some madman shot him in the neck—a refugee who had joined our party while we were on the river, not even one of my people. He paid for that murder with his life, as did almost everyone else. We even sent scouts right away to find the victim's troop and try to explain what had happened. They were killed, too."

Dorje closed his eyes for a moment. "Ah, I see. That explains much. What a strange and terrible end for all those people. I will add my prayers for them to yours."

He sat by me in silence while I fought back tears. "Well, it is too late to undo that tragedy," I finally said. "But I don't see how we could be unaware that Argamon's troop was nearby. We sent out Black Mask scouts every time we camped. They come from the steppes, too, and they are famous trackers."

"Ah, my dear, a Mongol is spotted only if he wants to be. They have better eyesight, better hearing, a better sense of smell, and therefore better stalking abilities than anyone else in the world, including other nomads. They hunt people just as they hunt game, and they are masters of both."

"But they stink so! How can they smell anything? Even animals must notice."

Dorje smiled. "They once stank to me, but I got used to it. In fact, they delight in their stench—it frightens their enemies. And their sense of smell is keen; when they greet each other by smelling one another, they know where the other has been."

"Something else: how could Mongke Khan's army move so quickly? My Papa was in Kyiv when those envoys were there. He thought the Mongols were moving north."

"Mongol armies travel like the wind, and well over a month has passed since then."

"It has? I lost all track of time. Why, it must be 1240 by now!"

"Mongke Khan and Kuyuk Khan were probably pursuing rebels through the southern steppes while you were traveling down the river and being captured and brought back to camp. These ordus have been slowly following the armies."

He paused uncertainly. "Should I continue?" I nodded. "Qacha's ordus had been encamped at a stationary base where supplies are stored for future use, and they were preparing to advance when one of Argamon's homing pigeons arrived and the message was brought to Qacha: he had captured a red-haired Kyivan princess. Argamon's arrow messengers arrived a few days later bearing the same news.

"Alas, Qabul was with his father and he fell into a rage. I know; I was there. I think Qacha already felt guilty that he had mistakenly allowed one son a greater chance at the prize than the other, but he is not one to admit any error. Hot words flew between them, and they came close to a breach with each other.

"You reached the ordu the night before the troops were to leave. Many were curious to see you, Qabul foremost, so a great press of people was there when Argamon brought you to his father. When you came in, did you see Yulta Beki standing next to me, nodding? When he told the noyan that you are indeed the princess he saw in his vision, Qabul flew into a rage. Qabul cannot help it; he is like a scorpion that has to sting. He first accused

Argamon of violating Mongol law, since any captured prisoners or spoils belong to one's commander until he shares it out. He argued that Argamon should not have raped you before bringing you to his father." Now I had a word for that appalling abuse. "It may mean little to you, but Argamon felt he had to do it to 'make you his.' You recall those words from Yulta Beki's prophecy?" I nodded. "He feared you might not stay in his hands unless he did that.

"No one knows if this is even what it meant, but Qabul would have raped you as well, even though he tried to use the law against his brother. Beyond that, Qabul tried to shame Argamon by calling him a little girl for not slaughtering all of the other captives."

What a pair of vicious, petty children! "So, I am a talisman for the man who 'makes me his.' And this quarrel was over whether Argamon had a right to—rape—me? Neither gave any thought to me. How can such an act do anything but make me *not* his?"

Dorje looked at me keenly. "You are a most unusual girl. Many women would have given in to their fate. Likely, Argamon expected you to do just that." Almost to himself, he added, "How often deluded actions lead us away from where we want to go!"

He seemed lost in thought. Finally I said, "And then what?"

"They nearly came to blows right before their father, a serious breach of Mongol custom, and you stopped them—although I think you only cried out in fear, yes? But it turned everyone's attention to you. Now many people think you are more than a talisman, that you also possess some special power that stopped the brothers. Perhaps that is why Kamileh called you 'Beki' as well as 'Begi.' Nonetheless, Argamon's standing with Qacha has risen because of you. He may even become Qacha's chief heir.

"Now that Qabul knows your name is Sofia just as prophesied—we know of the church of Hagia Sofia—he is probably both furious and afraid. If Argamon has any sense, he'll guard you carefully from now on. He probably will; he was frantic last night. Had you fallen into Qabul's hands easily, it would have signaled that he, not Argamon, should have you and all the fruits of Yulta Beki's divination. Let us hope *that* never happens. It is one thing for Argamon to hit you, another for Qabul to lay hands on you. Argamon is a young pup who has yet to grow real teeth, but Qabul is a fully-grown, dangerous wolf.

"Anyway, after Argamon brought you back, he went to war, the ordu followed behind, and yesterday he returned victorious. You know the rest."

A hopeless future stretched endlessly ahead. "What happens to me now?"

"That is up to you. I will do what I can to help you understand life here."

"I don't even know what 'here' means when we keep moving all the time. I suppose I should ask what these armies will do next."

"Hard to say. There was a terrible battle over Maghas, and Qacha's tuman suffered many losses because they had to fight hand to hand—that is why he took vengeance not only on the Alan khan his warriors captured, but on his wife. It was a sign of deepest contempt. Most captured noblewomen would simply be raped and enslaved."

He paused while I tried to shake off that horrible headless memory. "As for what comes next, Qacha's tuman might move north and join the main army or continue fighting here. Either way, we summer on the steppes and prepare once again for the assault on Kyiv."

I refused to hear that. "And why do you befriend me?"

The old man looked past me, and I followed his gaze: rows of tents, herds of animals, people at work, and beyond us the craggy mountains scraping the sky. He replied, "There are two reasons. First, I would have befriended anyone in your desperate plight, even before I felt that link to you. You could say helping others is what I live for. As for the second reason, you are not ready to understand it yet; but I believe that someday you will be, and it will make sense then. I will only say that you have another kind of power: to benefit both the Mongols and the peoples who fall beneath their yoke."

Was he mad? Why would I want to benefit a Mongol? And what link to me? Perhaps my trust in him was misplaced.

Dorje jumped up. "We should return now. You are turning blue with cold. Princess Sofia, try not to harden your mind toward these people. When you start to understand them, I think you will discover wells of kindness in unlikely places. Then perhaps we can explore what it means to do good unto your enemies."

In using our Savior's very words, the monk brought me back to His teachings—and to how far had I strayed from them since my capture. But the only way I could see how to do good would be to follow Saint Paul: my deeds would be as coals of fire heaped on their heads! And Dorje clearly was not seeking revenge, so *that* hope was lost.

With Asetai shadowing us, Dorje briskly led me back to Argamon's ger, already explaining Mongol speech. "As you may have noticed," he began, "it bears a likeness to your Kipchak Turkish, so you can grasp it quickly, although not all words mean the same. Take the word 'yurt.' In many forms of Turkish, it means the same as ger; but in Mongol speech, yurt means the lands belonging to a tribe: its summer and winter pastures."

"Oh, I wondered. But how could these Mongols claim land? Don't nomads just roam about like wild beasts?"

"Not at all. Though they take their homes with them, every tribe has its own territory. Within it each clan travels to its allotted pastures as the seasons change. When at war, ordus are bases and supply lines traveling behind the armies. Scouts find the best places for them to encamp and even store goods ahead of time, so when the armies rejoin them, they can repair equipment and so forth with no waste of time. So back to our lesson, you can see how important it is to understand someone's true intent when they use a word."

Dorje chattered on, linking words together with dizzying zeal, but I *was* beginning to see how Mongol speech worked. I felt a surprising burst of joy as words began to fit together. He was opening a door back into life.

When we reached Argamon's ger, my captor and his men were still bent over their weapons, singing. What a horrid droning, I thought. How the great piles of arms had grown: knives, lances with hooked tips, battle-axes, deadly looking curved swords, round shields, many kinds of arrows! Argamon stopped and stared up at me. He and Dorje gabbled together briefly, and then he jerked his head toward the tent. The old monk led me inside, but thankfully, silent Asetai rejoined the other men.

For much of the afternoon, while the other women worked quietly around us, my new friend taught me Mongol speech and I was able to forget my fate. After he took his leave, calling a cheery goodbye to Argamon outside the tent, I sat alone by the fire, my arms wrapped around my chest, feeling curiously empty, with nowhere to go, nothing to look forward to, nothing to remember with untainted joy. But if I stayed in the present, I could rest in simple sensation: the warmth of the flickering fire, the colorful patterns of the carpet beneath me, the voices of the women working nearby, each a tiny island of respite encircled by an ocean of unease.

After the evening chants, Argamon entered the ger and my quiet mood fled into the dusk. I struggled to my feet along with the others, though I refused to cup my hands to him. He seemed not to notice. Planting himself by the fire, he pulled me down beside him. I decided to be daring; it could make things no worse.

"Greetings, Argamon. I learn Mongol tongue."

He laughed and beckoned to his servants to bring in the evening meal. "Good!"

Argamon's manner toward me changed that night. After he and Asetai had eaten, he was attentive, even offered me a choice chunk of meat. He supplied some words of his own, like arki, the potent drink he kept trying to press upon me and which I steadfastly refused. But, though his crude kindnesses could not banish my dark feelings, something felt different. He had ruined my life, but sharing even a little of his speech made him seem less of a beast. My attempt to escape had led nowhere, so until I could see a way—and a good reason—to try again, I must accept that I was there to stay. At least I could seek a suitable revenge, perhaps somehow deny him my so-called protection!

That night, with no choice about either ill, I ignored Asetai and did not resist Argamon when he took me. He was much gentler when I stopped fighting him. Dorje's words haunted me, too. Doing good unto my enemies was at complete odds with my desire for revenge. But what could I do? A wordless prayer formed in my mind: to find goodness again, and love. I drifted off to sleep, Argamon's bare arm draped over my body.

And I had a strange but strangely comforting dream. I was at home with Papa, Alexander, and Baba Liubyna as though that wretched journey had never happened. We were awaiting a special guest, a great archbishop who was to preach an important sermon. He finally arrived, but by the back entrance, which confused us all; and when he entered the Great Hall, it was Dorje. Even his vestments were the saffron of his monk's robe. He smiled and blessed each of us, and said, "Love comes in many guises, my children." I felt his love, too. When I awoke, I knew that the old monk and I would become friends.

I had hoped for more lessons with Dorje the next day, but after some messenger had arrived for Argamon—I heard the name Mongke Khan—I was again made to put on my finery and Argamon's heavy jewelry before being whisked off amidst a company of horsemen. It seemed I was being taken to see the wicked Mongke.

To my gratitude, Dorje joined us at the last moment. "I talked Qacha into letting me interpret for you," he said, smiling toothlessly. "I also thought you might need to know who the different khans are, so you can make some sense of this world ... and of its pitfalls."

Argamon contented himself with holding the reins of my horse while Dorje happily described this khan and that. I was soon prepared to hate them all, especially Batu Khan, whose goal it was to impose his rule wherever Mongol ponies had tread, as Dorje put it. Of course, Batu also had no hesitation about treading in new places: namely, all Christendom.

"But it is already home to people far more civilized than Mongols will ever be!" I cried.

Dorje shrugged. "Alas, the idea of more conquest appeals to every Mongol warrior, not to mention the Golden Kin. Several eager relatives brought their armies, too, like Batu's brother Berke. And cousins Kuyuk and Mongke, both of whom you will see today."

"Armies or packs of wild wolves?"

"You may think to insult the Mongols, but the cunning and loyal wolf is one of their ancestors. They model themselves on wolves even to the way they plan campaigns."

Recalling Argamon and his company howling with their wolf kindred, I hastily changed the subject. "Why would Mongke Khan be interested in me?"

"Let me think ... Mongke is related to Qabul and surely wishes to see this rivalry with Argamon resolved. He may wonder whether your presence will inflame it further."

"Why should he care?"

"Because harmony is so highly valued in the army. But as members of the Golden Kin, both Batu and Mongke sometimes find their loyalties divided. For instance, Batu became enamored of his half-sister, Har Nuteng, when they were both young, and—"

"Has this Batu Khan no more shame than his father had?" I cut in. "And that Har Nuteng must be soaked in sin. She springs from an unholy coupling, and then she allows attentions from her brother! She probably *is* a witch!"

Dorje lifted his eyebrows. "Remember, Mongols see these things differently from you. If Batu had married Har Nuteng, that would have been incest. But Jochi gave her to Qacha. The point I wish to make is this: seeing his sister's bitterness over being second wife to Qacha, Batu continues to show favor to her and to her son, but he and Mongke Khan will always put the needs of their armies first. Now that Argamon has shown promise in battle, at least in his raid on your party, they must honor him, too. Mongke will understand that Qabul feels threatened and that you could tip the delicate balance between the brothers toward trouble in the army."

"What does that mean for me?"

"I don't know yet, but do not fear. Both Mongke and Batu respect Qacha, and since he accepts you, Mongke likely will, too. He may ask you a few questions—oh, there is another reason he might take an interest in you. He admires your city of Kyiv, and he may want to see a Kyivan prin—"

"Oh yes, to prove his admiration, he demanded a tenth of our wealth and people. He is vermin—they are all vermin, and I hate them all!"

After that Dorje had no more to say. He took his prayer beads from around his neck and began reciting a prayer under his breath, counting with his beads. After riding for some time, I shook off the gloomy thoughts that clung to me like burrs. Best not to dwell on those wicked khans. I would show this Mongke Khan how a true noblewoman behaved!

At least riding at an easy pace on a reasonable saddle revived me. We passed through valleys that seemed to overflow with milling herds of animals and tent cities. In every camp, smoke curled up from chimneys and campfires; people moved about laughing, singing, and working. Had I not known their aims, I'd have been impressed with their industry. The snow sparkled like crushed diamonds until the sun set aside her thin cloud cloak and turned it to blinding white steel.

We crested a final hill where mounted guards stopped us long enough for Argamon to show them some kind of metal pass. Below us lay Mongke Khan's ordu, smudging the snow with shadows. At first the camp seemed not much larger than Qacha's, or even much grander. Grand Prince Mikhail's palace, retinue, and clothing always outshone Papa's; how else could we all know our places? Only when we got close to the khan's cluster of colorful gers, encircled by windbreaks and carts, guards and horses, did I see how grand they actually were. A tall standard stood outside the huge main ger, topped by a crescent-moon insignia and decorated with black animal tails. Instead of one tent standing isolated beyond the ger, there were three.

"Dorje, what are those grim-looking gers out there? Qacha's ordu has one, too."

"The shamans live there and maintain the shrines that guard each ordu. Yulta Beki and his wife live in Qacha's, along with his apprentice." We reined in near another pair of fires. "You must pass between them to prove you bring no evil magic on them." I nodded. So that was what it meant. Such base superstition. I almost laughed.

Seeing our company approach, one of several guards entered the huge tent for a few moments. We dismounted before the broad corridor of chest wagons, and Argamon gave me a little push toward the fires. "You go." I tossed my head, gathered my cloak close around me, and strode between them, scarcely feeling their heat on my cold cheeks. Resolved to stand steadfast before Mongke Khan, I did not feel the same bodiless panic this time, either. Argamon was waiting at the entrance, his cap and girdle off, his belt laid on his shoulder. A guard pulled open the brightly decorated door and waved us in.

Someone had just finished a song, and the hum of his stringed instrument lingered in the air. While Argamon genuflected, at Dorje's prompting I prostrated just inside the entrance between a pair of idols. We passed a table set out with silver and gold vessels; a servant was filling a goblet of liquor from one. The fumes trailed behind us as Argamon self-importantly thrust me past a throng of people and into another prostration before a group of men seated at their ease. A voice spoke, and Dorje whispered to me to rise to my knees. A group of gaudily attired men sat on low chairs heaped with furs, all staring at me.

At first I tried to find fault. There should be more ceremony for a prince. How can I know who is of greatest standing when they all sit at the same height? And so on. But there was really no mistaking Mongke Khan, who was sitting directly before me dressed in gold brocade robes figured with intertwined beasts of red and deep blue. He set aside something he was reading—this barbarian could read?—and I glowered up into a lean, stern face with an amazingly flat nose.

Another khan sitting to one side of Mongke signaled for more drink. I glanced over at him. He had the usual big head and broad face, and he wore rich furs and vivid orange robes patterned with blue and gold roundels. Everything about him proclaimed arrogance. He was also clearly drunk. Then I realized that most of these men were, which was why liquor fumes hung in the air. And they looked so cruel.

My protective armor of righteousness suddenly vanished.

Mongke and the drunken khan had turned to Argamon, who had launched into some long report, leaving me on my knees. After an eternity, my legs began to cramp so badly that I thought I might never be able to stand again. Finally, Argamon spoke my name, and both khans looked down at me. I hoped they could not see how I trembled. But it was to Dorje, who was standing close behind me, that Mongke Khan spoke.

"Tell your name and what city you come from," Dorje said. "I will translate."

I commanded myself not to surrender to fear, to behave with nobility. Giving all my names, Christian and pagan, I said, "I am Princess Sofia Olga Volodymyrovna, daughter of Prince Volodymyr Yuri Petrovich of the Seven Fields. My mother was Princess Vera Olga Vasilyovna the Gracious. Both are descended from Prince Rurik, father of all Rus', and I belong to the proud and beautiful city of Kyiv." Suddenly rage surged through me again. I staggered to my feet and glared up at the khan. "Were it not for your wicked threats against my mother city, my Papa would never have sent me away from my beloved home!"

After listening to Dorje, Mongke Khan smiled grimly, exchanged a few words with his fellow khan, spoke to Argamon again for some time, and then waved a dismissal. My part of the audience had lasted but a few moments.

Outside I asked Dorje, "That was Mongke Khan? He was not very grand for a prince. And why did he summon me all this distance and then ask me so little? Is he mad?"

"Yes, that was him, but he did not summon you. Qacha sent Argamon to report on his behalf. And he sent you with him on a whim." So I was just a piece of baggage!

"As for why Mongke said little to you, who knows? He is the commanding general on the Alan campaign, and his word is law. If he had wished to see you for only five breaths, then so be it. Be grateful he made no effort to question you. You would have felt true fear then! But he saw enough to decide you truly are a princess of Rus', and he confirmed Argamon's right to you. He only remarked that being such a little filly, you cannot kick anyone very hard. He told Argamon to waste no time bringing you to the bit.

"Also, since Argamon is already here, the khan now sends him as a courier to Batu Khan. He is to report on the victory over the Alani and announce that Mongke will send Qacha's battered battalions north. With this campaign almost over, Mongke and his fellow princes will soon join

Batu to hold a kuriltai—a council of all the main generals. So Argamon's luck already begins; acting as the khan's messenger is quite an honor for him. And Mongke Khan orders Argamon to take you with him so that Batu Khan can see you."

"Why?" I groaned. I might feel insulted that I was not the main object of this visit, but I wanted no other khans staring at me, especially that Batu Khan!

"I suppose he thinks it might amuse Batu as much as it amused him," Dorje said. "Oh, did you see the man in orange sitting to his right? That was Kuyuk Khan, son of Great Khan Ogedai. People call him a bigheaded rooster behind his back. Alas, he *is* endlessly jealous of his position, somewhat like Qabul." Why was Dorje always saying harsh things about Argamon's brother? As far as I could see, all Mongols were the same.

"And those other khans taking their ease around Mongke were more brothers and cousins. Batu Khan's brother Berke was there. He will control the southern steppes as far as the Caucasus and Persia.

"Hmm ... I think I will ask Qacha to let me join your party, since he will soon move north. He can spare me until he arrives, and you will need me."

We returned by nightfall, a wearying ride, but I still had to endure my master's lust. He tried to make me respond in kind, but I neither knew how nor wanted to learn. Only his ready anger kept me from resisting, and my thoughts turned to murder once again.

Dorje was right. The next day Argamon was ready to depart with Asetai and Bow Legs, whose name I had learned: Bayartou. A few others joined us, too. Happily, the old monk had gotten permission to go with us. Before we left, Argamon led us to the main camp to bid goodbye to his mother. As we were all remounting our ponies, Lady Q'ing-ling approached me, her little dog peeking out from the overlap of her fur coat. To my surprise, she handed me a tiny packet of blue silk. I barely had time to bow my thanks and tuck it into my mitten before Argamon briskly set off into the icy wind. How I dreaded another long journey across a frozen wilderness, but the thought of her gift, even if she was an enemy, warmed my heart.

I turned to Dorje. "How do I say thank you in Mongol speech?"

"They use no words. If you are grateful for a favor, you do one in return."

When our company stopped for the evening, the wind was so fierce that after setting up a single large tent, the men had to hack pits in the frozen earth before they could get a fire going. That night I waited until everyone else had fallen asleep before opening Lady Q'ing-ling's packet. It contained a square gold cross with a small loop on one arm for stringing onto a cord. How did this stranger know or even care enough to give me such a gift? That it might be plunder made me pause only a moment; it seemed a gift from Heaven. I must find some way to repay the Lady's kindness. After whispering a prayer of thanks and kissing it, I added it to the cord that held my ikon. I still wear it.

Dorje smiled knowingly when he saw it the next day. Had he suggested something to Lady Q'ing-ling? He was a good if strange Christian, and she must be a good pagan.

We rode north into a wind that bludgeoned us like a mallet. Only the smelly grease Asetai had smeared over my face and body kept me from freezing. Argamon led us across flat, featureless terrain that stretched like white silk in every direction. The sky arched over us, a great impenetrable dome of palest blue. We traveled painfully fast for several dreary days with no sign of settlements and few landmarks beyond a few frozen rivers and their stiff crackling trees, yet Argamon's band seemed to know just where we were going. But dwarfed by endless snowfields, I felt utterly lost, not to mention sore from riding.

Late one afternoon, scattered ordus began to appear again, and we spent the night as guests of another noyan. A crowd of men and women shoved their way into his ger to stare at me. They spent the evening singing or playing horse-headed fiddles, while our hostess kept pressing us to eat more tasteless stew. But warmed by thick furs and hot food, I had to feel a little grateful to our rowdy hosts, even if they were enemies.

The next day, we reached another series of encampments. Their numbers grew until ordus lay spread out in every direction as far as I could see. This could only be the other army. At one point, bow-legged Bayartou galloped ahead of the party and disappeared into a huge encampment, a marvel of gaudy color. He returned at the head of a knot of horsemen who escorted us to the head of the main camp.

No one could mistake Batu Khan's cluster of huge gers. Painted or appliquéd, hung with rainbow-hued banners, and shimmering as though the world of the ancient gods had sprung from the earth, they did seem royal— although, I reminded myself, how could such vermin possibly know what true royalty was? The khan's colossal main tent was a miracle of brocades and appliqués, trimmed with massive ropes and tassels of gold. The bright felt windbreaks and corridor of wagons, even the horses and soldiers on guard, all in colorful gear, surrounded it like the setting for a great crude jewel. Before the entrance stood another standard, much taller than Mongke's, but with the same black animal tails hanging from it. The symbol atop it was a crescent topped by a trident.

Dorje spoke. "Batu Khan's chancellor sent a message. He says the khan will see Argamon—and you—right away." I tried not to care.

Our party halted. In his eagerness, Argamon almost ripped me off my pony. I thrust his hands from my waist and hurried between the usual twin fires, hoping to get out of the wind as soon as possible. It felt strange to know what was expected of me, almost as if I belonged there. No, never! What was I thinking? Argamon pulled me past several guards and into the great ger. I glimpsed many men, smelled liquor before beginning my usual prostrations.

A stab of fear punctured my false courage. Soon I must face the monster who wanted to destroy my people. Slowly rising, I noticed a gaudy idol-filled shrine at the back, in its center a tall golden statue of a man clothed in embroidered brocade robes. Dorje whispered in my ear, "That is a statue of Chinggis Khan, who is now the Mongols' guardian deity."

I touched my ikon and crucifix, afraid to cross myself in this hostile place, felt the statue's blank eyes on me even after I tore my eyes away to look around. Smoke and light radiated from the hearth and from scattered braziers, making the room almost as bright as outdoors and as stifling as a stable on a hot day. Around the hearth stood four thick support pillars, with four more pillars around the room to hold up the vast felt ceiling. The floor was strewn with gorgeous carpets, some as large as an entire room in my father's country palace. The walls were lined with cloth of gold and hung with tapestries.

Argamon led us past a long low table on our right, upon which sat various beakers of liquor. Servants were refilling huge golden goblets for their masters, who were ranged at ease around the ger. Many of them seemed drunk, although it was not yet midday. Most bore livid battle scars. The leading khans were seated along three sides of a large low table opposite the entrance, looking at something on it while a fat old man talked and pointed. At first I thought he was Batu Khan, but when a younger man in white next to him looked up and saw the three of us, he spoke and the fat one stopped. So that must be Batu Khan. After thrusting me down into another prostration, Argamon genuflected. When he pulled on my arm again, I rose to my knees and met the khan's eyes. I quickly averted mine.

As if to disguise his foulness, Batu Khan was dressed entirely in white samite, shot with gold and trimmed with gold brocade. Though he wore no armor, beside him sat a silver helmet ornamented with gold. He began softly stroking the white plume atop it. His oversized head was shaven in front, and the rest of his hair was drawn tightly back. A huge pearl earring dangled from one earlobe. Despite his yellowish skin, his cheeks were as red as beets, perhaps from exposure to the elements, perhaps from wine. After several moments, he turned to a golden goblet so huge that he needed both hands to lift it. He drank silently and seemed to stare at me again, smiling secretively. His face was rather plump for a tough warrior's, with its soft chin and drooping whiskers.

Suddenly he spoke, though his gaze never left me, and Argamon respectfully sat down at the table before him. While I remained kneeling, the two of them spoke together for some time. I recognized Mongke, Kipchak, Alani, Qacha, Kyiv, and begi. Once more my legs began to ache terribly. My mind wandered to the pain in my knees.

Dorje interrupted my painful trance, whispering in my ear, "Argamon has finished his message and told Batu Khan about capturing you. Batu wants you to go up closer to him." Rising painfully, I hobbled toward the table. Now I could see what was on it: maps. These men might well be charting their assault on Kyiv! Argamon turned and pulled me down slightly behind him.

When the Khan spoke, I dared a quick glance into his cold, cat-like eyes, which were deep gray and as hard as steel. Now my hatred had a truly worthy object. His smile broadened.

I heard Dorje's voice. "He asks if you are indeed a Kyivan princess."

For a wild moment, I thought of denying it—perhaps they would free me then—but common sense rescued me. Dishonoring Argamon before all these khans could only lead to my torture and death. The strange prophecy about me was my only weapon, even if I didn't yet know how to use it, and to throw it away would be foolish.

Casting my eyes downward for fear of unwittingly betraying my feelings, I finally spoke as steadily as I could. "Yes, I am a princess from Kyiv. My father is Prince Volodymyr of the Seven Fields, a lion among men." But a last wild hope overcame me and I blurted out, "He is wealthy and would pay everything he owns to ransom me." Worse, overwhelmed by panic and rage, I looked back at Dorje and cried, "No, tell him that Papa is very powerful and knows what they plot here. When he hears they have kidnapped me, he will come for me and kill them all!"

Clearly my threats failed to impress anyone. After Dorje spoke, they all whinnied with laughter. The khan's response made them bray even harder. I turned to the old monk. "What did he say? Why do they laugh at me?" I felt so helpless before these hard men.

"The khan replies that little birds swept along in the storm do not frighten him. However, he adds that you convince him you could only be of royal birth, because no one else would have the arrogance or perhaps innocence to speak to him as you did." I stared up at the khan in confused outrage. He was still smiling at me. He spoke again.

Dorje said, "Now the khan says that your cowardly Prince Mikhail has fled. He asks if Kyiv's people will foolishly try to defend it or if they will have the sense to surrender and perhaps still save their city. It seems that Mongke's wish to spare Kyiv gives it a second chance."

So Prince Mikhail had fled—a coward indeed—and I had thought him so dashing and proud! Recalling Papa's quarrel with him, I hardly knew what to say. Finally, I answered, "I have no idea. I am only a woman, not a warrior, and no traitor to Kyiv. But the warriors of Rus' are all very brave."

Batu Khan laughed softly at my answer, looked me over from head to toe, and said something that made the other men horselaugh again. Dorje did not translate for me, merely said, "He dismisses us now. You must prostrate again." As if I had a choice—the defiant glare I tried to shoot at the khan missed its mark, for Argamon pushed my head down to the floor before backing me out amidst hearty laughter. He steered me outside and through the windbreaks into the camp, where a servant waited to escort us.

As we walked, trailed by a few of his men, he barked something to Dorje. "Argamon says you have the courage of a she-bear and the disrespect of a jackal. He cannot decide whether to admire you or to beat you," said the monk. "I think he is mostly pleased with you. And Batu Khan was quite taken with you. Of course he does like a pretty face."

"That is disgusting. The khan is older than my father," I retorted. After a pause, I added, "But tell Argamon I want no more beatings. I will guard my tongue from now on."

Dorje and Argamon spoke together again. "He says he will never strike you as long as you obey him." If his pledge was meant as reassurance, it failed.

The rest of Argamon's men were waiting in the ger where we were to stay. Bedding was laid out, and a fire already burned in the hearth. They leapt up and disappeared with their young captain, leaving me alone with the old monk.

"What happens next?" I asked.

"We all stay here until the kuriltai. There will be a feast to celebrate the victories in the south, and then they will finish planning their next campaign. Argamon will be allowed to serve the khan, a great honor for him and his father, though I imagine Qabul will not like it. Meanwhile, we can continue your speech lessons."

That night in my sleep, row upon row of gers appeared before me, and out of each leapt a wolf. I turned and tried to run, but I could only take slow, agonizing steps. The wolves converged on me, and I looked down to see why I could not run There were the bloody corpses of my people underfoot. With a cry, I jerked awake. Argamon's eyes were glittering at me in the faint hearth light.

"Make still your heart. I am here," he whispered.

'Yes, but that is why I am afraid,' I thought. He renewed his iron embrace and drifted off to sleep again.

The next few days were almost pleasant. Argamon and his men always left early, so I either studied with Dorje or wandered about the camp with him among soldiers, blacksmiths, bow makers, fletchers, cooks, seamstresses, jugglers, musicians, slaves, and a surprising number of merchants from as far away as Cathay and as near as the Crimea. Wherever we went, Argamon's friend Asetai went, too.

Menials brought me food. Dorje never ate after midday, this being a vow he kept as a monk, perhaps as a penance. I enjoyed my meals, though: thin boiled ropes made of flour paste served with meat, pickled onions, and garlic; and sometimes sweets made of fruit and honey. As well as pretty faces—Dorje said Batu had twenty-six wives and innumerable concubines, some of whom had come on campaign—the khan clearly liked good food.

In the evenings, Argamon's men were caught up in endless games of knucklebones. They ignored me and I ignored them. But nights were bad. Argamon unfailingly satisfied his lust while I endured the shame of knowing the others could hear him taking me. And of course nighttime was when ghosts haunted my dreams.

One day when Dorje and I were out walking, we heard drums pounding and bugles blasting. "The khans must be arriving for the kuriltai," he said. "Shall we go see?"

We hurried toward the front of the camp in time to witness the stately approach of Mongke, Kuyuk, Berke, and the other leading khans. Asetai, who seemed eager for the best view, wedged Dorje and me through the crowd that was gathering along both sides of the broad cart avenue leading to Batu Khan's ger. Some people waved banners or shook standards, some clapped in unison, all sang and, as the procession passed them, stopped briefly to bow and cup their hands respectfully. I bowed to no one! Ignoring Asetai's attempts to move even closer, I stopped before we reached the front. I could see well enough.

The Golden Princes rode by on beautifully caparisoned horses, looking neither right nor left, dazzling in thick furs and bright robes. An attendant rode behind each khan, holding a huge parasol over him; behind them rode many more attendants dressed in fine brocades or armor, some carrying battle standards. The thunder of the drums and the shrill trills of the bugles were almost deafening. Bright banners fluttered and snapped in the wind.

Batu Khan, again dressed in white and gold under lush furs, his helmet flashing with jewels, rode out to meet them on a sumptuously bedecked white mare. He was surprisingly graceful astride a horse. His vast and grandly attired retinue included two servants who together bore *his* gigantic parasol of gold brocade trimmed with golden loops and tassels. Stern majesty was written on his face. I glimpsed Argamon among Batu's honor guard, trying to look dignified among older, hard-faced warriors. In bitter truth, the display was far more imposing than anything I had ever seen in Kyiv.

With a final flourish of horns and drums, the khans halted before each other. Batu Khan solemnly greeted his brother and cousins and gracefully turned his horse, his retinue parting and then attending him and his guests back to his huge ger. After the greatest khans had gone by, Noyan Qacha passed near us with the much-defamed Qabul just behind him. Qabul was not angry today. His eyes were alight with joy or perhaps pride. He flashed a bright smile at a pretty maiden standing near me. She giggled and clapped louder, but Dorje was suddenly pulling me out of sight and back into the crowd, saying, "We have seen enough. Time to return to lessons."

Toward evening the monk stretched and said, "I suspect that because of the kuriltai, you may be forgotten tonight and get no supper. Let us walk over to the feasting tent. Perhaps one of the servers will let you try some princely food."

As we made our way to Batu Khan's great ger, Asetai right behind, laughter and music floated across the chill air. Were Papa and his men sitting in the Great Hall, eating, drinking, laughing and singing right now? How I missed him! Did he think of me?

Khans were still entering with their retinues, forcing us to stand aside, and streams of servants were bearing jars of wine and trays of food into the ger. Happily, Dorje was able to stop one and talk him into giving me a small roast bird. We were turning to leave when Qacha and Qabul and their men came striding toward us. Dorje stiffened and muttered something. Asetai grew uneasy, too, and moved even closer to me as they approached. Qacha stopped briefly, spoke with Dorje, and moved on. But Qabul paused, a surprised frown on his face. In a gruff voice, he too asked the monk something. I watched with interest, wondering if he knew that Dorje mistrusted, perhaps even hated him.

The old man launched into one of his endless answers, but it was beyond my power to follow. Qabul kept glancing at me, foolishly holding my bird. Finally he cut him short with a sharp word, something I too had secretly wished to do more than once. My master's rival then turned to me, looked deeply at me as if we shared some secret, and smiled in the warmest way. I was so dazzled, I could not help smiling back and blushing so deeply that even in the dusk he must have seen. Nodding to me, he moved on. His men passed us, too, and one of them jostled Asetai.

"What did he say?" Qabul had smiled in just the way I had once hoped my husband would smile at me on our wedding night.

"He had no idea you were here. He was back in the eastern wing with his jaghun when you left. By bringing you before Batu Khan, Argamon has spoiled his brother's chances to find a rival princess, so I suspect that Qabul's hopes are now transferred to you. Do not be seduced by that friendly smile. He is a sly, dangerous tiger. Never forget it."

"Why do you hate him so? I see no difference between him and Argamon."

"I do not hate him. But even a child puts his hand into a fire only once, and Qabul burns everyone sooner or later." Before I could respond, a man came out of the ger and threw offerings of liquor into the air in four different directions.

"Look, the feast begins. Batu's man is offering to the spirit world: to the south for fire, to the east for air, west for water, and north for the dead who have returned to the earth."

Such pagan nonsense! Out of habit, I crossed myself and suddenly realized that despite Dorje's warnings, my mood had brightened on account of Qabul's smile.

Argamon did not return that night, but nightmares did. I startled awake to see Dorje sitting cross-legged by the fire, so still that he seemed asleep but with eyes half open. Sleep drew me back into an uneasy embrace. When I awoke at dawn, he was tending the fire. Had he slept at all? Argamon appeared at the ger later in the morning and barked an order to return the ordu to await him—I understood that much. My heart sank.

"Does this mean we have to ride all that way back there?" I asked the old monk.

"Oh, Qacha's ordus have moved north. They are only a few days away now."

He was right. With our backs to the wind, the return journey was much easier; plus several men leading a caravan of two-humped camels joined us, so I also felt less lost.

We arrived just ahead of a huge snowstorm that I will never forget, only partly because it freed me from Argamon for many days. The tent sides heaved alarmingly, and the ger grew stuffy and smoky after the women closed both the chimney hole and a flap over the door to keep the wind out. Kamileh and the women jested or sang while they worked. Asetai, when not gluing long, thin strips of wood together, played his fiddle.

Dorje practiced with me almost daily, though I wondered how he and his escorts braved that blizzard so easily. He not only taught me more about Mongol speech but also tried to instruct me in their customs. I say tried because I was not a very good student at first. For one thing, I often asked him several questions at once. He would always say, "Wait, slow down. Too many questions at the same time, even for an old talker like me!"

He tried to quickly give me a big picture of Mongol life, but I was never able simply to listen and learn. I wanted to argue.

For instance: "You can see that all the ordus are laid out in the same way," he began. "Great Khan Chinggis decreed that all entrances face south to get the most sun and the least wind."

I snorted. "It is the same in the camps of Papa's nomad dependents."

Dorje frowned. "Do you want to hear what I have to say?"

Blushing, I nodded, and he continued, "East is the feminine direction; west is the masculine. To honor the darker powers of the world, on which they heavily rely, Mongols consider east the greater of the two. For example, Qabul, the more experienced warrior, is in the eastern wing of the ordu, while Argamon, who is still proving his worth, is here in the western wing for now. And forward and rear camps guard south and north, all of which reflects the heavenly order and pleases the Mongol gods."

"That is so absurd," I cut in again. "You began with a useful practice, but now you wrap it in pagan nonsense. Only Christianity reveals the truth!" Dorje fell silent until I finally said, "I am sorry. Please go on."

The old man nodded and continued with more of the same.

But I did learn much from him, some of it surprisingly familiar to any-one from Rus', as when he explained that each ger is the center of the universe. "Its hearth is the axis joining heaven and earth; gers are round because the world is bound by cycles, and the arch of a ger's roof mirrors the arch of heaven. The same axis runs through people, too, and joins heaven, earth and the underworld, embodying the great world tree."

"At least they got that right. My Baba Liubyna taught me the same thing."

Dorje raised his eyebrows but merely continued, "In gers that are homes, the east side is for women only. A man entering it brings bad luck." Beyond Argamon's reach! If only I could …

"Mongols regard their gods almost as family, and they regard their family, not only distant forebears but those to come, as almost gods." He pointed at a rope tucked under the ceiling spokes. "See how it is shaped like a wolf's head? Through it the Mongols' spirit ancestor the Blue Wolf protects the ger—" I gaped as though the rope might turn into flesh and teeth and leap down on me, "—as do the felt effigies around the ger, the ongghon: like the 'brother' over your master's bed or the one next to it, the 'mistress's brother,' that protects his wife. Perhaps for now it watches over you." I wanted no Mongol demons pro-tecting me, but I checked my protests. "On the shrine are felt ongghon of gods and ancestors. Foremost are Natigai, who guards families, herds, and so forth; and Itugen who, like the earth, is mother of all, yet who always remains a virgin."

I could stand no more. "What idolaters, what superstitious rubbish! Everyone knows that Veles was god of herds until Christ transfigured him into St. Vlas. And the Virgin Mother, other than Moist Mother Earth, can only be Holy Mary, Mother of God!"

"Do not be too hasty. These 'idols' may serve the same purpose as your ikons."

"Except that ikons are windows onto Heaven and idols are works of the Devil!"

"Why, surely you Rus' are aware of unseen beings and forces, some base, some sublime? And you probably respect some and fear others." I grudgingly nodded. "And do you not use charms and make offerings to appease fearful forces or make them obey you?"

"Of course we do. Any good Christian knows there are legions of devils and angels. And yes, fickle spirits sour our milk overnight or make us drop things, and naturally we make offerings or use charms to appease them. But these Mongols wallow in superstition and black magic!" I neglected to mention that my priest had denounced *all* spell-making.

"Well, gods and spirits are as fleeting as everything else and are neither to be feared nor relied upon," said Dorje gently. I tried to argue more, but he raised his hands in a sign of peace. "Let us set the subject aside for now," and he turned to another matter.

He left early that day. I knew I had overstepped myself; he was only trying to help. And what a strange form of Christianity he practiced—had it been tainted by living among pagans? Still, I must try to listen better. I spent the rest of the day staring into the fire censuring myself while the others amiably worked together, an invisible wall between us.

Over the next few days, I made every effort to behave patiently, while Dorje tread lightly on my prejudices. Little by little, and with more subtlety than I realized at the time, the old monk fit together a mosaic of information that I might find useful, some of it as trifling as why Argamon and other warriors always sat with one knee up: to be ready to spring up to fight attackers at a moment's notice. At first, I could not see how everything fit together. Some bans seemed sensible—putting a knife in the fire could ruin it, and I might drop and waste meat if I tried to take it from a pot sitting over the fire—but so much seemed mere superstition, like avoiding the threshold of the ger: to touch it might bring bad luck on the household. And there were bans that made no sense at all, like not bathing because it disrespects Mother Earth. In that case, Mongols should never cross rivers, either!

I tried to be patient, but finally I burst out again. "Why must I learn all these superstitions? I'll never do most of these things, nor do I see sense in many of them."

Dorje looked surprised. "There is sense. Every Mongol custom respects the unity of the spiritual and the practical. This whole world is alive, and there is spiritual power everywhere." I'd have liked him to say more, but instead he picked himself up, offered a few words of encouragement, and departed with his escorts. There was little to do for the rest of the day but pace about reciting phrases and sentences while the winds howled around the ger, piling up snow against its sides.

Once I knew more words, Asetai and the women allowed me to practice their speech with them, and I began to feel more at ease with them. Kamileh was kind if a bit simple. Besides, I thought her so very old, what with such wrinkled cheeks and that net of gray braids. I was more interested in the other two: sisters, Bourma and Tsetsegmaa, broad-faced, plain, cheerful with each other and shy with me. Bourma was the older, but I could not have told them apart at first had Tsetsegmaa not been pregnant. Out of delicacy, I never asked about the father, probably some warrior who had had his way with her.

So I asked Dorje about the women. "Kamileh was enslaved as a girl around the time Chinggis Khan accepted the submission of the Uigur, 'The Rich and Strong,' as they still call themselves. Someone gave her to Qacha, and as you know, she now belongs to Lady Q'ing-ling. Bourma and Tsetsegmaa were born into slavery. Their grandfather was a chieftain who tried to defy Chinggis Khan. It cost him his life and his family's freedom. Their entire clan suffered the same fate. The girls' mother belonged to Qacha, but she died a few years ago. And your guard Asetai has an interesting story as well."

"Don't bother." Dorje looked at me queerly but made no protest. He could not know that the sisters had made me question my life. How could they, born to slavery, be so happy, at least with Argamon gone, while I was so full of self pity? I had never cared about slaves before, but now that I was one, it seemed only right to befriend them. And perhaps I could even learn the secret of their happiness.

In some ways Argamon's dog was my best company. He was so huge that at first it took all my will not to flinch in fear when he bounded up to me, especially when I learned his name was Wolf. But Wolf had decided to be my friend. I finally surrendered to his rough wet kisses and his way of dropping down next to me and sighing. He was not beautiful like Papa's Swiftwind, but he had a good heart.

Nonetheless, loneliness and sorrow clung to me. Many nights I barely slept, what with evil dreams crowded with bloodied ghosts calling out that I must redeem them. But how? To my shame, I woke the others with my cries. They went back to sleep, but not I, afraid and alone and scratching endlessly at bug bites.

I refused to try their remedy. They would sometimes groom each other, picking off one bug at a time and popping it into their mouths. Perhaps they reasoned that it was only fair to eat the pests since the pests were eating them. But I felt defiled by vermin and grease, and even more so by the rotten smell of Argamon that still clung to me. How I wished I could exorcise my despair and find my own clear nature again.

Finally, I decided at least to do something about feeling so filthy. I would approach Kamileh, whom I trusted most. Happily, the storm abated and once the sisters and Asetai were outside, I said, "Kamileh, I wish to become clean." I mimed washing myself.

She shook her head, her braids whipping around her shoulders. "Mongols say water is sacred, that we must not taint it with our dirt! *Never* bathe in running water! Even what you ask *might* bring bad luck." I thought she was being foolish, though truly no one bathed. At most people spit water from their mouths onto their hands to rinse their faces and heads. I started to ask how they could swim across rivers, then, or use water for anything, but she lowered her voice and continued, "But I am no pagan Mongol. I am Christian Uigur. And Christ was baptized in a river. I will help you, but in secret."

Kamileh was Christian! "Tell me more, please," I begged, but she would not. She was now only interested in my secret bath, in which she seemed to take a childlike pleasure. First she came up with complex errands for Asetai and the other women that kept them away all afternoon. Then came an almost ritual bath: pots of snow melted and warmed over the fire, several changes of water, and much care taken not to spill any. I got the cleanest I had been since leaving Kyiv, even without a handful of nice birch leaves to scrub with. Relieved of its burden of dirt and the nits that Kamileh had picked off and eaten, my hair gleamed like a crimson dawn. I almost felt renewed when I looked in a polished steel mirror, even after she made me smear fresh grease on myself. She was as kind as my Baba Liubyna.

"Kamileh, you do much kind thing for me. You are best Christian," I told her. We smiled at each other with new affection.

But my pleasure was short-lived. That evening the storm returned like some howling demon, and the next day Dorje brought the shaman to see me. "Yulta Beki insisted on meeting you. He even braved this new storm." Asetai disappeared somewhere; after a keen glance from the shaman, Kamileh and the sisters huddled as far from us as they could manage. The old woman looked terrified. So just the three of us sat by the fire in silence while the wind prowled and screamed outside the ger.

The white old man wanted only to stare at me, so I stared back. I refused to let him frighten me. He was so unlike our village shaman, who looked much like everyone else whenever I saw him. Yulta Beki was clad all in white, from his odd swooping hat and grimy tunic, painted all over with designs of trees and birds and stars, to his loose leggings and curl-toed boots. His long white hair streamed past his waist, and his eyes were the pale blue of a winter sky. Strangest was his skin: pale, pinkish-yellow, like candle wax through which a flame shows.

He finally spoke in a high-pitched nasal voice, but his meaning just escaped me. What could black snow cracking white sky mean? I thought it was because I was still learning Mongol speech. From a small bag hanging around his neck, he pulled out an ornately carved red stone and placed it on the edge of the square hearth where we were sitting. It began to rock slowly back and forth while he chanted in time with its movement. I could not take my eyes off it. He stopped suddenly, picked up the rock, stowed it back in its pouch, spoke to Dorje, glanced at me sharply, stood, and left.

I stared after him in bewilderment, while Dorje eyed me sternly. "Yulta Beki said you had bathed in secret, and then he did a protection chant for you and Kamileh."

I felt as if a door had opened up in empty space and dark nothingness flown into the tent. "How did he know? It was only once, what harm in that?"

"He just knows things. More important, you violated an important ban and you must not do it again. I thought I had warned you about that. But you are lucky," and he included Kamileh in his glance, "Yulta Beki was unready to punish either of you. He said he had read your hearts, and though you meant no harm, he needed to appease snow demons that you had drawn to the ordu. I think you have an ally in him, young one.

"And Kamileh, you must not disobey any other bans for Sofia, even if you think they are wrong." Kamileh and I both nodded shakily. I suddenly realized that without Dorje, I might be dead already! I sent a remorseful look to Kamileh, but though she was as white as the snowstorm, she shrugged and tried to smile. She and the others went back to work, all somberly silent.

Dorje continued, "Sofia, you *must* respect Mongol beliefs or you may run afoul of Yulta Beki again—or someone less patient. Perhaps I failed to explain things clearly enough before. I think I will start over again, this time at the very beginning."

I bowed. "Thank you for your patience."

His severe look faded. "Of course; I am glad to help." He paused thoughtfully. "All that exists, including us, is part of a great whole, alive and full of power."

"Yes, my nursemaid taught me that."

"The entire Mongol way of life is connected to this natural power, even to their mystical origins from a union between Blue Wolf and Red Doe. They honor this power in everything they do. Beyond the Sun, they worship the Moon, Earth, and Water; and they honor all the cycles of existence, from human birth and death, to the seasons, to the four directions."

"Our old Slavic religion is like that," I said, trying to banish the taste of fear from my mouth. "Our peasants still perform the ancient rituals, though our priest forbids—"

"Well, we needn't debate anything; I am merely telling you what you need to know. The Mongols' rituals and bans keep their link with sacred power clean and their windhorse, their life force energy, in balance, to bring good fortune their way. Water is sacred, so one never leaves wet boots inside a ger or *bathes* or washes clothing. Springs and running water and lakes are especially sacred, and you must *never* bathe in *them*. In spring and summer, sudden storms and thunderbolts often strike water—and people—which means that Tengri, the Eternal Blue Sky, is angry. I myself once saw a boy struck dead when he fell into a river. So, as I tried to explain before, the spiritual and practical are one, and these bans reflect both. The same with fire: honoring it brings harmony and strength, so Mongols never chop wood near one. If they swung an ax wrong, it would cut them off from its power. And, joining spiritual with practical: that way, no fires start on accident, either!"

"I suppose our spirits of home and woods and water are like that: we honor them so they will protect and not harm us. Our local spirits were my friends—" I stopped short and blushed. How deeply rooted my own paganism was!

"Yes, your people think of it in your ways," Dorje said, a smile hovering on his lips. "But now you are here, and you must follow Mongol ways. Just remember that they are only fleeting shadows in a fleeting world, and you may find that easier to do."

I did not understand what he meant, but since he went on to tell me just what I could and could not do, I didn't have to.

But he could not exorcise my unease over Yulta Beki, especially after the storm settled into softly falling snow that night. How could God allow him to see into my soul, much less control the elements with pagan charms?

At least the next day I could go outside again, although stolid Asetai hovered behind me wherever I went. Was he supposed to protect me or keep me from running away again? I stopped and lifted my face to the sky, letting stray flakes stroke my cheeks, and defiantly opened my mouth to catch some on my tongue. How sweet they tasted. At least I was still free to do this; it surely could cause no harm.

Harm. Shame crushed me like a falling boulder. My hiding in the woods the day the messenger had come from Chernihiv was behind everything that had befallen both me and my ill-fated companions. Papa would not have left for Kyiv without me, I'd have been sent straight to Constantinople alone as Oleg had advised, and nothing else would have happened. Meddling with Oleg's judgments had caused delays, and I had as good as invited that stranger from Pereyaslav to join us. I had meant well, but so what?

Worst of all, my folly had cost me my beloved Alexander—good God, he had been a slave, too! Never had I wondered about his life before coming to us. He must have lost *his* family. He had gotten sick when Oleg mentioned bandits. Had he been captured and enslaved? What an ungrateful wretch I had been when he was alive, and I had destroyed him. I had even endangered gentle Kamileh twice! How dare I take pleasure in anything?

I fell to my knees and cried aloud to Mother Earth for forgiveness. No answer came, just cold, wet, white blankness. In panic, I fled back to the ger and rushed to the small chest that Kamileh had given me for my belongings. Finding my ikon of Mother Mary, I fell to my knees and held it and Saint Anthony before me, trying to search every corner of my heart, to seek out my sins and ask forgiveness. But when I tried to enter the Lord's world of grace through the ikons' tiny windows, the saintly faces stared back at me like corpses. I could only weep and cry, "Please forgive me. Please help me." The other women stopped work and stared as if I had gone mad.

In truth I had usually tried not to think about religion. It was easy simply to rely upon the Holy Family and our saints, whom I thought of as being just like Papa and Mama and Liubyna. After all, at Mass, especially in Hagia Sofia, Heaven seemed to descend onto Earth and kindle it into splendor, surely a sign of God's love. I could not believe that this life was useful only for preparing my soul for Heaven or Hell because it was too wondrous.

Baba Liubyna had taught me that the world was always in balance—light and dark, man and woman, even good and ill—which had made perfect sense to me. And it had always spoken to me directly. Water sang, trees and rocks radiated an earthy clarity, light danced, and clouds spoke through their shapes. All carried the same simple message: we live, we are one. I had assumed that God was the life of the world and that to love life was to love God.

But if I had lost that special feeling, it was not just because of the Mongols. I had never looked deeply into my own heart, and now Lord God's wrath surely awaited me! In terror, I tried to confess my every sin—but how could I know them all, so how could I ever be forgiven beyond throwing myself on Christ's mercy?

And what if my pagan loyalties had tainted me? On that fateful day in the woods, my mind had not been with Godor Christ but with the spirits. Nor had my charms or amulets protected me from evil on my journey. How I wished I had listened to Father Kliment. I *was* an inferior daughter of Eve, and now God was punishing me!

In despair, I gave up and simply stared into the low fire, where the spirit in the flames danced mockingly before me—what matter if it was Dolya or some Mongol spirit—while the ongghon sightlessly gloated over me. Finally, hard though it was, I knew what I had to do, even if it meant risking the spirits' enmity. I solemnly vowed to leave the spirit world behind. From now on

I would trust the Holy Family alone. I took off my amulets, wrapped them in one of my dirty linens along with Baba Liubyna's little mother goddess, and buried them at the bottom of my storage chest, feeling that I had thus parted with all my misguided loyalties. Though it gave me little comfort—I felt even more alone—it did pacify some of my inner warfare. I slept better that night than I had since my capture.

The next day when Dorje arrived, I realized that just as with Alexander, I had never shown him gratitude or taken any interest in his life. I must make amends for that. After our lesson, after thanking him profusely, I asked how he had fallen into Mongol hands.

"Oh, that was so many years ago. When I was young, the Mongols invaded my kingdom not once but twice: Hsi-hsia, west of Cathay and east of Tibet. The first time, our ruler submitted to Chinggis Khan and agreed to send troops if they were needed. But a few years later when the Great Khan called for the troops, the new king refused. That was the end of my people. To ensure that no one under his rule betrayed him again, Chinggis Khan had his armies massacre almost everyone, both as punishment and as an example to other kingdoms.

"But a few of us were useful to them in some way. I was a novice in a small Buddhist monastery founded long ago by a great Tibetan missionary, Tusum Khyenpa Karmapa. The Mongols killed all the others, and they beat me for sport—that's how I lost some teeth—but they spared me because Qacha needed a scribe. I kept learning new languages over the years and became his interpreter. Now he trusts me. And I can practice the Holy Dharma best where things are most difficult, so I actually received a great gift."

The way Dorje described it, his terrible tale seemed almost ordinary. "Did your family and friends all die?" He nodded. "You must have suffered terribly."

"As did many others, but that was long ago, and this is now."

After a long pause, I asked, "And what kind of Christian is a 'Buddhist'?"

He looked at me strangely. "I am not Christian. Buddhist means a follower of the Buddha, the Fully Awakened One."

"Really? I thought ... I never heard of ... Well, then, what is 'dharma'?"

"Dharma means both the Buddha's teachings and the truth that he pointed out, which we can discover for ourselves through clear seeing."

That was enough for me. "Well, if you convert to Christianity, not only will you find the truth, you will save your eternal soul!"

He sighed. "I will never argue religion with you, for no one ever truly wins."

He seemed loath to go on, but I persisted. "Please say more. I won't cut in again."

Dorje thought for several heartbeats. "I will try to tell you much in a few words, and then I will say no more, agreed?" I nodded. "Perhaps this will help: we are each like ocean waves, rising and falling yet never separate from the water, perhaps from what you call God. When we fight that truth, we suffer and we cause others to suffer as well. The Buddha taught a way of life based on awareness and compassion that leads us back to the ocean of unity underlying all the little waves of being. Instead of wasting time on an imagined separate self, we can help others become free of the self-delusion. And that is the Buddhist path."

Indeed, he had said a lot in very few words to me, but I understood almost none of it. I certainly felt separate, especially from my Mongol captors! But the part about compassion sounded like what our Savior taught, so I did not close my ears as I might have done.

"As I said," he continued, looking at me intently, "clinging to ourselves, committing evil deeds, and believing confused thoughts bind us to more suffering. For instance, if you always thought of Mongols as your enemies, you would never see their good qualities and you would slowly sink into a poisonous lake of hatred. After a while, your whole being would drown in poison, and you would be hard put to see goodness anywhere. Then your actions would become poisonous, and you would die wretched and mean, destined for the lower realms. And now I have said enough." He smiled sweetly at me. Such talk hit too close to the bone, and I flushed.

To ease my discomfort, I asked, "Will you tell me more about yourself?"

"There is little to say. I could have given up my robes after I was captured and no longer had a monastery or a teacher. But life became my teacher, and my years with the Mongols have borne out what the Awakened One taught. When I became a monk I vowed not to go to this world for refuge, and the world kindly obliged by providing none. But I also vowed to benefit all living beings, and this I can do daily. There is so much suffering, but there are so many interesting people, too, so my life is quite delightful."

"Is that what you meant when you found me and you said that you keep going?"

"You remember that, do you? I hoped you would. Yes, you understood me."

"Well, if you gave up this world," I asked, "why you are still interested in it? And if it is soaked in suffering, where does your delight come from?" I suppose it was quite saucy of me, but I meant it innocently and Dorje just laughed.

"We all have our weaknesses," he said, "and mine is curiosity. But I try to use it to serve others. As to delight: with clinging gone, it is vaster and deeper than suffering."

"But what about God? What about atonement for your sins? The only true God sent His Son to us as sacrifice for our sins, to redeem us and lead us to Him."

Dorje gave me a penetrating look. "Is God somewhere else?" My mind stopped short. Before I could ask what he meant, he was rising to leave. "God is a very good idea, and it's time for me to go. I shall see you tomorrow, child."

After he left, despair descended on me. How much I depended on Dorje, yet how little I understood him. He was not even Christian and would likely go to Hell! Yet he had recalled me to my own faith, though in a way that left me feeling more stripped bare than comforted. He had even pointed out that hatred would be my undoing. It made me curious about his certainty that I too could do good. Was that how I might atone for my sins?

So a few days later before lessons began, I asked him what he had meant by saying I had the power to do good. "Even though I have no wish to aid any Mongol," I added.

"I know how you feel about them," he replied, "but your actions clearly led you here. And though they may live for war, they are not demons, only deluded. What they lack is compassion—they neither understand nor care about anyone but themselves. If they are not to destroy most of the world, they must learn to accept and respect ways of life other than their own. At the very least, you can help Argamon see this. He will someday wield power, possibly over many subject peoples. His mother already tries to teach him that people who fall beneath his sword are not just beasts." Beasts? I wanted to protest ... but then had I not always thought of our smerdi as little better than beasts?

"You can lead him toward a larger outlook. I have become quite useful to Qacha and even Batu Khan, and now that Qacha trusts me, he often asks my advice. Whenever I can, I guide him toward actions that benefit him without causing others harm. And when I translate for him or Batu Khan, I try to bring good into my words. You see, when you sway the right people, you are like a lever lifting a heavy burden. So if we can help lift the minds of the Mongols, we will benefit millions of beings."

"That is well beyond *my* power," I said. "I just want to find good works to do."

"Helping someone learn compassion is the best of works," he replied. "You needn't worry about finding good works, though. You're not one to stand idly by when you see something wrong, like when you rebuked Argamon for killing that woman who lost her child. He told me about it. He thought you were very brave."

"He gave me a black eye for it," I answered sourly. "You may believe good things about me, but I'm not that person. I learned a harsh lesson. I'm a slave now, and all Argamon wants me for is to satisfy his lust and somehow magically protect him! I am grateful that you teach me Mongol, and in return I'd be happy to teach you my speech, or Greek or Latin or Arabic. But do not ask the impossible."

Dorje leaned forward. "How many languages do you speak?"

"Those and Kipchak Turkish. I just know enough to deal with other merchants."

"Oh ho," he exclaimed. "And you think you have no influence! Do you know how important people like you are to the Mongols? They rarely learn other languages; they just use translators. Your skills make you doubly powerful!"

"I know nothing about that, but I know I won't help Mongols!"

"I understand. Of course it is still too soon. Let us turn to your studies."

Just before he left, though, I did have one thought about helping a few others.

"Dorje, may I ask a special favor of you?"

"Of course, child. What is it?"

"Can you find out what happened to my fellow captives? Perhaps I can help them."

The old monk looked grave. "I'll do what I can."

Finally, a few things happened to relieve me of my burden of shame. First, Dorje arrived with news of my peasants. "The women are all menials. They aren't ill-treated by Mongol standards, and I doubt they work much harder than they ever did. But I let it be known that Argamon wants their owners to treat them well. The men, for the most part, are in the army now, so what treatment they receive is up to them. I doubt more can be done for any of them, but I can bring you news from time to time if you wish."

"Yes, please." And Dorje kept that promise until they had all died of fever or hunger or despair or had been killed in battle. And only once was I able to give any of them old clothing or utensils, because the Mongols mostly used such things until they were worn beyond repair. Yet at the time, Dorje's news eased my guilty heart.

It was sometime around then that I remembered my book and began to write in it again. Someday I would turn what had happened to me into a story, just as I might tell it to my Papa.

On the first calm, bright day after the storm, to my surprise Lady Q'ing-ling summoned me. Riding over to the main camp with Asetai and another guard revived my stale spirits, which rose further when servants brought us dried jujubes and a hot green drink, fragrant and earthy, which she called tea. Her tiny, fluffy dog, whose name was Lu, peered at me from his mistress' lap like a little prince on his throne. She was so patient with my halting attempts at Mongol speech, and she even invited me to use her name, although at first I felt ill at ease doing so with an elder. I could not express thanks to her for the cross very well, but she seemed to understand.

An elderly man arrived with a stringed instrument as long, thin, and flat as the music he began to play on it. It hurt my ears, and I was glad to escape when Q'ing-ling dismissed me. Back in Argamon's ger, I realized that I might never again hear the haunting melodies of my own people.

Lady Q'ing-ling soon invited me back. Several of her women were working embroidered panels onto some new brocade jackets. I was delighted to watch and mustered the courage to ask to help. Both Lady Q'ing-ling and her servants looked surprised: this was usually a slave's task, I was given to understand. "But I *am* slave," I pointed out.

With her amused permission, I sat down to the only domestic task I had ever liked. Temulun, her main attendant, soon taught me their style of stitching, and I spent a bittersweet afternoon enduring strange music and thinking sadly of the times I had sat with my servant women in the weaving room, trying to avoid spinning or weaving. How they had loved teasing me about my marriage prospects, always suggesting men far too young or old for me or beneath me and then laughing at my vexation. I missed them now.

When she dismissed me, Q'ing-ling offered me some pieces of silk for a new garment. I gratefully chose a length of deep green brocade with a red and yellow bird motif worked into it; another piece, red with gold and blue roundels; and a third of golden samite. The kindness behind the gift meant even more to me than its beauty. I set to work at once making myself a new gown, and I was so delighted to be creating something lovely that I forgot to feel guilty.

As I sewed, a happy idea came to me. If I could show Argamon that I was not the princess in the prophecy, then he and his brothers could go back to seeking the right one and I would no longer need a guard or be liable for his well-being. Then I could escape someday and somehow redeem myself!

The final lift to my spirits came when Dorje brought a fellow student to the ger late one morning: an older man wearing a Musulman head wrap under his heavy, hooded cloak. The man kept his face slightly averted while Dorje spoke. "This is Selim al-Din, a merchant from northern Persia. Batu Khan sent him and his caravan here to learn Mongol speech from me— remember, they joined us on our way back here? He speaks Persian and I think Arabic, which is one of the tongues you speak. I had only just begun teaching him when you told me about your skills. Now you can help me instruct him in Mongol speech, which is certainly a 'good deed.'

"And you can warn him right now. Though his master in Persia swore submission to Chinggis Khan years ago, we all know Selim is a spy, or his men are. In Batu Khan's ordu, they were a little too curious about the layout of the camp, especially the section for siege engines. Had they not brought some fine trade goods with them that Batu wants more of, I suspect he'd have killed him and his entire company. But until they leave, they will travel with this ordu, which should keep them all out of harm's way."

The thought of Batu Khan carelessly murdering this man and his servitors shocked me terribly. I had never met a Persian face to face, though Papa had trade relations with Persia. And while I might despise all religions but my own, I also knew all the proper greetings for dealing with foreigners. So I greeted Selim al-Din in simple Arabic, "Blessings upon you from the God we share," and waved to him to sit.

"Dorje says to warn you. Batu Khan knows you are a spy and might kill you. Please take care."

The merchant was startled into looking directly at me for a moment. "A mere girl," he murmured. Then he smiled, looking at the floor in front of me. "And may All-merciful Allah's peace be upon you. Yes, that is what they seem to think!"

I did not like the sound of his first mutterings, much less his reply, and retorted, "I was trying to help you. And if you wish to study with me, know that I was born a princess of Rus' and am newly made a slave by capture. You must respect me."

Now it was his turn to be taken aback. "I offer you a thousand regrets. Please forgive me; I did not mean to be rude. I do not know how to treat a strange female, and I shamed myself by looking at you directly. I will be most respectful in future."

Selim al-Din's manner seemed entirely sincere, but I could not be certain, since he would not look straight at me. I looked *him* over, though. Hale enough for an old man, possibly in his forties, with a full mustache and liquid brown eyes. Under his furs, he wore a flowing robe, sash and vest, loose-legged payjamas as I later learned to call them, and fine boots. A bulge where his payjamas were tucked into his boot tops betrayed a knife.

Over the next few days, Selim often came with Dorje, and once we got to know each other better he proved to be good company and a quick student. Stumbling along in Arabic and Mongol, we three spent several hours at each lesson, laughing together at our patchwork sentences and slowly forging a special bond. After several lessons, the Persian lost his distance and even looked directly at me once or twice, though he always seemed a little surprised that nothing bad happened. But he still bowed to me on arriving and leaving and deferred to me whenever I spoke. His extreme courtesy finally began to amuse me. He did it to tease, I was certain.

At last I laughed, "Please, Selim, enough courtesy! Be more at ease."

Selim bowed and, closing his eyes, placed his hand over his heart. "I will do my utmost, Princess Sofia. Perhaps with Almighty Allah's grace, I can find the perfect way to address you: neither too formal nor too informal, with a certain poetry of speech but without implying—" Dorje and I began laughing so hard that he had to join us.

ate one day I was sitting by the fire, Wolf resting at my hip while I
recited new phrases and stitched on my new gown, when Argamon
suddenly strode into the ger. Wolf leapt up in greeting, as did Asetai. The
men smelled each other and clapped each other's arms, and my lean shadow
disappeared outside into the red-gold light. All the other slaves had jumped
up and cupped their hands, but I was covered in fabric and blocked by a dog.

Yet Argamon broke into a smile and said, "May blessings flow to you
from all-seeing Tengri, Sofia. How go your lessons? You sound like a Mongol already, I am told."

I was caught unawares, and missing my usual mind armor, I was struck
by how handsome he was—for a Mongol. Before I could stand and bow, he
sat down beside me, setting aside a pack he had been carrying, and sniffed at
my hair and clothes.

I almost froze to the spot. Could he tell that I had bathed? Trying to
hide my worry, I haltingly replied, "And may your days be fill—filled—with
good ... heart."

To my dismay, the women vanished outside, too. He leaned over my
work. "What do you make?" Was he using simple speech for me?

"I sew new gown. Your mother give—gave—me this." I almost asked him
if he liked it, then thought better of it, since why should I care what he liked?

"I like these colors for you. They make your hair look redder," he said. I
tried not to flinch as he reached out to touch it lightly. "You must not braid
it and spoil its beauty." I wasn't happy about that, but I had to undo my long
braid.

"I have some things for you," he went on. From his pack, he handed me
an ornately carved birch box, decorated with a frieze of beasts seizing their
prey. Not a promising container for a gift, I thought. "I carved this box for
you. Open it." Inside lay something wrapped in a square of red silk: a gold
torque shaped like a snake almost biting its tail, with emeralds for eyes and
pearls for scales. There were also bracelets and ear pendants of equal rich-
ness, all utterly lovely.

"They come from Khwarizm, once a great empire," he said, "now gone."

"It is a gift of—wonder," I stuttered. "I have no thing for to return."

Argamon laughed. "Your smile is my gift," he said as he fitted the torque
around my neck. After I had put on the pendants and bracelets, he said,
"They go with your eyes. Now you will look like a true princess again. My
princess."

Seeing my chance, I plunged into the speech I had been preparing for the past few days. "Argamon, I must tell you this. In Rus', many women are princess from first grandfather, Prince Rurik, he who make us one great tribe. I am one of many girls with hair of red. I am wrong one, too young like Mongke Khan says, and you are not safe."

He shook his head. "You are the one. We have eyes and ears in every city. We know who your father is and who you are. He runs with Grand Prince Mikhail's wolf pack, speaking smooth words, but he seeks the throne of Kyiv."

"No!" I cried. "Papa is good man, not wolf who spring on sheep of others!"

He just smiled. "And Yulta Beki saw you with his inner eye on the river. He knew you when I brought you to Father. When that bitch Har Nuteng tried to make him unsay his words, he would not."

He drew me into his lap. "You are of noble blood like my mother. She too came to the world of felt tents against her will. She told me you must feel as she once did. But now you are mine, and if you please me, I will always be kind to you."

I could think of nothing to say. Dorje was right: Argamon was *trying* to be good to me. He wound a hand in my hair and turned my face toward him, then took my chin and guided my mouth to meet his. He kissed me deeply. Pulling away slightly he said, "Now, put your arms around me and kiss me in the same way." I sighed, seeing no way out. We kissed again and this time I tried to follow his lead, though all I wanted to do was flee.

He pulled away again. "Do you like this better now?"

"A little bit," I lied, blushing deeply.

"I will teach you more. It is better now that we can speak to each other." He kissed me again. "I like kissing you," he murmured.

The door opened, and Kamileh poked in her head and smiled. "Master, Tengri's blessings upon you! Welcome home. Your mother joins you for supper. And look at the fine needlework your princess does, and hear all her new words."

She bustled in with a huge pot of meat in broth, heedless of Argamon's frown and my blushes. I moved off his lap. Asetai returned, bringing the smell of horse sweat inside. With a shock, I realized that I too could smell events: he'd been grooming Argamon's pony!

"Yes, she has learned much since I last saw her. And now she will learn more." Argamon gave me a glance full of meaning that set my cheeks further on fire.

His mother entered with her retinue, and we all stood and cupped our hands respectfully. Argamon spoke. "Greetings and Tengri's many blessings upon you, Mother."

"Greetings, and may good fortune attend you always, Son."

She turned to me and added, "Greetings and blessings, Sofia. Ah, let me see your work." I held up the outer garment, hoping she would like it: a long tunic of the deep green brocade, constructed in the traditional fashion of Rus'. I had edged it along the loose sleeves and hem with bands of the golden samite. It would hang gracefully, I hoped, over a gown of the red brocade that I would make next.

"You have not only skill but an eye for beauty, Sofia." Q'ing-ling had seated herself while she spoke. I bowed thanks and quickly folded up the tunic, putting it and the box away in my chest. But then I had no idea what to do. I had not been welcome at their last meal together. Behind me, Argamon was speaking softly to his mother and Asetai. I slowly turned and waited. Q'ing-ling was watching Argamon, her graceful brows lifted slightly.

He glanced over at me and beckoned. "Come sit with us, Sofia."

A smile flitted across his mother's face, making her even more beautiful.

Bourma and Tsetsegmaa came in with a roasted sheep haunch on one platter, its fatty tail on another, and its raw heart on a third. The women set the low table by the hearth while Kamileh set a pot on a trivet over the fire. Tsetsegmaa placed a slab of dough to bake on the hearth stones, while Bourma put out a dish of almonds and raisins.

While I joined the Lady, Argamon made offerings to his idols and Asetai took the sheep heart outside, perhaps for the outdoor shrine. Bourma and Tsetsegmaa began preparing his—our—bedding.

The sisters withdrew. I expected talk, but after Kamileh served Argamon and Asetai, they ate in silence. When it came the women's turn, Q'ing-ling hardly ate anything. The silence grew until it felt as if a cloud of woe hung over Argamon and his mother that might rain sorrow at any moment. Had it been me welcoming Papa home, I'd be celebrating. Then I remembered Papa's last homecoming: such a cloud had hovered over him, too.

Finally, Argamon broke the silence. I could follow better than I could speak, but his caring and concern for his mother, more than I had imagined any Mongol could feel, was what made his meaning clear. "Any more trouble while we were away, Mother?"

"No, at least nothing new. Time will take care of the rest."

"Well," said Argamon after a pause, "our plans are now firm and there are no surprises. With some southern regions left to subdue, another year must pass before our armies push through western Rus'. Then we can spring upon all these lands that call themselves Christendom. Noyan Subodai allows Father's ordus to remain here until summer's end to rebuild our supplies and weaponry, and when new warriors arrive from our homelands, Father will receive many of them. We also need more captives to use in battle, so I'll often be away on short campaigns."

Both Q'ing-ling and I were unsettled by Argamon's news, but for different reasons. She spoke sadly. "As I feared, this war drags on even longer. And what about Qabul?"

"All stays as it was: me here in the right wing and Qabul in the left. That keeps us apart. I used to dread what lies he might tell Kuvrat Khan about me." Dorje had spoken of Kuvrat, who oversaw the mingghan, the thousand soldiers, attached to this ordu. He was one of ten generals, one for each of Qacha's ordus. "But no such fears beset me now. I have Sofia." He touched my hair, but I barely noticed. I was worrying about Kyiv.

"I fear only for you, Mother. With Father and me gone so much of the time, Har Nuteng may try to harm you again. That woman is a scum pond of evil."

That caught my attention. "She does you harm, Lady Q'ing-ling?" She lifted her hands hopelessly and let them fall. Threads of silver in her hair caught the firelight.

"If intent counts as deed, she nearly murdered her," Argamon cried, "and her minstrel—not this one, a young Chinese man. The bitch wanted Father to think the fellow and Mother were lovers. Yes he did love her, but we all do. And Mother would never betray Father!" Forgetting my uneven mastery of his language, he warmed to his story.

"She spread ugly lies about Mother and the minstrel to other generals' wives. Mongol law bans telling false tales, so she never spoke straight, just dropped dark words here and there like stinking dung. Their stench reached Father. It shamed Mother, and he had the minstrel beheaded. He'd have killed Mother, too, had he believed any of it. By Mongol law, both man and woman caught in adultery must die. But now Mother endures sneers and insults from noblewomen in other ordus, while Har Nuteng hides behind her ancestry feigning innocence!"

How unfair! Q'ing-ling was so kind to me and, at least within her own circle, seemed to be loved and respected. How disgusting that anyone would treat her with contempt without knowing her; and what must she feel for such a husband? Dorje had been right about Har Nuteng. I *would* avoid her!

"I can do little, but I try helping you, Lady Q'ing-ling, if I may can." Mother and son laughed at my halting speech, but their delight was clear.

Q'ing-ling rose and prepared to leave. "We shall talk more then. Come see me tomorrow."

After she and her people had left, the two sisters returned and Bourma began pulling the curtain divider across the room. Trying to put off what must come next, I asked Argamon, "You and your mother not angry your father killed her minstrel?"

My question surprised him. "Father had to uphold his family honor. The man was only a slave, after all." Only a slave? I shuddered. Argamon frowned and added, "Alas, Father thinks to ease Mother's heart with a new minstrel, but that old man's bad music only reminds her of her loss. And when Father and I leave this summer, Har Nuteng will be free to spread more slander. I dislike leaving Mother for long."

Argamon paused pensively. "I wonder if you can...."

"Let us talk no more of this."

He pulled me down beside him. "I believe you were learning to kiss me," he said. "You need more practice."

The next day Argamon plunged back into his duties with his men, but Lady Q'ing-ling did summon me. Plump-cheeked Temulun served us tea and dried jujubes. She and the other attendants hovered over their mistress with such care. Clearly slave and servant alike loved her. Even her dog adored her.

Q'ing-ling spoke. "You wish to help me. I wish to help you, too. You will see much here and that you will not understand, no matter how many words you learn. Someone must help you. And I doubt any man, even Dorje, would think to tell you about us women."

"You are kind, Lady Q'ing-ling," I said, hoping I sounded humbly grateful, though the thought of more lessons on top of Dorje's did not really appeal to me.

She was so eager that she began straightaway, as if she had been carrying a heavy burden and was at last allowed to set it down. Happily, she did stop to help me with words I did not yet know.

"The women who are not menials are mostly wives of soldiers. But whether in war or peace, our daily lives are much the same. Most of these women know no other life than war, and some even ride with the men into battle. Others are concubines—and then of course there are the whores and other camp followers."

"What is a whore?"

"A woman who accepts pay from men in return for sex," she answered in surprise. I was aghast. I had thought I was worldly, but I had never imagined that!

Q'ing-ling added, "I suppose you are Argamon's concubine, since you lie together. But beyond that you have a strong power for good—unlike most concubines, who get so caught up in rivalries. But we can speak more of that later." It seemed unlikely that I had any "strong power for good" after the calamity at the rapids. Besides, there seemed little difference between a whore and a concubine, which likely meant I was damned, no matter how much good I did.

She continued, "Often women go to the battlefield after a victory to slit the throats of enemies and gather up useful things like arrows or boots." Just as Argamon's men had done to my companions! And because of a few kindly faces around me, I had thought Mongol women a little better than the men—but then, most of them were slaves. I grimaced and Q'ing-ling added, "Try to think of it this way: they spare the dying a slow, painful death. Of course, they only do it so their enemies will never be a threat again—"

"No! These Mongols like hurting and killing and cutting!" And I falteringly told her about them slitting Alexander's belly and chopping off Oleg's and Kateryna's ears.

"No, Sofia," she said. "Argamon and his soldiers were obeying orders. Once, a merchant tried to hide some pearls from Chinggis Khan by swallowing them. The Khakan was enraged. He had that man gutted and then decreed the same fate for any merchant taken as an enemy. Argamon's soldiers mistook your man for a merchant." Tears started from my eyes, and my throat grew tight fighting the sobs that tried to escape. Q'ing-ling waited patiently until I had control of myself.

"As to your slave and your guard, they were merely enemies. Had Argamon carried out his vow to kill you all, his men would have slit your throat and taken one of your ears, too, as a measure for how many they had slain."

She took my chilled silence for a willingness to hear more, for she then told me about Chinggis Khan. She insisted that it was important to learn about the man whose vision lay behind not only the invasion of Rus' but also of many other nations. He was a noble—even among nomads there are gentry and commoners—and still a boy when his father was betrayed and poisoned. Then his family was abandoned by their own people. Always pursued by enemies who wanted to kill them, he and his family survived against all odds, even eating field mice to stay alive. Yet he triumphed over misfortune, united all the Mongol tribes, and brought many kingdoms, nomad and civilized alike, under his heavy yoke. "But," Q'ing-ling added, "his eyes were always turned toward my homeland, which is split between the empires of the Kin and the Song." It took me a little while to realize she meant Cathay and that Dorje's Chin were her Kin. "It is—or was—a land blessed with rich soil, great wealth, and millions of people. The Mongols, like other nomads before them, always coveted both its riches and its grasslands. They overran us and camped around our capital city. Only when our emperor offered tribute and one of his daughters as a bride did the Khakan withdraw for a time. It was after that siege that I was brought to live among them."

I tried to ask her more about herself, but Q'ing-ling shook her head. "Perhaps I will tell you another time. For now you need a larger view. Chinggis Khan believed that God had sent him to unite all the ulus, the tribal nations in felt tents. Together they would take the whole world as their prize. His sons and grandsons still follow his will, and now we are here, halfway across the world. He is a god to them now."

"You seem to—look up at—to—him. I think he most wicked man ever live, outside of Judas," I said. I was also beginning to see that Dorje's views might differ from Q'ing-ling's: what he called universal peace, she called "the world as their prize!"

"What he did to other nations was often wicked, but he wasn't alone in that! And I came to respect the good in him. Betrayed as he had been, he could have become a monster. But if the khakan showed no pity to his enemies, he gave from his heart to those he loved and trusted. I lived in his court for two years and he was kind to me, a mere bug under his foot. But this is important: Chinggis Khan was willing to learn from those he conquered. He could read men, and he surrounded himself with good advisers—some were even his captives. At first he only wanted to learn more arts of war, but he soon had an empire to govern, His new counselors taught him how to do that as well.

"You see, when he was young there was no law, only customs like raiding your enemies; stealing their wealth, women, and children; and if you could catch them, killing their men. Usually the men ran away and sought revenge later. So endless rape and pillage and murder were taken as givens. Chinggis Khan and his advisors worked out a new, just law code for all people in felt tents. They say that nowadays a virgin can safely carry a pot of gold from one end of the Mongol empire to the other.

"Another example: the Mongols had no writing system, but the Khakan saw its worth and ordered Uigur scholars to make their script work for Mongol speech. And another: he learned the value of trade. They tax merchants now instead of killing them, and Mongol law protects them across the empire. Not that a Mongol of high standing would stoop to it himself. His place is on the battlefield, and plunder or tribute is his just reward."

"Well, I was virgin! And they cut my people down!"

"But your people were enemies. They killed a peaceful envoy." Too wretched to correct her, I bowed my head and blamed myself.

"I feel as you do," Q'ing-ling finally said, "but it seems to me that the strong have always taken what they wanted and the weak have obeyed or died...."

We parted soon after that. I wondered what the Lady wanted from me. It was as if she was hinting at something I could do, but I had no idea what it could be.

Lady Q'ing-ling began summoning me almost daily, and thanks to her I rapidly mastered Mongol speech. She often spoke of Chinggis Khan, whose memory seemed to prey on her mind, and no wonder. He was utterly ruthless. He did not destroy all the kingdoms that fell under his sway, but because he wanted no one attacking Mongol backs, he ordered his armies to totally destroy any peoples who resisted them. They blotted out vast empires and sometimes poisoned the soil where they had stood. When his warriors captured a city, they chose those useful as slaves—smiths, artisans, beautiful women and so forth—then led all of the others out of the city gates, beheaded them in long lines, razed the city to the ground, and came back later to find and kill anyone who had escaped the first time! I could scarcely credit such brutality. And why did people not all run away when they saw the beheadings begin?

But then I put myself in their places: even if I could outrun a Mongol horseman and his swift arrows, where would I go? Into the wilderness to starve while my family lay dead behind me? No, I would probably surrender to my fate just like everyone else. Q'ing-ling said the Mongols still do this to terrify other nations into submitting and to ensure that no one will rebel against them later. With far fewer men than their enemies, and despite their superior tactics, they know they are always at risk of being overwhelmed by larger armies. She also told me that the Mongols always invade other lands claiming revenge for some ill deed done against them—usually killing their envoys, as Grand Prince Mikhail had.

"Such savages," I once exclaimed during one of her 'lessons'.

"Every warrior is savage in combat," she replied. "A kind of madness descends on him, a feeling of power and a lust for killing. But Mongols do not kill blindly. They mostly kill other warriors, and they treat those they conquer just as they treat their animals: capture them, herd them, use them. I once thought them utterly alien, but I came to see that they spring from a harsh land. Mongolia's soil is too poor to farm, so herds and good grasslands are treasures; if drought strikes, entire tribes starve. Before Khakan Chinggis, there were constant wars and blood feuds over land and water. Yet a Mongol can surprise you with generosity or mercy, and no one can deny their loyalty to one another now. They are not entirely without goodness. Do try to see it, Sofia. This is your world now."

My world? Never! But the Lady had clearly endured so much, and she was so good, so wise. How could I turn my back on her advice? "I will try," I sighed.

"No one can ask more of you. I know it is hard for you here, and I will try to help.

"Well, here is Dorje to collect you for your language lesson." Leaning close, she added, "He is a good man."

As we rode back to my master's ger, I stared at the soldiers we passed. How many innocents had they killed—Argamon, too, and him so young? I could barely attend to my lesson. That night I lay stiff in my master's arms, feeling his temper rise. Finally I cried, "Argamon, I fear you. You Mongols love killing, but it makes hate and fear in me."

Argamon sat up and turned on me. "And your warriors are different?" He was right. Papa had often spoken with disgust of his fellow princes' bloodlust. They slew men who were almost their own brothers, too! Some claimed they fought for justice or revenge, but the misery they caused was the same, from the helpless smerdi who lost their masters to noblewomen widowed, their children orphaned. And it always led to more. Yet the Mongols seemed much worse to me—they were so thorough and so unfeeling. I searched for a way to tell him, but in vain. After a long pause, he lay down again and whispered in my ear, "I like making love much better than killing." He kissed me and stroked my body. "I wish you no harm. I would give you pleasure if you would let me."

I saw no choice. "I will try to do as you wish."

WINTER TO SPRING, Anno Domini 1240

I soon came to love Lady Q'ing-ling. She was helpful, gentle, and quietly dignified, and she cared about everyone who served under her. Slowly she began to reveal more about herself. For instance one day she was going on about Chinggis Khan again and said, "He also decreed that everyone be free to follow their own faith. Christians, Jews, Muslims, Buddhists, pagans all live side by side in peace. Indeed, the Mongols support all holy men, which means that they in turn urge their flocks to support their new masters. Of course, that gives the Mongols a tighter grip over everyone. Still, none of their subject nations was ever so tolerant as they are. I've even learned that Christians from Western Christendom would call me a heretic and kill me for my beliefs."

"You are Christian? How did I not know that?"

Q'ing-ling smiled. "I thought Dorje would tell you after I gave you that cross. There are many Christians in the ordus, some of them great khans. But Kamileh taught me at first. It gave me such comfort to find a religion of love and to feel our Savior's blessings. But a Roman Catholic monk who came here to convert us told me I follow the false doctrine of someone named Nestorius and demanded that we all submit to his true faith. Alas, he stirred up so much trouble that Qacha had him beheaded." I crossed myself and whispered a prayer for the martyred priest, even though he was Catholic. "We call ourselves the Church of the East, though. And you are called Orthodox?"

"Yes. Polish and German merchants lived in Kyiv and followed the Roman faith. Their priests call us heretics, too, but it seems wrong to kill them. Catholics even seized Constantinople." Q'ing-ling looked a question. "You never hear of Constantinople? After Jerusalem, is our holiest city. I maybe heard of a Church of the East. Is it King Prester John's Church? Some say he or his son David will come destroy the Mongols someday."

Q'ing-ling shook her head. "I never heard of a Prester John, but all the Christian kingdoms between my homeland and here already fell under the Mongol yoke." So I finally had to dismiss Prester John as Kyiv's possible savior.

Another day at my suggestion, we took a walk together, something Lady Q'ing-ling said she rarely did. Wherever our rather large retinue passed, people stopped to bow and cup their hands to her. She even halted a beating without seeming to. A soldier was shouting at his slave and whipping him across the face and body, but he stopped and cupped his hands to her while the poor victim cringed on the ground. She spoke in a friendly way with the soldier, and somehow his anger vanished. After we moved on, I looked back. The slave was busy at some task, and the soldier had gone into his tent.

Q'ing-ling sighed. "Such sights weary me. I want to return to my ger." We had almost reached it when she said, "I have long pondered this glut of brutality among the Mongols. Perhaps it is because in their homeland, even the weather is merciless. I know; I suffered under it for two years. Lightning often struck men and animals. I was terrified to go outside on a cloudy day. The first winter was so dark and cold that I almost went mad. The next summer the heat killed several people one day, yet it hailed and snowed the day after! And when a sudden storm flooded Karakorum, some nearby ordus were swept away. When the weather is so cruel, why should not people be? They seem to see kindness, especially to outsiders, as weakness. And life is but a brief dream. They believe the door of death opens on the other side to eternal life in a place of plenty."

"But God sees and judges! Evil deeds lead straight to Hell," I cried.

"True, but if it were not also God's will, would He not have stopped them? Indeed, when Chinggis Khan went to war, he not only called on the Mongol gods for aid, he summoned the aid of every god and even demon on earth!"

"But why does our true God not stop them?"

"I do not know. I can only suppose that He tests our faith through them. In all fairness, though, I have traveled far and met many peoples, and everywhere I found the same outlook. Those we call our own are human and worthy, and everyone else is less than human and deserves no kindness. Where you come from, is it not so?"

How could I deny it? Many Rus' scarcely regarded each other as their own, though we all looked down on foreigners as lesser beings. At least I could say with a certain pride, "Yes, true of many, but not my father, a good Christian. He shields people on his lands and in Mother Kyiv and is friend to strangers and the poor."

"He must be a lion of a man. I begin to see how you, so young, have those traits. You must keep his example before you." I blushed, knowing how unworthy I was.

We had resettled in her ger when Q'ing-ling said, "I was thinking about your father and recalled something most important about Chinggis Khan and his heirs." I stifled a sigh. Why did the man haunt her so? "You see, he was like your father. He too cared for his people. And though he cared nothing about those he conquered, his readiness to change did help them, too. Like in my homeland. At first he destroyed our cities and killed most of our people, especially peasants, in order to turn all the land into pastures for Mongol herds. But once he saw that the dead produce no new wealth, he stopped."

My horror must have shown, because Q'ing-ling touched my hand lightly. "This is most important to understand: why he changed his mind. One of my countrymen was captured in the same campaign that brought me to the ordus, Yeliu Ch'u-tsa'i. I knew him and I still admire him. He was a minor noble—a Buddhist scholar and astrologer who spoke several languages—and the Khakan saw he was special. For one thing, he was so tall! And his beard reached to his waist even then, when he was young! But foremost he was honest and unafraid to speak the truth to the Khakan. Yeliu Ch'u-tsa'i became one of his most trusted counselors, and he now advises Khakan Ogedai. Thanks to him they both have spared our people."

"But how?"

"He told them they could not rule from horseback, and he pointed out that wealth comes from cities, which need the peasants' grain to thrive—and Mongols covet both grain and wealth. He showed them how to enrich his Mongols by taxing their subjects' wealth. They listened and stopped the killing."

"How very kind!" I snorted softly.

"Sofia, one man saved an entire people, proof that a single person can make a difference. When the Mongols collect slaves, from the educated to the menial, they learn from them all, for better or worse. And they learn from those who join them knowing they will receive special favor—like an excellent blacksmith in this ordu who fled here after killing a boyar who had raped his wife." My eyes opened wide. I knew who she meant—the rude one who had called me a fox. My sympathy was all for the wife, but Q'ing-ling misunderstood my look.

"Perhaps an escaped felon is not the best example, but many who serve the Mongols work to civilize them. You can help, too. Nothing will stop them in battle, but we can win them over from barbarism, even if it takes lifetimes. I know because some of my ancestors were Jurchen, wild tribes from Mongolia. Long ago they toppled a dynasty and founded their own. But my homeland is the most civilized on earth, and no one can resist its culture. Many Jurchen became civilized. Now the Mongols will do the same, sooner or later, if they do not destroy us first. We cannot let that happen. I know this much: God sent you and me here to help save the remaining kingdoms of the world." She paused while I considered her words. Her face had taken on a new radiance.

"How? What can I do besides be lucky charm?"

Q'ing-ling laid her hand on my arm. "You already do more than that, Sofia. You have touched Argamon's heart in a very short time. He admires you, and he is gentler with you than with any other woman he has ever been with, even his wife, I think."

My mouth almost fell open. He had a wife? I had never thought about Argamon with other women, much less with a wife. Tsetsegmaa—*he* must have been the warrior who had had his way with her. Now I felt both jealous and afraid. Q'ing-ling had bent over to admire Temulun's handiwork and did not see my face, or she would have realized I'd known nothing about this. "My son needs your influence," she went on. "Qacha wants Argamon to be like him, and Argamon wants to please his father. Yet he already senses there is more to bravery than what his father teaches him. *You* are brave, which he understands. He told me that only because of you did he spare your fellow captives. But you are also kind. Dorje tells me you still look after their welfare. And Kamileh tells me that rather than use your higher position in Argamon's household for your own gain, you befriend his slave women. Even his dog likes you. You already teach him by example."

I pondered her words. Here was a way I could get at Argamon without murder. He already had a few good qualities—at least he wanted me to enjoy his embrace! And the night before he had sung a song he'd made up for me while Asetai played his horse-headed fiddle, so he had some finer feelings. "I can try. Dorje says this, too."

"Yes, he and I think alike about this. And something else: others may see your power as magic, but I know that God answered my prayers by sending you to my son. Be loyal to him and follow your heart. Time will do the rest. It was so with Qacha and me."

I could not imagine Qacha being any worse, but I said nothing. She saw my grimace, though, and said, "Qacha *has* changed, my dear. For example, Kamileh grows old, and it is Mongol custom to let older slaves starve to death rather than waste food on them. He could have bidden me to stop giving her real food, but he sees how much she and I care for each other and he has never spoken a word. He shows me so many small kindnesses, too."

What must she have faced in her years with her husband if that was the best she could say of him? I could not voice my thoughts, so we just sat in silence until Dorje and Asetai appeared to take me back. I knelt before her and we clasped hands. "I do offer help, Lady. You give so many good words and deeds to me. I hope to return good to you."

"You need never think of repaying me for simple kindness, my dear," she smiled. "And remember, you are always free in one way: to live in hatred and despair or to use life to do good." I glanced up at her in alarm. Had she, like Dorje, read my dark thoughts?

As I left the ger, I looked back at my new friend. She had stood up and was nodding approval of her seamstresses' work. She looked so slender and elegant, yet so lonely. This was not really her world, for not once had she said 'we' when describing the Mongols' many wicked deeds. Yet she had spent most of her life surrounded by brutes and made her peace with them without becoming cruel or bitter. Could I, a mere girl, ever do the same?

But I had a more pressing challenge to face. Riding back to Argamon's camp, I tried to think of how to approach him without revealing my fears. Nothing presented itself, and I stiffened that night when he drew me into his arms. He pulled back, anger at the ready, but I blurted, "Argamon, I must ask. You have a wife and … you lie with other women?"

Argamon beamed with delight. "Well, my only wife so far is in Karakorum for now with our son. She serves Great Khan Ogedai's wife Toregina. My other women are mere slaves like Tsetsegmaa and Bourma and those I— They are nothing, any of them."

"Even your wife? Do you not miss her? She not mind other women?"

"No; she was given to me to bind two noyans in friendship. And I can have as many other women as I want. Although right now I want only you." His flattery failed to reassure me. How thin was the thread from which my life hung! I had already begun to fear that if Argamon were wounded or killed, I would be tortured to death. But even if that never happened, what if he tired of me? He was forever pinching or slapping Bourma and Tsetsegmaa, and someday he might treat me that way. I had thought to show him that bedding me was not the same as possessing me, but pushing him away might be a mistake.

Well, for now I was his favorite. Once his lust was sated, I said, "When others hear us do this, I feel shame. If they go away at night I can please you better."

Argamon frowned. "Their feelings count for nothing. Besides, when people live close together as we Mongols do, we are deaf to what is not meant for us." But he did call to the women on the other side of the curtain. "Kamileh! Bourma and Tsetsegmaa! Go stay with the other slaves tonight. Come back in the morning. Asetai, go to Bayartou." Asetai grumbled and I heard a few murmurs from the women, but soon we were alone. "Now, please me." And so I did, even if I felt like a whore who bartered sex for privacy.

A few days later, it now being customary for Argamon and me to be alone at night, I knelt down by the two sisters while they cut up dried meat for a stew. "I must speak for sleeping alone with Argamon. You both did lie with him, and Tsetsegmaa, you carry his child?" She nodded, looking puzzled. "I will never try to come between you and him."

They both looked more puzzled. Bourma said, "We feel no ill will. He treats us better since you came, so we are happy you are here." We all smiled, suddenly allies.

Bourma's answer also showed me that I had already swayed Argamon for the better. I decided to regard his nightly rape as just an unpleasant task and to put my mind elsewhere. In a sense, I was even doing a good deed!

As the days began to stretch longer, Qacha's ordus moved again, spreading out over the immense grasslands. On a clear day I could make out nine lines of smoke around us. I often felt like a wisp of smoke myself: one small, smudged soul, fading away in the camp's routines. Ironically, I scarcely saw Argamon. Mornings and evenings he made me genuflect with him to the sun, but he was gone with his men all day. At night he satisfied his lust and then fell asleep. My nightmares no longer woke him.

Dorje was often attending Qacha, so Selim al-Din would stay away as well. I had little to do beyond sew more garments or write in my book. Kamileh came and went between Argamon's camp and the Lady's, and when it was not snowing, she brought me to the main camp to visit, though I tired of endless stories about Chinggis Khan.

I became ever friendlier with the other slaves and Asetai: Kamileh so kind, the sisters so gentle, Asetai so cheerful. He and Bourma shared many a shy glance of affection. He always seemed to be stepping outside with his bag of koumiss, or airag, as they called it, probably off refilling it. He often took long pulls, yet it never seemed to empty, like our Rus' fables where tables set themselves and pots of stew never emptied.

One day he passed out, but no one moved to revive him. After he was awake again, he could not see very well for awhile. Later, when he went outside for more airag, I whispered to the sisters, "Is he ill? Can we help him?"

Bourma sighed. "It happens more and more. But he always gets over it...."

Whenever Yulta Beki and his wife sought omens in the heavens or performed sacrifices, I had to be there with Qacha's family. I tried to see it all as beneath me, but it was difficult not to be afraid, especially on the first of each month when Qacha's family visited the shaman's ger to offer candles, incense, and food; they smeared these straight onto the idols. I had to offer, too, but in my heart I was praying to Mother Mary to save me from those bloody, greasy idols and those bloody, greasy people—or at least to send me a sign that God had forgiven me.

The first time Argamon took me there, it seemed as if his brother Qabul was staring at me no matter where I stood. When Argamon noticed, he seized me around my waist and rubbed a hand over my privates, grinning triumphantly at his rival. He didn't notice my distress, much less care, but Qabul winced and looked sorry for me.

That night Qacha held a feast to honor his generals. Q'ing-ling even invited me to sit near her, but it put me amidst Qacha's family. The noyan and his men could not open their mouths without saying something gross or mean; the food was forgettable; Argamon was opposite me, talking and laughing with his friends and drinking heavily; and Q'ing-ling, though she was kind to me, seemed as quietly unhappy as I was.

At one point she whispered into my ear, "I saw what Argamon did to you today. He ... he tries to be good, but so many forces work against his best nature."

Asetai got both drunk and sick straightaway, but instead of going outside he simply turned and vomited on the carpet behind him. I could hardly believe it. When Papa's men had gotten that drunk, he'd made them leave! Argamon laughed, but Qabul sneered, "You can't hold your liquor or your piss. Make sure you don't mistake piss for airag."

Argamon half rose from his seat, fists clenched, but Asetai stopped him with a hand on his shoulder, a whisper in his ear, and the offer of a cup of arki. He finally shrugged and poured more for Asetai, too. Later in the feast, ironically, several men, including some of Qabul's, vomited where they sat, too. The stench in the tent made me ill. But Qabul and Argamon both just laughed at their friends and urged more drink on them.

Qabul was full of crude jests that night. And every time he caught my eye, he smiled so warmly that I blushed. At one point he leaned forward, arm on his table, and looked at me as if we were alone together, alone and in love. Argamon noticed and began glaring at him, but Qabul just smiled and raised his cup to me in a mock toast.

What if I were to smile back? He was no grosser than Argamon, and he had shown me sympathy that day. Why not see, and perhaps hurt Argamon a little, too? So I smiled sweetly and then glanced at my master, whose face had turned dark as a tempest. I didn't bother to look back at Qabul to see how my smile had affected *him*.

When the feast was finally over, Argamon almost threw me on my pony, seized my reins from me, rode in grim silence back to his ger, dragged me off my horse, and thrust me inside, where he shook me so hard I thought my neck would snap. "You look at Qabul like that ever again and I'll beat you until you cannot stand!" he shouted.

"I beg you, stop hurting me! I'll never do it again! Please! I only tried to—"

"What, you little bitch? Make trouble?" he snarled. He shoved me and I fell backwards, tears streaming down my face. He poured abuse on me relentlessly, but on his face was less anger than a haunted look. He finally ran dry of words. The only sounds in the ger were the hiss of the low fire in the hearth and my sobs.

Finally I summoned courage to speak, though not to tell the full truth. "Today you mocked Qabul by shaming me, and *he* showed me kindness. I smiled because ...," with no word for thanks, I searched for the right words, "I wanted to repay it!"

Argamon's face fell. "That is why?"

I nodded, secretly ashamed of my little game, and wiped my tears.

"Then never do it again! He's a wicked man, and any kindness from him is falsity. He means you no more good than he means me." He stood frowning over me in silence for some time, his hands on his hips. Finally he held a hand out to me. "Come to bed now."

With his anger worn off, he was almost gentle with me when he took me. And I felt even more ashamed of myself for my mean-spirited game.

From then on, Argamon did treat me better around Qabul. Alas, I found I must now constantly avoid the elder brother whenever the family gathered. He always seemed to be nearby, watching and smiling in a way that made me blush. And, though Argamon never shamed me again, he still delighted in parading me before his rival.

Finally the weather improved, and so did my life. Argamon, claiming I must learn Mongol ways, sent me to explore his wing of the ordu with Asetai. I was willing to do anything to get outside that stuffy ger, and Asetai allowed me to wander at will, though I avoided the area where that rude blacksmith worked! I soon discovered that though Asetai was often drunk, he was an unpolished gem of kindness. Indeed, he did not even begrudge my dislodging him from Argamon's ger at night. And I did learn much from him. How many false notions I had held about nomads, whom I had always dismissed as lazy leeches sucking at us civilized people. In fact, from young to old, everyone was busy repairing something old, making something new, tending to animals, and so on. Asetai explained it all.

Of course the slaves did all the heaviest work. Papa had never treated our slaves as Mongols did—beating them for no reason, scarcely feeding them, giving them the worst rags to wear. I knew that because of me, my fellow captives were being treated better than most, but it was not enough. So much unthinking cruelty broke my heart. Powerless to do more, I prayed for them all, but with little hope that my prayers mattered.

With time I learned to steel myself against painful sights and to seek out what was pleasant, like the singing. Everyone sang while they worked, as we did at home, whether fletching arrows or stirring pots of stew. Men even sang their laws aloud in order to remember them! I especially liked listening to the women. Once I exclaimed over a particularly charming song, and Asetai smiled. "This kind of work song pairs with its task. The women follow its cadence, which lends strength and beauty to what they make."

The women themselves were often cordial and kind, not only to each other but to me. They all knew who I was, even in other jaghuns. At first little children would stare at me in curiosity as I passed, then dart behind their mothers if I smiled at them; but before long they gave me their names. Some even followed me around. I learned their mothers' names, too, though I kept a certain distance. It was one thing to befriend an innocent child, but the women were my enemies.

The section of the camp devoted to the soldiers' pleasure, though, Asetai would not allow me to enter. I found it one day, attracted by hearty laughter and cheers coming from a circle of tents. A group of soldiers were standing around a fire-eater and a jester. I wanted to watch, too, but Asetai caught my arm and firmly turned me around. Too late: I glimpsed a soldier following a whore into her tent. I knew what she was; he was already groping at her breasts and privates. He couldn't wait to get inside before he was at his business! Asetai was almost dragging me away, but I looked back and saw her shove her customer away and hold out her hand until he dropped some coins into it. Her painted face was hard and unsmiling. I shivered: both of us doomed to eternal fires. I was less eager to explore after that. Besides, we all milk animals or toss fodder or boil water in the same way.

Evenings were often rather pleasant, filled with heroic poetry and song that was often performed by skilled minstrels, one of whom was Asetai. Like him, most minstrels played horse-headed fiddles that sounded like bees humming in harmony with each other, only deeper. Their songs were all about Mongol greatness, bravery, and victories, even the beauty of Mongol horses.

Indeed, you were more likely to hear about a man's love for his horse than for his woman. They reminded me of the heroic tales Matvei the Bard would recite while playing his kobza, except they celebrated the wrong heroes.

As the weather grew warmer and the days grew longer, my heart rejoiced at the first signs of spring: brooks swelling with melting snow, the sweet bright green of early grasses, the glad song of returning birds. After so much snow and such stench in the camp, I even welcomed the chill rainstorms that washed the air clean, but my Mongol captors looked up in worry at the rumble of thunder. As soon as lightning forked over us, most people raced for shelter, while those who could not, like shepherds, had to face the storm alone. I thought it a farce, the first time Bourma made me hide under black felt blankets for extra protection.

The men especially seemed to fear it. Asetai had mentioned that many warriors wore special straps covered with precious stones to ward off Tengri's thunderbolts. Qacha and Qabul wore them, and now I saw why. Fearless warriors indeed, I sneered—until I remembered that most of us Rus' feared God's thunderous wrath in much the same way. Baba Liubyna would shut the windows tight and make me huddle with her and chant pagan and Christian prayers, while all I had wanted to do was to watch the magic of clouds alight with lightning, the very sky thundering out greatness. And crouching under those black blankets, it came to me: did I not deserve God's wrath? Perhaps I should fear storms after all.

Around the equinox, spring's arrival was celebrated with a great festival. Argamon had me dress in the garments I had made from Q'ing-ling's gift. My gold gown and blue tunic seemed to have shrunk, anyway. We joined his family in front of his father's ger where a crowd of onlookers stood, as many as would fit, all jostling each other cheerfully. Hundreds more spilled out onto the steppes. They parted hastily when Yulta Beki and his wife and apprentice galloped up on their white horses and dismounted almost before the beasts had stopped.

Noyan Qacha reverently offered the shaman gifts of the fattest sheep and horses. While the boy drummed, the wife chanted, and Qacha's men held the animals down, Yulta Beki slaughtered them; offered their hearts; sprinkled liquor, milk, and blood about; and studied their entrails before burning everything in a smoky bonfire.

Dorje spoke softly into my ear and I almost jumped. "This festival honors Natigai and Itugen. Remember them? Protector of cattle and virgin fertility goddess? And those ditches over there will hold burnt offerings to the dead who watch over the Mongols."

"You speak as if these false gods and dead souls really do something."

"Perhaps. But only as if," he smiled, leaving me puzzled and annoyed.

More mares' milk was wasted on the yak-tails that hung from Qacha's standard. He poured an endless stream of it over them while Yulta Beki droned some chant and the assembled crowd looked on in silent awe. But with all that over, everyone plunged into several days of eating and drinking vast amounts of meat, flat bread, liquor, and honeycomb; playing wild music; and dancing just as wildly, since everyone got drunk.

I could not help contrasting it to our spring celebrations at home: happy ring dances, jolly pipes and tambourines, songs full of glorious harmony, all to honor Lada, goddess of love and beauty. Instead of sacrificing animals, *we* burned a straw effigy of winter to welcome longer days, the new green of plant and tree, and the birth of bright flowers. I hoped that somewhere maidens were adorning birch trees to celebrate spring and to give thanks for the useful bark. And feasting with friends and family: blini pancakes, cabbage soup, sturgeon and carp—Mongols detest fish as fit only for emergencies— roast meats, berry jams, honey cakes, calves-foot jellies, berry-scented kvass, mead …

But then I had to admit to myself that our people got drunk and rowdy, too.

I truly did enjoy the contests during the festival, mostly the Three Manly Sports: horse racing, archery, and wrestling. Every day there were races, some of which women and girls could join. While most were short and about speed, others must have taxed people of any age or sex, as they also tested cunning and endurance. One race lasted all day and took the riders far from the camps. Most archery matches were on horseback, too, to see who could shoot farthest and truest while riding away from a target and so forth.

But one archery contest seemed absurd to me. The archers lay flat on the ground waiting for a flock of birds to fly past so they could shoot straight up at them. When I sneered, Asetai said, "This is a favorite Mongol sport, Sofia Begi, and very hard to do."

"Well, it sounds impossible to me—and dangerous." He and I were watching Bayartou try his skill along with a few other madmen. Nothing happened for a long while and my attention wandered. Suddenly several arrows streaked up into the sky. I looked up uneasily, hoping no stray arrows would hit me. Instead, three jackdaws fell to the ground while the crowd roared. Luckily the other arrows fell safely to earth. But I was not humbled. After all, what did they get for their pains but ugly dead birds?

On the last day we watched a wrestling match, which seemed strangest of all to me. The players fought almost unclothed but for gaily decorated loincloths, heavy boots, and odd long-sleeved jackets that only reached halfway down their backs and left their chests mostly bare. Argamon had to prepare for another event so he left me at the front of the crowd with Bourma, Tsetsegmaa, and a harsh-faced guard named Temur, to watch Asetai fight another man. There was the usual circling about to find the right grip, but then each tried to seize the other by the sleeves and hook his leg around his rival to throw him off balance. It looked just as hard as the way we Rus' did it! Finally Asetai managed to throw his man, and his friends all burst into cheers. Bourma could barely contain her smile.

I shook my head and was about to turn away when she stopped me. "Do our men's wrestling costumes seem strange to you?" I nodded. "There is a tale about them. Once, many years ago, men fought with jackets that covered their chests, and among them was a very tall and strong wrestler who won easily every time. One day, this wrestler's jacket got torn open in a fierce match, and to the surprise of all, 'he' was a 'she'!"

I laughed. "And their jackets are cut away so no woman can fool a man and win?"

"Yes," smiled Bourma. "That's right!"

Just then Asetai joined us, glowing with pride and holding his prize: an amulet that he offered to Bourma. She blushingly tied it around her neck. He turned to me. "You must stand with the noyan's family now, Sofia Begi, for I must join my team for the polo game. It's the high point of the afternoon, and only nobility can play in it. Will you come this way?" I followed him toward a large area protected by stern-looking guards, looking forward to this new game. Asetai gallantly ushered me through, jesting with the guards as we passed. It struck me that Argamon had expected Asetai to guard or protect me, but he had done something else entirely. He had shown me what my master lacked.

We reached a playing field with men on horseback milling about and a crowd of finely dressed people surrounding it. Asetai left me with Q'ingling, who, unfortunately, was standing on the other side of Qacha from Har Nuteng. It seemed that Argamon and Qabul were to lead the opposing teams, which were composed of sons of Qacha's generals. Once the game began, the Lady tried to explain what was happening. Its object was to hit a small ball made of some kind of root down the playing field with long-handled mallets. Each end of the field belonged to a team, and someone had to hit the ball outside of their rivals' end of the field. But with horses plunging about, players shouting and cursing, and spectators screaming for their favorites, I could scarcely follow what was happening. Polo seemed almost as vicious as the one battle I'd witnessed, but Qacha and his generals were in such a happy frenzy that they could scarcely stay off the field.

Toward the end of the game, Qabul darted behind Asetai and struck him across the back of the head with his mallet. Luckily Asetai moved unexpectedly and it only grazed him, or he might have been killed. He toppled off his horse and barely avoided being trampled, while Qabul galloped off to send the ball sailing through the goal. Asetai crawled away, but he was clearly hurt. Even for such a violent game, this surely was not right. I tugged at Q'ing-ling's sleeve. "Did you see that? Qabul just hit Asetai from behind with his stick! Is that allowed? They must stop the game! He needs help!"

She looked over at Asetai. "No, I didn't see, but Qabul has been doing vicious things to him since they were boys."

"But look at his head!" Asetai had stood, but his head was bleeding from a gash.

"No," she said, "we cannot stop the game. That would shame Asetai further. He knew the risks when he insisted on playing. What a beast that Qabul can be!"

I glimpsed Har Nuteng glaring over at us. She must have overheard Q'ing-ling. But her face changed to scornful triumph. Qabul's team had just won, and Qacha was already striding onto the field shouting happily. "He *is* a beast. He's a real man," she sneered. "Not like some who suckle under their mother's skirts." Even I caught her double meaning.

Lady Q'ing-ling flushed but said nothing. I frowned at Har Nuteng, unable to think of something cutting to say. So I turned back to my friend. "That Har Nuteng is mean. You are to her as a jewel is to rock." My friend smiled her thanks, but she still looked upset.

Qabul's men were roaring and clustering together on their horses to pound each other's backs, yet even they could not drown out an angry shout from Argamon. He pushed his way through the horses to confront his brother. "You could have killed Asetai, you cheating son of a whore. You struck from behind like a coward!"

Qabul just laughed. "Go cry to your mother, little girl. If you cannot play like a man, don't play at all." Argamon swung at his brother with his own mallet, and shouts broke out from all sides. Men from both teams jumped off their horses and struck wildly at each other before Qacha and the other generals could step between them.

Qacha was laughing! "Enough, enough! You can settle your quarrel tonight. I demand a rematch then, with words. Now go, all of you, and soak your hot tempers in drink. Enjoy!" Laughing to himself, he marched off to follow his own advice. I followed Argamon and Asetai off the field wondering how he could find their enmity amusing and glad to see that my guard's wound was not as bad as it looked—at least he could walk on his own. What a wicked thing for Qabul to do! Now I understood Dorje's warnings.

That night I joined Q'ing-ling in front of Qacha's ger to witness the word duel. I had never seen one before, though Dorje had mentioned them. Mongol warriors pride themselves both on their poetic abilities and their ability to withstand insult, and the loser was the one to lose his temper. Until late into the night, their faces lit weirdly by flickering firelight, Argamon and Qabul circled around each other trading insults: crude, bawdy, and all in rhyme, surrounded by laughter when one of them scored a good hit. I followed well enough to catch most of their double meanings, some of which were quite witty.

Finally, Argamon called out an especially crude thrust that compared Qabul's manhood to a broken sword that needed constant repair by soaking in hot blood. But while I was puzzling over what he meant, Qabul leapt at his younger brother with a shout of rage. Several men jumped up and held them back, and Qacha stood and cried, "Qabul, be content! You won the polo game, Argamon the poetry duel, each of you according to his strengths. You are two fiery steeds of different breeds, and neither need envy the other!"

Qabul threw off the men's arms, barely cupped his hands to his father, and stalked out into the night. His mother started to follow him, but Qacha gripped her arm and pulled her to face him. "Leave him. You rot his mind, letting him gorge on golden visions."

She sank her gaze to the ground and murmured, "As you wish, my lord." When he released her arm, she looked up again and, with a nasty gleam in her dark eyes, added in an insulting tone of voice, "Do you grant me leave to return to my ger? My lord?" He stared her down, pushed her aside, and strode into his ger, waving to Q'ing-ling to follow him.

As Argamon came up to me, flushed with victory, his mother paused long enough to say softly, "I fear your insult will bring harm on some innocent one, my son."

He shrugged. "Now or later, it always ends the same way with him."

She turned away without answering, and Argamon led me back toward my pony. I started to ask him what he had meant by his insult and what Q'ing-ling had meant, too, but Bayartou and others were already slapping him on the back and praising him, and I was thrust aside. My question was lost in the celebration that followed, which Asetai joined, his head wrapped in a bloody rag. They all drank late into that night, hooting and pounding on each other as they recalled this or that witty verse. But they never mentioned the last and winning rhyme. I finally crept into the ger for Argamon's other slave women and fell asleep.

The next day marked the end of the festival, and I was glad. A surfeit of food, drink, and merrymaking. One good thing, though: while neither of us knew the exact date, in honor of Easter Q'ing-ling gave all the slaves in the ordu castoff clothing and food. I handed out ruined clothes all afternoon—but some people were wearing shredded rags. Two of my former peasant women were among them. We wept when we saw each other, and they insisted on kissing my hands.

That evening at Qacha's final feast, knowing two pairs of eyes were on me, I kept my own down for the most part. After the meal a bard played a horse-headed fiddle and sang a song that made the hair rise on the back of my neck. Not merely a melody came from his mouth but echoes and chords, unlike anything I had ever heard before! And skilled performers pranced about like horses or danced on their knees, shaking their shoulders and arms fancifully. I quite enjoyed it. Qabul and Argamon even joined the dancing, laughingly trying to outdo each other.

Once Qabul landed directly before the low table where I sat with Q'ing-ling. He smiled at me, his white teeth gleaming, his skin glistening in the firelight, and leapt away again. The force of his gaze robbed me of thought.

Not long after the festival the ordus moved again to seek out new grass and fresh water. A month later, we moved yet again; and another month, another move, always northwest, always toward Kyiv.

Despite my unease I could not resist the beauty of the steppes, stretching endless and serene from one curving horizon to the other. On days when great towering clouds sailed overhead, the land was like some green sea-bottom and I a mermaid staring up at cloud ships. Each day the grasses turned brighter and more bespangled with many-hued flowers. Huge dancing butterflies appeared as though the flowers had taken wing.

The animals were fattening and giving birth, and the herds, so immense already, doubled in size. Milking became an ongoing chore, and though men tended the mares, Bourma and Tsetsegmaa were often gone to do milking. I was left with little to do most days but pray, write, and practice with Dorje and Selim.

Tsetsegmaa's baby was getting huge inside her, and one day, weary with simply standing at the edge of things, I had an idea. Here was how I could perform a good deed! Feeling most virtuous, I offered to replace her at heavy chores. She gratefully accepted and let me help Bourma while she took up lighter tasks. Though I found real joy in hard work that day, I soon discovered how hard a menial's life really is, although I only churned butter and set wide bowls of whey on the roof of Argamon's ger to keep them safe from animals. They would dry into the white rocks for the drink Argamon's soldiers had forced on us—not magical after all. Asetai worked nearby, fletching arrows. He and Bourma smiled at each other whenever they thought I wasn't looking.

Another time I helped Bourma cut meat into thin strips to dry in the wind, lay out moist chunks of curdled milk onto trays, and set them on the roof, too. "We ate too much of this all winter. I tire of it. I miss our grand feasts at home," I grumbled.

"Or cheese made from cream—Master let us taste it once, and I never forgot it!"

"With so much butter, why not make more of that? And why not have fresh meat?"

"The creamy cheese is only for the noyan's feasts. Butter has better uses. And if we eat fresh meat now, what will we eat in winter? Or if drought strikes or plague kills the herds? But we can have marmot now that they're getting nice and fat, and plain cheese now and then, and milky tea, and sometimes airag!"

Asetai, endlessly busy with his arrows, added, "You wait for one of our great hunts, Sofia Begi. Then you will feast. Meanwhile, who could not be happy with marmot and airag? You may not like ground squirrel that much, but I know you like airag even if you don't drink much of it. Fresh airag marks the best time of the year!"

I smiled. "Even if it's only mare's milk wine, it gets me drunk if I have too much. I think you Mongols drink far too much liquor."

Asetai laughed. "Impossible, Sofia Begi! To be drunk is to live among the gods." I held my tongue. Many Mongols were drunk all the time, even more than at home where Papa was forever trying to curb his servitors. And Asetai really couldn't hold his liquor, for he had recently passed out at a feast and had to be carried out.

One day I learned how to make felt. We used old felts as supports for making the new, so they were called the mothers and the new pieces the daughters. When a felt was finished, the women stood around it and said, "Now a sweet daughter has been born." I liked that. We made light pieces for hats and clothing, but Bourma explained that in the autumn we would make heavier pieces for tent walls and such.

One morning Asetai brought Bourma a gift, which she shared with all of us: curds left over from making mare's milk wine. They were delicious, and without realizing it we all ate too much and got giddy from the liquor left in the curds. When Argamon returned to the ger, he found the four of us lost in laughter.

We slaves stood up in alarm and cupped our hands, but he only smiled. "So my princess is not always so solemn. You should laugh more often."

My smile faded. "I will try, Master."

Such a scowl crossed his face! He stalked out of the ger, Asetai at his heels. Asetai returned shortly thereafter, looking secretive, but Argamon did not come back until the evening meal, Bayartou following him with a large wine sack. They looked like a pair of wolves stalking a doe. The men had finished eating and were reclining tipsily when Argamon said, "Here, Sofia, eat up. I saved this good piece of meat for you. And drink this, much tastier than wine curds. After airag, it's my favorite." He poured me a great goblet of liquid from Bayartou's wine sack. So *I* was the doe he was stalking. It was arki. I would never mistake it for water again!

I sipped it slowly this time. "It is good."

"Have more. Drink up!" I glanced over at Tsetsegmaa, sitting patiently on her heels waiting to serve, and made a wry face that Argamon couldn't see. She smiled slyly.

The men spent the rest of the evening trying to get me drunk and helping themselves to more arki when I refused it. Argamon kept eyeing me hopefully, as if to win a smile or even more from me. If so, he failed. He had to be content with my usual dutiful surrender that night, and the next morning he disappeared with his men without a word.

Spring stepped lightly into summer. I still missed my home, but I had friends now, and each showed me kindness in his or her way. I could not help but respond. Every friendly gesture seemed to stand on its own at first, but there were so many of them, each a small, unseen chip at the wall of my defenses.

Argamon was *not* my friend. He learned about my working with his slave women and forbade it. "You forget who you are. It's wrong for you to work like a menial."

"But there's nothing for me to do. I cannot study with Dorje and Selim every day, or visit your mother all the time," I retorted. "Or—"

"Well then," he cut in, "whenever you aren't with Dorje and that Persian, Asetai can teach you more about the heart of our ways, the work of the men!"

"But I have alread—"

"Enough! Say no more about it."

So I was forced to visit parts of the ordu that held no interest for me. Asetai led me to the main camp all too eagerly, where to my surprise we went to the area where airag was made! He showed me an empty churn of stiff leather and a wooden paddle that swelled into an upside-down bowl. "Only men milk the mares and make the airag. Every time we pass a churn, we work it a little, and the next day it's ready to drink. But some we allow to get stronger in special bags. Airag is sacred; it gives a warrior his strength."

"Or perhaps it makes him drunk and gives him visions of power!"

"No, I'll prove it to you. Come meet a friend of mine who has been training me." Asetai then led me to the ger of, not a warrior as I had expected, but a bow maker. When we arrived, the old man was gluing together slices of horn and wood for a new bow, just as I had seen Asetai do. He waved us inside and continued working. Asetai picked up a half-finished bow and handed it to me. "This is one I was working on before you came to us."

"Oh dear, did I stop you?"

"No, I'll come back to it. I have one in the ger I'm working on. And I am proud to be your guardian. It's a sign of Argamon's trust in me that he gave me such an important duty. Now, look over here." And he showed me several other bows of various sizes that were finished. They curved like half-moons, and when I tried lifting one it seemed light and springy but lacking in power. The old man stopped and took the bow from my hands.

"No, no, this is not their final shape. These bows are unstrung. When we string them, we bend them back against their natural curves, like this." He deftly strung it. "Look, this is what gives our bows such might." The bow now curved like an upper lip, the handle resting in its center. "Try the bowstring now." I could not move it at all.

Asetai and his friend laughed. "It takes great strength to bend this kind of bow, Sofia Begi. Some bows need two men to string them. Men used to make their own, but now skilled craftsmen make even better ones. Only our most powerful warriors can handle the best bows, and few of the captives in our ranks ever master them." I tried to assure myself that a Kyivan warrior could, but unease gnawed at my heart.

Asetai was a far more eager guide than I was a listener. Now he had too much to say while we watched soldiers fashion arrows that would carry fire or whistle like ghosts like the ones that had wakened me that dreadful night at the Dnieper; or visited the rear wing of the ordu to watch Chinese and Turkish engineers oversee slaves building massive siege engines that could be dismantled for travel; or fashion new arms amidst the din and heat of smithies. The men sang work songs, too, but the work had but one dark purpose.

Last of all, Asetai took me to watch his fellows train their horses. That at least was amazing. Spread out as far as the eye could see, clusters of men were working the ponies. And this was only one camp. "Airag is sacred, but our horses are our souls," he said. "They serve us in so many ways: as mounts, for food, for leather. When traveling fast on campaign, a warrior will even slit a vein in his mount's neck and drink her blood while he rides. Horses are a man's true wealth." Drink blood from a horse's neck? I shuddered.

Sweeping his arms to include the entire herd, Asetai added, "Now, all these mares are three years old. Some have just arrived from our Mongol homelands along with the youths who are now old enough to fight. The trainers teach the mares to be fearless through the noise and smoke of battle.

Each pony learns her own summoning song, too. Later I'll show you with one of my own how we call them."

Later, Asetai led me back to our wing of the camp, talking all the while about the glory of war. Several of his main ponies were hitched near Argamon's ger, but now he untied his favorite mare. She stood stock still while he backed up to where I was standing. Then he warbled a call to her. Pricking her ears, the mare trotted up to him and nuzzled his chin while we stroked her rough coat.

"I've heard you and others do that before," I marveled. "She reminds me of my Shchap at home. I miss riding."

"Argamon may give you your own pony someday. Meanwhile if you wish to use a borrowed mount, I'll be glad to take you."

"Yes, please!"

"I shall ask Argamon after this year's mares are trained."

War followed me everywhere, even just outside Argamon's ger. Once I found him and his men absorbed in making strange spears from long, stiff plant stalks with rings around them every few inches. They were stuffing them with a greasy, smelly substance. Argamon saw me and grinned, as eager as a little boy to show off a new toy.

"We're making missiles. They'll carry our version of Greek fire! You know of it? Selim al-Din brought us naphtha and sulfur from Persia and bamboo from Cathay."

Of course I had heard of Greek fire. It never dies, and people and buildings perish once it touches them. Since I had never seen a single dragon, Greek fire must be how the Mongols set cities ablaze. I was shocked at Selim. Surely he knew how it would be used. I wrinkled my nose. "It smells bad."

"Perhaps because it comes from the bowels of the earth," he laughed. I shrugged and pointedly turned away.

At last Asetai could show me no more. I still feel the irony: when I was at King Louis' court on Cyprus years later, I could have shared everything I had learned with any of the king's advisors had I been free to speak. It would have spared the king some illusions.

Days passed with little way to tell one from another. Q'ing-ling sometimes invited me to visit, and now that she had finished lecturing me on Chinggis Khan, being with her was most pleasant. And with our tours of the ordu over, Asetai took me riding daily. Of course I also sewed and prayed and wrote. But what I truly enjoyed was secretly helping Bourma and Tset-segmaa, which I saw as both good deed and defiance in one.

Argamon somehow found out. One day he strode into the ger where we were working and pulled up both women by their hair. He struck each in turn, shouting, "Get out!" As they fled, he turned on me. I too had risen and was steeling myself for a blow, but he only snarled, "You still disobey me! I won't have you working like a menial!"

Without thinking, I retorted, "Then give me something else to do!"

He drew back in surprise. After several deep breaths, he calmed down enough to speak again. "I will think on it." And he strode out.

As for my friends, I felt almost as much pain in my heart as they did where they were hit. All my attempts at good works had come to this. But the sisters both smiled and shrugged when I tried to tell them how sorry I was. They took it as their due for allowing me to disobey their master, while I, who was simply from another world, was of course spared. But I vowed that if Argamon struck them again, I would defend them better.

I got my chance very soon. Kamileh had trained me to serve Argamon at meals, so she was rarely there anymore. Had she been, perhaps it would not have happened. Though other food was ready, my master suddenly decided he wanted a certain marmot soup. He was downing cup after cup of airag and impatient, so Tsetsegmaa hurriedly prepared it and I hastily placed a steaming bowl of it before him. "About time!" he said, swilling a big mouthful. He nearly choked and then gulped it anyway. Throwing his bowl on the floor, he shouted, "It's too hot! Tsetsegmaa, you little bitch, come here!"

The poor girl immediately began sobbing, threw herself at his feet, and begged his forgiveness. Yet still he raised his fist to strike her! I laid my hand on his arm. "Don't hit her, Argamon! You usually let your soup cool a little. You may as well hit me for handing it to you. And she's carrying your baby—you could hurt it!"

Argamon flinched as if I had hit *him*. He stared at me for a moment. But then he seized my arm and shouted, "Don't you tell me how to treat my slaves, or I *will* hit you!"

"Then do it," I snapped back, surprising us both. Now it was too late to back down. Argamon and I glared at each other for a small eternity, him squeezing my arm ever tighter, me refusing to bend, though it hurt so much that tears started from my eyes. Finally he growled and shoved me backwards. Tsetsegmaa brought him another bowl, but he ended up downing more airag than soup.

Later as they cleared the dishes and the mess on the carpet—Argamon was off seeing to some errand, no doubt made up to salve his pride—Tsetsegmaa saw to my bruise. "Master had every right to hit me," she said. "He had to swallow the hot soup or break Mongol law, so his throat was burned bad, I think."

"Well, he won't let greed rule him next time," I said, though I was actually worried about where defying him might lead. To salve his anger, I would have to swallow hot pride.

When Argamon returned in the middle of the night, drunk, I was waiting alone in the half-dark. He ignored me until I knelt in front of him, hands cupped and head bent. "I am sorry for meddling tonight, Master. I did not understand. Please forgive me."

He made the most of that moment. After a long silence he finally said, "Yes, you could hardly know. I forgive you. This time." I thought he was talking about the soup.

The next day Argamon announced, "I have decided what you will do with your days: study more with Dorje. You've mastered Mongol speech, and I am pleased with you, but you can now learn writing and such. I'll ask Father to send him more often, and he can bring Selim al-Din. But no more helping my slaves. Remember who you are!" I made no reply. I had never been trying to please him. As for remembering who I was, that was getting harder all the time. I only knew I didn't want to be anyone *he* wanted me to be.

When I next saw Dorje, he said, "So you've offended Argamon by helping his slave women." I nodded sadly. "Your friendship with them means much to you."

"Yes, doubly so. Not only do I like them, but they gave me a way to atone for my past sins." Dorje raised his eyebrows. "You see, I've hit upon the truth. God is punishing me for my arrogance. I hoped to atone for my wickedness through good works and by taking on the ways of humble people, but now Argamon denies me that."

"Ah, dear child, if only life were that simple. The ups and downs in life are not reward and punishment but a path to truth. Is this forbidden friendship merely atonement? And why limit your compassion to slaves when the whole world cries out for it?" He must have seen my blank look, for he only added, "Well, let us leave that topic and turn to one that is much the same and no less difficult: learning how someone else thinks as well as speaks."

From then on I also spent time each day with Dorje learning the Uigur script. Writing from top to bottom was a charming novelty. Sometimes we practiced on scraps of fabric with brush and ink; sometimes we scratched letters in the dirt, and once or twice I even used Papa's book, though that seemed a waste. I missed the lovely thin peels of birch bark that we Rus' used instead of paper.

Sometimes I became the teacher and taught the speech of Rus' to Dorje and Selim, and sometimes Selim took a turn with his native speech. Soon the three of us were pattering away in simple Farsi. It was easier to learn than I expected, being a blend of Persian and Arabic.

Once Selim offered me what he clearly thought of as high praise. "Admitting, of course, that I know few of them, but, you, an infidel *and* a woman, learn as well as any man I ever knew!" I had to laugh. For one thing, from my point of view he was the infidel!

"I thank you, I think. Perhaps you just never met an educated woman before."

He paused thoughtfully. "Yes, you may be right."

Once we spoke each other's language well enough, he often made us laugh with tales from his home. Here is the one I remember best, less for its humor than for its aftermath. We three were sunning ourselves in front of Argamon's ger.

"Three holy men were lost in the desert: a Muslim, a Christian, and a Buddhist. They had been sharing their food, but one night there was only one meal left. While trying to decide how to divide it, one of them suggested they each pray overnight for guidance from God." Dorje smiled wryly.

"So they all went to sleep hungry, praying for a revelation, and in the morning each shared his dream. The Christian said that Jesus Christ himself had appeared before him in glory and told him that since his was the only true religion, he should have the entire last portion. Then the Buddhist said that the Buddha had appeared from heaven, surrounded in splendor, and said the same to him. Then the Muslim holy man spoke. 'In my dream,' he said, 'Muhammad, praised be his name, appeared to me and commanded me to wake up right then and eat the last meal for myself … so I did!' "

Dorje laughed politely, but I just looked at Selim in dismay. Since my capture, I saw no humor in taking advantage of others. What a puzzle he was—like selling Argamon the makings for Greek fire when he knew how it would be used. And he and his men made such wild claims for their wares and cheated people so baldly. If I pointed him toward honesty, would that atone for my sins *and* help others? I did not know, but surely I must try.

A few days later, Selim had just sold the last of his dried apricots to a friend of mine for an absurd price, and I summoned my courage as he was packing up his goods. "You should not cheat these women, even if they are Mongols. And it's a sin to sell wares to Argamon that you know he'll use to kill innocent people. Our God sees and judges us."

Selim flushed. He finished his packing in silence, then stood and looked down at me, frowning. "Two years ago, Sofia, my ruler sent envoys to the Christian kingdoms warning them that the Mongols would invade them next. He asked for their aid. Had they fought side by side with us, we might have driven them out of our lands and they would never have reached yours. Instead, your kings turned them away. They rejoiced in our sufferings, so now they can suffer, too! If unbelievers die in Mongol flames, they have only themselves to blame!" I had never heard Selim speak bitterly. It was a shock.

"As for your women friends, I do them all a service," he continued in a milder tone. "Even with all the war spoils the Mongols bring back, there are still things only a merchant from afar can bring you to better your lives."

"How are you making *our* lives so much better?" I wished I had never started this conversation. I was not a Mongol just because I had a few friends among them!

"Think of everything you'd go without: spices, fruits and vegetables, sweets, wines—not to mention things like blown glass that never survive looting. Admit you like adding cumin and carrots, even old ones, to your master's dull stews!" He smiled grimly. "If we cheat or strike hard bargains, it is fair payment for the hardship and danger we face to reach here. But you, child, are forgetting something. Though you and I must act as their friends, these people are still enemies to us both."

Feeling I must wrest some kind of victory from this disheartening conversation, I replied sullenly, "Then perhaps you should warn your men not to boast in others' hearing. I've overheard them a few times. I may not be the only one who understands them, and I doubt Qacha would care for their frauds."

"Ah, in that case, I will warn them to be more discreet, my young and very honest friend." He bowed politely, his face a mask, and left.

Still feeling I must rescue my good intentions from defeat, I even tried to warn Bourma and Tsetsegmaa, but the girls laughed. "Those merchants think they get away with something, but they never even see that they are the true slaves—to gold and shiny things. Those are nice, but you cannot ride on them or live in them or eat them!"

After that I dropped my little campaign. It was painful to admit, but I was becoming a self-righteous meddler again, just as I had been with Oleg, and where had that led?

Besides, why did I care if merchants cheated Mongols? Selim was right: they were my enemies. The next time I saw him, I felt obliged to ask his pardon, which he graciously granted. He even seemed secretly amused. And with that, I had to admit that each of my attempts to redeem myself had borne little fruit beyond trouble.

SUMMER, Anno Domini 1240

s the summer grew hotter, people stripped off more and more layers of felt from the sides of the gers until in effect we lived outside.
Bursts of wellbeing would sometimes fill me, perhaps when I was
awakened by melodious birdsong or was picking wildflowers among the high
grasses or when I took great breaths of air as sweet as honey. I still felt the
strength of the spirits who dwelt there, though without their friendship I felt
as if I was seeing with only one eye.

The troops began leaving just after dawn and returning at sunset, leaving the ordu as empty as if they truly had left for battle. I could see jaghuns
in the distance, wheeling and racing in unison, and once Argamon ordered
Asetai to take me out to watch. One of Kuvrat Khan's lieutenants signaled
each company with a particular banner, and its captain would wave a certain
pennant and his bugler sound a special call. The soldiers obeyed silently,
galloping in a tight v-shaped formation, shooting from the saddle, whirl-
ing around, and falling back while shooting behind them. They all rode so
straight and unmoving, even drew their weapons in unison, while the ponies
flowed over the ground like a flood.

Qabul was not far away with his jaghun. Despite myself, I could not help
admiring his elegance on a horse. He handled his men superbly, and they

responded much more crisply to his signals than Argamon's soldiers did. He was clearly a gifted leader.

When we left near sunset, my master rode beside me, boasting. "Today we practiced the Chisel. It's one of our many battle formations: Moving Bush, Wolf Lope, Spreading Lake. Sometimes we feign a disorderly retreat to draw out overeager enemies. We lure them on and wear them out, and then we cut them down. Like your Rus' in Chinggis Khan's time. The fools didn't stand by each other, and one of the largest armies out-raced the others. We led them on a wild chase for three days until they were too tired to fight well. Then we turned on them and slew them all. The rest of their forces were easy prey after that. Almost 80,000 men to our mere 20,000." He laughed, deaf to my chilled silence.

"The jest is that our troops were merely chasing down a renegade shah who gave us trouble during our Persian campaign. But once he was dead, they swept west of the Caspian Sea just to see what lay north of Persia. They passed through northern Persia and Georgia, crossed the Caucasus, and attacked the tribes living beyond the southeastern reaches of Rus' just to set fear into the hearts of all nations. But Rus' was far to the northwest. Our envoys went to your Grand Prince in peace to warn him not to support their Kipchak enemies, and he murdered them. Had he listened to us, we'd have left Rus' alone. When the generals returned and reported, the Khakan vowed to destroy Rus'."

Argamon's battle was where Papa's father and brothers had died. Mongols had feasted sitting on my dying grandfather's back, and now Argamon boasted of it! Worse, he had said it was our fault, though clearly he and his kind just looked for excuses to invade other kingdoms.

One time he and his men left for several days. When they returned he boasted, "Father gathered all his tumans together for huge mock battles. He says that until we all act as one great living beast, we're unfit to call ourselves warriors. Thousands of us trained together. You should have been there, Sofia. It was uncanny! At the start, even our ponies were still. But the instant we heard the signals and saw the banners rise, we charged, silent and side by side! Around us drums pounded, trumpets called, gongs clanged, and pots of smoke hazed the air! It was if the sky and earth had shattered together! Some day if you are fortunate, you may get to witness such a glorious sight." As I listened to Argamon's praise of battle, I recalled my Papa's noisy, self-willed knights. How could they ever resist such a disciplined force?

"Soon we go on a battue, a great war exercise that is also a game hunt," he added. "Wait until you see the bounty we bring back for the table! We slowly encircle all the game from horizon to horizon, driving them ever inward until the tiger stands next to the deer, both too weary to lift paw or hoof. Then we pick them off at will. We entrap our human enemies in just the same way—just as I caught you!" He laughed gleefully.

Argamon's boast was not idle. Qacha did host a great feast after they returned: deer, boar, gazelle, a wild ass, foxes and small field animals—even a wolf! Most meats seemed unfit to touch, but I did enjoy eating something besides the usual drab fare. It was another crude celebration. All Qacha's generals with their wives and sons were there. While musicians scraped away on horse-headed fiddles and shrilled on flutes, servants moved about with monstrous roasts. People lunged forward with their knives to carve off huge hunks of meat and stuff them into their mouths, hardly chewing before they swallowed. The men took turns forcing giant goblets of liquor down each other's throat; it seemed a miracle that no one choked to death. As for the women, their lewd jests seemed endless.

The high point of the evening was a kind of drinking game. Kuvrat Khan stood drunkenly, holding a goblet of liquor, and pranced toward Qacha, laughing and singing, to hold it out to him. But when the noyan reached for it, his general drew back while his fellow generals doubled over with laughter. Then Kuvrat offered it again—and again drew back. This game continued for a small eternity until Qacha finally seized the goblet and downed it in one draft, grinning like a jackal. Then another general began the game again, and another after him. None but me seemed to weary of it, so I dully looked down at nothing and dreamt of escape. At one point, though, I looked up. Qabul was staring at me. I flushed and looked down again.

The next day was blessed with bright sunshine and sweet breezes. Argamon had left with his jaghun, the sisters were busy, and I looked out past the camp to the waving grasses and felt so weary of everything. Finally I decided I would visit Q'ing-ling. Surely I need not wait for an invitation. I turned to my guard. "Asetai, would you take me riding?"

He looked up from the arrow he was fletching. "I would, Sofia Begi, but the horse you usually ride is in use today. There are few trained horses in camp right now, mostly just the half-wild three-year-olds that arrived a few days ago."

"Oh, please. I would so love to visit Lady Q'ing-ling, and you must tire of watching me when everyone else is gone. Would you not enjoy stretching your muscles?"

I tried all my charm on him, and soon hapless Asetai had found a sweet-looking young pony for me. She was what they call a summer mount—less hairy—and frisky as a colt. But after accepting his help in mounting her, a fancy seized me to circle around the entire main camp. "Come, Asetai, I'll race with you!" And I was off.

"Wait, Sofia Begi," he shouted, calling for his own horse, but I took his words as a challenge, not a warning, and waved at him to join me. Kicking my pony to a full gallop, I sped toward the rear of the huge main camp, as giddy as the child I had once been. I laughed aloud at the clean rush of wind on my face. Butterflies, red-gold as the sun, flew up from the grasses before me like flocks of flying flowers. How good I felt. Asetai was far behind me and not gaining. I rode so fast that I passed the very end of the rear guard camp without him.

Suddenly a bright butterfly flew up from the grass and into one of my pony's eyes. She shied and bolted. "Easy, easy," I leaned forward and tried to croon to her. She did calm somewhat and slowed her pace slightly. "There, there, that's better." I leaned to one side and tugged gently on the reins. "Come, horse, I want to turn back now," but not having a song to obey, she did not understand me. I panicked. How was I to stop her now? Up ahead I glimpsed a troop of warriors, but then my vision narrowed to a tiny point as I finally got the pony to turn but not to slow down any further. Growing desperate and almost weeping in panic, I pulled on the reins as hard as I could, but to no avail.

A man's hand gripped the reins and tugged them so hard that my mare's head was wrenched back, her eyeballs rolling. She danced sideways and almost fell, and it took all my effort to stay seated. The creature finally stopped and stood trembling and heaving while I stroked her neck and tried to soothe her. I looked over with mixed anger and gratitude, expecting Asetai and ready to chide him.

Instead, Qabul was staring down at me, catlike, a slight smile on his face.

"What a graceful little dove you are. Not trying to fly from your master, are you?" he asked, as Asetai finally galloped up, wide-eyed with alarm. A group of Qabul's men had gathered around us, and none looked friendly.

"Of course not. I lost control of my pony, that's all. It was kind of you to help me. Asetai can escort me back to camp now." I reached to take the reins away from Qabul, but a tiny sharp spark leapt between our hands and snapped my hand back.

"Oh, but *he* might not be able to find the way. I would be most honored to escort you back myself, my men and I. Asetai can come too." He smiled broadly. "Come, princess." He had my reins, and there was no way to retreat. We rode slowly back toward the encampment, my horse still breathing hard. The ring of men fell behind, swallowing Asetai up like a giant mouth. I could not have felt more alone and exposed.

We rode in silence until Qabul leaned over and said softly, "So fate brings us to each other at last. You felt it, didn't you? That spark that flew between us? It was a sign."

"A sign of what? Tengri's displeasure?" But my voice came out in a squeak.

"Hardly! There's a prophecy about you and lightning, and I think it was just fulfilled. You and I are destined for each other. I felt it the first time I saw you—no, don't pretend not to understand after the way you smile or blush or look down with false modesty whenever I am near you. You are always as aware of me as I am of you. I saw your desire the first time you smiled at me, and last night your blushes made your feelings clear! You know you were always meant for me, not for my little girl brother. Just as you know where I will take you now. And what will happen when we get there." He almost smacked his lips.

Only then did I see that Qabul had turned toward his own camp in the east wing. Alarm gripped me, and I cried, "Qabul, I smiled at you only once with intent, and then it was partly to hurt my master. Since then I've given you no signs at all! I feel nothing like what you—"

Qabul's laughter cut off my words. "You wanted to hurt your 'master' then? And not much has changed, I would hazard. I see how he stares at you with fear whenever I am near. For almost five full moons he's held onto you, yet one smile passing between you and me terrifies him. It shows how little you belong to him! Under me you will learn what mastery truly means." The way he said this made sick fear rise in my throat. We rode in silence for a while, me cursing myself for not waiting for Asetai.

Suddenly Qabul spoke again. "Ha! My brother is such a little girl, I wonder if he's even been able to waken your passion. From me you will learn its full measure!" I said nothing, for despite his insults, Qabul was right. I knew nothing about passion. Another long silence followed. He broke it with, "I know things Argamon cannot even imagine. I will do them to you. *I* will arouse the bliss sleeping inside you. And you will learn how to please me. How I will enjoy making you mine."

I looked up, feeling faint. His face filled my vision, his teeth glittered like polished bones, and beneath his skin lurked a leering, grinning skull. I looked around frantically, praying to Mother Mary not to let this man harm me.

As if in answer, a man in white on a white horse hove into view, galloping at full speed toward us: Yulta Beki. I could not imagine why he might be out there, nor did I expect help from *him*. At the same moment, to my right a large body of riders burst from the main camp, cutting across our path as if to stop us. When I recognized Argamon foremost among them, I rose in my stirrups and waved wildly. "Argamon, here I am!"

Qabul cursed softly and looked back at his men—only a dozen of them—while Argamon was leading at least three times that number. He reined us in and sat waiting. The shaman and Argamon's company reached us at the same time. I feared they would run us down, could feel the horses' pounding hooves in my body, but they drew up so suddenly that the ensuing silence seemed loud. For a small eternity no one said a word. I searched the faces of the men before me and saw grim determination in each, even that of the old shaman. It came to me that I must do something or there would be fighting and perhaps killing, and it would be my fault.

"Master, my mare bolted. Qabul did me a service: he stopped it and was returning me to you." I turned to Qabul, tugging my reins from his unwilling grip. "I must learn to handle such half-tamed beasts." But my words came out as if I meant him and not my pony.

He smiled with mock sweetness. "I'll happily service you anywhere and at any time." My cheeks aflame, I prodded my mount forward to stand beside Argamon's. I remembered my guard.

"Asetai, are you coming?" He rode forward, his face ashen.

Qabul mockingly saluted Argamon and bowed toward Yulta Beki. "Until we meet again, then." He smiled at me secretively before turning back to his troop with his men.

I looked up at Argamon and then at Yulta Beki. The shaman did not even glance my way, only nodded to my master and turned his horse away, while Argamon wrenched my reins from me as if I might flee him. Then he leaned over to look closely at my mare.

"Her mouth is ruined. We'll have to butcher her," was all he said. So I was responsible for a killing anyway. And on the way back to camp, when I tried to explain about the butterfly sprite and my losing control of my pony, he barely heeded me, though he had many harsh and, to my mind, unfair words for Asetai. Only once did he speak to me.

"He did not touch you? He might have taken you right there ... or perhaps he feared he might not— You were so fortunate: the power you bear, perhaps. But never be such a fool again!"

He left me at his ger without a word. I felt deeply ashamed. Asetai at least forgave me after I stammered many words of regret. Alas, he still had to lead my doomed mount away.

That night, though I begged Argamon's forgiveness again and again, he responded with a silence deeper and colder than any abuse. After he fell asleep, I lay awake half the night. I had meant no harm. It was that butterfly's fault! Some wickedness must have been afoot for Qabul to appear from nowhere like that. Had I offended the spirits of the land? Since my vow to trust only in the Holy Family, the world felt as if it had slowly changed its code and begun to keep secrets from me. Perhaps the spirit world was allied with Qabul. But Yulta Beki had come, and powerful spirits served him.

Still, if Qabul had been able to carry me off, I'd have stained my master's honor and destroyed all hope of escape. And have lost Q'ing-ling and Dorje and all my new friends.

Dorje already knew when he arrived the next day, but he let me pour out my woes. "And Argamon refuses to listen. I don't even know how they found out I was in trouble."

"I can tell you that. One of Argamon's slaves saw you racing off alone and hurried to tell him and then, on his master's orders, to tell Yulta Beki. When Argamon set out in pursuit, he had no idea whether you were trying to escape or simply amusing yourself, but either way he feared the worst for you. I was right to warn you about Qabul, wasn't I?"

I nodded, feeling like a naughty child. "All I wanted was a fine gallop, not to fall afoul of Qabul. Evil spirits are to blame. Why cannot Argamon see that?"

"Whether that butterfly was a spirit or not, do you give him reason to trust you?"

I snapped, "Why should I? If I could escape, I would! But I am no fool. Why would I seek to trade him for a man who causes harm for his own amusement? Besides, I think Qabul just likes power over others—he only wanted to see if he could frighten me. He would never have truly dared to steal me."

Dorje just sighed and shook his head.

setsegmaa went into labor soon after that bad day. Being off with Dorje and Selim, I found out when she was not there to help with Argamon's supper. Bourma cooked and I served him, but neither seemed uneasy or excited. After supper, remembering Mama and Cousin Irina, I asked, "Are you not worried about Tsetsegmaa? She could die."

"She's only a slave. If she does, that is Tengri's will. If she does not and she has a son, I'll raise him to be a fine warrior." He motioned to Asetai, who reached for his fiddle.

"Listen, I made a song for you to show you I've forgiven you. Only you can sing it—and me, of course. All Mongols have one."

I hardly wanted my own song, but I sat politely as he sang:

> *I am Sofia, called the wise.*
> *I am Argamon's noble prize.*
> *I enchant him with my green eyes.*

I thought it was stupid. Besides, my mind was on Tsetsegmaa and the baby. I wished I could go and help. That night while Argamon satisfied his lust as usual, my prayers went out to my friend. She might not even be alive in the morning.

But at dawn I awakened to the faint cry of a newborn from close by and knew it was her baby. Instead of hurrying to see his new child, though, Argamon delayed his visit for three days! Every morning he would linger over his bowl of gruel as though it had developed new, interesting qualities, and then he would disappear with Asetai. At least he allowed me to go alone to the black birthing tent where Tsetsegmaa lay on a pile of dirty skins, attended by Yulta's wife. How tiny and wrinkled he looked, with dried blood still caking his black hair and skin. When I returned, Argamon seemed maddeningly calm about having sired a son.

But when he finally went to her, me following, and she held out his tiny son to him, he melted. Perhaps she would receive more kindness from her master now.

"Look, Sofia," he told me proudly after he had lifted the sleeping baby and rested him against his shoulder. "See, he's a true Mongol. There is the sign." He pointed to the base of the baby's spine, where I saw a pair of birthmarks that looked like small dark bruises, one on each side. "I name him Kuchan." He handed Kuchan to me, but the baby awoke and began crying hungrily. Tsetsegmaa took him back from me, opened her robe and tickled his cheek, and he turned to her breast.

To my surprise, my throat swelled with a mix of joy and pain. I praised Kuchan to Tsetsegmaa, but then I had to leave the tent quickly to stand outside. Why would I want to cry? When Argamon joined me, I hastily composed myself. But it threatened to slip again when he spoke. "You will bear me sons, too. Great warriors."

NO, my mind screamed. Yet …

I thrust the thought away. A child would tie me to Argamon forever. Did I want that? Never!

As if in mockery, not a week later my first moon cycle began. Bourma showed me what to do, praising the day that I had become a woman and seeing no twist in the fact that I had long ago become one in all ways but this. And now I might become pregnant.

The lightning raids began, as Asetai called them—sudden, sharp, and deadly. Argamon and his jaghun were often gone, sometimes with all the soldiers in Qacha's ordu. Our skeleton camp would sometimes await them and sometimes follow. The returning warriors mostly brought in boys to train as soldiers. Asetai mentioned that they would be thrown first into battle, simply to wear out the enemy army and use up its weapons. The raids also brought back loot and enslaved captives, since slaves died quickly from poor food and too little of it, from abuse, and from despair.

I began to worry: while Argamon's absence meant I would not get pregnant and could freely help Bourma and Tsetsegmaa in small ways, what if he were killed? And we were moving ever closer to Kyiv. Once more my thoughts turned toward escape, this time to warn my people. I didn't know how I could get away, or even whom I could approach, but I might redeem myself if I could, for I had learned so much about my captors. I dreamt of arriving at the Golden Gate, weary but strong, to deliver valuable secrets that would save the city. After that I would become a nun, forgiven for my fall and honored by all Rus'.

Instead, I had to stand before Argamon's or Qacha's ger with the other women who sang and clapped to honor the victorious, while I waited to see if Argamon was a shrouded corpse slung across a pony.

Once after a raid, I saw Freckled Hlib striding by dressed as a Mongol warrior and carrying some trifle that was his portion of the loot. So my old playmate and loyal servant had been reduced to this! I called out to him, and he stopped to greet me, although without any deference. I asked if he ever saw any of our fellow captives.

"None of the women," he said. "We men were put into the Mongol army, and some are dead already, though they trained us well enough. I'm a Mongol warrior now. Really, there are few true Mongols in our armies. Most are like me, captured men pressed into service. It's better than being killed outright, and I have a chance to prove myself. I've been on two campaigns already," he said with pride. He spoke just like a fifteen-year-old youth, I now see.

"You mean you killed innocent people!"

Hlib shrugged. "They give me a share of the booty." Seeing my dismay, he frowned and added, "It's different for me than for you, Princess. At home I was a worm beneath your feet. I had to submit to your every whim. And I could never become a real hero like your father's knights. Well, now I can become a Mongol hero, not so different! Nor am I alone. Many other peasants from Rus' escape their masters and join us on their own. And I'm not sorry when I see some boyar or his widow hauling water or being beaten instead of me. Oh yes," he smiled grimly at my shock. "Those from the northern cities are all dead by now, but a few from Pereyaslav and Chernihiv still live. And I can see that *you* are thriving."

We parted with no good-byes. To think I had pitied, even missed him! What would happen when he must fight and kill his own countrymen? Had he no conscience? I understand better now: the knights he so admired fought and killed their own cousins. But I could not see why any peasant would flee safety under their masters for this world of war. Could life be that harsh for them? And I resented Hlib's jibe. I was not abused, but I must live with my heart in my throat while awaiting Argamon's return, or endure his rapes, or go to Qacha's gross feasts and be ogled by Qabul.

My master began returning from his forays with gifts for me. Although I accepted them civilly, I always packed them away in my chest with scarcely a glance at them, feeling they were bought with blood. But Argamon did give me one gift for which I was truly grateful: a pony of my own, fully trained. He made me promise never to ride without Asetai and that sullen brute Temur. I agreed gladly. Since my mishap with Qabul, I was grateful to have men protecting me. I named my pony Little Liubyna and learned how to summon and direct her with her special songs. Although I never ventured far and or went out unless the army was gone, those rides meant much to me.

Meanwhile, despite my folly toward him, Asetai and I developed a close bond. With him no longer trying to teach me about war and me giving him no trouble, we found we had much in common: a love of riding, of beauty in small things, of the deep quiet we found on the steppes away from the ordu. Once when the camps were on the move again, I asked him a question that had been in my mind for some time. "Asetai," I shouted over the screeching wagon wheels, "why do you never go with the army? Surely I'm not in danger when it's gone. Do you regret not being with your comrades?"

"Oh, I have no regrets, Princess," he shouted back. "I'm just happy to be with my nokhor and of service to him. I could never fight, as I cannot see clearly past the length of three men laid end to end. Beyond that the world is hazy as smoke. My eyes grow weaker and the world grows darker every year. And as you know, sometimes everything turns black on me! Once I was the best of wrestlers, but I had to struggle to win that last match! I'm only suited for close tasks or for guarding you. Even so, I can never ride out very far alone or I might get lost. I was mastering bow making to avoid becoming completely useless."

"I had no idea you were short of sight!" So my galloping off that day had been doubly foolish. Plus Argamon's faith in Asetai had been at risk if he was Argamon's nokhor. A nokhor is loyal for life, even closer than an anda, for brothers can fall out with each other.

"You've known Argamon for long, then?"

"Since we were small boys tumbling together like wolf pups. My father was a khan. He sent me to Noyan Qacha to become a warrior, but then plague killed my family, so his family became mine. When we saw that I could not become a warrior, Argamon shielded me from the gibes and beatings of other boys—especially Qabul. I cannot marry and sire children, but thanks to him I could join this campaign." So there was no future for Asetai and Bourma. No wonder he drank all the time.

"Argamon is a true friend to you," I mused.

"Yes, and I to him. We stood together against Qabul and his friends many a time."

"I see. I am glad that you told me, Asetai." How full of contradictions Argamon was: good to Asetai and his mother, but so brutish and arrogant in other ways. So far I had done little to civilize him beyond getting him to stop beating his slaves.

Soon after the summer campaigns began, Selim al-Din came to say goodbye. "Thanks to Merciful Allah, I've sold everything and without too much cheating, you may be glad to know," he jested. "Do not look so doleful. If Allah wills it I will return. Here is a gift to thank you for your lessons, Princess Sofia, and may the blessings of the only God rain down upon you." He offered me a glass vial as blue as the evening sky.

Because he was not family, I had to pretend to reject his gifts at first—I had learned much about Persian customs by now. But after the ritual was over, I said, "Thank you, Selim. May the God we share protect you on your journey. I wish I had something for you, but I possess little, and none of it would be of value to you."

"Do not be sorry. You helped me learn Mongol speech, an excellent gift. And I learned that a woman can be as intelligent as a man," he laughed. So did I—in surprise!

After he left, I opened the vial. The air filled with the delicate scent of roses, a reminder that somewhere a world of beauty and refinement still existed. I put some on my wrists and felt as if I had wandered into a lush garden. I would miss him.

Once Selim was gone, Dorje's lessons changed. Besides improving my writing skills, I must master all the Turkish dialects he knew. He had also found some books in Latin and Greek that he wanted me to study on my own. "Someday you will use your skills, perhaps in Batu Khan's service. How you interpret something might tip the balance toward peace and away from cruelty and war." Seeing my scowl he added, "He is but another small wave in the painful ocean of existence, Sofia, and if you can divert even one wave to the shore of kindness you'll have been of use to this world." When Dorje talked like that, he sounded like Alexander and Father Kliment rolled into one. But he was right: that was what my Savior had taught. I would try to be kind to everyone, but especially slaves!

Whenever I visited Q'ing-ling, Kamileh and Temulun greeted me with smiles; and although the lady was often busy, she seemed glad to stop and visit for a while. Once I arrived to find her alone before her shrine, most unusual, as she usually worshipped before the others awakened. I'd have left, not wanting to intrude, but she signed for me to stay. I waited inside the door and watched with more curiosity than shared devotion. Her shrine had a square cross and some carved angels and felt idols on it. Like we Rus', she was burning candles and incense, but the idols made it look strange. And with all that bowing and clapping, her way of worshipping seemed strange, too. How odd to be friends with a pagan like Dorje or a heretic like her.

I realized Q'ing-ling truly was a heretic that day, the one time we discussed religion. "Why do you have no ikons to pray to?" I asked as we sat together outside, soaking up the sun's warmth and watching her dog Lu chase a grasshopper.

"They are not part of our way of praying."

"Please say more. I know nothing of your religion."

She thought for a moment. "The Catholics pray to an image of Christ on their crosses—do Orthodox Christians?" I shook my head. "Then I doubt my Christianity differs much from yours. We know that Christ the God was never crucified, only Christ the man. Why would we want to worship before something that symbolizes his human degradation and death? We prefer the empty cross, which symbolizes the risen Christ." I wasn't sure about the God and man part of what she said, but I too had been taught to worship the risen Christ, so I just nodded. "And the idea that Mary was the mother of God, as that Catholic monk said: she was the mother of His Son. How could a mere woman, born from sin, give birth to God any more than an image be the source of blessings?"

I had never thought of *my* faith like that. Mary was the Mother of God and my special patron. And I had never questioned that ikons bestowed blessings. I was tempted to retort that we of Orthodox faith looked on statues like hers as suspicious, but that would have disrespected an elder and a friend. I changed the subject.

But it was too late. Doubts about my faith arose seemingly from nowhere and attacked me from all sides. How could everyone else be so sure that their religion alone brought salvation, while I had no idea what to believe? My old confidence in the life and beauty, in the very balance within God's creation, had withered away, while Selim was certain that Dorje was going to hell, Q'ing-ling dismissed my precious ikons, and even Dorje, who would not argue or even discuss religion, seemed at ease with whatever it was that he believed.

Meanwhile, these pagan Mongols prided themselves for respecting every faith, claiming that all are fingers on the hand of God, a hand that holds *them* up over every other nation on earth! It felt to me as if God was not only holding them up but gripping—nay, strangling—this world through them. It made me fear and doubt Him. How could He love us and yet allow so many innocent people to suffer so horribly? Were we all so tainted by sin that we deserved the hell on earth that the Mongols brought wherever their ponies tread?

I could not shake my doubts for many days. I blamed Satan and spent a week or more on my knees praying in frenzies of despair. I even fasted, which made me faint once. Bourma caught me just before my head hit the hearth, but my braid got singed. She chided me for my silliness, as she called it. Nor did my self-mortification bring any relief.

When Q'ing-ling heard of my fasting and fainting, she summoned me to her ger and forbade me to continue my excesses. Without caring that her women were there sewing and listening, I poured out my woes, including not being allowed to atone for my sins by helping my fellow slaves. She paused and answered carefully, "Everyone has doubts, Sofia, and feels guilt, too. But how will starving yourself resolve them? We who have no spiritual guide must still try to follow Christ's teachings. As to good works, you can be kind every day to everyone." Her down-to-earth advice made sense, and my guilt loosened its grip.

She added, "And if you want to please Argamon, you can sew shirts for him. My women are doing just that today for Qacha's men."

Plump-cheeked Temulun looked up from her work, smiled, and made room for me to sit with her and the other women. "We always need more silk shirts for the soldiers, and you can appliqué banners for signaling, too."

"Silk shirts for common soldiers?" I asked in surprise.

"Oh, don't your soldiers wear them?" I shook my head. "Well, that explains why their armor cannot stop our arrows! We protect our soldiers properly. Silk doesn't rip, you see. Instead, it twists around the arrow tip and stops it from boring through flesh. Then a man can untwist the arrow shaft from his wound and remove it cleanly." I recalled the time those bandits had attacked Papa's party. One of his servants had been hit by an arrow. He had died when Papa's men had gouged too deep around the arrowhead trying to get it out. The man's chest had looked like a piece of bloody meat.

But commoners were not allowed to wear silk. The arrow that had killed Argamon's envoy! There was a twist, indeed—of fate. Had it hit him anywhere but in the neck, he'd have survived and I would not have been captured. I went to work with a will. Now I could truly protect both Argamon and myself.

When he returned from his foray, my master was delighted. From then on he eagerly wore my shirts into battle, certain they were filled with magical power. And he even arrived home from one raid with a shallow arrow wound in his arm: a little round hole with no ripped, rotting flesh. Bourma gave me a small pot of honey to use as a salve—just as we did in Rus'. More surprising, Argamon was not angry with me for failing to protect him.

Instead, he boasted, "Your shirts do give me luck. That arrow was aimed for my throat, but your magic made me raise my arm just at the right moment."

So even if he were wounded, Argamon would believe I shielded him. But was there any magic working through me? If so, then God did watch over some of His creatures … unless the Master of Lies was using me. Well, I was stoutly resisting the doubts Satan had planted in me, and surely I must consent for him to use me for his evil purposes.

My master's arm healed cleanly, and within a few days he was gone again.

More and more Rus' captives were brought into camp. We often had to change direction to avoid a battle site; and more than once out on the steppes with Asetai and Temur, I stumbled upon destruction as bad as the massacre at the cataracts. The first time, we found the remains of a nomad camp, perhaps Kipchak, littered with dismembered corpses, human and animal; goods strewn and trampled; tents and wagons overturned and burned; and huge swaths of steppe grass scorched and stinking.

I was foolishly drawn to it, my mouth hanging open in horror, but Asetai seized my reins. "Never go near such places! Plague demons might follow us back to the ordus! We must leave now!" I fearfully obeyed. Plague demons sometimes attacked Kyiv. It was said that a man could rise from his bed healthy in the morning, be struck on the street by invisible arrows of illness, and be resting in his grave that night. In my own household, plague had taken Papa's mother before I was born, and Baba Liubyna had lost her husband and children.

On another outing, I came upon the charred remains of an isolated Rus' settlement: trampled fields, orchards chopped down, charred skeletons of homes, bloated body parts befouling a stream. I turned my pony and raced straight back to the ordu, aflame with rage and despair. When Dorje next visited me for a lesson, he tried to comfort me, although he did not react with horror to my gruesome description.

"Yes, I understand. I had to watch my own friends die. It is heartbreaking, but war is a mighty spoke in the endless wheel of suffering. It reminds us to be kind to others rather than add to the misery of this world." I wished I could share his composure.

I began to realize that Argamon was on another kind of campaign: to please me. He gave me things he had carved himself, like a beautiful comb of ivory from the northern seas. Once he brought back some lengths of bright silk, filmy as clouds. "Here, Sofia, you can make yourself lighter clothing now that the days are so hot," he smiled. I bowed and promptly set them in my chest, for I never welcomed plunder. I could see he was disappointed, but I did not care. The silks stayed there until the weather grew too miserable; besides, I was outgrowing my old clothing. I reluctantly pulled them out but defiantly stitched them into loose Kyivan-style summer garments. However, when he saw one, Argamon only said, "You look beautiful. I rejoice that you liked my gift." I had to admit that he was doing his best.

The season passed with neither a pregnancy nor a moon cycle, and I began to wonder if I was barren. It seemed a sad answer to my prayers, but I tried to be grateful. I was certainly growing into a woman in other ways. I shot up almost as fast as the steppe grasses. By summer's end I was half a head shorter than Argamon, though he too was growing taller.

He liked the way my body was changing and redoubled his efforts to give me pleasure. When he was in camp, he often took me riding with him, always with a few guards behind us to stop intruders, and always carrying one of those supple herding poles with a noose on one end. It served another purpose as well. He would stop and pull me off my pony. Planting the pole in the ground like a standard, he would turn and with a sly smile say, "Now you have no reason to fear other eyes or ears!" And he would pull me down into his embrace.

The feathery grasses were so tall that we were hidden in a rippling world dotted with dazzling wildflowers. Invisible birds sang high above, bright butterflies flitted just beyond reach, lacy clouds dappled the brilliant blue sky, and I was enfolded in beauty. It was hard to resist the lusciousness of sun and soft breeze on my bare skin, the perfume from the grass under our bodies, and even Argamon's passionate embrace.

Then he would do something arrogant or foolish, like insist I go hawking with Qacha's household, even when I pled with him to leave me behind. I had often gone out with Papa but had never really enjoyed it, having always felt too much sympathy for the prey. And it was difficult to be around the noyan's household. Asetai never came with us. Qacha's other sons leered at me, his concubines had no idea how to treat me, Har Nuteng either stared at or ignored me according to some private whim, and only Q'ing-ling and a few other attendants were friendly.

And I must steadfastly avoid Qabul. He seemed ever to lurk at the edge of my sight like a malicious spirit.

Worst was the time Argamon galloped off after his hawk, Temur close behind him. I tried to follow, but Little Liubyna stumbled and nearly fell. I reined in and looked around for help, but he and his men were all bent on the chase and too far away. I dismounted and knelt in the long grass, examining her hoof for a stone bruise. I failed to notice the shadow that fell across her flanks.

When I finally looked up, Qabul was staring down at me like a tiger about to pounce. He swung off his horse and stood over me, smiling insolently. I felt as transfixed as any prey.

"And where is your so-called master now? Now I can make you mine after all, as I should have done that day."

The spell broke. I stood up and retorted, "How dare you! Go away!"

Qabul's smile was like a gust of chill air. "I've dared as much with my little brother before. All my life that Chinese bitch and her little-girl whelp have made me fight for what was mine by right. Besides, how could I resist such a choice little morsel as you?"

He moved toward me and I stumbled backwards, but Little Liubyna stood stupidly in the way. His hands slid swifter than snakes around my waist, his lips sought mine. I twisted my head aside and beat my hands against his chest, terror coursing through my body. He whispered into my ear, "It's not merely the power and wealth you will bring me. I want more! You are the one I have awaited all my life, and in your heart you feel the same."

"No, you're wrong! Get away from me, you ... you thief!"

Qabul just gripped my head and tried to kiss me, but Little Liubyna finally took alarm and shied away, and I tumbled to the ground. Qabul lost his grip and I rolled away and struggled to stand, but he was on top of me in an instant, laughing. "So like a woman—she claims she doesn't want what she actually desires the most. As for thievery, if that weakling Argamon cannot hold fast to you, he deserves to lose you. The strong always take from the weak! That's what makes me a better warrior than him—and a better lover! Ah, pretty dove, don't tremble so."

"Stop! Let me go!" I cried. "I see your father. I'll scream!"

Qabul looked over and seeing his father swore and then shrugged. "Ah well. Today only adds spice to what is to come. But fear not, little dove. Some day I will carry you off to your rightful destiny. Until then, dream of me!"

He was on his pony and gone. But I was unable to move or even to catch my breath, my whole body was so atremble. What a foul beast! Was one brush with him not enough? And why hadn't I screamed for help anyway? Was it because of fright? Because I mistrusted Qacha? He might well have misread what had happened between his son and me. I dared not tell Argamon. He had been so angry with me over Qabul before that he might blame me again.

But there was something else, and I could not admit it then, for it was too hard to face, but Qabul's animal vitality appealed to something in me, something so deep that I feared it as much as I feared him. It made me feel vaguely guilty, as if I actually had been sending him false signals. At least I knew this much: from then on, I must be on constant guard whenever he was near, for I could count on no one to help me a third time.

That night I did dream about Qabul. I was walking alone in the dark, lost on the empty steppes. I saw a fire and made my way toward its light. But as I reached it someone raced up from behind. I turned just in time to see a knife raised to strike me in the back and to be pierced by Qabul's cat eyes. His knife plunged down and I awoke, clammy with fear.

SUMMER TO WINTER, Anno Domini 1240

By late summer, the days were wretchedly hot. Dusty winds often forced us to roll down the sides of the gers again, and when we went outside we had to protect our faces with scarves that whipped and billowed as though alive. Dust demons whirled and danced across the plains in the hazy distance, and sometimes shimmering water and trees appeared on the horizon, surely shades from some other world, for the long grasses were now withered and gray. I was resigned to camp life, to Argamon's comings and goings. I no longer flinched when Mongol soldiers led in lines of defeat-faced captives. But I could never forget that one day the prisoners—or the dead—might be my own friends and family.

Autumn arrived, and the camp seemed charged with expectation. Although no orders had arrived, everyone knew that soon Batu Khan's combined armies would assault central Rus' and Mother Kyiv. The ordu began preparing for winter and for war. Half the herds were slaughtered and the meat preserved, hides were cured and shaped into armor, and great sheets of tent-weight felt were strengthened with oil or milk to withstand heavy storms. And as if the troops were not armed enough already, armorers fashioned even more weapons!

They celebrated a fall festival, too: more sacrifices and contests and gorging, more avoiding Qabul's insistent gaze at Qacha's feasts. I was now thirteen, for the feast day of my patron the Virgin Mary was around this time. But what good was it to compare these festivities with the harvest celebrations of home? At least Q'ing-ling welcomed my suggestion that we hand out winter provisions to the slaves.

Winter came early that year. The ordus had finally moved onto what I was certain was Kyivan soil because trees began to appear in abundance. Branching out from the immense northern forests, they stretched along the frozen rivers and streams like great fingers gloved with sparkling snow. Qacha's tuman met up with others heading west until the world seemed infested with ordus. Thoughts of escape haunted me, perhaps after we crossed the next river or moved a few versts closer. Or the Mongols might see Kyiv was too powerful and sweep past her into Hungary. Once I said so to Dorje.

"Child, when the people of Kyiv killed the Mongol envoys a second time and nailed the corpses to the city gates, their fate was sealed. It's just a matter of time."

"They did?"

"Yes. Mongke Khan prevailed upon Batu Khan to give them a second chance and send envoys again, but after that foul deed … There is no hope for Kyiv now."

Dread began stalking me like an enemy in the dark.

One frosty afternoon, Qacha summoned his family to a family ceremony with Yulta Beki. I knew why. Throwing myself at Argamon's feet, I pleaded, "I cannot seek your victory against my own city! I beg you, let me stay here."

"Sofia, forget Kyiv. You belong to me, now. My father honors you by including you, and you insult him with this babble? Come!"

All the way to the main camp, I dwelt on the injustice of this world and of my master. Clouds covered the sky like smothering shrouds, the bitter wind tugged at me like a demon. Tramping to the shaman's ger, I dragged behind Qacha's people. Qabul edged toward me, but Argamon was straightaway by my side, gripping my arm. During the ceremony I stood in a dark trance as the shaman sacrificed and burned a fine horse, and the family smeared all the ongghon with butter and milk and blood.

I recalled telling Dorje once how I hated Mongol rituals with their bloody, greasy, smoky offerings, and he had asked how they differed from the Christian ritual of eating the blood and body of our God—to a Mongol, *that* seemed disgusting and irreligious. I had tried to explain that it symbol-ized God's love for us and he had countered that it seemed a strange way to show love, leaving me upset that I could not express myself better.

A public ceremony followed that lasted late into the day. Yulta Beki sac-rificed more animals before Qacha's standard—his Spirit Banner, as they called it, a source of sacred power. And late that night when the full moon would be high in the sky, the shaman would perform a divination about the next great battle. When Argamon disappeared with most of his men, Q'ing-ling invited me to stay with her. We women all waited in silence, doing nothing.

That evening after sunset, I slipped outside to stretch my legs and saw the sky flame out and the cold lunar light slowly flood the steppes. Friendly Father Moon was now only a dead white disc. Even the wind had died down as if holding its breath expectantly. With a shudder I turned back into Q'ing-ling's ger, my heart as chill as the air.

Finally we received the summons. I straggled behind Q'ing-ling to the area before Qacha's ger, where his family, closest generals, and their women were settling into a large circle around a huge roaring conical fire. They whispered and stirred and stared at nothing. I had never witnessed a major divination and once might have armed myself with disbelief, but now I just wished I could be somewhere else.

The sound of hoof beats, and Yulta Beki rode in from the night, fol-lowed by his white-clad wife and apprentice. Over his white garment he wore a colorful cape and an apron painted with strange designs, and his face was covered by a nasty black wooden mask with red eyes, fangs, and lengthy whiskers and eyebrows. From a belt around his waist hung long wedge-shaped sticks and metal disks that clacked together as he moved. The mask made him seem taller than usual, and malign. Qacha solemnly offered him a great chunk of raw meat, which Yulta Beki passed on to his boy. Then with his wife's help, he swept the space around the fire and sprinkled it with airag. Beating his drum, he began to sing and dance slowly around the fire, his skirt of sticks and metal clanking together eerily. Little by little we all fell under his spell as the beat pulsed faster, the dance grew wilder, the chants became more disjointed.

The night came alive with weird taps, creaks, and high-pitched voices crying out from nowhere. I looked around but could see nothing, though the space seemed crammed with spirits. Wind arose, began to moan and whip around us, the felt walls of nearby tents sighed and snapped, their ceiling spokes groaned. Yulta Beki whirled and danced faster and faster until he seemed to be in two places at once.

Suddenly he cried out in a high, hoarse voice and fell into his wife's arms like a tree struck by lightning, gasping for air, writhing like a snake, foam streaming from the corners of his mouth. The apprentice held aloft the chunk of meat. This must have been a sign, for Qacha began asking questions. A series of voices totally unlike Yulta Beki's answered, sometimes with deep moans and growls, sometimes with clear yeses or no's, and sometimes with what sounded like ancient words from some unclean world. A shudder ran through me. This man indeed held great and dark power, and dreadful spirits spoke through him, as real as any I had known in Rus' but far darker and more dangerous.

Qacha finally finished questioning Yulta Beki. Slowly the shaman pushed aside his wife's hands and rose to his feet as if gathering thunderclouds around him. In a raw voice he uttered the only thing I understood. "These curs of Rus' bay at the mighty tempest, but they will all be swept away by the Mongol storm!" I felt like I was falling into icy blackness.

He paused, seeking out the gaze of Qacha's eldest son. "Yet out of this conquest I also see blood, loss, and calamity. Take heed, Qabul. A perilous time comes toward you. Your future lies hidden in storm."

The shaman turned and sought the arms of his assistants, who helped him reel away and mount his horse. They rode off into the dark, the sound of hoof beats rapidly fading away. Everyone was dead silent. Har Nuteng, looking slightly ill, turned and stared at me. Although I stared back, trying to hold my ground, my eyes dropped first. She then moved to kneel next to her son and whisper into his ear before bowing coldly to Qacha and asking to leave. He nodded slightly, and she too vanished into the night with her retinue.

Slowly people got up and left, murmuring to each other about this strange and terrible prophecy. I now knew that the mention of Mongol blood was avoided, and certainly no shaman would willingly predict calamity to his master, so for Yulta Beki to say such a thing was utterly shocking.

Qabul got up and swaggered over toward us women, but he could not hide his unease. I tried to shrink from his sight, but he saw where I was sitting and stood as close as he could, directly in front of me. Though I refused to return his gaze, he waited for a short eternity as if for some sign from me. Finally, receiving none, he turned and left. I was certain he would be out there, somewhere, waiting. If only I could escape back to Q'ing-ling's ger unseen! Asetai was signaling to me to join him and my master, standing near the dying fire. But instead of going back to his ger, Argamon began to talk eagerly with Bayartou and Asetai about the prophecy while I stood outside their circle, shivering, feeling sure that Qabul was lurking nearby.

Qacha had retreated to his ger, and I glimpsed him through his doorway, alone, staring into his fire. A servant passed me with a broad, flat sheep bone and entered the tent, closing its door behind him. Why Qacha did need a further divination? Rus', Kyiv, my family and friends had been cursed and doomed. As to the rest of the prophecy, who knew what it meant until events revealed their sense? Qacha's muffled chants were barely audible, but I heard the bone cracking in the fire before Argamon led me away.

Within days, Qacha received his orders. When Argamon bade me fare-well, he told me to abandon all hope for Kyiv. There would be no feigned siege or feigned withdrawal to draw out her defenders. She would be sur-rounded and destroyed, along with her citizens. So, numb with dread, I stood with my fellow slaves as Qacha's divisions passed by in formation—row upon row upon row of horsemen—while drums hammered a haughty fare-well and horns blasted loud enough to crack the dome of the sky. Behind them rode more soldiers leading extra ponies, and behind them others drove the wagons carrying siege engines, missiles, and extra gear. Other armies passed by in the distance, leaving broad swaths of dirty snow and trampled grass like a road to hell. I could do nothing but pray.

The next day we began to follow, deep into Rus'. Although I stayed with Q'ing-ling, who tried to keep me busy, despair was ever ready to entrap me. Her ordus made camp a few days later within sight of a procession of trees that surely marked the Dnieper River. I thought I could see Kyiv's walls in the far distance, and perhaps a flash of copper from the Golden Gate. Having crossed many a frozen river by then, I knew just how easily Mongol tumans could swarm over the Dnieper and surround her; that must be why they had waited for winter. Hoping to see more, I climbed a little rise near the ordu and glimpsed the burnt remains of a village in the distance. I turned back with a sigh, wondering how many months would pass before Kyiv fell, as of course she must.

But I was wrong. It was the very next day—December 6, 1240—a date I learned later but will never forget. That morning, smoke bloomed against the western sky like a dark weed. At first I thought another village had been put to the torch, for surely not even Mongols could overcome Kyiv so quickly. The day seemed endless. Each time I went outside, the sooty mass had relentlessly spread further until it was a great black cloud, lit from below by a flickering glow. As the sun set behind it, it turned deep blood red. In the deepening gloom, little bursts of flame shot up. All night I repeatedly abandoned my bed and went outside to look. Above the bloody glow a smear of darkness was slowly blotting out the stars. Finally I knelt in the snow and prayed for my people.

The next morning, several hundred armed women rode out, laughing and shouting war cries. Papa had told me about the corpse-eating Valkyries of the old Norse legends, but these were the real-life women Q'ing-ling had once described to me. They would soon be slitting throats. Some must be women I saw every day, friends who had shared their memories of disease or famine with me, who sang and jested as they worked, treasured their little ones, loved their men at night, and kept the flesh-eating spirits from the gers with their prayers. How could they carry kindness and ruthlessness in one heart?

For two days smoke stained the sky while my heart turned black with desolation. Finally the armies returned. I stood with Q'ing-ling this time, watching as seemingly thousands of people rhythmically clapped and sang a joyous welcome to the victors. Qacha rode in looking straight ahead, all his sons directly behind him this time. Argamon had no marks upon him—though I felt not a shred of relief—but Qabul had not been so lucky. Something had happened to his face, perhaps a sword slash, for a vivid wound ran down his nose and onto his upper lip. Qacha's retainers followed, shaking the tall yak-tail Spirit Banner aloft, carrying banners marked by smoke and sword, and shouting victory. With them rode Kuvrat Khan and other stern-faced generals. Behind them came the orderly ranks of horsemen, including the women who had fought by their sides, their heads held as high as any man; and behind them marched men with pack animals laden with equipment, plunder, or corpses. Some led a few ragged prisoners bound together in lines—so few.

After a long and boastful speech from Qacha—at least there were no executions—everyone greeted their heroes with a joy bordering on madness. Women rushed to their husbands, clapping their hands and shouting greetings, while senior officers began dividing up the plunder. Women's song, children's shouts, and happy laughter mingled with the miserable wails of widows in an unbearable din. I stood there burdened by pillaged finery, my heart shattered into frozen splinters. And that night I must join a victory feast!

The first few soldiers were staggering off laden with loot when I glimpsed a pitiful handful of prisoners lashed together, mostly beautiful young women and older children, and a few men clothed like artisans, all of them lost in a waking nightmare. Before they were given away, I must hear a voice from Kyiv again! I slipped away from the others as Qacha dismounted. Asetai seemed not to notice; he was calling greetings to a friend. I slowly worked my way through the crush of people. Not even the guards around the prisoners paid me any mind. Squeezing close to the nearest captive, a tear-stained beauty about my age, I whispered, "Please. Are you from Kyiv? What happened?"

She turned toward my voice and stared at me dully. Finally she said, "I was. Now … nowhere. My city, my home, my family … gone."

"Gone? How can Kyiv be gone?"

"They destroyed her, killed almost everyone. Only a few walls are left—and Saint Sofia. We were praying there. They pulled down the ikonostasis. Raped me before the altar … many men, many times. All around screams of the dying, of women and girls hurt like me. They killed my baby and my husband … if only they had killed *me*."

Fresh tears began flowing down her face, and she began to wail as guards came to claim the captives. I reeled away, her words a knife twisting in my heart. I stumbled through the crowd, trying to grasp what she had said. Gone, gone. Papa, Baba Liubyna, my friends and cousins and servants, my beautiful city, all cruelly gone. Even after all those months of dread, I simply could not believe it.

All those innocent victims: I must pray. But how, to whom, for what? A stern Father, a loving Mother, a sacrificed Son? What if it was all a lie and the world had always been ruled by fickle spirits and evil demons? What if everything I had been taught about God, religion, or even goodness was a lie and it never mattered how anyone behaved?

A whimpering animal seemed to be following me. Looking around, I realized that the sounds came from my own throat. I want to die, they cried. I want to die. I pushed through the crowd, while grief gushed from me like blood from a severed artery. I found Q'ing-ling's empty ger, fell inside, tripping over the threshold, and landed in a heap before her shrine. I sat there with my arms wrapped around myself, rocking and moaning, for what seemed like an eternity.

Once again it was Dorje who roused me. "Sofia, are you all right?" He knelt beside me. "Child, I know, I know."

I drew away. "Don't try to comfort me. I wish I had died with everyone else."

I sank back into despair. Distantly I heard Dorje calling for Kamileh, then felt her kneeling beside me saying, "Here, drink this." Asetai was there, too, sitting nearby.

I cried, "Leave me alone, I don't need your potions." But she insisted until I gave in. A liquid burned my throat, the drink took effect, and I floated into a calm, cool space.

Dorje, floating with me, took my hand. "Sofia, you must be brave and go to Qacha's feast now. It's vital for you to be there. He must see you as one of them or he'll feel insulted and the poison of mistrust might eat into his mind. You might be its victim."

"I don't care. Why should I? Let him kill me. That would be best, anyway."

"No, it would not. Just sit as quiet as a mouse, and it will soon be over."

Dorje pressed at me again and again, and then Kamileh joined in until I could think of only one way to rid myself of them. "All right, I'll go. Just let me be!"

The old monk stood stiffly. "Come, Asetai will take you over."

Somehow I lurched across the clearing behind Asetai and entered the tent of my enemies, to be deafened by drunken shouts and song. The noise seemed to beat inside my head and heart until I could bear no more. I turned to my wine cup, emptying it I know not how many times, and then sat sodden in front of uneaten food. At one point, Qacha shot me a look that penetrated my foggy mind. Poison of mistrust. And well he should mistrust me, I thought. If I must live, it would be to see his undoing! I finally ate a mouthful. But he continued to note how I behaved, just as Dorje had predicted.

At one point he said, "I wager our little princess is glad to be feasting here tonight with us Mongol wolves instead of being a feast for the wolves herself!" His men slapped their thighs with mirth. Encouraged by their horselaughs, he continued. "Qabul, you saw no flame-haired princesses trying to escape Kyiv, did you? I'm certain we can find you one of your own.

We surely didn't kill them all. And you do seem to need one to fend off further damage to your beauty." Qabul's nose and upper lip were bleeding into his food, though he had tried to bind them with a ghoulish looking mixture of spider's web and green mold. We both sat woodenly through jests that grew cruder with every word.

Afterward I had to face Argamon all bloated with triumph. "I fought like a demon, Sofia," he boasted. "You should be proud of me! Your magic has brought me such glory!"

Proud? He was more a stranger and enemy than ever! And if I had possessed any magic powers, I would never have used them to help my enemies, let alone destroy my city and my homeland. Yet somehow Argamon—and others—had begun to think of me as something more than what the prophecy had foretold. In bed while he tried to coax me into pleasure, I felt only despair now that Kyiv was gone. How pathetic that I had hoped for a heroic escape. To be done with his lust, I tried every trick he had taught me. He fell asleep content with yet another conquest while I lay grieving.

He awoke as usual just before dawn and announced that Batu Khan was to host a great victory celebration beginning the next day. Qacha and all his family were expected to attend. He was lolling at his ease for once while I dressed. "I forgot to tell you last night. Batu Khan told Father to bring you, too. He wishes to see you again."

I flared, "I won't go anywhere near that butcher! What could he want from me, anyway? My heart has been ripped out and—well, *you* could never understand!" Instantly regretting my words, I steeled myself for Argamon to leap up and strike me.

Instead, though he frowned, he said, "I understand well enough, but you must set aside your weakness. You have no choice." I turned away, but Argamon surprised me again. He stood and lightly touched my shoulder. "Batu Khan heard about your skill with words, and he wants you to show him. That would raise my standing with him. But don't be uneasy, I'll be there by your side." As though that could be any comfort!

"Kuchan is crying. I must go see what he needs, Master," and I bowed and fled.

While Tsetsegmaa stirred a pot of gruel, I sat with Kuchan in my lap. How could Argamon dismiss my grief as weakness? Perhaps if I went to Q'ing-ling, I could persuade her to tell Argamon to leave me behind. I even came up with an excuse to avoid going.

As soon as I could, I rode over to the main camp, threw myself at her feet, and burst into tears. "I'm summoned to Batu Khan's feast. How can I be expected to rejoice in this of all victories? I might do something rash and disgrace everyone! Must I go? "

Q'ing-ling said nothing until I had calmed a little and wiped my tears. "I am sorry, Sofia. I know how you grieve, but if the khan wants to see you, you must obey. I must go with Har Nuteng lording it over me with her ancestry. I wish I could stay away, too."

"What if we both feign illness? We could send word and neither of us have to go."

"No, you've been summoned and I must be seen. Others still suspect me of wrongdoing, and this is how Qacha shows them his high regard for me." She took my hand. "I'd be very glad to have you by my side."

I looked up. Her face was pale with concern. She was a target for so many arrows of judgment, but she was bravely facing them. I must, too. I took a deep breath and nodded.

The next morning while Argamon and Asetai arrayed themselves in their finest, Kamileh came to help me dress. The old woman insisted I accept some drink that left me a little dizzy but calm. My Mongol-style gown was a gift from Argamon: deep blue-green brocade with a russet-colored motif of intertwined dragons. It was trimmed with narrow bands of gold, deep russet and white, and edged with fur. Argamon had chosen well: it set off my red hair perfectly and was clearly meant to stress my worth to Batu Khan. He had also given me colorful high-heeled boots of appliquéd leather, with turned up toes. If a millstone of woe had not weighed on my heart, I'd have liked them.

Kamileh wound my hair into coils. I felt immodest with no koruna and veil, but a Mongol would not understand. Only married women wore headdresses. In honor of my dead countrymen, I did have her secure the coils with long pins from which hung chains of pearls. She added some with coral beads as well, claiming that both pearls and coral were for wisdom. I said nothing. I had chosen pearls because in Rus' they stand for tears.

Just before we left, Argamon brought me a magnificent silk-lined coat and a warm cap, both of mink. He handed the coat to me, saying, "Your old cloak isn't fine enough. I want your beauty to shine in every way."

But my heart almost stopped when he picked up my "old cloak" and began to hand it to Kamileh. I fell to my knees and cupped my hands. "Master, please may I keep it? My father gave it to me, and it's all I have left to remember him by." Of course that was true; but if I ever did escape, its hidden riches would secure my future. I added, "Please give my blue gown and gold tunic to Kamileh instead, since I've outgrown them and she's so small. They will fit better than the cloak." She looked satisfied, so he slowly gave it back to me.

I bowed deeply and cupped my hands. "I will never forget this greatest of gifts."

Argamon beamed with delight. "It pleases me to please you, Sofia."

Outside, I scarcely knew Little Liubyna at first. Her bridle and narrow red saddle were beautifully tooled and ornamented with real gold, and the saddle blanket was of yellow brocade trimmed with tassels. On the ride to the main camp, Asetai was right beside me, looking cheerily about at what must have been mere misty shapes. He had been following me all along on that day—was it only two days ago?—when I had collapsed in Q'ing-ling's ger. Bless him; it was he who had found Dorje and Kamileh for me.

When we arrived, Qacha nodded at me approvingly, but Har Nuteng gave me a long, inscrutable stare. And to my dismay, Qabul rode up right next to me for a moment, pushing Asetai's pony aside. His face was a mockery of its former comeliness. He said something, but the scab on his lips had stiffened and his words slurred. I just stared at him blankly. Argamon, riding on my other side, made a point of taking my reins from me.

"Stay away from what isn't yours!" he snarled. They glared at each other for a moment before Qabul nudged his horse forward, close to their father.

It only took us until midday to arrive at Batu Khan's ordu. We plowed through the rowdy throng, not only soldiers or their families but musicians, jongleurs, acrobats, tightrope walkers, men leading dancing bears, puppeteers, jesters, and fire-eaters. Where had these entertainers come from? They reminded me of our seasonal festivals at home when everyone had rested from their toils. We had feasted and danced, too, or gaped at just such vagabond performers. How the puppet shows had made me laugh. When I was small I had believed the mimes' gaudy masks were real faces. Perhaps these were the same people?

Batu Khan's huge ger, its gold fittings and embroideries gleaming in the sunlight, was surrounded by several large new tents. Finely dressed people were making their way inside them based on rank. One man was arguing with the guards when they refused him and his retinue entry to the khan's, but when Qacha led us to it, we were all bowed in.

It was already stuffy and foul-smelling inside. The mingled voices, shouts, laughter, fiddles, tambours, and song sounded like a great beast snarling. People were seated on carpets before low lacquered tables set with dishes of gold, silver, or copper according to rank. The only empty space was in the center of the tent between Batu Khan's dais and the hearth. Qacha made straight for a long table right in front of the dais, while his sons pressed into tables to each side. Har Nuteng found a seat at the front of the women's section amidst a group of grand-looking ladies, perhaps some of Batu's wives. Q'ing-ling led me to another forward table, stopping to greet a few women here and there. One of them stood and hobbled over to embrace her, tears on her cheeks.

After we passed, I asked, "Who was that?"

"A Han princess who was sent with me into Mongol slavery. We would never have become friends had it not been for that, for the Han hate anyone not of their pure blood." Seeing me about to ask more, she added, "I will tell you about it someday."

"But why does she walk with such a strange gait?"

"Oh, among her people tiny feet are highly regarded. When she was a child, her feet were bound and not allowed to grow. She once told me it was like having them roasted in a fire. Some of her toes even fell off. Han men find it sexually arousing for some reason. I suspect that they also do it to set themselves apart from upstarts like the Jurchen. Thank God my father was against the practice, or I might have shared her fate."

She stopped at a table near the front dais and greeted two women seated there, reeking of scent, their faces painted with heavy black eyebrows and bright red cheeks. One was the fattest Mongol I had ever seen—until I looked around. Many of these fine ladies were painted like whores or were as corpulent as she was. I discovered later that to be fat was a much-envied sign of wealth. The two women stopped their chatter to welcome Q'ing-ling with smiles, inviting her to sit.

"Sofia, these are my friends Kulan and Yisui. They are both wives of another great noyan." They smiled at me, too.

"Are you two friends?" I burst out in surprise. "I thought wives hated each other."

"Heavens, we are closer than sisters! You're thinking of what Q'ing-ling has to endure." Kulan gravely shook her head. "That is a shame, but it is rare. Generally we wives get on with each other very well. After all, when we share a man, none of us has him in our way so often!" Both women laughed knowingly.

I stared around at this cream of Mongol society. Nearby sat a young woman dressed all in red, wearing a tall headdress. Her companions were admiring her hands, which were covered with elaborate lacy brown patterns. I had never seen such a thing before, although I met with it again in Persia and the Holy Land. Q'ing-ling smiled when I pointed the woman out. "A noble bride, a gift to one of the noyans as a reward for his success in this last battle. Her red gown and jewelry stand for prosperity. She wears henna paint called mehndi that will fade in a few days. I think it came from Persia or Africa."

There was more to see. Like Har Nuteng, many women wore red brocade and tall crowns, sometimes topped with fans of pheasant or peacock feathers. But other headdresses were made of hair and decorated with turquoise and coral beads, jeweled spangles, strings of pearls, and gold beads. These were wigs, since Mongol women usually cut their hair short after marriage. A few wigs were shaped into black horns that curved around past their faces and brushed their shoulders.

Q'ing-ling smiled at me. "You've never seen such an assembly before, have you? You see, Chinggis Khan grouped soldiers from the same clans in units of ten and one hundred. But then he placed men from all the different tribes together in the great tumans, to force them to abandon their old enmities. Still, they didn't abandon their own customs. Each married woman wears the traditional headdress and costume of her clan. In a way I do the same. My hairstyle comes from my homeland."

"Ours, too," said Yisui, whose hair was shaven in front, making her seem bald under her headdress. "Is that your traditional way of wearing your hair?"

I touched my own bare head and answered slowly, "No, at home I would wear my hair in a braid with a headdress and a veil, but my master likes it loose most of the time."

"And what tribe are you from, and what clan do you belong to?"

"I belong to a rod—or I did." This was hard to explain, even had I wanted to go into it. The best I could say was, "A rod is a lineage of ancestors dating back from the beginning of time. Some of them lived in tribes centuries ago, but not since mingling with the Norsemen and settling into cities. They watch over us ... or they did."

"So no clan? No tribe?" asked Kulan. "Don't you feel alone without them?"

Tears rushed to my eyes. "I do feel alone. I miss my family."

Q'ing-ling squeezed my hand and quickly said, "Look, Batu Khan is arriving." The music melted away and in silence we all rose and bowed, cupping our hands to the khan as he and his fellow dignitaries entered, several of them already reeling from drink. Nodding to favorites here and there, stopping to talk with a favored few, he made his way to his dais accompanied by his brothers, Berke Khan foremost; his cousins, including Mongke Khan and Kuyuk Khan; one of his wives; and various retainers. I noticed that Kuyuk was dressed in the same orange and blue robes again—and looked drunk again, too. And Batu was limping slightly. Perhaps he had been injured in war long ago. I hoped it still hurt!

He and most of his cohorts seated themselves along the low table on the dais while others sat in front and below him according to their rank, pushing Qacha and some other noyans further down. Everyone waited quietly while the khan's major domo took out the airag offerings and Batu solemnly poured a libation on the floor. Only when he motioned for the musicians to begin playing did people speak to one another. While the servers poured cups of wine for the khan and his royal guests, the musicians drew out a lively tune. Batu stood, took a gulp from his cup, raised it toward his fellow princes, and started to speak. But he never did.

Kuyuk Khan slammed down his cup, jumped up, and shouted, "Why do you drink first, you wretched dog sired by a bastard!"

At that, another drunken prince whose name I did not know jumped up, too. "He's right, you old woman with a beard! You're unfit to lead an army. Without Subodai you'd be nothing, you pretender from nowhere!" The musicians wavered, stopped in mid-note. Like deadly vapor, silence spread across the room.

Batu Khan had turned beet red. He shouted back, "How dare you insult me and violate my hospitality! You sit here tonight by my grace—to celebrate *my* victory!"

"Hah! Drinking first was my privilege! I'm eldest son of the Great Khan, not some bastard's whelp," Kuyuk shouted. "You deserve a common beating!"

A voice chimed in, "They ought to tie a wooden tail onto you like a donkey. Then you'd know who your betters are." Mocking laughter mingled with roars of protest.

Batu and Kuyuk leapt toward each other and would have come to blows, but Subodai and Mongke Khan just as quickly jumped between them. After a brief struggle, Kuyuk turned and stalked out with his retinue. Several other princes and their men joined them, shouting further abuse as they left. Batu Khan sat down heavily, still as red as fire. Mongke Khan seated himself next to him, his face a mask. Angry voices outside called for their mounts, followed by clatter, shouting, and the sound of horses galloping off. Batu sat breathing raggedly and staring straight ahead while the rest of us sat like dumb stones. I had no idea what they were quarreling about, and although I would have loved to fling insults at Batu, too, it would never have been at an event like this!

Finally, Mongke Khan whispered something into Batu's ear. Batu Khan took a deep breath and looked out at us all. "And why should the foul tempers of a few spoiled little children ruin our celebration? Music, wine, food! Let us begin again, friends. I toast all my bold warriors, my *true* brothers and boon companions." At Batu's signal, his musicians threw themselves into the loudest possible music, though some hit a few sour notes. The khan turned to Subodai and Mongke, offering each of them a hand clasp, and quietly made some jest that had his men pounding the table with mirth—all forced, to my eye.

But the tension had broken. Batu raised a series of toasts to each of his noyans, his troops, his favorites; and the musicians added a special flourish to their music each time. Indeed, whenever Batu Khan reached for his cup, that flourish signaled us all to join in. As well, his companions offered so many toasts in return that soon no one had a clear head. Finally, Batu speared a huge chunk of meat upon an ornate, oversized long fork and gave it to one of his servants, who passed before his favorites and generals for each to slice off a bite for him- or herself. Meanwhile, servers began to bring in food and liquor for everyone, and people settled down to eat and drink. And gossip.

I looked at Q'ing-ling in amazement. "What happened? Do you know?"

She nodded. "Qacha says that bad blood has been rising between Batu and some of his cousins from Mongolia, especially Kuyuk. Now it has burst open most poisonously. The other young nobles are taking sides. Of course, Kuyuk was already deeply drunk."

"Let's not think about it," suggested Yisui. "I just want to enjoy the food! Try these, Sofia. I know you'll like them." She pointed out some plump horsemeat sausages.

"And this wine is wonderful," added Kulan. "Let the men settle their own quarrels! Best thing is to make the most of this feast. There won't be another like it for months. Here, try some of these, too," and she lunged sideways to seize a huge helping of skewered meats from a maidservant. "You're much too thin. Your master cannot enjoy riding a bony mare. A man needs his meat, you know." She grinned slyly when I blushed.

"We'll be here all afternoon, Sofia," Q'ing-ling warned, pulling out eating implements for both of us from a pouch at her belt, "so try not to take too much of anything. And be wary—the wines are potent." She need not have worried. Between heartache and too many toasts, I wanted neither food *nor* drink, though our table was soon laden with both.

Our companions eagerly set to work. Like Q'ing-ling, each brought out a pair of carved ivory eating sticks, a cutting knife, and a toothpick. You hold eating sticks in one hand and pinch them together to pick up food. The Lady had once told me their Chinese name means "nimble ones" and that many Oriental people use them. They are tricky to use at first, but once you know how, they're much less messy than knives and fingers. I had recently mastered them. Many Mongol women had brought nimble ones, but others were making do with fingers and wiping them on their own napkins—another borrowed custom, no doubt, since they were as filthy as any common Mongol.

The food, however, was unlike anything I had eaten in Qacha's camp. There were birds and game in rich gravies, meat dumplings, pickled vegetables, dried fruits, honey cakes, sausages, and roast meat in truly astounding quantities. Servers constantly offered us wine, mead, airag or arki. I finally gave in and bit into a spicy, savory dumpling. Hunger overwhelmed me, and I tasted something else. "It's all so delicious!"

Q'ing-ling smiled ironically. "This is a crude copy of the feasts in my homeland. No one with breeding would use a knife at table. Food was already cut up into bite size pieces, beautifully arranged and subtly flavored … Well, it's better than dried meat stews, and I can only be glad we Kin taught the Mongols more than mastery of siege machines!"

Knowing no different, *I* found no fault with the food, although after a few more bites I fell back into my dark mood. I prayed that at least I would not have to meet the khan that day. With luck, he would call off the rest of the feast and forget about me entirely.

People often wandered over to other tables to greet each other. Several women from Har Nuteng's group came by our table and stared at me while ignoring or even sneering at Q'ing-ling. How could she behave with such grace in the face of their insulting behavior? I felt a surge of warmth for my friend and at one point whispered to her, "My Lady, I see why you wished not to come. You're so brave."

Q'ing-ling smiled and briefly pressed my hand. Her bones felt as fragile as a glass bauble.

By the next morning, rumors about the khans' great quarrel had spread throughout the camp. Qacha and his sons left for a gathering of Batu's advisors, so I stayed with Q'ing-ling to await news, not that I cared. Finally Argamon appeared, excitement snapping in his eyes. He waited impatiently until his mother had dismissed all her servants before announcing, "When Batu Khan took the first drink, he offended most of his cousins from Karakorum." He turned to me. "That is an honor due the eldest and most senior khan, in this case Batu, but this pack of spoiled pups thinks itself his equal or better because they were raised around Khakan Ogedai in Karakorum. Without understanding what it means to grow up with only the wilds for a friend, they are as arrogant and ambitious as any city-bred fool, especially Kuyuk, who thinks himself a near-god because he's Khakan Ogedai's eldest son. How dare he trot out that old tale about Jochi Khan!"

"Sofia," his mother added, "you may not know that Batu's father might not have been Chinggis Khan's blood son because the Khakan's first wife was kidnapped in an enemy raid and raped. But he always accepted Jochi as his first born."

Argamon continued. "Worse, Kuyuk claims that before Jochi died, the Great Khan suspected him of disloyalty and thought to disown him. Kuyuk forgets important details, foremost how the Khakan wept at the news of Jochi's death. Such gross insults to his own uncle! Our family is faithful to the line of Jochi, who was ever a true heart son of Chinggis Khan. We've always laughed at these Karakorum princes' airs, but now they put our war plans at risk!"

"What will happen?" asked Lady Q'ing-ling.

"They must find a way to patch this rip in our campaign's fabric. We'll wait a little longer while Batu and Subodai take counsel together alone, but something is afoot."

After Argamon left, all the serving women poured back into the ger, chattering about the great quarrel and what it might mean. He didn't return with further news until late in the day. "Messages have passed between the rival factions, thanks to Mongke and Subodai. The feast and kuriltai must go on, and everyone must at least feign unity. We're all summoned back. And Batu Khan spoke of you to my father, Sofia. He thinks you may provide a much-needed distraction."

Q'ing-ling and I exchanged despairing looks before trudging back to Batu's ger. Although it soon filled with people again, they were all rather subdued until Kuyuk and his men strutted in as if nothing had happened. Batu came forward with a false-looking smile and escorted his rival back to a seat of honor. With harmony seemingly restored, the feast continued with more food, drink, shouts, and barks of laughter, and a stream of entertainers from magicians to acrobats to dancing girls. It seemed even louder than the day before; perhaps people were trying to mask their disquiet over the falling-out.

By late afternoon, almost everyone was filled to bursting and utterly drunk. Many a man was guzzling from an animal horn while his friends held his mouth wider so he could swallow more. Some people vomited where they sat and then ate and drank more. Others reeled outside for awhile and on returning attacked the food as if they were starving.

Snatches of obscene conversation floated to my ears. Although I'd heard plenty of bawdy talk at home, my upbringing had included many strictures on public behavior. From hosting the Grand Prince to bargaining with merchants in the marketplace, a noblewoman's second veil was modesty. Yet here women lifted their skirts and scratched their privates right in front of the men—or gestured at them obscenely! I whispered a disapproving comment to Q'ing-ling, but to my surprise she disagreed.

"Yes, they are gross, but they're also completely faithful to their husbands. They expect to receive as much pleasure as they give to their men, and that was so in my homeland, too. I see no real problem. Some Christians are too ready to brand women as daughters of Eve."

Q'ing-ling's words took me aback. I had been told often and at least partly believed that as daughters of Eve and snares to men, women must always behave with decorum. Indeed, according to Father Clement, our only saving grace was that we were also heirs to the wisdom and compassion of Mother Mary.

As the afternoon dragged on, it seemed as if Batu Khan *had* forgotten me. But just as I thought of going outside to ease my stiff knees, Argamon approached the women's side. Several ladies shouted lewd suggestions to him. He just laughed, shot back an obscenity, and waved to me to join him. I sat staring at him foolishly until he called, "Come, Sofia. The khan wants you now."

Forcing myself up felt like pushing a boulder uphill. We walked toward Batu Khan's dais, engulfed by laughter, shouting, chewing, swallowing, gulping, belching, and vomiting while music blared and pulsed around the tent, but my heart was pounding so hard in my ears that I could scarcely hear.

Several girls were performing a traditional shoulder and arm dance before the khans and casting inviting glances at them, while the men pounded their tables and shouted coarse proposals. The music stopped and the dancers filed away, one of them tossing a last alluring smile back at the men. When Argamon led me before the khan, the empty floor was suddenly too large. Before me sat a row of khans and noyans, Qacha among them, laughing together as if they were all the greatest of friends, even though a few had stalked out with Kuyuk Khan just yesterday.

Their talk stopped as we approached. They seemed to know some secret about me, for I saw sneering amusement on several faces. Qacha's neighbor poked him in the ribs. He frowned at his friend and then at me. Behind them, surrounded by his cousins and friends, my enemy sat on his dais. His wife of the day lolled beside him, dressed in a red and gold brocade gown and gaudy feather-topped headdress. Once again he was dressed all in white—heavy brocade trimmed with gold-shot samite. On his head sat a helmet-shaped silk crown topped with white feathers; a piece of brocade hung behind it to his shoulders. Altogether, he glimmered like a huge pearl, as if he had clothed himself in his victims' tears.

As Argamon genuflected, so did I, but I remained on my knees without falling to my face as I was supposed to. It was a daring gesture, but one I had planned. If they thought I was one of them now, I should no longer be forced to prostrate like that! Argamon froze in alarm, but the khan's eyes gleamed with amusement.

Still, my legs turned to jelly when he looked straight into my eyes and smiled secretively. I tried to make a mask of my face. "So here you are again, the famous princess who means so much to my young Argamon and who provokes so much envy in my dear nephew Qabul. I hear you now speak the Mongol tongue as if born to it. Come closer."

I rose and forced myself forward. My mouth suddenly felt drier than a riverbed in drought. His smile broadened as his cold eyes traveled over my body as if undressing me in his thoughts, while everyone around him looked on in approval! "You are growing up, I see. I have need of your ... services," Batu Khan leered, while his companions snorted with laughter, even his wife. He glanced over at Argamon, standing rigid as a board, and added, "I mean your services as a translator, of course. I wish to test your new skills. I have made friends with a warrior of Rus' named Dmytri, whose life I spared on account of his bravery. He led the defense of Kyiv. You will ask him some questions for me and tell me what he says." He looked over to a servant. "Bring in Commander Dmytri."

As the man stumbled in between two guards, I could scarcely believe my eyes. He was Prince Danylo's man, who had once carved wooden toys for me! He was trying to hold himself straight though he was clearly in great pain. His head and an arm were wrapped in bloody rags, and his dark beard was matted with blood from a face wound. "Uncle Dmytri!"

It took several heartbeats before he recognized me. "Princess Sofia? Is that you? Great God! I thought you were in Constantinople."

I gave him my hand, and he bowed as best as he could. "Mongols—Tatars—captured me at the Dnieper cataracts," I said. "They killed almost everyone, but Argamon here enslaved me a year ago. There was a Mongol prophecy about me."

We were both trembling with emotion, but remembering where I was, I turned to Batu Khan. "I know this man. He served one of my father's cousins. He says he thought I was in Constantinople, which is where I was traveling when Argamon captured me."

Batu betrayed no surprise. "In that case you may ask him your own questions. Doubtless you'll find much to say to each other." He beckoned to a dark-haired Turkish woman seated just behind the dais, and she came to stand by his side.

Dmytri and I stood as if we were alone in that roaring sea of noise. "How came you here? What happened to Grand Prince Mikhail? To Papa? Tell me everything."

"Ah, Princess Sofia, it was like a tragic tale from the olden days." Dmytri flung his good arm about like a drowning man. "I do not know when you left—did you know that the first time envoys came, Prince Mikhail had them killed and their bodies thrown off the walls? Then he fled with many princes, claiming he must visit King Bela of Hungary. His son was to wed the king's daughter, most opportune for him!" He snorted contempt while I shook my head. Such base cowardice.

"Then reports came to Prince Danylo's court. Envoys had come to Kyiv a second time demanding that the city submit completely and pay tribute to Batu Khan, but her remaining leaders killed them, too. It spelled doom for Kyiv. Later I learned that the only one to oppose their foolish action was your father. *He* insisted that killing them was suicide and that Kyiv must surrender and offer homage this time. No one listened to him.

"But once the envoys were dead, he helped organize the defense—and not only against the Tatars. Instead of standing together, several princes began fighting over the Golden Throne. Your father sent word to us. We made peace with him, and his army and Prince Danylo's triumphed. I proclaimed Prince Danylo Grand Prince, as we hoped the Tatars would spare Kyiv then, since *he* had already submitted to them. But we were wrong. They refused to parley with me, and it was too late to retreat. I thought we could hold out for months, but we'd never met an army like theirs before!"

He was so choked with emotion that he could not go on for some time. "When they poured across the Dnieper, your father was by my side on the walls praying for deliverance, but I doubt God could even hear us. The din of drums and siege engines and camels and horses crossing the ice was more deafening than thunder. First they built their own wall around us so no one could escape, and then it truly began. Sofia, they had infernal machines, worse than dragons. Some threw monstrous stones that shattered our walls; others sent balls of flame into the city—Greek fire! They shot flaming arrows over the walls, too. Everything was ablaze—you know how much of

Kyiv was built of wood—and we could do nothing! But as they broke down our outer defenses, we built our own walls inside the city.

"The last time I saw Prince Volodymyr, he was leading his men toward a breach in one of them. A church falling in on itself separated us, and I had to fall back with my warriors. People trapped inside the church were shrieking as they burned or were crushed to death. Dear God, how I wish I had never gone to Kyiv. We thought we were fighting nomads, not demons! I will never forget seeing screaming women and children put to the sword like cattle.

"Now these monsters claim they spared *me* for my bravery. As though no one else was brave! But I think it was only because I'm Prince Danylo's man. Batu Khan claims he wants to keep me as an advisor, and now he leads me around like a tame bear. What can I do but obey? My only hope is that if he begins to trust me, I might talk him into sparing other cities of Rus'. There's little more I can do to atone for my arrogance." Dmytri began sobbing, deep dry hacks more terrible than tears.

I was weeping, too. "And all were killed? Do you think my father might still live?"

He shrugged. "Even the warriors who surrendered were struck down. A few captives were taken, but … I am kept apart from other prisoners."

A wild hope flared. "Papa might be held in one of the other ordus, then! Perhaps I gave up too soon. Thank you, Uncle Dmytri."

Lifted by this slender thread of possibility, I turned to Batu Khan. The dark haired woman had been translating into his ear while we spoke; perhaps she was the one who, rumor said, had demanded Ryazan's surrender. The citizens had thought she was a witch and turned her away with arrows. The Khan continued looking at me expectantly, and I realized she was merely there to confirm or deny what I said. I repeated my conversation with Dmytri. Most of the other khans had lost interest while Dmytri and I were speaking together, but now they stopped to gloat over the story of their victories. How I hated them!

Batu nodded. "Well done. I may indeed use you to translate for me someday.

"Qabul," he called, "I see why you are envious. She is a prize worth possessing." I turned and saw Qabul sitting scowling at a nearby table, near his father.

"Friends and brothers," Batu continued, "shall we reward our young Argamon for uncovering a double treasure in one woman? What shall it be?"

He patted his chest as though the answer might lie there, while he looked over at Subodai, who shrugged and continued to gnaw on a bone already stripped of meat. 'Just as you gnawed on bones over my dying grandfather, you cur,' I thought! None of the other khans bothered to respond, either. "I know: a fine horse and new armor for our lucky warrior. And for you, young princess, I will find something special. I'll send it to you soon."

Argamon took a huge breath, flushed with pleasure, and bowed deeply. "Yes, yes, very good, my young warrior," said Batu. "You must see to it that your fair flower continues to bloom. You may go now," and he waved a dismissive hand. I barely had time to bid Commander Dmytri farewell before he was dragged off.

"Bow again," Argamon ordered me in a whisper, for I was stupidly staring after Dmytri, wondering if we would ever meet again. But once we had genuflected and backed away, my master guided me out into the chill late afternoon with only a light hand on my arm, so unlike the last time he had presented me to Batu Khan. After we left the tent, he took another deep breath. I had not realized that facing the khan might be an ordeal for him, too, and that he might be as glad as I was to be dismissed. I felt grief-stricken and giddy at the same time. Although Kyiv had been horribly destroyed, Papa might be alive after all.

Argamon spoke. "You were splendid, Sofia. Batu Khan was impressed, and you brought honor to me and my family. What did you and that man say to each other?"

"He used to come with Prince Danylo to visit my father. He was kind to me. You heard what he said about the battle for Kyiv. I am proud of Papa for not fleeing like that cowardly Prince Mikhail! I hope he still lives, but I may never find out."

To my astonishment, Argamon touched my cheek softly. "This feast has several days to go, but Father orders me to take you and my mother back home the day after tomorrow. She has fulfilled her duty, and you need time for your heart to heal. You can stay with her tonight while I rejoin the feast."

I was struck dumb. Argamon truly understood? And he cared? Tears welled up. I looked into his eyes and saw, for lack of a better word, his goodness. For me that was a turning point of deepest import. We continued speaking with our eyes without regard for the people passing by us.

Finally he glanced back at the tent. "Bayartou and Asetai should have brought out my mother by now. The dogs—probably guzzling another round of arki. Stay here by the entrance guards. I'll go find them." He darted back inside.

The sun was touching the horizon while the clouds flamed carmine, rose, and fiery gold. On the opposite horizon, the sky was fading from shades of violet into a liquid blue gray. Long purple shadows stretched from the gers, but where the sun still shone on them their decorations glowed as if from within. The moment's perfection smote my heart.

Someone lurched out of the ger behind me, and the spell broke. I turned, and there was Qabul's injured face leering down at me. He broke into a mockery of a grin that cracked the scab on his lip and made it bleed. "Oh, little princess, is it really you, and are you alone again?" He looked around. "Where is Argamon this time? The fool keeps losing you, and soon he'll lose his luck. And his loss will be *our* gain!" I backed toward the guard at the door, but Qabul brushed by me, sliding a hand across my breasts. He reeked of liquor. Three of his men swept after him, smirking at me.

Argamon reappeared with Asetai and Temur just before Qabul disappeared into the crowd. "Did he speak to you? You look frightened."

"I am. He mixed insult with threat."

"He would never violate the khan's hospitality, but Asetai, you keep a special watch in case he tries to trouble Sofia again." Asetai nodded solemnly, too drunk to speak. Bayartou and Q'ing-ling appeared, and we hastened through the thickening blue dusk past drunken revelers and rows of tents into a finely appointed ger where Kamileh and Temulun were waiting with the other servants. Bedding was already laid out.

"Rest well, my princess. Good night, Mother." As Argamon left, he spoke to Asetai. "I'll send Temur over, too."

After I was abed, I thought about what had just passed between Argamon and me. His words were not flattery or a gift to seduce me. They came from his heart. How strange: he fought to destroy my homeland yet also cared how I felt. What use was my endless resistance to him? Argamon was but one warrior in a vast empire, raised to believe in his people's destiny, and the end to life's story was always the same for both conquerors and conquered. Eventually the debt of all flesh, as the Franks say, would be exacted from us all.

At that, something inside me broke. Whether Papa was alive or not, or anyone I had known and loved in Rus', we would never meet again, except in

Heaven—if lost souls like me could find it, if it even existed. But I was here, and to this world I must belong.

The next morning began with more gorging. How could people eat so endlessly? I finally went outside to relieve myself at a midden just beyond the camp. Asetai was trailing behind me, already drunk enough to stumble over every little bump on our path, but after that brush with Qabul I was glad that Argamon was taking no chances.

At the midden, several men and women were forcing themselves to vomit. I was too revolted to go back to the feast.

"Come, Asetai. I want to go to Q'ing-ling's ger." He looked disappointed. "Then you can go back to drinking. I'll be safe with the women."

"All right," he answered, casting a longing glance back toward the feasting tent.

I started off in what I thought was the right direction, but soon I was so jostled and turned about in the crush of people that I was no longer sure where I was. That was when I realized that Asetai was not behind me or anywhere among the shifting faces. Alarm rising with every heartbeat, my heart beating ever faster, I called his name, but my voice was lost in the hubbub. For months I had only been unguarded when *I* had abandoned *him*. Surely he would never leave me, especially after Argamon's warning. I tried to turn back, but some grand entertainment was starting, and a wave of eager people carried me along. I finally squeezed out of the flow and stood by a ger, frozen by worry. I would wait here for Asetai—no, I would find the Lady's ger by myself and he'd seek me there. Someone could surely point the way.

I was about to ask a passing woman for help when I felt a hand at the small of my back, most unlike Asetai. I looked around to see Qabul smirking down at me. Cracked scabs clung to his face like evil spirits.

"Do you think yourself lost again, princess?" His speech was slurred, but triumph lit his face. "No, you are *found* at last. Little girl Argamon and that weakling Asetai are gone from your life forever. Now you are mine." His arm crept around my waist. "We've both waited too long for this."

Panic lent me strength and clear sight: a path miraculously opened through the crowd. I pushed back against Qabul, threw him off balance, and twisted away, bumping hard against a passing menial laden with heavy bags. They toppled off his shoulders and landed, I hoped, right where we had been standing. Behind me I heard the man bellow in alarm, while Qabul cursed him and called my name in turn. His voice sounded close, but he could not see me, as I had already ducked beneath the river of people.

I pressed forward blindly, weaving around people to get to the tents on the other side, twisting down lanes made by gers and wagons, frantic as a rabbit running before a dog and fearing that Qabul's hot paws might still seize me. His shouts faded behind me, but I kept going. When I finally stopped beside a large black tent, gasping for breath, I was more lost than ever. Before it women were turning meat on spits, cutting off chunks for people, or filling bowls of stew from huge cauldrons. When no one was watching, I slipped inside the tent and hid behind a stack of bulging leather bags, shaking with fear.

After crouching there for an eternity, my legs turned into knots and chill oozed into my body. There were rustling noises in the tent, and once a big black rat raced across the bags. Someone came inside and rummaged about, but not near my hiding place.

At last I peered over the top of the bags and cautiously edged outside. The sun was well past her zenith. I huddled by the tent while pricks of pain shot up my legs.

A voice spoke in my ear, almost stopping my heart. "In the name of All-Merciful Allah, what are you doing here, Sofia?" I whirled about and there stood Selim al-Din, surprise written on his face. It was a miracle!

"Selim! What are *you* doing here? Please, I'm lost and in danger. Can you lead me toward Batu Khan's feasting tents? I can find my way from there."

"Of course. Come this way. My men and I will gladly escort you." Behind him stood several men, a few of whose faces I knew. An unspoken question hung in the air.

"I was at the feast and decided to return to my ger. My guard disappeared and—" I could not say more; after all, he was a spy. Could I really trust him? With barely a pause, I continued, "I saw something that frightened me, and I fled and got so lost."

"Yes, you're shaking all over." Happily Selim asked nothing more, and soon he was carving a path for me through the crowd while his men surrounded me protectively on all sides. None came close enough to touch me.

He finally turned to walk beside me. "It was Qabul. I know more than you think, child. Who are you trying to protect? Yourself? Your master? I would never harm you."

"I am sorry, Selim. You must understand. I trust no one anymore. Except Dorje and perhaps a few others." Then I realized how many others I did trust: Q'ing-ling and her servants, Asetai, Argamon's slaves, and even Argamon in certain ways. They were my people now, by necessity if not by choice. I could not betray them to an outsider.

"But when did you return, and why here?" I hoped to avoid more acute guesses.

"We just arrived yesterday, thinking to go to Kyiv first. But it was gone. I was in the Crimea, only a few weeks' journey from here. It is—or was— much easier to reach now that the Mongols have made the route safe. I grant them that! Venice and Genoa have trading colonies there. I did well, Praise Allah. Now it seems that I will join the ordus for the rest of the winter. Even tonight I may find some custom. I make large profits when my customers are drunk, although they act like pigs—an unclean people in every way."

"Yes, that's why I left the feast. People make themselves vomit so they can eat more! Why not save all that food for another time if they're so frugal? It makes no sense."

The crowd suddenly seemed to surge and ripple toward us. Soldiers were pushing through, apparently looking for someone. I was still so afraid that I almost turned back in case they were Qabul's. But Selim said, "Sofia, those are Argamon's men, I believe."

Then I recognized faces. "Bayartou," I called out. "Are you looking for me?"

He rushed up to me. "Here you are! We found Asetai's body in Argamon's ger! Someone had broken his neck. Argamon seeks you everywhere. We feared the worst."

An icy hand clutched my heart. I cried, "Dear God, no! Qabul—"

I hastily thanked Selim and was led off to Argamon. He was shouting at someone, but when he saw me he stopped and ran toward me, his eyes wild with grief and rage. I fell into his arms, reeling with horror yet so glad to be returned safely. He gripped me so tightly it hurt.

"Where were you? What happened? Are you all right?"

I could not speak fast enough. "Asetai disappeared and Qabul tried to seize me, but I escaped and hid. I was terrified. Then Selim al-Din found me and brought me here. But Asetai can't be dead! Your nokhor—my friend!" Argamon turned, and the men behind him stepped aside. There lay Asetai's limp form.

"I'll kill his murderer, even if it's my own brother!" Men picked up the corpse and Asetai's head lolled back suddenly as if it might fall off. Its empty eyes caught mine and held them. A wave of blackness swept over me, and only Argamon's grip kept me upright. To Bayartou he said, "Go ask Batu Khan's chancellor for an audience tomorrow—I know the khan sees other petitioners then. Tell him it's urgent."

He turned to me. "I will think on avenging Asetai later. First I must see you safely back to my mother. How dare Qabul lay hands on you! I'd kill him for *that* if I could!"

"What will you do?" I was drowning in a dark flood of grief, confusion, despair.

"I'll take you before the khan! Let him see what his dear nephew is really like!"

He hurried me to Q'ing-ling's ger, leaving several of his men on guard before stalking off to arrange for his friend's funeral. The lady's servants surrounded me, crying out at the terrible news, and she soon arrived, pale with concern.

"My God, I cannot believe it! How could even Qabul do such a foul thing to Asetai? And why? You, too, endangered in the khan's own ordu! Here, drink this. You're half frozen. Kamileh, wrap that coverlet around her."

I lay there shaking with cold. Worse, it suddenly came to me that by stumbling over the threshold of the Lady's ger, I might have brought bad luck to my friend. He had been right behind me that day. I dared not confess my error. Bursting into tears, I cried, "Poor Asetai. I bring more ill fortune than good, and *you* end up needing to protect *me*!"

"Not so. We never know why things happen the way they do, or how they will end, but Qabul's evil deed must come back to haunt him. You will see. Here is some soup. No? Then try to rest. You're safe now. I will sit beside you."

The sunlight faded while my tears came and went. The Lady was right: there was no way to know anything for certain. How fickle fate truly was! And what a grievous blow to Bourma. My sorrow over Kyiv spilled over into a new pool of pain. One foolish smile to Qabul was why I had ever needed guarding. By now Asetai could have been a master bow maker.

As I lay in the thickening dark, remembering his kindness, his loyalty to Argamon, and his bravery in the face of so many regrets, I fervently prayed that no one else would ever come to harm on my account. I even repented, and recanted, my early curse on Argamon.

The next morning at some distance from the camp, my master and his retinue held his nokhor's funeral. After chanting, pouring offerings, and sacrificing Asetai's favorite pony, they buried the remains as best they could, the winter ground being so frozen that they had to finish with piled stones. Perhaps Asetai's pony would hear her master's special song in the afterlife and come to him. Surely he deserved that much. But Argamon showed no grief, only anger as hard and cold as winter.

That afternoon Argamon brought me to Batu Khan, this time in a ger beyond the feasting tents. Music, laughter, and coarse shouts poured from them as if nothing had changed and people would revel forever. White-clad as always, the khan was seated on a brocade-draped chair on a high dais. A different gaudily dressed wife sat beside him, and Qacha and other noyans sat before the dais on a low bench. Qabul was sitting in front facing them, arms crossed and a scowl on his face. Har Nuteng was also in front with some court ladies, no doubt to remind her half-brother that his own nephew stood accused. I wondered if Batu's sense of justice—if he had one—would override loyalty to a relative. When I sat down by Q'ing-ling, Qacha stared at me coldly.

We had to wait for some time. Before Batu could listen to those with claims for justice, he must deal with several envoys from other cities of Rus' who, Q'ing-ling whispered, had arrived just after the great quarrel and been sequestered since then. Batu Khan was probably eager to send them on their way before they heard any rumors. They were seated near the tent entrance on the women's side. Each emissary came forward bearing rich gifts for the khan, but after he had presented his prince's offers of submission on bent knee, Batu sternly told him through a translator that he must bid his prince to come and submit in person. The khan's only sign of goodwill was to allow the envoy to cross to the men's side of the ger and then to be escorted away.

Then Batu settled disputes between senior officers in his armies. The wait seemed endless, and sorrow and anger and dread swelled in me until I felt like bursting. I tried to thrust aside these feelings, to be ready to speak if Mongol justice allowed it.

Finally our names were called. We three came forward and bowed to the khan.

Batu began. "I understand there is some trouble between the sons of my Noyan, Qacha. First I will hear from Argamon, who requested my judgment."

Argamon stepped forward and bowed, hands cupped in respect. "My lord, yesterday Qabul waylaid my concubine Sofia. Her guard, my nokhor Asetai, had mysteriously vanished. She fled Qabul, and while we were looking for her, we found Asetai dead in my ger. Someone had broken his neck! I am certain that my brother and his men are to blame."

"I see." The khan glanced at his nephew's sullen face before turning to me. "Is this so, Sofia?" People stirred and whispered. Was it rare for a slave to be asked for proofs? Afraid to put myself forward, I merely bowed and cupped my hands as Argamon had. "Go ahead, speak." Batu eyed me curiously.

My mouth had gone as dry as a field in drought; I could not keep my voice from trembling. "My Khan, it is as my master says. Yesterday Asetai and I were separated in a crowd, by accident I thought at first. But then Qabul tried to seize me. He said that I belonged to him now, and that both Argamon and Asetai were gone from my life forever. I fled in terror and hid. Through someone's kindness I found my way back to Argamon, to learn that Asetai had been murdered! From the way Qabul spoke, he had to know already."

Suddenly I saw my chance to destroy all Qabul's mad convictions. I turned and looked him in the eyes. His damaged face went as still as stone. "I must also add that I do belong to Argamon, who is a young lion of strength and growing wisdom, and that I will never belong to you, Qabul!" To my shock, he stared back with disbelief!

Turning back to the khan, I said, "I do not know what the penalty for murder is, but he and his men are surely behind Asetai's. I beg you, great Khan: see that justice is done."

Silenced blanketed the room. Batu Khan finally spoke. "You now speak as if you were born Mongol. Very good, princess. Now, Qabul, what is your answer?"

A shadow had swept over Qabul's face. Stepping forward and forgetting to bow, he cried out through his scabs, "The girl's very words reveal the truth. She 'must also add' them because my brother forces her to speak them against her will! Yes, I found her, wandering around like some lost mare. From the first, she has slipped out of Argamon's hands again and again. I hear that the night his jaghun attacked her caravan, his men captured her, not he. And she tried to run away in midwinter last year and again in the spring, when I returned her to him. And fate *keeps* sending her my way.

"Uncle, if I could have carried her off before and did not, why violate your hospitality by trying to seize her now? Yesterday I needed to do nothing—once again she just fell into my hands. It was surely a sign." My mouth almost dropped open. He was twisting everything! And how low to use his kinship with Batu to try to best Argamon!

"Alas for her," Qabul continued, "a man carrying several heavy bags stumbled into her and nearly crushed us both when they fell. She pushed me out of the way and saved me, but then she fled from him in panic. Had I wanted to kidnap her, I could easily have followed her! This I ask: if her powers were meant for Argamon alone, then why did her magic protect me as well? I believe this girl is destined for me and that the gods frown on her serving Argamon. Her being there to save me was an omen. That Asetai could be murdered here of all places is but one more sign of their displeasure.

"As for Asetai, it is a shame that my brother lost his nokhor, but he was lucky to live as long as he did. He was losing his sight and was unfit to be a warrior. Anyone could have lured him away and killed him: he was drunk all the time. And if one of my men did it, he will be punished!" He looked around boldly and met with a few murmurs of support.

"Indeed, he was not the only one with limited sight. Her own bleary vision is all that keeps Sofia with Argamon! But fate makes these choices, not slaves, and again and again it guides her to me. When the right time comes she will understand who her true master is, no matter what Argamon forces her to say today." Qabul paused as if pondering some great wisdom he had just discovered. "I *never* believed she belongs to him. They have been together for a year, yet she has yet to bear him a child. Why is this so if she is truly his?"

I could scarcely believe his brazenness. I started forward to retort, but Argamon caught my arm, whispering, "Let the khan decide who is to speak or you'll displease him."

For some time Batu Khan sat looking at the three of us. "Somehow we have veered from this murder to a question of property. How do you answer Qabul, Argamon?"

My master stepped forward and bowed courteously with cupped hands. "My Khan, Qabul is your nephew, but he does not live up to your greatness. He has hurt Asetai many times, even struck him a near-fatal blow from behind during a polo game. And he did try to seize Sofia before. Not only I but our shaman had to rescue her, and I only regret I was not there this time, too. He is surely doubly guilty." He bowed and stepped back to my side.

Batu turned to Qabul and gave his nephew a penetrating look—a knowing look, even. "First let us settle this question of property. Despite your passionate claims, Qabul, Argamon captured her; and to judge by her loyalty to him, you would be hard pressed to keep her even if you did take her from him. She belongs to Argamon. So be it." My master and I share sighs of relief, while Qabul paled and then flushed.

"As for Asetai's death," Batu added, "whether you ordered it or not, you knew something about it. You must not let this insult to your brother go unpunished. I order you both to pay a fine and to find those who killed his nokhor, and *they* must be put to death." He looked at his nephew significantly.

From the voices raised in agreement around us, Batu's courtiers all seemed to think his decision was brilliant. But why the khan did not hold Qabul to account personally for Asetai's murder and have him put to death, or at least banished, was beyond me. If Qabul only had to pay a fine— assuming he even bothered finding someone to blame—that meant nothing! Papa had once ordered one of his knights to pay a fine for killing a free peasant. He had given the money to the man's grieving widow who had come to him for justice, but she had thrown the handful of coins onto the ground. At the time I'd thought her mad, but now I understood: how could mere coin ever replace the hands and heart of her man?

Lost in thought and believing the audience over, I expected to bow and leave when the khan spoke again. "You, young Sofia, how did you learn to put such magic into our speech? Are you a shamanka?" He laughed, but most of his audience failed to follow his lead this time. I saw several courtiers looking at me coldly.

"My Khan," I bowed, trying to keep my voice from quavering, "I am not. I have a fine teacher, Noyan Qacha's interpreter, whom you yourself sometime use: the monk, Dorje. With much time on my hands, I simply worked hard to master your speech, just as I did with the others I know. Once you learn one new language, others follow easily."

Batu leaned forward in surprise. "What other languages do you know?"

"I speak Greek, Latin, Arabic, Farsi, and several Turkish dialects, my Khan."

"Impressive. Perhaps Argamon should give you to me and you could become one of my interpreters. That might resolve this quarrel." I shivered at the thought of having to be anywhere near that snake, with his hard eyes and self-satisfied smile.

On impulse I cried, "Please forgive my forwardness, my Khan, but the rivalry between Argamon and Qabul goes far back in time. Taking me from my master would not resolve it, while it would break the force of the prophecy surrounding me. And that might displease the gods." I fell silent, shocked at myself. Now I would pay for my bold tongue.

Happily, though, after a few moments' thought, Batu nodded assent. "You may be right. But one thing is clear: I cannot allow this rivalry between Qabul and Argamon to continue with no effort to mend it." He eyed the brothers sternly. "I order you two to sleep in the same ger and eat from the same bowl until you can reconcile. If a month passes and you cannot, then I must set you into different armies. As it was done in my grandfather's time, so it shall be done now. All of you, go now. Who else wishes to speak to me today?"

More names were called and two angry-looking men stood up. The three of us bowed and left, each brother's retinue jumping up to follow. My mind reeled. These two would never reconcile. All Batu Khan's decrees seemed like errant nonsense to me.

Qabul had stalked off, his grim-faced men right behind him, but before he disappeared around a ger, he turned and called, "Our time will come, little dove."

Argamon and I stared after him. "He is mad and always has been," he finally said.

Q'ing-ling came out. "A breath of freedom for us all, Son," she smiled. Argamon looked less certain, but I smiled gratefully.

We returned to her ger in silence, but I stayed outside after she had gone in. "Please forgive me, Master. Sharing a ger with Qabul ... I thought only to help you—"

"No, Sofia, don't blame yourself. Batu Khan's judgment was right, even if it was late in coming. It's the Mongol way. Father should have made us settle our quarrel or be set apart long before now, but he could never believe it was that bad. And had Batu Khan ordered me to give you up, I'd have done so gladly. Instead, he let me keep you."

"Could you really let me go so easily?"

"Of course not. But I cannot allow you to come to harm, either. You'd be safe from Qabul if you stayed here. I see how my brother looks at you and how you give no sign to him. I also know what would happen to you were you to fall into his grip. But I relied on the prophecy, too. Batu Khan would never challenge fate; only Qabul is crazy enough to do that! You are mine and he knows it. And so does the khan."

"What about Asetai? Your brother *is* behind his murder. Surely Batu sees that."

"Naturally he does. Qabul has always sought to harm Asetai, and this time he got what he wanted. But remember: Har Nuteng is the khan's half-sister. One of Qabul's men may die for the murder, but Qabul will only pay the fine, as is right for a Child of Light." He snorted cynically.

"And I will take my own revenge someday. Asetai's death pains me deeply."

"Father says we'll all leave tomorrow morning, since we've lost all sense of celebration," he added. "I will return to Batu Khan's ger for now; I must speak with my father. But I'll leave you here with a few men on guard."

He lifted my chin and gave me a lingering kiss. "I miss you in my bed," he whispered. Once I might have shuddered at such words, but my world had just changed. If he was willing to part with me for my own safety, Argamon truly cared for me beyond his own gain. Now that all hope had vanished, I could only feel deepest gratitude.

That night Argamon summoned me to his side. To my surprise, he had sent his other men away, leaving only a few guards outside. He took my hand and drew me onto his divan at once. A flagon and goblets sat on a nearby table, and he poured for both of us. It was that strong opium-laced wine again, and I took only a few sips.

He looked so young, so sad. I said, "Master, I share your grief over Asetai."

As soon as I spoke, his face returned to a hard mask. Yet he did say, "Yes, I do grieve, but life is short for us all. He is happy in the next world, with plenty of airag and many horses. With new good eyes, he can enjoy death as he never enjoyed life."

"I hope so, too. I will keep him in my prayers."

Again Argamon's grief briefly showed, but he hooded it. Downing the last of his wine, he said, "Let us speak no more about him." He pulled me close. "I'm so glad you are safe. I never want to lose you."

"I'm glad you care for me, Argamon." I looked into his eyes and for the first time saw tenderness there—or perhaps I had been unwilling to accept it before. The fall of Kyiv had frozen my heart with sorrow; his caring, so unexpected, melted it. I felt so sad for him and Asetai that I reached up and kissed him, the only time I had ever touched him first.

He responded with a passion I could no longer resist. For over a year, he had tried to teach me to enjoy lovemaking, but it was shared grief that opened a new door to me. I wasn't expecting what happened. In a great surprising surge of pleasure, I discovered the secret that lies between a man and a woman.

Looking back, I have often wondered if I could have kept resisting him, kept denying my own body. I think I was a rarity for having taken so long. Fighting your captivity wears you out and kills you more quickly. But I yielded not just to Argamon, but to something in myself that freed me to love the right man fully one day.

WINTER, Anno Domini 1240-1241

The next morning as we were about to leave camp, a court offi
cial brought Argamon a fine mare laden with armor. He also handed
me a bundle wrapped in blue silk. "From Batu Khan," he said before
marching off. I opened it to find a pair of small leather-bound books, a set
of writing utensils, and an ink block. I opened one; its pages were blank. I
could only feel grateful, as I had almost filled Papa's book. I decided to begin
writing my full story in Batu's book, an irony I rather liked.

A small, flat object was strapped to the other book: an exquisite ikon of
my ancestor, St. Volodymyr Equal to the Apostles, the Grand Prince who
had brought Rus' into the Christian fold.

No doubt it was loot, perhaps from Kyiv herself, but the hair on my neck
prickled and tears sprang to my eyes. Papa had been named after St. Volodymyr. Did Batu know that? Was he being kind or making a cruel jest? It didn't
matter. I would treasure it always.

Riding back in Noyan Qacha's retinue, Qabul seemed to hover at the
edge of my vision. I paid him no heed. If he and Argamon would have to
"share the same bowl" for a month, where would they stay? I prayed not
in Argamon's ger. The idea of living near that man filled me with fear, so I
asked my master about it when we reached his ger.

"We'll live side by side on the next campaign, which starts within days."
He paused.

"I know you wish to be of use, and I've decided: while I'm gone you
will oversee my household. Kamileh has already passed on many duties to
you, and you know what work there is to do—I credit your friendship with
my slave women for that, at least. Your loyalty to me before Batu Khan has
earned you my trust."

So he *had* been hoping for loyalty from me. "Master, I'll try to be worthy of it."

"But," he added in a low voice, "take care while I'm gone, Sofia. If
Qabul knew what happened the night I captured you, then there's a spy
among my servitors. Don't go anywhere without Temur. He's trustworthy."
A chill ran down my spine.

Argamon and I had but a few nights of pleasure together and then the armies
were gone. It was the first time I was sorry to see him go. When the ordus followed, they would move toward the principalities of Prince Danylo of Halych.

Ironically, through listening to Argamon and Bayartou I had already
pieced together the Mongols' plans, little though it meant with no one left
to whom I could betray them. The armies would settle in northern Halych
and Volhynia for the winter and in the spring would pounce on Hungary
and Poland. The Kipchaks were Batu's first objective. He claimed that they
had committed treason by fleeing and that King Bela had affronted Mongol
honor by harboring them.

But all this talk of honor was just a stratagem, since they had always
meant to invade all the Christian lands. As for Poland, it was simply at Hungary's back and Subodai wanted no Polish armies coming to King Bela's aid.
I wondered what that coward Mikhail of Chernihiv would do now. I hoped
he would suffer some day for betraying Kyiv.

I always traveled with Q'ing-ling, so after seeing to Argamon's packing
I went to her, shadowed by Temur. As a rule we would have already been
on the move by then, but that day she seemed somewhat weary and less
able to manage. I had just begun to help when Dorje appeared at her door,
his nose red and dripping.

"Dorje, how good to see you! I thought you were on campaign with
Qacha."

"Not this time. I was ill, which is why you haven't seen me lately. I'm better now, just sneezing a little, but Qacha gave me leave to stay behind. Lady
Q'ing-ling, may I take Sofia off for awhile?"

"Yes, of course. Don't worry, Sofia, we'll cope," Q'ing-ling smiled. I bowed and followed Dorje into the icy morning.

"Come with me where we can be warm and trouble no one." He led me to a covered wagon already hitched in a line with several others. "Let us sit here and talk, and then we can ride with some of Qacha's senior servants." As we settled onto a heap of furs, Temur pushing in behind me, he asked, "How are you? I missed all the great and terrible events in Batu Khan's ordu, but I heard plenty of rumors. And you were there."

So I told him about the feast, the princely quarrel and its aftermath, even about my having to perform for Batu Khan like some dancing bear. I hardly needed to describe that quarrel, though. Dorje knew more about it than I did.

"Subodai worked out a truce," he commented at one point, "and Kuyuk and the other princes returned to the feast. But the damage was done. Kuyuk and several other princes left for Karakorum after that, which disrupted the kuriltai. Batu sent out both homing pigeons and arrow messengers to protest to Khakan Ogedai. The Mongols have such good roads and horse stations that the message may get there before the princes do. Though Kuyuk seemed not to see it, he has dishonored himself and will only meet with disgrace when he arrives."

"Well, I only wonder how such fierce warriors could behave so childishly. I wish this Khakan Ogedai would call off the entire campaign, and then all these Mongol wolves could slink back to Karakorum and quarrel there to their hearts' content!"

"We both know that won't happen."

I sat in glum silence until he added, "Do you wish to tell me what happened to you?" So, as painful as it was to recall it, I recounted Qabul trying to kidnap me, Asetai's murder, and the audience with Batu Khan. I felt the strangest mix of self-importance and grief while I talked—it was already a *story* in my mind, and I was the heroine. But the way Dorje listened, though he seemed sympathetic enough, made me feel that I was curving events to surround and enhance myself. I hated seeing my own small falsities.

But he only answered, "Qabul has behaved badly before, but this time he went too far. I think I know why. You've seen his belt to protect against thunderbolts, and under his coat he wears every amulet and charm that his mother gives him. Once when he was just entering manhood, she even followed him to Qacha's ger trying to get him to wear a new one. I had just gone inside and was still near the door. Before they came in, I heard him turn on her in anger and ask if his skills as a warrior were not enough. She said, 'Look at your father's missing eye—he's a skilled warrior. Believe me, his skills counted for nothing against dark spirits!' And then she whispered something. When they came into the ger, he was as white as ash. He's been terrified of spirits and magic ever since.

"Yulta Beki's latest prophecy was aimed straight at him, so when he received that bloody slash across his face he must have feared that loss and death awaited him next. Perhaps he thought kidnapping you would avert further danger to himself. And maybe he hoped Asetai's death would fulfill the prophecy."

I flushed with guilt. "I must confess something to you, Dorje. I've been feeling uneasy about it for some time." And I told him about stumbling over the threshold of Q'ing-ling's ger, how I feared Asetai had picked up bad luck from me.

He raised his eyebrows in surprise. "You once dismissed all Mongol beliefs as superstition and nonsense. Have you changed your mind, Sofia?"

I shrugged. "I'm no longer certain of anything. And there is more. When I was first enslaved, do you remember how I smiled back at Qabul that evening in Batu Khan's camp? You warned me then about him, but I didn't listen. Well, not long after that he smiled at me when I was in distress and I mistook it for sympathy. I was angry with Argamon, so I smiled back. I knew that woman is a snare for man, but I violated decorum without even thinking. After that Qabul mistook everything I did for secret passion, which is why he tried to seize me, including a time I never told anyone about. Asetai died because of my folly."

Dorje sighed. "My dear, you take on too much blame. It's common to believe that women are at fault for lust, and certainly many women use wiles to get their way with men. But I've seen too many men take the mere flutter of a robe for an invitation to open it all the way, and they rush in whether they are right or not! Why blame womankind for that? It's just deluded mind. Think: was it not Qabul who has continually tried to ensnare *you*? And he has been tormenting Asetai for years. Give up blaming yourself. It does you more harm than good and it helps no one else, either! Enough said, yes?"

I nodded.

"Now, will you tell me more about Selim al-Din? His very words if you can."

I was puzzled, but I did as he asked, adding, "I've not seen him since we left Batu Khan's ordu. I wish I could thank him."

"He travels with our ordu again. I'll bring him to see you. Argamon has already sent him a reward, by the way, and Qacha, too. The noyan is quite torn between his sons, but he saw that Qabul was wrong, and he had to repay Selim al-Din's kindness for helping you. Batu Khan even granted him an audience, and Selim gave him a Jewish physician who is also a master of astrology. Batu is always happy to add to his collection of such men. Yes, Selim is doing quite well, especially since Batu knows he's a spy."

I did not care if Selim was a spy. More interesting was this Jewish doctor, since I had been taught that Jews had only one goal in life: to get rich by lending money.

Several other people crowded into the back of our wagon just then, and we had to shift to the very front. With a great lurch and screeching of wheels, the cart began moving. We could not talk with each other after that, but it was a comfort just to be together.

Yet as the morning passed, I began to feel uneasy, as though something was creeping up on me from behind. I looked around wondering if Qabul could have returned and was spying on me, but there was no sign that anyone was interested in me. Yet the feeling kept growing. Finally I realized: to move west, we must cross the Dnieper near Kyiv.

By noon we were almost there. The ice was thicker than a spear's length by then, but with thousands of people, wagons, and animals upon its back, the river was groaning like a wounded creature. While I could not see the ruins, I knew they were north of us, just around the river bend and hidden behind hills. An unseen hand began squeezing my chest. The wagon ahead of us lurched between trees and down the river bank.

Just as we reached the ice, a frigid blast of wind hit my face, carrying such a smoky, putrid odor that we all covered our noses. Our wagon plunged down the bank and rocked so hard that I had to seize the side. I looked out to see what had so nearly overturned us. A frozen, half-eaten corpse stared back at me, its mouth open in a silent scream.

A matching scream rose in my throat. I half-stood and nearly flew out of the wagon as it swayed and slid on the ice. I'd have fallen under its wheels, but Temur snatched me back.

I burst into tears. If only he hadn't saved me! Now I knew what had been haunting me: how could I forget everything I had lost, even for an instant?

The heart must find ways to shield itself if it is not to turn to rock or be crushed by the woes of this world, but I did not know that yet, and mine found none. I was crushed in another way, by shame that my petty dramas and the pleasures of the flesh had chased away the grief I should be feeling. I must be damned!

All afternoon I tormented myself until I thought of Q'ing-ling. She never spoke a harsh word to anyone, was married to an idolatrous killer, and had lived amidst carnage for years. She was so good, so strong. Even though she was a heretic, she might be able to advise me, to show me how to atone for my faulty heart.

That evening I sought her out and asked for guidance. She sat silent for several heartbeats. "No one ever said that the path Christ laid out for us would be easy or even clear. But to lose confidence helps no one. I believe that no matter what, He is always in our hearts, seeing our travails and loving us without pause.

"As to your fear of damnation, I leave it to someone more learned than I am to decide about reward and punishment. But this I know for certain: we cannot act in hope for heaven or fear of hell. Some people choose to live in love and some do not, and some who call themselves Christian do not choose love.

"Then I look at Dorje, who seems to worship no god and yet acts with loving kindness at every turn, and I believe he has found Christ in his heart far more clearly than any Christian Mongol who ruthlessly slays the innocent."

Perhaps some would say her advice was heretical or simple-minded. I leave the question of heresy up to the Church, but as for simple-minded: it was never simple to follow. And at the time it gave me comfort.

"What about Argamon? I have no idea how to behave toward him when he returns."

"I understand, my dear," she said. "I've often had mixed feelings about Qacha. All I can do is love the good in him and pray for his soul. As for guilt, remember that having fallen from grace, it is our nature to put ourselves first. But in surrendering to Argamon you showed him your loving nature. And love defeats Satan.

"Besides, God chose you to be here. He uses you to redeem Argamon, so He must be glad you yielded to him."

Her advice lifted my mood a little, but that night I began to sneeze and cough, and then fever and chills felled me. I had never been so ill before, and I saw it as punishment for my sins. I was certain I would die without receiving forgiveness. But Kamileh assured me it was just a bad cold and gave me a bitter brew of wormwood and willow bark to bring down the fever. To dispel the sickness demons, she also hung a little packet of dried magnolia leaves and spices around my neck; otherwise, I might have been banished from the ger.

Dorje visited, and straightaway I blurted out my shame. He sighed. "Sofia, everyone's minds go up and down—one moment we're drowning in sadness and the next moment we're scratching an itch." I nodded, but with no spirit or understanding. "You take on such blame," he added.

"Yes and deservedly."

The old monk cautiously continued, "I've heard that you Christians have a rite of confession, as do we Buddhists. Since you have no priest to hear you, might you consider me? You once said that sharing your thoughts with me helped ease your heart."

I pondered his offer carefully. "You've been as wise as my own priest was, and much kinder. I think in such times as this, I could trust you." Still, I confessed my sins, nothing more. I was not about to share my doubts about my faith with a pagan.

After hearing my long list, Dorje smiled gently. "Sofia, consider yourself free of your guilt over the deaths of Asetai and your other people, and for all your other misdeeds. I must add something else. In Buddhism, when we do something wrong we regard shame and remorse as good first steps. We vow to do better and go on, trying to avoid repeating our error, but we don't reproach ourselves endlessly. After all, our own faults are just like everyone else's; seeing that leads to compassion for others. Look at yourself with less censure. Then you'll see what things cannot be helped and you can let them go. It's time to move on, yes?"

His words did me good. "Yes, Dorje. Thank you."

While I was ill, the Mongols were vanquishing the westernmost principalities of Rus' as if by magic. If no one stopped them, all of Western Christendom would fall. Dorje once mentioned that uprisings had swept like steppe fires through communes and villages across western Rus' and Halych. But when the peasants had killed their old masters and welcomed their new ones as deliverers, the Mongols accepted their new subjects and then set up their own, equally harsh rule.

Had Papa been harsh? I didn't know, though he had refused to force his smerdi into serfdom, unlike some princes who made laws binding them to the land to keep them from running away.

Having destroyed much of Halych, Qacha's armies returned laden with spoils. Prince Danylo's submission to Batu Khan had not protected his principality at all.

Argamon and Qabul were still obliged to live with each other, so I stayed with Q'ing-ling when he was home, although he visited us daily to boast about his triumphs. He said that Prince Danylo had fled to Hungary. Several of his cities had surrendered without resisting but the Mongols had slaughtered everyone anyway. He seemed to think this a great jest!

It made me realize that Kyiv might have suffered the same fate, too, even before Prince Mikhail had killed the envoys, and that all of Papa's efforts might have been in vain.

When Argamon paused, his mother asked, "How are things between you and Qabul?" I sat at a little distance, trying to contain my sneezes.

"Like a wolf and a tiger forced to share the same prey. Father demands that we behave with respect to each other, and he forbids me to take personal revenge since Qabul paid a huge fine for Asetai's death. Father even puts our troops far apart during battles, so none of our men can do each other any mischief …

"Mother, I may be bound to obey my father but I'll never forget. Qabul and I are enemies for life. The month is almost over, and then we return to our own gers. Batu Khan must decide what to do next." He glanced at me. "What worries me more is you, Sofia. You've never been ill before." I blinked and shrugged.

Soon he was gone again.

Dorje began bringing Selim al-Din to visit. The merchant had a new stock of jests and was able to make me laugh again.

Selim offered to teach me a board game, too. The board looked familiar, but not the pieces. "These little carved statues stand for kings and generals, war elephants, knights, chariots and common soldiers," he began, setting out the game pieces as he talked. "It's good training for planning a war or any difficult undertaking."

"Oh, we call it chess! Papa and I used to play it sometimes, but we have queens, not generals, and bishops instead of elephants. Why would they include mythical beasts?"

"Elephants aren't mythical! I've seen them. Look at this piece closely," he said, handing me the little statue. "My set is ivory, from India, and the likeness is true." Tiny horns came out of its cheeks, and a small house sat on its back, all cunningly carved.

"Now, do you wish to test yourself against this humble challenger?"

We often played together after that. I learned new ruses from him and tried out my own. A rush of delight swept over me the first time I was able to cry out 'Shah-mat'.

"So, the Shah is dead, is he? Perhaps you would care to try again and see? Allah the All Merciful surely won't let a young woman kill an old Shah twice," he laughed.

Once I was well, Q'ing-ling insisted that I do something useful, so I decided to make some wall hangings to adorn Argamon's ger. Planning how to piece the appliqués together engaged me completely, and I found that an entire day could pass without my noticing.

But one morning I awoke to the sound of wailing. Temulun was putting something into Q'ing-ling's hands. Both were pale as death. "He was poisoned, my Lady. With a piece of meat left right outside the ger. I let him out for his morning business and meant to follow right away, but I remembered you wanted me to—"

"It wasn't your fault. There are too many under her spell ready to do her bidding. I'm only surprised it took this long to find some new torment. How low she stoops!"

"Lady, what happened?" I hastened to Q'ing-ling's side. She was cradling Lu, whose tongue was hanging out, eyes staring at nothing, his little body till twitching.

"Dear God, who would do such a thing?"

"Who?" She made a ghastly noise—both bitter laugh and limitless lament. "Who but Har Nuteng? And who will believe me if I cry out against her?" She shook her head, tears rolling down her face, and handed the now-still body back to Temulun. "She has already cost me so much, yet still she is not satisfied."

The shock of this petty murder forced me to see past myself. From then on I insisted on serving Q'ing-ling and trying to comfort her in her loss, not only of her dog but of a serenity that had never before wavered.

In less than a month, the ordus reached their destination: the rich rolling lands of Volhynia north of Halych. There the armies awaited us, having left a trail of ruin behind them, some of which I had witnessed once I was well again and able to ride out with Temur: cities, villages, farms, churches, and so many ordinary lives wantonly destroyed.

Argamon and his brother had spent their month together and been separated by the time we rejoined the troops. I hoped to use Q'ing-ling's lack of spirit as an excuse to stay with her, but Argamon came for me right away. After greeting us and asking after her health, he held his hand out to me.

"Sofia, come. My slaves are packing, and you should be there. I've been ordered to move to the main camp. You'll still be near Mother." I had to follow him. The sky had laid a thick wet blanket over the world, and even the camp noises seemed blunted by moisture. The smell of smoke and animal dung and soggy felt clogged my nostrils.

In reality, when we reached Argamon's ger, no one was there and nothing was packed. Then I realized that my master wanted to take me right then. The instant we had removed our coats, he encircled me with his arms and kissed me deeply while backing me toward the divan. But when I did not respond, he stopped and pulled back. "I thought you'd be glad to see me. Are you still unwell?"

"No, Argamon. It's not easy to explain this. After you left, I came to feel guilt for betraying my people when I ... surrendered to you. I still struggle to find peace of mind."

As I sought to explain myself, his face flushed with anger and his grip tightened on me. "First, why do you still cling to 'your people'? They fell under the sword like beasts. You betrayed no one!"

"Please, when you lose someone you love, are you not sad?"

"No, I get angry! Sad is for weak foreigners, not strong Mongol warriors." He paused in thought. "Well, you were once foreign, so I must allow for your weakness."

That was too much for me. Struggling in his arms, I cried, "That has nothing to do with it! I cannot abide your lack of feeling, the way you Mongols kill and rape and destroy!"

Argamon flushed and gripped me harder. "Don't you ever judge me!"

"I didn't mean it that way! But I thought a tender understanding was growing between us when it's not me you want at all but some dumb mare to follow your song. All you want from me is to magically protect you and give you pleasure!"

Argamon's fingers dug into my arm. "It's all I *can* have! You made that clear!"

Suddenly everything seemed so hopeless. I drew a long breath and lowered my head. A lovely Persian carpet lay beneath my feet. Who had put such effort into making it? Now they were probably dust, just as Argamon and I would be someday. Why struggle?

"I was just hoping you might—" I shrugged and forced myself to look up. "It is nothing," and I leaned up to Argamon and kissed him as he had taught me. 'Nothing, nothing, just as I am nothing,' echoed my thoughts.

"That's better," Argamon muttered as he pulled me down onto the divan. While he blindly satisfied his lust, I wondered how many women he had raped or widowed or orphaned or killed while he was gone. When he finished and rolled off me, I felt utterly lost. Silence stretched between us.

Finally, Argamon turned toward me. "Sofia," he said softly, "Look at me." I unwillingly obeyed, tears stinging my eyes. How I hated weeping in front of him! "Listen. My ways are strange to you, as yours are to me. The great Chinggis Khan once said that the greatest pleasure in life is to kill your enemy, take his wealth, and hold his weeping wife and daughters in your arms. I once wanted only to be like him, but now I carry the memory of your face into every battle. Seeing it stops me from doing harm for no reason.

"When I first captured you, you were merely a means to bring me good fortune. I thought I only had to take you bodily to make you mine, but you were like a fish I was trying to grasp with my bare hands!

"Yet because of you I did become a great warrior. Batu Khan favors me, and he approves Father's plan to make me second-in-command to Kuvrat Khan. That is why we move to the central camp tomorrow." My indifference must have shown because Argamon reached out and touched my cheek.

"Listen. From the first I've watched you, though you never seemed to know it. It began because I wanted to make you mine in every way, to keep my windhorse strong and to protect my luck.

"But then I saw *you*. You still carry yourself like a princess, yet you gladly serve my mother. You befriend even the lowest slaves, and you have been loyal to me in surprising ways. I care for you, and I want you to care for me, too."

How could I resist such a balm to my heart? I put my hand to his cheek, and he took it and kissed my palm. We put our arms around each other, and he held and stroked me as I wept. He was so tender with me that I could not help responding to him.

Later I remembered Dorje's counsel. "Our own faults are just like everyone else's. From that grows compassion for others." Surely that was what our Savior had meant when he taught us to love our enemies. If I could be kind to Argamon in ways that held meaning for him, it freed him to be kind to me and to others. This I could do without betraying anyone.

WINTER TO SPRING, Anno Domini 1241

My surrender to Argamon seemed complete, and I thought myself happy. After we had relocated to the central camp, I did see Q'ing-ling daily. While the ordus rested, Argamon devoted himself to me whenever he was free. We played chess, or he took me gliding over ice and hard snow, long sheep bones bound under our boots as hunters do to catch game, but we did it just for pleasure. And passion became a sweet and abiding pursuit.

Around then came the news that Batu Khan had received a message from Khakan Ogedai. Argamon, filled with vengeful glee, announced to me, "Kuyuk is in disgrace! What a welcome his father gave him; I wish I could have seen it! Khakan Ogedai *has* to make an example of him. Our strength is our chain of command. Noyan Subodai may plan our campaigns, but our commander is Batu Khan, and insulting him as good as broke the chain!

"Now we can move forward in a great tide. Qabul is in the army that attacks Poland, far from us, while Father's ordus move into Hungary with Batu Khan and Subodai. A third army invades Hungary from the south." I knew that Qabul had been sent away but had never wanted to ask for details.

"And I'm glad I can leave Mother with you, Sofia. It eases my mind." Argamon and I smiled at each other, happy in our newfound bond.

Dorje appeared at our ger that afternoon to invite me for a walk, and the air was so crisp, the crunch of the snow underfoot so rich, the sky so cleanly blue that the thought of armies on the march seemed a distant fantasy. As usual, he wanted to gossip, this time about Batu and Kuyuk.

"I suspect they'll be enemies for life," he lisped. "But I wonder why Mongke Khan plans to return to Karakorum. He has nothing to gain by leaving. Indeed he and Batu have become great friends, and he could expect rich rewards at the end of this campaign."

"But don't you want everyone to love each other?"

"Oh, certainly, in time. Meanwhile, sticks fall from the bundle," he smiled.

"What do you mean?"

"I will tell you. When Great Khan Chinggis lay on his deathbed, he called as many of his sons and grandsons together as could come. When they were all assembled, he handed his eldest son a bundle of sticks tied together and told him to break it in half. Of course it couldn't be done. Then his second and third sons each had to try, and they too failed to break it. The Khakan sent the bundle around to every one of them, and none could break it. Then he took the bundle back, untied it, and gave each man a stick to break in half. Of course, each stick broke easily. The Khakan warned that as long as the Golden Kin worked loyally together, their empire would be as unbreakable as the bundle. But if they fell out among themselves, the empire would weaken and break apart, just like each stick. I think we are seeing the first sticks fall out of the bundle, yes?"

"I hope so, with all my heart!"

While Argamon was away with his men, Selim al-Din paid me a visit. "To travel farther west does not suit me," he said. "We can go south toward the Crimea under the protection of a party of Mongol scouts and, Allah willing, return home to Iran for a time."

"I am sorry to see you go." I had grown deeply fond of my Muslim friend—he had told me how to pronounce the word correctly—even if he did hide certain things from unbelievers like me. But since I did the same with others, how could I judge him?

A few days later, Selim came by to take his leave, exchanging courtesies with Argamon and giving us a pair of finches that, alas, died soon after. I had something to give him as well: a piece of fine white silk for a new dulband, which is what I had learned to call his head wrap. After several humbly polite refusals on his part and me politely insisting, he accepted with graceful thanks.

"Will we meet again?" I asked.

"If Allah the Compassionate wills it," he said. "May his peace rain upon you." He placed his hand on his heart and bowed farewell before joining his men and horses and camels waiting just beyond the camp. Bells tinkling from their colorful harness, the animals bore away slaves and spoils captured in Rus' and Halych.

I turned away.

Argamon was taking his son from Tsetsegmaa's arms. Kuchan crowed in delight as his father tossed him into the air and carried him over to his stallion. "A ride for my son, the future warrior!" With one hand cradling his boy, Argamon swung onto the horse's back and slowly rode in a circle while Kuchan laughed and patted its black mane.

I felt a pang of envy toward Tsetsegmaa, but if I still wished to escape someday, was it not better for me to be childless? I knew that Argamon was disappointed that I had never gotten pregnant. And with nowhere to go, did I still wish to flee? Would I welcome a child?

The call to arms came with the first thaw. The morning Argamon departed, the sun appeared in regal splendor above pleated golden clouds, throwing a thousand shafts of glory across the land and setting treetops and snowfields aflame. I had deserted the deities of sky and earth, yet they were still there, apparently blessing those who honored them.

Once again, the armies fanned out and the ordus followed behind. We passed more butchery on our journey through Volhynia and western Halych, lands just like my own. Though we avoided such things, there was no way to evade all the rotting corpses, burned manors and villages, and hacked-down orchards. It made me heartsick.

The lowlands swelled into hills and then into the mountains of Hungary. I had always dreamt of climbing over mountains, and those snow laden slopes cloaked in great wild forests were more awe-inspiring than I had ever imagined. Sometimes we passed through tunnels of trees, spangles of sunlight piercing the gloom and forest spirits darting behind mounds of snow. Sometimes we marched above the tree line, braving high passes where a long fall awaited the unwary. And far-off ranges stood like heaven-touched immortals.

A few times we passed great boulders strewn on either side of the highest passes as if giants had tossed them aside. Below them, spills of snow and rock had slid down the mountain and mangled the forest below. At first

I thought that was what mountains did in winter. But at the lower passes below the tree line, great chunks of felled trees lay on either side of the trail like tumbled walls, surely not natural. As Q'ing-ling and I rode through the first of these massive ruins, gaping in awe, she said, "This must be the second barrier."

I looked a question, so she added, "According to one of Qacha's messengers, boulder walls blocked the mountain passes—do you recall those great spills of rocks we passed? The Hungarians seemed to think they would halt the Mongol armies. But with Kin and Persian engineers to direct them, slaves soon cleared the passes. And felled trees were piled up in the lower passes, but newly enslaved woodcutters were brought to chop through them."

Back among foothills, brooks born of snow, flowers budding in greening meadows, and joyous dawn birdsong greeted us. All reassured me that Mother Earth still renews herself no matter what the Mongols might do to her.

During that journey Q'ing-ling had much free time, but without her usual duties her spirit seemed to sink lower. She seemed thinner and paler, too. On sunny days I got her to leave the ordu on short rides, accompanied by guards. With them on watch, we could sit happily by a singing meadow brook, perhaps glimpse a herd of deer flitting past like shadows, and pretend there was no war. On one such occasion, while idly poking at a mound of melting snow with a twig, I asked Q'ing-ling about her childhood.

"Oh, it's been so many years … My father was a great landowner, a scholar, and a distant relative of the Kin Emperor. We lived in a manor near Zhongdu, the capital. Our home was full of love. The land was so green and gentle in the spring. Mountains lay north of us, softly rounded and hazy in the distance. A great wall stands there, snaking on endlessly. It was built in ancient times to hold back invading barbarians, though it mostly failed. I remember a little quilted silk jacket I wore as a small child and fields of grain blowing in the sweet breeze outside the walls of our compound; a harvest festival; games and laughter with my mother and little sister; my father's kindly smile. Little more.

"My clearest memories are of the invasions, perhaps thirty years ago? Perhaps more, perhaps less: time's passage means nothing to me now. I was fourteen when refugees began to appear at our doors, begging for food and bearing terrible tales that even reached the women's quarters. A tribe of barbarians called Mongols had overrun the northernmost provinces, destroying the crops, killing or enslaving many peasants. The rest fled into cities, but those were besieged. If a city fell, the Mongols looted and burned it before putting almost every man, woman, and child to the sword—unimaginable then, but a common story now. Just as now, a few were spared and sent to warn other cities to submit. But even if a city withstood their siege, it might be stricken by plague or lack of food and water. In some places, starving people ate their own dead!

"We lived in constant uncertainty after the Mongols destroyed our defenses in the nearby mountains, even though they vanished suddenly. And rumors spread. In Zhongdu, the generals were quarreling while our emperor did nothing. Then plague struck the countryside. Many in my household died. We lost my oldest brother and my little sister, and my parents were weakened by illness and loss. I was betrothed to a young man of good family, but I never saw him after that. I sometimes wonder what happened to him.

"That spring the Mongols poured over the mountains so quickly that we barely had time to pack and slip away—it was night by then. We raced frantically for Zhongdu surrounded by hundreds, maybe thousands of others. I remember abandoned wagons looming up in the torchlight, fires burning in the dark distance, weeping children, old people left behind to die alone.

"We were lucky; our guards protected us. Father's cousin took us in when we reached Zhongdu, but there was no safety in the city. Mongol armies besieged it and burned the nearby fields and villages. Smoke choked us for days. Then they attacked. We lived near the center of the city, but even there inside the women's quarters, we could hear what was going on. We all clung to each other and wailed in fear every time we heard the great thuds and crashes and booms, the whistling arrows, the cries and screams. Some areas of the city began to burn; we could smell it. The attack went on for an entire day and night, and then silence ell. Finally a servant brought the news: the enemy was retreating. We had won!

"So Father led us home only to find our compound burned and his fields destroyed. Any servants and slaves who had stayed behind were dead. We faced starvation. In despair, he led us back to our relatives. But living in such close quarters was hard on everyone, though I hardly ever saw Father. He spent every day at the palace seeking a patron. No one seemed to need the talents of an aging scholar.

"Over the next year, with reports of Mongols sweeping over the countryside, the generals murdered our emperor and put his weak nephew on the throne, and then they turned against each other. Several died. The only good thing—or so it seemed—was that Father found work as a royal scribe, so we moved into rooms in the palace.

"And suddenly the Mongols were back. For countless days, their armies sat outside our gates and waited. I was terrified of starving or having to eat the flesh of corpses!

"But then a miracle seemed to happen. Their leader, Chinggis Khan, agreed to raise the siege in exchange for the emperor's daughter in marriage and much tribute, including five hundred fair youths and maidens. At first we rejoiced at our good fortune. Deputies were sent across our realm to find the most desirable youths and maidens, but then the emperor decided to also offer children of courtiers or minor staff, like me.

"We were lined up outside the city gates while our parents had to watch Mongol brutes wander up and down, looking us over. The stench was dreadful. I looked around and saw that the great protective ditch surrounding the city was filled with rotting corpses. I gagged and nearly fainted; some girls did. The Mongols had filled the ditch with peasants, just thrown them in alive and ridden over them to reach the city walls!

"There was a brief moment for goodbyes. Mother and I wept and held on to each other until Father made us part. He chided us for behaving so badly. After all, he was being brave. He said I should feel honored to be among the maidens sent with the Princess of the Kin. Then I was taken—dragged—away. I was not yet fifteen."

Why, if Kyiv had surrendered to the Mongols and been spared, Papa might have had to give me up in the same way! No wonder he had been so anxious to send me away. He must have known.

"So you fled from one horror into another, even more than I did."

"Yes. Like you I was both terrified and enraged. Chinggis Khan's army did not have ordus then. It was all crude soldiers on horseback. We were herded along like animals over the mountains to a rough, dry, unfriendly world. And the farther north we traveled, the worse it became until the hellish heat forced even the Mongols to stop for the summer. Until the weather cooled enough for them to take us past great deserts and mountains into Mongolia, they made us entertain them in ... various ways, while they lolled at their ease."

Her face grew rigid. "After we reached Mongolia, they continued their war against my people. I heard they killed sixteen million people—perhaps they counted ears. I doubt they counted the peasants at all, or those who starved to death with no one left to farm.

"Zhongdu was destroyed later, and probably my family with it. And now I cannot even remember my parents' faces."

All of which explained why she had been so kind to me when I arrived. We sat, each with our own memories, until I thought to ask, "What did you do in Mongolia?"

"I was given to a chieftain's daughter who was waiting to be wed to the Great Khan as the seal on some pact. I served them on their wedding night. That was how I came to his notice." Something in the way she spoke gave me a chill. I dared not ask, but this "great khan" might well have bedded my friend, too, which would explain her obsession with him.

"How did you become Qacha's wife?"

Q'ing-ling smiled softly. "Qacha first saw me at my mistress' wedding to the Khakan. He was there with Jochi Khan. He once told me he could never forget me. Over a year later, he saw me again and asked Jochi Khan to request that the khakan give me to him. My mistress had so many slaves that she cared nothing about me, so I became his. He was so dashing then—no fearsome scar yet—and I felt lucky to be given to such a promising warrior who would take care of me. I think I was pretty then."

"Lady, you're the most beautiful woman ever, inside and out!"

Q'ing-ling smoothed her hair shyly. "Do you think so? That is kind of you."

We sat in silence for a few moments more. There seemed little to ask about Qacha. Perhaps he was kind to Q'ing-ling, but he only valued his other wife for her lineage. He had certainly never won Har Nuteng's love, and perhaps that wasn't entirely her fault. I wondered about *her* life, but I could hardly ask Q'ing-ling about that. Qacha still frightened me: as cold as stone, as blind as his lost eye. Did he ever think beyond war, his men, his own pleasure?

I suddenly saw Qabul as a boy, petted and twisted by his vain, selfish mother and driven to constant toughness by his unfeeling father.

Q'ing-ling brought me back to her story. "But in the Khakan's court I found someone who became like a brother to me, who always reminded me that I come from a great civilization that will still be here after the Mongol empire crumbles into dust. I spoke of him before when I told you how Chinggis Khan found good men: Yeliu Ch'u-tsa'i. Because of him the Mongols have learned some civilized ways. He's wise and good-hearted as well as tall! I miss him."

"Was it he who told you we can sway the Mongols for the better?"

"Yes. He says that people like us are the only hope for civilization."

"That's what Dorje says, too."

"Dorje is a good man. Kamileh tried to convert him to Christianity some years ago. She was in love with him, and perhaps he with her." My disbelief must have shown. I had always thought of Kamileh and Dorje as ancient! "Don't be so surprised," Q'ing-ling laughed. "She's only about ten years older than I am. She has aged much in the last few years, and she wasn't too old to fall in love with Dorje thirty years ago. He nearly set aside his vows for her, or so he once told me. Did he ever tell you that?"

"No, he won't speak of his early life. I wonder what scars lie on *his* memory."

"I don't know, either. Hsi-hsia had fallen, and the Khakan had just died. Dorje was already in my husband's confidence. Qacha brought him straight to Karakorum for Chinggis Khan's funeral while I took care of his hearth camp and tried to protect Argamon. Qabul was already tormenting him, and Har Nuteng was causing me misery in small ways.

"With his anda Jochi Khan dead, it made no sense for Qacha to stay after the funeral, but he lingered on, reliving victories with his fellow noyans. Yeliu Ch'u-tsa'i sent me a message that my husband was in danger from Jochi's old enemies and that smiles and flattering words were fooling him. Yeliu Ch'u-tsa'i urged me to send word asking Qacha to return home as soon as Ogedai Khan was elected. Retribution might follow if enemies of Jochi turned him against Qacha.

"I was terrified! I did send word, but it was Dorje who talked Qacha into leaving. When they returned, neither would tell me how Dorje became his slave. Qacha only told me that he spared Dorje's life."

Interesting … I might ask Kamileh about him later. But I had other questions.

"May I also ask about your other children who died?"

Q'ing-ling looked down at the stream sadly. "Yes, I had two daughters and a son before Argamon was born. All three died within a year of each other, first my youngest, an infant boy, for no reason. He just stopped breathing one night while he was asleep. Qacha had his nurse tortured and killed, thinking she was a witch. Then my second daughter died of a fever. The eldest died when a horse threw her and her neck broke—she was only four. I thought I could not bear losing all of them so close together. And if there was witchcraft behind it, it couldn't have been that poor nurse. I don't know, perhaps Har Nuteng—no, that's unkind of me. But it seemed as if everything that went wrong with my children and my life happened after Qacha married her." She fell silent.

"What of Argamon? He survived."

"Yes, he did. For a long time after my baby boy died, I was unable to conceive again. Qabul was already a fat, frisky puppy when I realized I was carrying another child. Though I was so happy to be pregnant again, I was terrified something would go wrong. I even accepted the charms and amulets that Yulta Beki had always wanted me to wear. That's how desperate I was, for I never relied on him. And from the time Argamon came into this world, the shaman and Qacha both insisted I dress him as a worthless girl. Yulta Beki said it would confuse the demons that had killed my children. Argamon even wore his hair in ribbons like a girl until Qacha decided it was time to make him into a man. Qabul was so cruel to Argamon about that. He still never misses a chance to call him a little girl. But the charms and ribbons worked. The demons never got him!"

She looked straight at me. "But Qabul has caused my son pain in other ways, too, Sofia. I've wanted for some time to tell you about this, but it seemed best to wait until you cared for Argamon a little. I can tell you now. About three years ago at a spring festival, he met a young maiden his age, a lovely shy girl named Bolgana. He courted her quietly, and he had even begun to collect a bride price before he asked Qacha to approach Yulta Beki to arrange their marriage. But to his rage and dismay, Qabul had asked first, though he had never shown any interest in Bolgana before. Qacha and the shaman had already come to an agreement with her father and the bride price been sent."

"So Qabul stole her to spite Argamon?"

"To all appearances, yes. He stole her and he married her—indeed, custom demands that a young man prove his prowess by stealing his bride from her ger in the dark and outracing her father and brothers. If he can do that, she is his. And Qabul more than proved himself because, according to her younger sister Doquz, Bolgana truly did try to escape from him, but she failed.

"Qacha insisted that Argamon swallow his anger and take Doquz instead, so my son had to carry her off and marry her. My husband wanted to bind his family to their clan—he can never forget that he is not a true Mongol—and he saw this double alliance as a brilliant stroke. But how can there be true harmony of the spirit between Argamon and Doquz when she wasn't the bride he wanted?

"Qabul left the family quarters and took Bolgana to live in the east wing after that, so we rarely saw her. I thought it best, anyway, especially since it is customary for brothers to share their wives and that would never have worked between Argamon and Qabul!" I shuddered. Thank God there had never been any thought of sharing me! "But," she continued, "Bolgana seemed to suffer at Qabul's hands. At family feasts she sometimes bore bruises on her face, though if I asked her about them, she always claimed she'd had some accident.

"There's little more to tell. She died in childbirth. She hadn't yet come to full term, and she was in labor for far too many days. Her son was stillborn and terribly deformed. Qabul claimed that a host of demon mingghan had attacked Bolgana, making her go into labor too soon and turning the baby into a monster. But people always blame demons.

"I wasn't at the birthing—Har Nuteng would scarcely have welcomed me—but Doquz was. She came away grieving for her sister and deeply shaken about something. She refused to speak of it, but I heard whispers that began among the slaves. It was said that Qabul's constant cruelties had slowly shriveled Bolgana until she preferred dying over giving him a child."

I shuddered. "I wish I had never even looked Qabul in the eye!"

"Sofia, I must be honest with you. As little love as I bear for him, I think that in his own way Qabul did care for her. He may have married her to hurt Argamon, but her death seemed to make him truly unhappy. After that he passed beyond mere selfishness and grew twisted and cruel.

"Argamon kept the deep hurt of losing Bolgana to himself. He once told me it was both unmanly and dangerous to show any feeling. Until you came into his life, he was becoming almost as hard and cruel as Qabul."

Q'ing-ling's story was like a door opening and spilling light into a dark room of secrets. "Thank you. I might not have cared before, but now it means much to me."

"I knew a time would come when it would." Q'ing-ling smiled. "I felt a link with you from the first, and it continues to grow. I've come to think of you as my daughter, and it fills an aching hole in my heart left by all my little ones' deaths."

"And you have become the mother I lost when I was small," I said, feeling both glad and heartbroken. We shared a moment of such love that it remains one of my sweetest memories.

Once the ordu reached the broad flat plains of Hungary, the regular rhythm of camp life returned and Q'ing-ling and I could no longer ride out together. I loved this land that so resembled the steppes of Rus'. And though snows assailed us once or twice, they soon melted or turned to rain, and in turn the rain gave way to sunshine. With the grasses spreading carpets of vivid green and wildflowers adorning them, the world kissed my eyes with color. I could have been rejoicing in beauty every day. Instead, our ordu again had to find routes to avoid the destruction, but why repeat myself describing it?

That woodland conversation with Q'ing-ling also haunted me. Now I was curious about Dorje's past. I knew he would never tell me, so finally I took Kamileh aside and asked her.

"No, I cannot tell you. Ask him yourself," she said.

"But I need to know now, and I have an important reason. And he's with Qacha, so I cannot ask him." I thought to impress her with this "important reason"—namely my curiosity—but Kamileh only shook her head.

"Why won't you? Is it because if you tell how you know, I'd also find out you were once in love with each other?" She looked at me sharply, as if to see whether I was mocking her in any way. I kept my gaze steady and sincere until she softened.

"No, that's not why. It's a bad, bad story, that's all!"

"I've seen enough bad things by now not to be shocked by the past."

"All right, I'll tell you. But you must promise you'll never let Dorje know I did. And no questions about him and me. That is no concern of yours!"

"Yes, I promise. You are always so good to me, Kamileh!"

"Wait until I tell you before you say that," she answered tartly. "It was because of that new king of Hsi-hsia: his father had promised to send troops to Chinggis Khan, but he was dead and the new king refused, so the Great Khan came after him! Jochi Khan was dead, and the Khakan sent Qacha's tuman as a loyalty test.

"Hsi-hsia fell, but when it was almost defeated, Chinggis Khan fell off his horse and was hurt to the death. While he was dying, he ordered his noyans to punish the entire kingdom, even though the king was coming to him to submit. I think they flayed him alive when he arrived! And then—well, before killing every one of them, the Khakan's soldiers raped all the soldiers of Hsi-hsia.

"Oh, don't look so shocked. You know about Sodom and Gomorrah! What else can you expect of Mongols when they do the same to their animals?

"Anyway, wherever they went they killed, looted, destroyed and did all sorts of bad things. This time the soldiers wrecked holy places, too. People had fled to Dorje's monastery for refuge, but even inside the shrine room, Qacha's troops killed them. The abbot was in their midst praying for them. When Dorje tried to shield his abbot from the soldiers with his body, they laughed at him and beat him for sport.

"Then they dragged the few monks that were left outside to behead them before Qacha. Most monks wept and prayed, not for themselves but for their murderers, knowing that terrible hells awaited them. Others shook with fear, while their fellows tried to comfort them. And then there were only two left: the abbot and Dorje. The captain of the jaghun knew Dorje had tried to save his teacher by just standing in front of him, and he thought it would amuse Qacha to make the foolhardy monk watch his abbot die. I cannot think of this without seeing him with his teeth knocked out, his mouth all bloody, and headless corpses all around him. Horrible!" We both shuddered.

"But his abbot died with dignity and calm. And just before the blade fell upon his neck, he turned and smiled at Dorje and ... he smiled back!

"Qacha was so surprised that he spared Dorje. He kept him for several days as a curiosity, but when he saw how fast he was mastering Mongol speech and that he could read and write, he put him to work. Dorje became Qacha's translator, too."

"But why did Dorje smile, Kamileh?"

"It makes no sense, does it? What *he* said was that his abbot's smile stopped his mind and melted his heart. He lost all care for his life or death, and he was filled with love for everything and everyone—even for Qacha's murdering soldiers. He told me that as he walked forward to meet the bloody blade, he saw only 'terrible beauty, terrible purity, and terrible compassion.' He said it was his abbot's final and greatest teaching."

That story haunts me to this day.

One day Qacha and his regiments returned to repair equipment and add to their supplies. Argamon rode in, this time beside his father and Kuvrat

Khan, radiant about something—who knew what? He saw me among the other women and smiled with such joy that I realized he was looking ahead to being with me.

And I smiled back, seeing in my mind's eye a little boy in ribbons, first trying to fend off the cruelties of an older, stronger brother and later losing the girl he loved to him. I even felt faintly jealous of this long-dead girl who had captured Argamon's heart.

Alone with him after the feast, I utterly melted in his arms. Afterward he said, "Once before a battle, waiting with my men in silence to attack, I heard the song of a lark so high above that its voice seemed part of the sky. A joy sprang into my heart unlike anything I'd ever known before. And I thought of you, and my joy was complete."

A secret lake of sorrow evaporated. "I too feel such joy, Argamon, now, with you." I did not know I was merely reflecting his passion.

But my words acted like Greek fire on his lust and ignited mine in turn. For the next few days, I plunged into a new world where every sense was drenched in honey, where I utterly forgot myself in pleasure. Though he was gone most of each day and camp life continued as always, I thought no farther than his bed.

Even after the army left, my body smoldered with memory for days. But soon we were traveling again, avoiding destruction, and the embers of my lust died. From nowhere the pain of losing Papa arose afresh. Yes, I realized, I could lose myself in passion, but war and ruin would not go away. And confronted by it, I either felt too much pain or nothing at all. Both extremes frightened me.

At least the world was full of glory. If the sun shone when I was sad or if it rained when I was happy, were both not reminders to see beyond my own pain and pleasure? If God did not listen to me, I could still listen to Him through moments of beauty, from sparrows darting across the sky to grasses sparkling with morning dew.

Without warning, Qabul returned to Qacha's ordu. As ill luck would have it, I was stepping out of Q'ing-ling's ger when he rode into camp trailed by a few of his men. His left arm was in a sling, his face was gray with pain, and he was cloaked in such a cloud of bitterness that I could feel it. I darted back inside, already afraid.

By the next day, gossip had reached Q'ing-ling's ger. I heard it from her attendants while we sat and sewed. She was outside speaking with a messenger from Qacha or they might not have dared talk about it, but each was bursting either with curiosity or news.

"How did it happen?" asked someone.

"Just as Yulta Beki predicted," said another, shaking her head. "Danger, loss—and a storm, too! Qabul's injury isn't even from battle. I hear he ordered some soldiers to throw a bridge across a river, but it was sleeting and work slowed down. He got angry and tried to strike one of them—shocking, I know—and he slipped in the mud and hit the pile of logs. They fell on him and one shattered his left arm. Only now is he well enough to come here. He's covered in shame!"

Temulun added, "As he should be! And did you see his arm? It's all twisted."

Several women nodded, and one added, "He may never be able to draw a bow again. I wonder if his fighting days are over. A just reward for—"

Just then Q'ing-ling came inside and the chatter stopped, but I had heard enough. I wished we had never moved to the central camp! Well, I would not have left with Q'ing-ling's spirit often so low, so I must make the best of it.

Over the next few days, I tried to avoid Qabul, which was not just awkward but impossible. The first time, I had left Q'ing-ling's ger to fetch something from one of the wagons and he appeared around its corner as if he had been waiting for me. My heart leapt into my throat, and I fled back inside. After that our paths kept crossing too often to be by chance.

Luckily he began disappearing all day long. Once I saw him galloping out of camp alone, forcing his mangled arm to draw his bow—such stubborn resolve.

Qacha and Argamon returned to the ordu after almost a month's absence, and I went back to my master's ger. The next night the noyan held a feast for his family. Because Qabul sat on one side of his father, beyond my view, I could almost forget he was there—until he moved suddenly and drew my eyes to his twisted arm. I pitied him briefly. Alas, just then Qacha turned to speak to Argamon, and I think Qabul saw me. My feelings must have shown, though I never looked him in the eye.

After the feast, Argamon and I returned to his ger and drifted to sleep in each other's embrace. But later I awoke needing to relieve myself. I crept outside and inhaled the cool perfume of night. A man stood in the shadow of a nearby ger. Thinking he was a guard on patrol, I made my way into the grasses between the wings of the sleeping camp. It was farther to walk, but I hated the foulness of the midden. Half-asleep, I had forgotten all about Qabul. Moonlight painted each stalk of grass silver, a nearby stream burbled quietly, and the world seemed so peaceful.

When I was done, I was about to stand when a shadow fell over me. Qabul was staring down at me like a serpent eyeing its prey. He stank of drink and was swaying badly. I slowly stood and backed away, hoping he was too drunk to be a threat. When I judged I was far enough away, I tried to dart around him, but he was too fast. His good arm snaked around me and pinned my arms to my sides. Before I could scream his mouth locked hard over mine. I fell back and he fell onto me, knocking the wind out of my chest. As I regained my breath and tried to scream, he clamped his hand over my mouth. The stench of liquor almost overpowered me, and his weight crushed the breath from me. Even hampered by his hurt arm, he was so much stronger than I was.

"See, Princess, I told you our time would come," he whispered. "You could never stop wanting me, just as I never stopped wanting you. I saw it tonight at the feast, and I saw it again when you came out of the ger just as I willed it. You knew I was waiting, and you led me here. Now you can finally have me. Despite appearances and all the twists of fate, the prophecy about you always leads you straight to me. The bond between us was sealed by Tengri's spark. That bond can never be broken."

He shoved my legs apart with his knees while I kicked and pounded feebly with my fists, and he whispered, "That's right, that feels good, little dove. Do it some more." Struggling with his left arm to force my robe over my hips, he added, "I followed you and little-girl Argamon tonight. I listened at your ger, to the two of you fucking. Now it's time for you to have a real lover! When I fuck *my* woman, if I like the way she performs I don't slit her throat. That's how I make sure she'll satisfy me. And you'll love how I do it." He laughed knowingly.

Now I fully saw his twisted nature. Not even his drunkenness could account for this. He *liked* making me afraid, and he meant his threat. I was certain he would kill me. I almost fainted with fear.

Just then a shadow crossed the moon: an owl sailing close over our heads. In silence it dove, caught a mouse, and flew away. The little creature gave a faint death shriek, and Qabul heard it. He pulled his head back sharply, and perhaps he saw my terror. Or perhaps he felt an omen. Whatever it was, he suddenly dropped his cruel mood.

"No, little princess, I was merely jesting. I mean you no harm. You'll never suffer at my hands, not ever." He slowly lifted his hand from my mouth and rolled partly off me, pushing my robe up further and seeking my privates. "No, you are all mine now. And you'll bear my sons, invincible warriors!"

I gasped, "You'll never have such sons. You can breed only monsters like yourself!" I was not thinking of Qabul's deformed son, but I think I cried out the only thing that could have stopped him. Qabul flinched away just enough for me to club his groin with my knee. As he doubled up in pain, I wrested free and leapt up, hearing a ripping sound and feeling searing pain on my scalp. I ran like a hunted deer. Although Qabul still lay on the ground moaning drunkenly, I could almost feel his tiger's claws at my back. Not until I flung open the door to Argamon's ger and threw myself inside did I feel safe.

Argamon sleepily wrapped his arms around me as I lay down, shivering badly. A spot on my scalp burned like fire—when I felt it, my finger came away bloody. Qabul had torn a scrap of skin and several strands of hair from my head. At first I wondered where that guard had disappeared to. He should have heard something—or had that been Qabul himself and not a guard at all? Was that why he had spoken of my coming out to him?

How I wished I could waken Argamon, but for a host of reasons I did not dare, starting with the fact that I had unwittingly fed Qabul's fantasy by my actions. No one would understand my wanting to avoid the midden, so how could I explain myself, even to Argamon? Qabul's story would make far more sense to a Mongol than mine. Even if Argamon believed me, he might try to kill his brother, and I wanted no more spilled blood on my conscience! If Argamon only accused his brother of rape, it would still cause problems. Qacha already saw me as trouble, and that would further set him against me *and* throw suspicion on Argamon, who stood to gain by his brother's downfall.

Yet to live in the same camp with Qabul meant he might attack me again. I had no idea how far he would go. It was said that men had killed other men just to obtain their wives because the penalty for murder among royalty was merely a heavy fine like the one Qabul had paid for Asetai, whereas the sentence for fornication was death. I wasn't sure if the law applied to stealing concubines, but what if Qabul grew bolder and tried to kill Argamon? I lay for the rest of the night, worrying. In the end I decided to tell Dorje.

I sought him out the next day. He shook his head at my story. "Were you speaking of anyone but Qabul I'd hardly credit it, but I know him too well. This injury to his arm has affected his mind as well as his body. I see your reasons for not telling Argamon. Whatever he did to seek justice, it would provoke Qabul or his supporters to exact revenge. But if you fail to do anything, Qabul will surely try something wicked again."

"He didn't threaten me simply because he was drunk, did he?"

"No. Qabul has developed a name for cruelty to women. He has behaved worse than ever on this campaign. He's never been the same since—" He stopped.

"I know about the girl he stole from Argamon. Lady Q'ing-ling told me."

"Something happened between them, something that poisoned Qabul's feelings toward women and destroyed her. Rumor has it that Bolgana somehow unmanned him. Since her death he seems unable to love a woman in the normal way. He had Yulta Beki make offers to different nobles for one of their daughters, but each time he changed his mind without explanation and in a way that cast doubt on the girl's good name. Far worse is what I've heard he does to captive women he brings back from raids. He always kills them after he tires of them—which is sometimes the same night if they don't satisfy him—and who would speak out against him for killing a slave?"

My whole body grew cold. Now I understood the line from the poetry battle: repairing a broken sword with hot blood. And all this time had Qabul expected me to make him into a new man, to prove he could be with a woman in the normal way and sire normal offspring, and had I—*when I*—failed to produce any children, would he have killed me, too? What might he have done last night had I not escaped?

"Dear God, what should I do, Dorje?"

He frowned, deepening the creases on his face. "Let me think about this. Argamon doesn't leave again for a day or two, so stay close to him and Temur until then."

I did as I was told, mostly hiding inside Argamon's ger for the next two days. On the morning of his departure, it was raining and he told me not to come outside. After a long kiss, he dashed to his horse and left, rain streaming down his oiled felt cape.

By midmorning the ordu was ready to follow the army. The rain had stopped, and creamy clouds were parting to reveal a sky of delicate milky blue. As the ordu compacted into travel form, I nudged Little Liubyna into a trot to join Q'ing-ling's party, trailed by Temur and wishing I had eyes on all sides of my head. If Qabul had spies in the camp, I was too alone, too exposed to invisible threat, even with most of the soldiers gone. Temur was so grim and hard-faced that I never really felt safe with him. By ill luck, when I joined Q'ing-ling, there was Qabul riding next to his mother. He stared directly at me. I cringed.

"While Argamon is gone, may I stay in your ger with you again?"

"Of course, you're always welcome."

She looked over at Qabul. "Dorje came to me and told me what Qabul did. My women will keep an eye on him and his mother for you."

"You are so good to me. Once again I bring ill luck with me."

"No, Sofia. Ill luck has hovered over this family for over twenty years. You've done nothing but walk the narrow path of goodness, while he who would ambush you has been exposed for what he truly is! Ignore Qabul and tell me one of your Rus' fables while we ride, perhaps that strange one about the Baba Yaga and her chicken leg hut."

SPRING TO SUMMER, Anno Domini 1241

everal days passed, and Dorje seemed to have vanished. I was surrounded by women at all times and only saw Qabul at a distance,
but my lack of freedom began to chafe. Then one sunny morning,
a pair of messengers arrived from Batu Khan carrying two short letters.
Q'ing-ling and I sat together while I read and reread them in disbelief. Finally
I looked up at her.

"Well, now we know where Dorje is. This first letter summons me to
Batu Khan's ordu to be a translator. I'm to accompany these soldiers. The
second letter is from Dorje, and it says that he asked Qacha's consent to
serve under Batu Khan, since hundreds of prisoners are being questioned.
Batu was glad to use him, and when Dorje suggested I might also help, the
khan welcomed the idea. Dorje says I'll be safe there, but I don't want to
leave you! And why would I want to question prisoners?"

She looked as dismayed as I felt. "I'll miss you, too, but you must obey
the khan."

Soon I was packed and riding off between two battle-scarred veterans,
one a flat-nosed ruffian, the other, a shifty-eyed rascal. I kept casting fearful sidelong glances at them. Oddly, they bore scars all over their chins and
upper lips like Bayartou's and Temur's.

At least I felt freer after being almost imprisoned in camp. A brisk gallop over the broad countryside was a joy, especially since we mostly crossed empty lands untouched by war. And I had a normal saddle! The few people we saw fled in terror, so greatly did they fear Mongols. My guides found this amusing and discussed chasing a few to kill for sport, but luckily they knew their duty was to get me to Batu Khan.

That night, seated around a small campfire, I mustered the courage to ask my escorts about their battle scars. They both burst into laughter. "These are not battle scars, Lady," answered Shifty Eyes. We cut our faces to keep our beards from growing. Most of us common soldiers do it. Beards and mustaches are just in our way."

I had to laugh, too. After that they tried to outdo each other with gallantry to me, even gathering soft grasses to pile up under my bedding. I awoke in the middle of the night and heard one of them softly singing a protection song outside my small tent. Clearly my worry for my safety had been misplaced.

After two days, that first glorious gallop turned into a bone-rattling ride. I felt we had covered a shocking distance, but my escorts complained that we were taking too long. When I retorted in turn that, on the contrary, we were traveling too hard and too fast, Shifty Eyes laughed, "This is but a pleasure trip. We ride much farther than this in one day—one of our best ruses. These fools think we have twice our true numbers because we strike in one place one day, ride hard the next, and reappear far away on the third!"

Ruffian added with a grin, "They are so easy to trick. The night before a battle, we light twice the fires we need and they think our armies are double their size. Or we give a false sense of our numbers by placing stuffed armor on extra horses. Our enemies take them for real soldiers and flee headlong into ambush!"

"But that's cheating!"

"War is not a game that follows rules! War is to win," Ruffian smiled grimly.

Soon we began passing ordus spread over the valleys, and near sunset we reached Batu Khan's camp some distance from a tree-lined river. A huge gold rectangular tent in its center glowed in the waning sun's rays. Apart from this surprising sight, his war camp was laid out around the great tent in the same pattern as a full ordu.

Hills rose on the far side of the river, crowned by a beautiful little city with pearly walls and towers gleaming in the late sunlight, flags fluttering bravely from their ramparts. Shifty Eyes said he thought it was called Buda. "There was another city on this side of the river just across from it. It was a pretty little town when we took it—nothing left now!

"It was called Pest," added Ruffian. "Its so-called holy men came out and waved bones and other bits of dead men at us—vile! We had to raze the city to purify ourselves, though we kept some women for sport!" He laughed in a way that made my skin crawl.

When we entered the camp, the soldiers were taking their ease, if you could call it that: many men in rut, a handful of poor captive women—and right out in the open! By the time my guides had led me to the Khan's central camp, discovered that I was to see Dorje, and found him, it was nearly dark and I had seen and heard things that made my stomach turn. I was ready to go back and face Qabul rather than stay there.

"This is a haven?" I asked the old monk without even greeting him.

"Sofia, I had no idea you'd ride into the middle of a victory celebration. Those poor women! It is appalling indeed. At least you didn't arrive right after the battle when men were beheading captives." I groaned. "But it is good that you're here. Our translators don't understand Hungarian, and most captives speak no other language. A few who speak Rus' or Latin can translate for their fellow prisoners, but it's taking forever and I fear Batu Khan will simply kill them all. You are much needed—although part of the time you may attend the khan since he has taken such a liking to you."

"Dorje, I don't want to question prisoners *or* serve Batu Khan! And why go to such lengths for these people? I pity them, but they're doomed, anyway. Why not just end their misery? Q'ing-ling needs me more than they do."

He stopped and faced me. "Sofia, here you're safe from Qabul. Q'ing-ling has servants who love and protect her, but here are people in need who could end up changing their Mongol masters' outlook. If someone can temper even one person's savagery, it helps everyone who suffers under the Mongol yoke. Is that not a pressing reason to be here?" I bowed my head in shame.

"Now, come meet some of the other translators." Dorje led me to their campfire and seated me near the same woman who had translated to Batu Khan when I saw 'Uncle' Dmytri.

"Welcome Sofia, everyone," he said. "This is Toramun. She's a Volga Bulgar. Most of her people were put to the sword just before the Mongols invaded Rus'." She nodded to me and passed me a bag of airag and a crude cup.

"The yellow-haired man beside her is English John. He's from an island far to the west. After gambling all his money away, he drifted east and entered the Khan's service. He was sent to demand King Bela's submission and barely escaped with his life. A golden tongue saved him." English John bowed and winked at me.

"The man with the shaven head on the other side of the fire is Kipchak Kchiia." Kchiia wiped his mouth and smiled ironically at me, his former enemy.

"And the woman next to him is Maria. She's half Greek, half Venetian and hails from the Crimea." And so on until I had met a good dozen translators from across the world.

"You may have a chance to learn from them while you're here. We're quite the odd flock of birds, none alike, learning to chirp in each other's native speech. And tomorrow I am to bring you to Batu Khan. You probably saw his new tent; he captured it from King Bela. I hear the king fled south out of Hungary."

"Did Prince Mikhail of Chernihiv flee with him?"

"Possibly—that's one thing I don't know. Here, eat up."

Gloomily gnawing on a meat strip someone had handed me, I listened to words drifting around me. Maria, a handsome woman with dark hair bound back, and Kchiia, who was as homely as soap, seemed drawn to one another. At least they sat closer than necessary while they compared the way to say such-and-such in Kipchak and what she called Veneziano. English John was telling Toramun about some recent incident.

"I almost lost my head to the ax that time! Any of King Bela's German allies would gladly have done it. It's a shame the king didn't listen to me, but he at least saved me from the block. I wonder when I truly will meet my end."

"You never know. I still feel pain from that arrow in my shoulder—remember when I was sent to Riazan? They never even let us inside the gates. It was pouring rain, and I had to shout. I was still calling to them when a wall of arrows came at us. My escorts and I had to flee. One fell before he had time to turn—an arrow in the eye—but they got me home. I was feverish for days, but I survived that time."

"Well, here's to no tomorrows," said John, raising his cup of airag.

"To no tomorrows," everyone cried. I raised my cup, too.

After supper Toramun took me to the ger used by the lesser women translators and showed me a place to lay my sleeping mat and quilts. "It's crowded, but you'll get used to it. A few menials serve us all. If you prove your worth, you can earn a ger of your own, like mine over there. Call on me if you need to know anything." I bowed thanks to her for her kindness but spent a dismal night amongst strangers, dreading the dawn.

The next morning Dorje took me to the khan. *His* area was as grand as ever. An assortment of nobles sat with him in the huge gilded tent, whose walls were lined with golden hangings crafted in Hungarian style. The khans—fat old Subodai, Batu Khan's brothers, and a few others—were taking their ease. Many were drunk already.

Batu set down a huge goblet of liquor. "Welcome, little princess. Ah, not so little, now; you're growing into a young woman." A few of his company laughed knowingly. "Do you like my new tent? King Bela left it as a gift for me after we defeated his troops. I believe I'll send some of my men to find and reward him for all the warriors I lost. I must offer him my gratitude." Which meant that Batu's army would pursue King Bela to the end of the earth. When they caught him, and they would, they would roll him up in a carpet and suffocate him or trample him to death with horses so as not to spill any royal blood, just like that Alan khan.

He turned to a Turkish man in a tall, narrow hat who was seated at a low table nearby. "Mahmud, here is the young woman I spoke of who will help you with your work." Mahmud put down his ink brush and gathered a sheaf of papers together before standing and nodding to me. Batu dismissed me with a wave.

I cupped my hands and genuflected before following Mahmud to the tent entrance. He paused there and said, "I am told that you speak several languages. Can you write any of them?" I nodded. "Good, you can use them when you write decrees to the khan's subject peoples. And sometimes you will copy out messages to other ordus, though today you'll merely be making lists of captured goods and people. And every now and then you will question prisoners." This was good news, for it meant I wouldn't be around the khan or his captives very often. Dorje's plan might not be a disaster after all.

Just outside, a mustached man wearing a dulband was waiting. Mahmud handed him the papers. "Yusuf Ibn al-Jabar will take you over to the ger."

The new man, likely Persian by his name, bowed in my direction and led me toward a ger set at the edge of Batu's court. "Here is where we secretaries work," he said.

Three colorful shamans' gers stood together across the meadow along with several smaller tents. Sounds of chanting floated from one of them. "What are all those tents near the shamans' gers?" I asked.

"Oh, they house holy men. Batu Khan has collected them from every faith to seek blessings from their gods and spirits. I know that two Christian priests live over there, because one of the khan's sons worships Christ. There is also, praise Allah, a mullah who keeps the true word of God alive here."

"Could either priest be from Rus'?" Hope rose in my heart.

"I do not know, but you can go over when your work is done." Inside the ger, I found low tables where several men and a few women sat. He left me under the direction of a senior copyist, who sat me down and told me what to do.

For most of the morning I copied out lists of goods and newly enslaved people whose skills were needed, along with orders to send them to particular ordus. That afternoon we made copies of orders to various branches of the army, but these were in code. We wrote on real paper. In Rus' we had used birch bark for such lowly writing and parchment for Scriptures or histories. It seemed wasteful to use paper, but it was probably taken as loot.

Ibn al-Jabar came and went among us, collecting and, I supposed, sending things out by courier. It was dull work. I felt like a cat being held against its will, feigning compliance when all it wanted was to run away.

Someone entered the tent and greeted me by name in the speech of Rus'. I looked up. To my joy it was Commander Dmytri, dressed like a Mongol but for his full black beard. "Uncle!" I cried.

He strode over and bowed to me. "I heard you had just arrived, Princess Sofia, and I had to come see you before I leave."

"I am so happy to see you well! I never knew what happened to you—and where are you going?" My pent-up feelings escaped into words. "Oh, Uncle Dmytri, it is so horrible here. I am here to help Batu's staff with the translating, but—words fail me! I cannot bear more viciousness! And Batu Khan toys with me like I am his next meal!"

Dmytri looked puzzled. "Princess Sofia, this is what war is like even among us Rus'. Why, you are lucky to be under the protection of a great man like Batu Khan."

Blood rushed to my cheeks. "Well, my father was incapable of such cruelty! And how has Batu Khan transformed from a monster into a great man?"

Dmytri seemed taken aback. "Only a great man can achieve such great victories! Make peace with your destiny, Princess. Mine kept me at Batu Khan's side until I ceased to amuse him. He could have had me killed then, but instead he sends me home to help my Prince rebuild Halych. Had I resisted, I would be dead today instead of a free man."

"He freed you? You are so lucky!" I looked around to see if anyone was listening and whispered, "Could you take me with you? I hate it here so much."

Dmytri shook his head. "No, Princess, I could never betray the khan like that."

"So loyalty to Batu Khan is more important than loyalty to a fellow Rus'? After the way the Mongols betrayed Prince Danylo's trust over Halych?"

He frowned. "Princess, the khan would suspect me right away. His men would bring us back, and then he would punish us both, probably kill me. Your fate is kind, to be a concubine to a young man destined for renown, for I hear that the khan thinks highly of your Argamon. You should be grateful."

"Please, Uncle Dmytri, there must be some way you could help me escape. For the sake of my father's memory—he would have done the same for you or any Rus'!"

"No, you ask the impossible." Dmytri's voice rose, along with the color in his cheeks. "Your father would have said the same thing in my place. And you credit his memory too highly. *He* betrayed *my* Prince Danylo for that fool, Prince Mikhail. And then when he called on us for aid, he made a great show of being the wise prince, but he was just another petty noble grasping at power. Great God, he treated you like a son; did he never tell you his ambitions, especially since you were part of them?"

"What do you mean?"

"He was waiting to seize the Golden Throne for himself. Once he found the right ally, some prince powerful enough to support his bid for power, you would have been married to the man straightaway. And when he called for our aid in the end, he deluded himself into thinking Prince Danylo would support *him* as Grand Prince."

"I cannot believe it! You have lived too long among men who think only of themselves and betray each other like beasts." I sat back down and picked up my brush. Dmytri looked down at me in surprise. "Go!" I shouted. He shrugged and strode out.

I worked through a mist of tears. Why did people justify their wars and cruelty and pettiness by belittling others? Argamon had said the same hurtful thing long ago. To me, Papa was everything good, and I hated it when others sowed doubts about him! How bitterly I missed him right then. I tried to recall his face, but a gray veil had fallen over his image and even his strength and love for me seemed dim. Dmytri had spoken rightly about one thing, though. Why could I not accept my fate?

Worse, Ibn al-Jabar saw our quarrel and Dmytri's hasty departure and came over to speak with me. "How do you know him?" I shrugged. "Dmytri is a good man. Word is that he often stayed Batu's hand when the khan wished to destroy certain cities in Halych."

So I had judged Dmytri too quickly and too harshly. Besides, once I had calmed down, I realized that he was right in refusing me. And was not making his peace with Batu Khan just what I had done with Argamon? As for betrayal, was I not ready to fly from the Mongols at the least opportunity? Where was my loyalty to my master, who *had* earned it? Even Dmytri's cruel words about Papa were only petty gossip. He had never known my father well. Nor could I make up for my unchristian behavior to him, because when I went to search for him once my duties were over, he had already left the camp.

Worse, I realized that I had no idea whether I still was a Christian when so many doubts clung to my heart like burrs. Then I remembered: there was no need to despair about my faith when a true spiritual guide might live nearby. I must seek him out soon. Yes, confessing my sins and resolving my doubts would surely console me and renew my courage.

The next day Ibn al-Jabar, seeing how upset I still was, kindly gave me leave in the afternoon to visit the holy men's tents. To my delight I found the right "church" easily: a little ger with an Orthodox cross marked on its door. I knocked, and a voice bade me to enter. It was dark inside and almost empty but for some felt bedding rolled up to one side and a small altar with candles, incense, and a few ikons upon it where the priest was praying. Finishing his devotions, he turned to me with a warm smile. He was old but pink-cheeked and vigorous. Raising his hands in a gesture of welcome, he peered at me. "Why, you must be the princess from Kyiv. Welcome, daughter. I am Father Kyril."

I sank to my knees before him, certain I had been blessed already. "I come seeking spiritual advice, Father. Since the Mongols captured me, I have had no one to speak with about my faith, and I sorely need instruction."

"I am at your service. Do you wish to confess your sins?"

I nodded, the lump in my throat almost strangling my words. It was less a confession than a flood of grief and confusion, as if a dam had broken: parting with Papa, the massacre at the rapids, Argamon raping and finally seducing me; my rage and horror at the brutality of the world I was trapped in; my guilt over the dead—and the living, remembering my harshness toward Dmytri; my mixed emotions about Argamon, my loss of faith in the harmony of this world, and my doubts about God. Only the friendship of Dorje and Q'ing-ling stood out as lights in my dark world.

Father Kyril was visibly moved. He stood in thought for a good while. "My daughter, clearly you have humility and a sorrowful heart, and I forgive you in the name of our Lord God and our Savior, Jesus Christ. But you must banish your doubts, for did our Father not send us His only Son to save us as proof of His love? We pass briefly through this world of pain, and God's plan for us is far beyond our understanding. But He loves you and therefore chastises you for your own good. Pain purifies us. Never forget that suffering is noble and that we must accept our lot just as the first saints of Rus' did.

"However, I fail to see how you can blame yourself for the deaths of the other people in your party. Greater forces were clearly at work, and you must no longer cling to your guilt or you will fall into another sin, that of a particularly twisted pride." His words were a true balm to my heart. But then he added, "Your fall into slavery is part of God's plan for you. You must pray for deliverance in the afterlife and try not to be stained by your master's wicked and carnal outlook.

"What worries me most is the power your two friends have over you. However good you think their intentions are, one is a pagan who denies the existence of God; and the other is a heretic doomed to the agony of eternal separation from Him. They are wicked influences sent by Satan to lead you astray."

My face must have revealed what I felt. They had saved my life and given me heart in the darkest times. If anything they were the only signs of divine mercy I had received! Surely if Father Kyril knew them, he would understand. "Father, please do not condemn my friends for their religion. They are good people."

The priest shook his head. "I know them both. That Dorje is a sly gossip and an idolater, and Lady Q'ing-ling is under the sway of that Nestorian heretic, that lying drunkard, Mar Sauma. I would gladly help her find true faith, but she is lost to all hope."

"But when Mother Mary visited Hell, she had compassion for pagans and heretics—"

"My daughter, that is only a tale for the simple folk. You must live with your masters, but you must never trust them, for they will lead you astray. You must constantly pray for forgiveness and submit to God's will. These are the best penances a captive can perform."

I wanted to protest that I had been praying desperately for more than a year. Instead, I drew a long breath, trying to see how to submit to Father Kyril's direction, though I could not see why he would say such harsh things about Dorje and this Mar Sauma person. And how was I to distance myself from Argamon's touch or Q'ing-ling's gentleness? Why, the Father himself must have given in somehow if he was praying for Batu Khan! Just as disappointing was his command simply to banish my doubts. I could not.

I stood up to leave. "Thank you, Father Kyril. You have made some things clear to me. I must go now." I bowed, crossed myself at the altar in the old way, and kissed each ikon in turn. They gazed back at me sadly. The priest blessed me and I left, resolving to attend Mass when possible and to pray more and ask forgiveness for my sins. Even if I had doubts, it couldn't hurt to try. But I could not obey his command about my friends. I sighed, giving up one more hope. If this was truly what God wished me to do, then I was doomed to eternal Hellfire.

I looked back. The priest had already returned to his own prayers.

A defiant thought, one I tried to blame on Satan, flitted past. In the tale that Father Kyril had dismissed, Mother Mary had found a host of monks and priests in Hell, too.

Outside, I looked around. Large gers for the khan's shamans occupied the central place of honor. A dispirited looking bear sat tethered before one of them. What could a shaman want with it? And who else was praying for the khan?

Some thirty paces away from Father Kyril's ger stood another with a square cross painted on its door and a wooden sounding board set up outside it. I walked over and peeked in the open door, thinking it might be the Nestorian church. The dim interior did look Christian: an altar with burning candles and incense sat upon it and a plain square cross hung behind it. One wall was decorated with an embroidered hanging, and a statue of an angel stood on the altar.

A middle-aged priest was praying before it in a language new to me. He wore a pointed cap decorated with peacock feathers and earflaps, and his vestments looked equally unfamiliar. And instead of bowing from the waist in submission, he sometimes stopped speaking and raised his hands, clapped them together, and then prostrated before the altar as Q'ing-ling did. Perhaps this was Mar Sauma.

When he was done, he turned around and saw me, smiled, and waved me inside. I crossed myself and obeyed. We looked at each other for several moments. He had slanted eyes and flat cheeks, quite red, and a friendly smile. "You are Sofia, are you not? My friendly rival Dorje spoke of you. I am Mar Sauma. Welcome." He held out his hands toward me. An image of a square cross was dyed on his right hand.

Not only did he know Mongol speech, he knew Dorje! He seemed so mild-mannered and harmless, and he was friendly with the people I loved most. "Yes, I am she. It seems we share the same friends." I spent a happy interlude visiting with the priest. He told me that he was one of the few survivors from a city called Balkh somewhere deep in the wilds of the Orient. The Mongols had sacked it long ago.

After saying goodbye, I peeked into another ger that was empty but for a few books on a low table. The largest said Quran on it in Arabic script. Perhaps this was the Muslim mosque. Time was growing short and I must return to my duties, so I looked into only one other ger, which smelled of incense. Two men clad in robes of saffron and reddish purple were sitting inside it on the floor, still as statues, facing some kind of candle-lit shrine. They were the first men I had seen dressed like Dorje. There were statues against the walls and on the shrine itself. I slipped away, wondering what they were doing, and returned to camp, still uneasy over Father Kyril's counsels. Perhaps Mar Sauma could guide me.

No, I had Dorje. His advice was always sound and based on kindness. He was a virtuous pagan, and there must be special dispensation for people like him.

oded dispatches flowed out for several days, and then without warning the armies left. With no ordu, the rest of us had to take horse and follow far too rapidly for my liking. Leaving the flat plains behind for hilly country, we rejoined Batu's army a few days later. It overflowed with spoils and new captives.

Dorje met me with the chilling news that I was to start questioning prisoners. He led me to a tent full of wretched-looking captives penned and roped together like animals. Several other translators were moving among them, sorting them out in some way.

"Our task falls into two parts," he said. "One is to learn what trades the men practice and decide whether to put them to work or send them into the army. The other is to learn about other cities and countries if we can: their leaders, their quarrels, their strengths and weaknesses. Usually you can find a way to help everyone. I'll explain how to do that."

Although I hated questioning people at first, for they were so wretched that all I wanted to do was weep, I soon came to see that Dorje's method had merit. Asking in the right way showed me how to help them, so I could feel a little better about my new duty. If I could uncover a special skill that would be useful to the Mongols, I could give a man a chance for a new life. They were mostly well-to-do tradesmen, wealthy peasants, artisans, a few monks. Some prisoners spoke Latin or Rus'. All veered between grief, anger, and resignation.

At least I soon could speak simple Latin again. When I explained what I needed, some began to translate for those captives who knew only Hungarian, many of whom, to my surprise, were gold miners. I had never known that most of Western Christendom relied upon Hungary for gold, all now in Mongol hands. I also found several gold- and silversmiths whom I sent to the ordus of the noyans to fashion gaudy jewelry and so forth. Most of the educated men eventually went to other ordus, too, to act as scribes and translators, while craftsmen could repair damaged equipment or fashion new items.

But the rest of the men I had to send away. Those deemed worthy of training would be put in the army and made to fight in the forefront against their own people. Those for whom I could find no use would be beheaded or driven before the advance guard of the Mongol armies to be unwittingly cut down by their own people.

Then there were the women and children, most terrified almost into muteness or weeping for their lost loved ones. By the time I saw them, all the women and many of the girls had been raped at least once, and one woman told me through her tears that some of their number had already died from repeated assaults. All of them had been spared on account of their beauty, although I did find some who could cook or sew well. They could serve the khans and noyans. But I had no choice but to send most of them and all of the children to be shared among the troops as menials or concubines.

I also had to question a few people of noble rank. When they understood that they could avoid torture and death by being truthful, most came forward. They were spared a truly cruel end, for the Mongols were masters of using pain to pry what they wanted from their prisoners. We could hear the screams sometimes, which frightened me as much as it did the captives. Once they had told me about terrain and politics, I tried to find some skill that they could practice, too, but most men knew little beyond fighting and refused to join the Mongol army, while the women knew only how to play music or do needlework or oversee a household. I placed some of them as musicians or seamstresses. At least I found a few who spoke Latin, French, or German. Those who did not scorn their native Hungarian or refuse to treat with those beneath their station became translators or, if they could read and write, secretaries to the illiterate khans.

I weathered several of these ordeals and even felt I was doing worthwhile work until the day three soldiers dragged a knight or perhaps a baron into the tent, his arms strapped to a heavy Y-shaped stock resting on his neck. He had been captured trying to spy on a camp. He fought them at every step until they forced him to kneel before me, stared up at me with loathing, and sat stubbornly silent while I tried to explain.

He finally exploded in anger. "Listen, you bitch, why should I betray my fellows? Let these fiends do their worst—I feel no fear! I welcome my own passing. Mortal pain lasts but a moment, and then I will be in Heaven. And where will you be? Burning in hellfire for eternity! Look at you, dressed in finery stripped from someone else's back. Did you sleep with some Tartar beast to get it, you accursed whore?"

I was struck speechless. He raved at me until I gathered enough wits to send him away. As his guards dragged him off, he shouted, "Whore of Satan! God will punish you!" I was shaking like a birch in the wind. For the rest of the day, his abuse would come to mind and I would think up a belated retort. 'How dare you! I'm trying to help!' Or, 'You could have helped tame these "Tartars," as *you* so ignorantly call them!'

That night I took out my ikons and tried to pray before them. But to whom was I praying, and for what? Forgiveness for myself and others? Gratitude to God for His creation? Even the beauty of the world seemed trampled underfoot, and by an uncaring mankind that was made in His *image*. Nothing made sense.

Finally I simply sat and felt the pain of the cruel man's words slash though me. What would Dorje say? Shrug and ask me to forgive the man, or at least not take his words to heart? Dorje was so ready to allow for human frailty. And how I missed Q'ing-ling's kind words and soft heart.

But this much that man had made clear to me: I did *not* want to serve the Mongols through years of war. Even if war did end, the thought of life in an ordu filled me with despair. A little of my old spirit revived, and for the first time in many months I seriously considered escape. After all, my knowledge might prove useful if I could reach the right people. Perhaps Western Christendom need not fall if its kings would listen to me and unite to drive the invaders back, even out of Rus'.

How odd it seems now, as if such dreams often did come to pass, yet almost at cross-purposes to my intentions. Though I did eventually reach the right people, I certainly never saved Christendom, and I played but a minor role in King Louis' court on Cyprus.

The next afternoon, Batu Khan summoned me. He was taking his ease alone for awhile. When I entered his golden tent, a slave was filling his huge goblet with arki while a musician played a horse-headed fiddle. Batu was settled on a low divan, a terribly swollen foot sticking out over its edge. It turned out he had gout, not a battle wound. "Come here, Sofia Begi. Tell me about this man who dared to shout at you." He motioned to me to kneel beside him.

I haltingly recounted the knight's vile words.

"And what do you think? Are you a whore doomed to Hell?" he asked.

I looked up with tears in my eyes. "I do not know, my Khan. Perhaps I am."

He leaned over and clutched my arm. "Listen to me. You belong to us, now. A whore has some small choice, and you have none. You're a slave! All that fool wanted was to soar like a hawk in the sky of his own heroism, but he crumbled after a little well-applied pain. By the time my men were done, he was begging to betray his own mother! And he died like a weakling, drowning in his own tears. That taught him to harm those under my shield!" He let go of my arm and leaned back against his pillows.

"Don't be so shocked," he laughed. "He deserved his fate. These petty so-called warriors have no idea of true bravery *or* loyalty, and their so-called kings are no better. They're like wild beasts, ready to tear each other apart for the slightest personal gain. Or like a snake with many heads and one tail. They can never agree with one another, so they cannot save their own body. If he had been a Mongol and gone off spying on his own like that, we'd have executed him *and* his nine companions for disobedience. In *our* armies, soldiers always stay with their companions unless ordered otherwise. Loyalty to our fellow warriors is what makes us invincible!

"These fools value personal exploits above victory; even their kings expose themselves to needless risks during battle. No one doubts a Mongol's courage, but my noyans oversee our troops. It's far more important to know what to do next than to rush about trying to prove how brave we are! We Mongols are like a snake with one head and many tails. Working together under firm leadership, the one head saves the many tails.

"You are a tail, Sofia, not a head." He laughed. "A tail, not a head! Very good." I wanted to sink into the floor with shame. My feelings must have been clear to him, because he added, "Listen! Of course you have a head, and because you use it I now have some fine seamstresses, three new blacksmiths, and an excellent goldsmith from some city called Paris. I think of sending him as a gift to Mongke Khan. I know you try to help my captives, but if we all prosper, even to the meanest slave, that is good. Give no heed to the words of a madman." He took a great gulp of arki and stared at me with his cat eyes.

"You've earned high praise from my secretaries. Our spring campaigns draw to a close, and we will need fewer people to question prisoners. When we settle into summer pastures, I'll use you as one of my personal translators. And when the rest of my ordus arrive, I will need men to help me govern Hungary until I decide whether to stay here. My young warrior, Argamon, comes to mind. I think to bring him here, too. Will that please you?" He eyed me intently.

I had only had time to think about Argamon at night, but the idea did please me. Bowing my head, I replied, "You are most generous, my Khan." Then I remembered Q'ing-ling, left alone in Qacha's ordu. What petty cruelties might Har Nuteng be inflicting upon her? I looked up and tried my most charming smile. "My Khan, I know I impose heavily on your generosity, but may I make one small request? Not for myself but for another."

Batu smiled back. "Ah, a slave who dares speak out to her master. What is it?"

"Argamon's mother, Noyan Qacha's first wife, Lady Q'ing-ling: I fear for her wellbeing. She was falsely accused of adultery and still lives with the shame. She's so alone. Is there some way she could serve you as well, or one of your wives? While the campaign is going on ... until her husband returns." He could see right through my feeble wiles and was looking more amused with every moment. I blushed and ran dry of words.

Batu stroked his cheeks. "I must consider such a request from all sides. Qacha's family problems are slipperier than a stagnant pond. I know what you want: Q'ing-ling parted from Har Nuteng. My sister has become as bitter as wormwood, not like she was when she was young. Nor has Qabul lived up to his promise as a warrior. His injury has embittered *him*, too. Such a rash nature. Has he recovered from his broken arm?"

How could I have forgotten Batu Khan's link with Har Nuteng or the reason I was even in his service? I replied carefully. "Qabul's arm will always be crooked, my Khan, but it has healed. He tries to regain use of it, and I believe he practices archery daily."

"You so amuse me, Sofia Begi," he grinned. "I know you must hate him, but your speech is so honeyed, you're such a dove of peace. You'll make a melodious addition to my retinue of croaking ravens. Yes, I will find some way to make everyone happy, just as Qacha's Dorje wants us to do. Everyone happy," he laughed. "Go now."

I bowed and left, ignoring the knowing glances cast at me by the khan's attendants. Pleasing everyone included Har Nuteng and Qabul. Would he be summoned to the khan's ordu, too?

But it was out of my hands now. Batu's armies were soon sweeping over the green Hungarian plains like grassfires while I floated along like some tiny spark. But when the khan commanded even a small matter, it came to pass. I had half forgotten his promise when one evening a messenger from Batu arrived at my sleeping quarters and told me to gather my things. He led me into a small but well-appointed ger close to Toramun's. What different surroundings! Only senior translators merited such luxury. Argamon was sitting knee up by the hearth. He leapt up and without a word sniffed all over me, swept me into his arms, and carried me to the divan. It seemed that I had been growing again, for we were almost the same height now! I was glad to see him, too, and in his passionate embrace I found a brief, blissful respite from care.

Only afterward did he speak. "Yulta Beki's prophecy still unfolds, Sofia. I've won renown on the battlefield, Father bade farewell to me with praises on his lips, and now I'll be by Batu Khan's side with my hand-picked men. My whole family will prosper, even that cur Qabul and his bitch mother. And all because of you."

"I rejoice for you, Argamon. But I felt so alone here. And some bad things hap—"

Propping himself up on an elbow, he cut in, "Well, I'm here now to remove all bad things from your mind! Mm. You're not only taller; you've grown here, too."

I tried again. "When your mother arrives, perhaps everything will be better."

That at least caught his attention. "Sofia, have you heard any news from our ordu since you left? I worry about Mother alone with Qabul and Har Nuteng."

"No, I've heard nothing. The reason I asked Batu Khan to find a role for her here was to protect her from their ill will, but what real harm could they cause in such a short time?"

He sank back onto the bed. "You must be right. Doubtless she's safe, although I've had no word either. Father will escort her here, since the noyans meet for another kuriltai soon." He was quiet for a moment. "Fate smiles on us in so many ways. Is it not a cause of wonder?" He kissed me again.

Our reunion kept us up most of the night, and I fell asleep wondering, too: why I had ever wanted to escape. So much for my new resolve!

Qacha and Q'ing-ling arrived the very next day. Ibn al-Jabar had sent me to Batu's ger on an errand, and I saw them amidst a group of courtiers greeting Batu Khan. The khan noticed me as I entered and, motioning me forward, smiled benignly. "I will find just the right role for your lady, Sofia Begi. See how well she adorns my court, like a radiant moon." I bowed gratefully. Perhaps I had judged the khan too harshly. What a joy to see Q'ing-ling! She looked so weary from her journey.

When my duties were completed for the day, I found Q'ing-ling attending one of the khan's favorite wives, but she got permission to join me. The weather was as soft and sweet as the green grasses, and we decided to wander around the camp in the late afternoon sunshine.

"Has there been any trouble from Har Nuteng and Qabul since I left you?"

"No, dear. I rarely saw either of them. Qabul was off practicing archery, and Har Nuteng has brought a new shaman into her circle and is busy with charms and potions. I think she never forgave Yulta Beki for recognizing you, so now she's found her own man."

"Can she replace him?"

"Oh, no. Yulta Beki belongs to Qacha. He was once a nobleman from the forests north of Mongolia. Jochi Khan's army captured him in a raid long ago. He was another of Jochi's gifts to reward Qacha's loyalty, and this gift was a much happier choice. I don't know where this new shaman came from. He is handsome but with weasel eyes—truly, I do not care. I don't hold with contact with spirits, but if she's happy and no longer trying to cause me harm, then I too am happy." Q'ing-ling smiled and patted my hand.

"Now, tell me about yourself and how you changed everyone's lives for the better."

Not everyone's," I replied sadly. "I met Father Kyril and asked for guidance. He ordered me not to enjoy lying with Argamon and to give up my friendship with you and Dorje. He says it imperils my soul. It's hard to trust his counsel now." Q'ing-ling looked pained. "There is more."

I told her about the cruel knight. "He called me a whore doomed to Hellfire for serving the Mongols, and now I feel so ashamed."

Now she seemed puzzled. "Sofia, he was wrong; you have no choice. And what is so shameful about you and Argamon? Surely your princes had concubines."

"Well, I once overheard gossip about some nobleman's concubine. The servants spoke of her with such disrespect, and they stopped their talk short when they realized I was listening. Besides, even if Argamon married me it wouldn't matter. At least you are Qacha's first wife, so God surely recognizes your union."

"What do you mean?"

"There can be only one marriage in a lifetime unless one is widowed and remarries. But Argamon already has a wife. Even if he married me, I would still be a fornicator."

Q'ing-ling pondered my words. "It seems to me that we see some things very differently, and who is to say who is right? But no matter what, our Heavenly Father sees your efforts and your devoted heart, and you can trust our Savior's love and sacrifice for us. The rest is beyond your control."

I took her slender hand. "Thank you. I felt so lost after talking with Father Kyril."

"You can always come to me, my dear," she answered.

We had reached the edge of the camp and turned back when Q'ing-ling said, "Did you know that the Kipchak Khan Batu was pursuing died before the invasion of Hungary even began? He was murdered last year by a mob that thought he was secretly aiding the Mongols."

"Really? How strange fate is. Because the princes of Rus' once came to the aid of the Polovtsy—I mean the Kipchaks—Batu's forces invaded us. And their fleeing to Hungary was the khan's excuse for invading it. How different my life would have been had the Kipchaks not fled—Papa would not have dared trying to send me to Constantinople! Or had those remaining behind not rebelled, the Mongols wouldn't have moved south to crush them ... and Argamon and I wouldn't have crossed paths."

Another thought struck me. "Why, without that rebellion, the invasion of Rus' would have happened a year earlier and I would likely be dead—or enslaved, anyway!"

"Yes, fate is fickle in some ways and relentless in others," Q'ing-ling answered. "But war is always a cruel weed, no matter when or how. Its seeds unfailingly sprout into new wars. Once I took it all in stride, but lately ... I am so weary of endless conflict."

That night Argamon told me the khan's plan for Qacha's family. "Mother will attend Batu Khan's second wife from time to time and Har Nuteng his first. Har Nuteng can feel that hers is the higher position, which is something Mother cares nothing for. And the khan wants only one of them here at a time, so the other can oversee Father's ordu. Har Nuteng will have that duty for the first time. And best of all, they'll rarely see each other."

"That will do very well indeed!" I cried. The khan was surprisingly diplomatic.

"But there is more," said Argamon. "Batu Khan commands Father to encamp near him, another great honor, and to have his pick of Hungarian prisoners to impress into his troops. You have benefited everyone!"

Hlib suddenly came to mind. I had never seen him again. He was likely long dead, along with all my other companions. Many of the people I had questioned were dead, too. The men forced into fighting had been sent first into battle, and some of the others I had questioned and thought I had saved had displeased their masters in some way. They had been driven before the armies into battle as human shields, Mongol mockery in their ears, arrows shot into their backs if they tried to flee, while their own people unwittingly cut them down in front.

With the noyan's arrival near Batu Khan's camp, Tsetsegmaa and Bourma came to Argamon to serve him. Little Kuchan had begun to walk—nay, run!—since I had last seen him. It was good to greet my old friends and to see Bourma smiling again, and I began to feel as if we were creating a true household together, almost a home.

And Q'ing-ling was often in the ordu, free to spend however much she liked in the company of the khan's second wife, a fat cheerful woman who in her slender youth had often ridden into battle. Afterward, the Lady sometimes visited me. She seemed to be aging overnight, even to the stiff way she walked. We spent much time outdoors, either walking in the camp or riding together through the flower-dotted plains, soaking up the sunshine. My people always said that the sun and God are the same: the source of light, warmth, health, and wealth. Surely the sun's rays would revive her.

I was happy for myself, too. I no longer had to question prisoners. Now that Batu Khan's armies were at rest across much of Hungary, I merely copied dispatches or interpreted for an occasional envoy. Indeed, once when Q'ing-ling and I were out riding, we stopped on a green rise and witnessed ordus in every direction, as far as our eyes could reach. Argamon had told me that tumans lay all across eastern Hungary, fattening their animals on its rich grasses, but that Batu had decided that the plains were simply not vast enough,

To think that they might never have left Hungary. God knows what would have happened then. If fate had not stepped in, the Mongols would have vanquished the rest of Western Christendom, too—the great cities all put to the torch, everyone enslaved, and mighty kings and nobles and chivalrous knights strewn on the battlefield like chaff.

*S*ometimes Q'ing-ling and I visited the Nestorian priest, Mar Sauma. I liked him, though I was glad I hadn't asked him for spiritual advice. He had a warm heart, but he took life far less seriously than I did, and it was true that he was too fond of wine. When I went to Father Kyril for confession, I avoided asking for guidance that I could not follow, nor did he offer any. Perhaps he realized he had spoken too harshly of my friends. He surely knew about my visits with Q'ing-ling to Mar Sauma, yet he never spoke of them.

I also attended Mass when I could, along with a few other slaves from Rus'. I loved the beauty of Father Kyril's singing, the sweetness of his Scripture readings, and the sincerity of his intercessory prayers. The candles and incense revived shadowy memories of my former devotion, but somehow the Mass didn't satisfy my longing for that missing bedrock of faith, especially when I could hear the Nestorian service nearby. One of Batu Khan's sons was Nestorian, and whenever he attended Mass, Mar Sauma seemed to glory in chanting and beating his wooden board. Father Kyril would sing louder to drown out his rival, and Mar Sauma's chanting would turn into shouting!

Though Qacha had reclaimed Dorje, we could sometimes walk together, and his advice I did seek. He was a sharp observer, but I never found malice in him. And he helped me so often. For instance, once after I had agonized over some sin I thought I had committed—and probably wearied his ears with the same old story—he said, "I simply cannot understand this 'sin' you speak of. It divides you against yourself and gives you no path forward. Yes, we are all confused, but how does that make us evil? If you see you've done wrong, feel remorse for it, and resolve to do better, that's a goodness far deeper than evil."

"But I keep committing new misdeeds or the same ones over and over."

"You don't give up. Besides, that's how you learn compassion for others—they're doing the same as you! Be brave, trust your heart, and your life will bear fruit. If you need proof, look at Argamon."

I had to smile. "Yes. He says Batu Khan respects his advice, too. I think he got the khan to forbid killing peasants. Batu gave him King Bela's royal seal, which was captured in battle, and Argamon's agents show its stamp to the peasants. They think they're obeying their king's commands, and now they return to their fields. That means no famine! And Batu issues copper coins for trade and appoints judges, even though he wont stay here, so maybe he too grows more civilized!"

I hadn't had any say, of course, but surely I had indirectly helped shape these policies.

Dorje smiled. "In fact Qacha and his entire family seem happier these days, and I hear it's because of you—hardly the work of an evil sinner!"

Dorje's words were music to my heart. When I thought about it later, I realized his advice was much like Father Kyril's. Perhaps learning from my misdeeds was the same as the power of pain to purify my heart.

Even Qabul seemed happy. Batu Khan had ordered him to train new troops in a nearby ordu, and I only saw him at Qacha's family feasts—not just chunks of meat but, thanks to peasants who came to the ordus to trade or work, Hungarian bread, apricots, and spicy soup. I avoided Qabul's eyes, yet without ever looking at him I felt the heat of his gaze on me. If only he would abandon his fantasy about me!

But all in all, the summer passed pleasantly. The meadows slowly turned from bright green to soft gold, and after rainstorms the sparkling grass smelled so sweet. As we only moved a few times, I felt almost settled. Argamon was often in camp, ever ready to seek pleasure together. And though sometimes the pain of losing Papa would still pierce me to the bone, overall he seemed to be fading into soft memory.

Hungary's people were returning to normal, too. Sometimes I translated when princes came to the camp to submit and offer tribute. After a long ritual of greetings, gifts, praises, and an endless ceremonial meal, Batu Khan would confirm their rule over their old lands. I sat close behind him and translated for them, glad to help clear a path for these nobles, some of them my fellow countrymen, to return home and begin again. These events taught me to read people, too, a skill I needed later in my life.

But most of the time I was free to do as I wished. Because we had been on campaign, we had scarcely celebrated the coming of spring and no one had given gifts to the slaves. So I took to bestowing food, drink, and clothing wherever I saw the need. I also learned to speak Hungarian, a musical tongue, oddly akin to Turkish, which I learned mostly from the peasants who came to the khan's ordu to trade. Many of them were so desperate that they tried to trade their daughters for meat! I became known as the one who would give them free food. I also gave them stern words about selling their girls into slavery. They were in awe of me and thought it a great marvel that I knew several languages.

I made friends with the other translators, too. Some nights we gathered under the stars and English John would recall his wild adventures to us, or Kchiia would sing us a haunting steppe melody, or Maria would perform a stately dance. We all did teach each other our speech, and thus I learned simple English and Veneziano. I used up the last pages of Papa's book recording what I learned of the two languages, as there was scarcely room for anything else. Besides, now that Papa was lost forever, it mattered little what I wrote in it.

I spent many free hours with Toramun the Volga Bulgar, sometimes stopping at her ger. When she was there, she would offer me airag. She had an endless supply. Or she would come by the secretary's ger and demand that Ibn al-Jabar let me go early. We would sit together in the sunshine, drinking and telling each other about our homelands. Her story was familiar but for the details: her city invaded and destroyed, its khan captured, tortured, and hewn in two before her eyes by Mongke Khan himself when he refused to bow to him. And a handful of people like her spared and enslaved. A good woman, tough but kind.

In Argamon's arms my sins ceased to haunt me, too, along with the memory of the name-calling knight. I even found time to be alone now and then, something I had sorely missed since being enslaved. I had no special guard to watch my every move in Batu Khan's ordu and was free to move about on my own, even to riding by myself. I had heard from Argamon that there were many warm springs dotted across Hungary, and I wanted to find one. There were some in Rus', too, but far from my home. What a miracle that warm water could rise from the cool earth!

And when I was out riding alone one day, I did find a spring hidden among trees in a little rocky dell not far from our encampment. A secret place just for me! Water spilled into a small pond before meandering off into a meadow. Slipping off Little Liubyna, I dipped my hand into it. It was warm! Forgetting that I should never bathe in running water, I slipped off my filthy garments and slid into the pool. The water came only to my waist when I sat in it, but the bottom was soft sand. It was heavenly. I leaned back and looked up through the lacy leaves of the trees and felt like a child again, at one with the world.

The next time I saw Q'ing-ling, I suggested she go with me, hoping she might try the waters, too, for she seemed so tired and they had been so refreshing. She started in alarm. "Sofia, you broke Mongol law! Never do it again! What if Yulta Beki finds out?"

To my regret I never bathed again, though I was certainly glad at not being found out.

Still, when I could I stole away just to sit by my little pool. One morning I had just knelt down beside it when I noticed an object sticking up from the sand near the spring's mouth. I drew it out to see what it was. A chill passed through me. It was a small stone figure of the Great Mother, like a cousin to the one Baba Liubyna had given me so long ago, but with huge breasts and buttocks.

I felt as if my nursemaid had reached across the chasm of death to touch me. Unless she had died before the sack of Kyiv, she would have received no burial, much less last rites. Her body would be dust and corruption by now, but her spirit might still be wandering the earth, lost and frightened, crying for release. It came to me that I must return this little mother to the earth and put my own statue with it to honor my beloved nursemaid.

I hurried back to my ger and found it still buried at the bottom of my old chest. Pulling a scrap of silk from my sewing box, I wrapped both statues into one silken shroud. The next day I galloped back to the spring, where I scraped a hole under a little bush and buried the two tiny women side by side. I said a prayer for my Baba Liubyna and for all the women on this huge, sad, amazing earth who had lived and died as she had.

As if my prayer had been heard and Baba Liubyna's restless soul found peace at last, the air seemed to sigh and grow still. I looked up at the leaf-dappled sky and felt almost crushed by its vastness, its mystery.

I never visited that spot or rode alone again, though, because when I left the grove I saw a jaghun training in the distance. Qabul was directing it. I dug my heels into Little Liubyna's sides and almost flew back to Batu's ordu, praying that he had not seen me.

SUMMER'S END, Anno Domini 1241

In high summer, a stream of princes arrived to submit to Batu Khan and he needed me to translate, so I missed seeing the Lady for days at a time. One fine bright day, finally free again, I took Temur with me to her ordu.

As I arrived at Q'ing-ling's door, Temulun slipped out, tears in her eyes. "My Lady lies abed today, Sofia Begi. She has felt unwell for some time."

"I noticed, but she denied it whenever I asked her. What's wrong? Can I help?"

"She bleeds as if her moon cycle has returned, but it never stops and it grows worse every day. This kind of bleeding is not right. She is possessed."

Sick fear rose like swamp gas. "By an evil spirit? Surely not."

"She has been bleeding since we came to Hungary, at first just a few spots, but now more and more heavily. She wanted no one to worry about her, but now she is so ill she cannot hide it any longer. I think we should call Yulta Beki."

"But isn't he more a seer than a healer? Perhaps we should ask Batu Khan's Jewish doctor to come, the one Selim al-Din gave to the khan." I knew Ben Hasan slightly now, a soft-spoken man with thick brows and curly dark hair, possibly in his mid-thirties, who spoke Farsi with me and whose kindness had forced me to revise my ideas about Jews. "His cures work." His poultice of goat's milk and horse dung had actually relieved Batu's gout.

"Perhaps," Temulun frowned.

Inside, Kamileh was giving Q'ing-ling something to drink. "Lady, why didn't you tell me you were ill?" I took my friend's hand. How thin it had grown since the spring.

"Sofia dear, I just need some rest."

I did not believe it. I stayed with Q'ing-ling until the sun was low and rode back through mellow warmth and golden grasses, but I had no eyes for beauty. Argamon was standing before our ger when Temur and I arrived, and I was scarcely off my pony before I was telling him everything. It was the first time I had ever seen him show fear.

"I thought she looked unwell. Does Father know? He's on a battue. And has Yulta Beki been called in? He's a great healer. He can wrestle demons and cast them out. We must go to her as soon as Batu Khan grants us permission." Argamon straightaway sent my guard with messages for the shaman and for Qacha. It was too late to seek out Batu Khan, but early the next morning we both went to ask permission to leave.

However, when we got to Batu's ger, Mahmud stopped me while Argamon went in. When I tried to explain my need to him, he said, "You must stay through tomorrow, Sofia. Last night the khan issued several decrees to the troublesome Slavic princes under his rule. He wants you to write them out." He paused and gave me a meaningful look. "We've received word that some of them plot rebellion together. I suggest you use all your skills to warn them against such treachery. We both know the fate of those who try to thrust Mongol boot heels from their backs.

"And tomorrow Batu Khan needs you, as another prince arrived from Rus' to submit. Go; Ibn al-Jabar expects you."

It was midday before I finished, having added stern warnings to the decrees before sending them out. As I was hurrying back to my ger to tell Argamon not to wait for me, a shadow fell between me and the sun.

"So, we meet in light of day this time. No guard to keep the wicked tiger of a brother from carrying you off?" Qabul was walking beside me, smiling.

I almost jumped away. "What are you doing here?"

"Oh, I had an audience with the khan first thing this morning. He will let me lead my men again now that I've regained full strength in my arm."

He reached to take *my* arm, and I threw it off. "Don't touch me, Qabul. This is the light of day, with witnesses nearby, and I'll scream loud enough for even the khan to hear!"

Qabul stared and then barked a bitter laugh, the scar across his lip puckering horribly. "You still deny what lies between us. Do you remember that night? I was drunker with passion than liquor, and I was very drunk. When you kept silent afterward, I thought you were finally admitting what you felt for me. And then you disappeared." I stopped and glared at him. Had he forgotten what he had nearly done to me?

"Why look at me like that? I lost my comeliness, even my strength, from loving you!"

"Qabul, you did those things to yourself. I never told anyone but Dorje and Lady Q'ing-ling about that night because you tried to rape me and I feared for my life. Stop deluding yourself about me. Years ago you once charmed me with a false smile, which I foolishly mistook for kindness. But I soon learned what a hard and selfish man you are. What you call love hurts and kills. Just be glad I never told your father. Now, leave me alone!" I spoke boldly, but every muscle in my body was ready to flee.

Qabul's face was a map of pain and mounting anger. "So it was fear that kept you quiet. Well, I won't forget your smile and how you always blushed when our eyes met. I know what I know!" He turned and stalked away a few paces but paused in mid-stride and called back, "Just remember this. There is more than one way to love."

Where had I heard that before? It took a moment to remember: in that long-ago dream about Dorje as an archbishop. Qabul's words were their twisted reflection.

I raced to my ger, my heart pounding. He would surely leave me alone from now on, but I must tell Argamon about it. I found him ready to leave.

"I've been waiting for you, Sofia. Batu Khan told me about that snake Qabul coming to him. I want to leave right away. Hurry and pack; we'll stay there for some time."

"Argamon, I cannot go yet. The khan needs me tomorrow, so I'll have to follow you. But I want you to know that Qabul waylaid me as I was coming here—"

"Did he offer you any harm?" Argamon frowned.

"No, I spoke to him bluntly. I think he's given up hope that—"

"I'll leave some men to escort you to Father's ordu, but I must leave now."

After the next day's endless feast with yet another defeated-looking prince, I raced to Qacha's ordu, arriving at dusk. The noyan was in Q'ing-ling's ger with Argamon and Yulta Beki.

But when I entered, the shaman motioned me back outside, him on my heels. "Did I not warn you against bathing? You could forfeit your life," he whispered fiercely.

My heart dropped into my belly. "Good God, Yulta Beki, how did you know? I—in the joy of finding water that ran warm from the earth, I simply forgot!"

"A shaman knows things. And count yourself lucky that I see into your heart. You get the khan to help everyone in this family, but then you endanger their wellbeing with your rashness! You did it but once so I spared you again, but from now on you'll receive no more clemency from me!"

He stalked back inside, leaving me shaking with terror. How could he have known? Feeling utterly at the mercy not only of Yulta Beki but also of dark forces I could never understand, I began to pray not only for my friend but for myself!

Over the next month, Qacha, Argamon, and I spent nearly every waking moment with Q'ing-ling. Dorje often came to sit just inside the door, softly chanting, his prayer beads clicking. Mar Sauma came by often to pray for her, and Yulta Beki offered sacrifices. Yet as summer waned, she wasted away before our eyes. Whenever she flinched and cried out in pain, Kamileh and Temulun would help her drink one of the shaman's pain-killing potions, but mostly she lay staring into space. Then she began drifting in and out of sleep, as if already entering the next world. Lumps appeared on her body.

But when Yulta Beki wanted to perform an exorcism, she refused. Since Qacha had been called away with his men for a few days, Argamon had to decide. I watched him agonize for an entire day before he obeyed his mother and told the shaman. Yulta Beki, who was usually so calm, left in a fury.

Temulun and I watched him riding away, and we turned to each other, a shared sense of foreboding blotting out the warmth of the day.

However, at Argamon's request Batu Khan did send Ben Hasan to examine her. When Argamon described her symptoms, the Jewish physician shook his head. "It may be too late to save her," he said gravely. "Where I was trained, I was not allowed to touch or sometimes see or even converse directly with a woman patient. May I touch her?" Argamon nodded and Ben Hasan felt her pulse and forehead. Gently probing her belly, he said, "A cancer grows in her womb, and now it has spread elsewhere: see the lumps? This is a mortal disease."

He examined the potion that Kamileh had been giving the Lady, added some herbs to it, and left after asking that we save a sample of Q'ing-ling's morning urine. The next day it seemed to tell him something, for he made various observations about humors and elements before cautiously recommending another mixture from his herb chest. It smelled like spices and contained a tiny amount of a precious ingredient he called mummy.

"This comes from the faraway land of Egypt," Ben Hasan explained impressively, producing a pinch of gray dust from a bottle. "An ancient race once lived there. They preserved their dead and laid them in great tombs. Now these remains are ground up into a most efficacious medicine along with cloves, camphor, and dates. The Lady's case is desperate enough to warrant its use." Alas, she could not swallow it.

"I can think of no more to do," he said. "Bleeding her would be of no use, and it is far too late to cut her open and remove the growth, as the other lumps would keep spreading. Besides, for that you would need a surgeon, and I am a physician."

No one could imagine cutting Q'ing-ling anyway, and Ben Hasan returned to Batu Khan. The next time Mar Sauma visited, he performed the last rites for her. I could not believe that everyone was giving up. Surrounded by our love and prayers, she must recover!

Qacha returned. When he heard that his shaman wasn't treating Q'ing-ling anymore, he rounded on Argamon, fury straining his words, "Why was he sent away? He should have exorcised her by now!" Argamon's face went gray and he sped from the ger.

As soon as Yulta Beki and his people arrived, he marched into the tent, shooing out all of us but Qacha, and shut the door in Argamon's face.

"I blame myself," my master cried. "I should have listened to him, no matter what Mother wanted. All this time Yulta Beki has been waiting to return. What a tongue beating he gave me on the way here!"

I had my own guilt. What if my bath in the spring *had* brought this on, or my tripping over the threshold of her ger back in Rus'? I had slowly forgotten my terrible fears about not knowing what was true, but now they all attacked me at once. How cold and malign the world suddenly seemed, how full of entrapments waiting to drag us all down.

Yulta Beki's apprentice had brought a spear wrapped in black felt, which Yulta planted in front of the ger before he and his wife went in. Argamon shook his head. "That signals the presence of death. Now, except for close family and one personal servant, no one will even want to enter. The evil spirit in Mother's body might enter him."

"It won't stop me!" But I was never allowed back in.

For three long days, we who loved Q'ing-ling spent all our free time waiting just beyond the black staff, sometimes catching glimpses of the old shaman and his helpers when they opened the door or of the half-drawn swords lying at the foot of Q'ing-ling's bed. Even outside, we could hear Q'ing-ling breathing heavily and sometimes gasping. Only Kamileh was allowed in to serve her.

Each day when Yulta Beki first arrived, he brought out a small meteoric lump and placed it in a sacred cup before entering the ger. My master explained: sometime during the morning he would pour in a potion, let the lump give it further power, and down the drink. As well, each morning the boy and the wife brought mare's milk and spring water inside.

"The shaman will bathe Mother to purify her," Argamon whispered to me while we listened to the three chanting. Each morning the shaman commanded all evil spirits to leave her at once.

On the second day, we all heard the shaman demanding that her illness be drawn into him! Although nothing seemed to happen to him, I had to credit the old man with courage. I would never invite illness into myself!

But Q'ing-ling seemed to revive a little, which was when she asked to speak with Qacha alone. They spoke in whispers and he left without a word, hurried to his ger with his head down, and stayed there for the rest of the day.

On the third morning, we were waiting outside when Yulta Beki suddenly shouted, "Be gone, evil demon, by the power of mighty Tengri and the white spirits of the upper world, the wandering spirits of this world, and the black spirits of the nether world. Be gone forever!" The door of the ger flew open, the cup and lump rolled out, and the shaman was standing by Q'ing-ling, shaking as if possessed. He suddenly screamed and fell to the floor clutching his belly. Struggling outside, he fell onto the ground, while his wife and apprentice tried to hold him down. He seemed in such agony that I thought he had poisoned himself!

Q'ing-ling began tossing fretfully and I tried to rush into the ger, but Argamon gripped my arm hard. "No, stay here. You'd invite the demon back if you went inside now! Trust Yulta Beki. He knows what he's doing."

I wrung my hands. "He seems to be dying! Can we do nothing?"

Argamon simply wrapped his arms around me tightly and I clung to him, sobbing. Qacha strode forward, closed the door, and turned away. Yulta Beki's cries and thrashing grew weaker until he finally lay unmoving. Very faintly I heard Q'ing-ling draw in a long, shuddering breath and then sigh, but no new breath followed.

Almost as one, everyone in the camp, it seemed, began wailing together. I sobbed, "She died alone. I cannot bear it."

"Shh-shh." Tears were coursing down Argamon's face. "No one can stay with a dying person. The demon in her would have tried to possess him, and there are some that even a great shaman cannot exorcise. If Yulta Beki had stayed with her, even he would have been banished from the ordu for months. Mother understood. She was prepared."

This only made me cry more. What a harsh way to die, all alone and without Mar Sauma there to comfort her!

Yulta Beki slowly arose and staggered over to Qacha, who sat by the black spear with his head in his hands. The old shaman leaned over the noyan and spoke softly into his ear. With a savage howl, Qacha jumped up, called his closest men, and summoned his horse. He spoke briefly as he mounted, and Kuvrat Khan was streaking to Har Nuteng's ger, while a handful of others called their ponies. Still weak from his trance, Yulta Beki stumbled after Qacha, mounted his own horse, and galloped off, too. Argamon and I stared after them in amazement before grief engulfed us again.

At least that evening I was allowed to help. Kamileh, Temulun, and I tearfully wrapped Q'ing-ling's body in felt sheets and placed the angel statues from her shrine around it. It was so shrunken that it might be a child's. We sat with it through that long night, them wailing and beating their breasts, me weeping while I tended candles and incense at the shrine. Grief blotted out everything but a constant prayer that Q'ing-ling's soul would find Heaven. Outside, Argamon sat rocking back and forth and sobbing, his men solemnly gathered around him, more women wailing to the night sky.

Late in the night I heard Qacha and Yulta Beki return, their horses' clatter mingling with the howling of the women. We retired at daybreak, and others took our place. I looked around outside for Argamon, but he had vanished, so I sat down before our ger, worn out by our vigil, and dozed fit-fully, wakened by every sound.

I did not sleep for long, for we had to bury Q'ing-ling. Qacha had returned with Mar Sauma, whom Batu Khan had given leave to conduct the Christian part of the funeral. The noyan's scarred face was a granite mask, as were his men's. While the priest beat his wooden board and chanted, they buried Q'ing-ling with her shrine and special belongings. Yulta Beki performed a rit-ual to free the Lady's spirit and send it to the heavenly realms. And at the end, her people gathered all her belongings onto her carts, even her dismantled ger, for a purification ceremony. Once again two fires burned before Qacha's ger, this time with a long spear planted beside each, multicolored ribbons dangling from their tips and a rope stretching between them to create a symbolic portal. Yulta Beki sprinkled water over us as we all passed through it to be purified. Slaves then led the lady's carts and animals through while the shaman chanted and his wife and boy beat drums. It gave me a headache. Once a bundle of silk slipped loose and fell to the ground, but when I started forward to put it back on a wagon, Temulun stopped me and the shaman's wife seized it.

"That belongs to the shaman now," she said.

At day's end, Yulta Beki held a feast for the family to honor Q'ing-ling's special deity. At the time I was too sunk in sorrow and self-blame even to notice the irony of a shaman sacrificing a lamb to God. His wife handed small portions to each of us while he chanted. I did not think of it then, but now I see it was almost like taking communion. They left soon afterward, carrying away the skull, entrails, and bones.

Qacha, Argamon, Kuvrat Khan, and a few other men continued to drink, so I returned to bed and fell asleep. I had a terrible dream. Dark horsemen rode into the ger, threatening to trample me, and someone was screaming again and again. I awoke with a start to mid-day sun. Argamon was sitting by my side, staring down at me. He seemed uneasy. And the screams were real and coming from nearby.

"Are you well, Sofia? Do you hurt anywhere?"

"Everywhere. Q'ing-ling was like a mother to me."

"Yes." He stroked my hair and looked at me intently. "No special place?"

I sat up. "No, why?"

"Come with me."

In silence he led me to Qacha's ger. As we bowed and entered, another ghastly scream shredded the air. Several of the noyan's senior retainers were grouped around something on the floor, but they made way for us. There lay Har Nuteng, naked, hands tied behind her back, her body covered with bruises, scratches, and welts. She must have been in agony, yet she still flung curses at the men around her. Qacha stood over her with a whip, his sorrow entirely replaced by rage. Yulta Beki, next to him, stood like stone.

Har Nuteng caught sight of me. Her obsidian eyes glittered. "You! You'd have been next, you little bitch! You were destined for my Qabul, not that Chinese mongrel. I wish I'd had more time, you ro—" Qacha kicked her in the face, stunning her senseless. Darkness nearly engulfed me. I leaned against Argamon's chest and gulped air.

"I've heard enough," Qacha growled. "She should have been named Black Heart, not Black Eyes! Sew up every hole in her body, take her to the nearest lake, weigh her down with stones, and throw her in." He scooped up some objects from the floor and handed them to Yulta Beki. "Take these atrocities. Destroy them."

The old shaman examined them curiously. Vaguely human in shape, they were made of twigs bound together, dirt-encrusted felt, and scraps of fabric. Several strands of hair were wrapped around each. One bundle with black hair was matted with dried blood. A scrap of silk from one of Argamon's old war shirts dangled from it, and a long needle was thrust through what would have been its neck. A second one was so bloodstained and filthy that it seemed ancient. It looked as though someone had hacked at its middle. Again, the hair around it was black, and dangling from it was a strip of silk from Q'ing-ling's oldest gown. Three were small, almost childlike. They too had been savaged. And one bundle was new. A scrap of blue silk from the gown I had given Kamileh hung from it; its hair was auburn.

"Good God. She put a curse on Lady Q'ing-ling ... and on us?"

Argamon nodded grimly and whispered, "And my brother and sisters! For years she's used powerful spells to conceal her wickedness from Yulta Beki. Only when Mother died and Har Nuteng's demon ally entered him and was bested did all come clear at last. That was why he and Father left after she died. They rode straight to Batu Khan.

When he heard it all, he disowned Har Nuteng and sent Qacha back here with Mar Sauma while his own men found the witch. She was with Batu Khan's main wife, possibly cursing her, too! They dragged her straight to the khan. By then Kuvrat Khan had found these hidden in her ger and sent them to Batu.

When she saw she had been exposed, she admitted it all. She even boasted that her last curse on me had almost succeeded despite your magic—remember, an arrow nearly hit me in the neck? She had been waiting for Qabul to seize you, or she'd have cursed you sooner, too. She had just made this last abomination. I wonder why she stopped waiting."

Qabul was why. He had told her to do it! "More than one way to love," he had said. More than one way to hate was closer. I began trembling so violently that Argamon had to tighten his arm around me to keep me upright. I tried to speak. "Qabul did—"

But Argamon was still talking into my ear, his voice thick with rage. "The khan sent her to Father. An ugly death awaits the bitch, but she deserves worse! I would choke her until she fainted, then wake her again. Then I would drag her behind my horse until every bone was broken, then I would …"

I put my hands over my ears. I felt sick.

While Argamon was talking, Har Nuteng stirred and opened her eyes. Qacha's men didn't wait for more curses; they all added a few kicks of their own to silence her. At a motion from Qacha, they lifted her up and dragged her out to her doom.

After they had left, Qacha sank onto his seat, his features dark with grief and rage. "That vile woman always hated me! Oh, my anda, oh Jochi Khan," he groaned. "You thought to reward me! Instead, you gave me a serpent cloaked in woman's skin. And now she has killed the only woman I ever loved." Qacha was capable of love?

He looked at me. "Worse, she admitted—nay, she boasted—that her witchcraft killed my other children by Q'ing-ling! Had you not been here, Sofia, she'd have found a way to murder Argamon, too." His gaze wandered around the ger as if he was lost.

"And did she tell Qabul? That would be the witch's final stroke of wickedness … Oh, Tengri, you cursed me with blindness. Yulta Beki tried to warn me, but how could one of the Golden Kin stoop so low?"

Pain squeezed Qacha's voice into a whisper. "I have lost my beloved." He buried his face in his hands. "And I never once told her I loved her!" His shoulders shook, a raw rasping sound came from his throat, tears dripped from his fingers. We all stood quietly, none of us knowing which way to look and feeling as raw as if our hearts had been scraped by knives.

Who knows how long we'd have stood there, but one of Qacha's men entered. "We have the witch's sorcerer, Noyan."

Qacha quickly dragged his hands over his eyes. "What? Where was he?"

And then Qabul was thrusting his way in. Terrified he would see me and somehow do me harm, I slipped from Argamon's arms and hid behind him. There was suddenly so much rage and grief in the air that I felt I was breathing smoke. Scarcely pausing to cup his hands and genuflect, Qabul knelt on one knee before his father, already spilling out words.

"I have brought you a felon, Father! He appeared at my ger shouting that Lady Q'ing-ling was dead and my mother was arrested for a witch, that Batu Khan was hunting him! He made terrible claims: that Mother had wanted him to destroy Argamon and curse you with a painful, lingering death. He claimed that Mother's witchcraft and not his had killed the Lady! Such wicked lies about my mother! My men and I tortured the truth out of him. *He* was to blame for it all!"

I stared at Qabul. Why would Har Nuteng's sorcerer attack Q'ing-ling if not in obedience to his mistress? Qabul must have known, too!

He added, motioning to his men, "I brought him here so you could clear her name." Several of them dragged the sorcerer inside, his hands and feet bound so tightly they had turned purple, his features almost lost to blows. A faint noise bubbled from his bloodied lips.

"The stinking murderer!" Qacha's face was black with rage.

How could he be so blind to Qabul's guilt? I wanted to protest, but my voice froze in my throat. Qabul spoke as though he was alone with his father and had secret knowledge that he was loath to share.

"Father, there is more. The brute first claimed that Mother had promised him he could replace Yulta Beki once you were dead and I had taken your place. But she would do none of these things!" He paused dramatically. Everything in his manner seemed false to me. "Father, I can scarcely bear to tell you what else he said: that she promised him sexual favors."

Qacha seemed stunned for a moment. "Well, she deserves her death even more!"

"Father, you don't believe these lies about my mother?" Qabul looked so sincere, but his story sounded to me like one massive lie—and he had certainly made sure of the shaman's silence. I tried to speak again myself, to beat away the darkness rushing over me.

"She confessed her wickedness, and now she's being executed as a common witch!"

Qabul almost fell backwards. "No!"

And then, with hardly a pause, "You don't believe *I* had anything to do with such crimes!" How quickly he had changed his loyalties! Did no one notice but me? Why was my voice turned to stone?

My tongue remained entangled in silence, but Qacha was now staring at Qabul as if searching his son's soul. He slowly picked up a bloodstained rock lying at his feet and held it up. "I only know that that bitch consorted with a stupid man and a poor sorcerer. And I would do this to anyone who dared harm the woman I loved." He knelt over the man and began striking him in the face again and again, just hard enough to call forth a scream.

It was so horrible that darkness and a sweet stillness descended on me. When sense returned, only Argamon's arms held me up. The noyan was still pounding on the remains of the man's face, faint squeals still bleating from what had once been a mouth. Qabul was still on his knees, grimacing at the bloodshed—or was he smiling? I shut my eyes.

Finally Qacha said, "Sew this thing up and crush it under the heaviest rocks you can find." The bloody moans had faded before I could open them again.

Qacha was standing, staring at Yulta Beki with wild-eyes. "Others are to blame, too. I should have shielded her better. And Argamon dismissed you before you could divine the truth. If only I had never left, she would still be alive!"

"No, Noyan Qacha." The shaman gripped his shoulder. "Do not blame Argamon or yourself. Har Nuteng's powerful curses were buried deep, long before I came to you. They have slowly poisoned this family for years and deceived both me and my wife! After Argamon brought Sofia here, Har Nuteng accused me of siding with him, even threatened revenge! But her sorcerer merely hastened Lady Q'ing-ling's death. Too late did I see and root out her evil. But as is said, 'Whoever digs a pit to entrap another falls into it himself.'

"And you, Sofia," he added, looking at me with meaning, "never caused any harm to this family. Har Nuteng's confession made that clear." Happily, he added no more or I might have been Qacha's next victim! To the noyan he said, "I must go now and destroy these twisted tokens of evil." He bowed and left.

Qabul was still frozen in place, staring up at Qacha as if in a trance. Qacha suddenly turned on us all, his face distorted with rage. "All of you get out! And find Dorje. I want him." He turned toward Qabul, gripped his arm and forced him up. "I *will* have the whole truth from you, Qabul!" He seemed like a mad dog, ready to bite anyone. Argamon pulled me out of the ger as the others left, grimly silent. Qabul's guilt might yet be exposed, but I had failed to speak up.

Well, I could still tell Argamon. He was hurrying me toward our horses, saying, "I've seen Father in moods like this before. It's best to stay away for awhile. Luckily when Batu Khan sent that witch here, he summoned us back. We are fortunate to remain in his favor. There's nothing to do now, anyway, but to leave that bastard brother of mine to his fate! I'd like to grind *him* to dust, too, but Father will soon do that."

"Please, Argamon, I must tell you about Qabul. More than once he tried to harm me. I'm certain he helped his mother—"

"Of course he did! He's as much a murderer as that witch who spawned him. But father sees that now, and he'll banish him. You need think of him no more. Hurry up. I want to get back to Batu Khan's ordu before dark."

I mounted Little Liubyna, wishing I had been permitted to speak. I was certain I could have sealed Qabul's fate. Why had my tongue failed me? Fear of Qabul? Fear of Qacha? Or was it Har Nuteng's final curse? I did not know.

rgamon and I returned to Batu Khan's service the next morning, both of us confident that Qacha would at least banish Qabul. Alas, a few days later the truth reached me through Dorje. Qacha had sent him to Batu Khan with a gift of gratitude for his aid, and the monk sought me out afterward.

"Qacha was wild with rage. Qabul was at his father's feet swearing on his guardian spirits that he knew nothing about any witchcraft. And the noyan asked *me* whether or not he spoke the truth."

"Qabul never told the truth in his life!"

"Please listen, Sofia. It's important. I thought he already knew that his son was privy to his mother's sorcery and I did not trust that anything I said could help, so I told Qacha that he must decide for himself."

"Of course Qabul was privy to her designs! He saved the hair he ripped from my head and gave it to her! I only wish I could have found my tongue when I was there."

"Well, Har Nuteng's curses seem to have reached Qacha even from the grave. He stared at Qabul for the longest time. Finally he reminded his son that a true Mongol warrior is bound to speak the truth to his superiors, even knowing he'll be executed. Qabul flinched, but he didn't change his story.

Qacha didn't know what to do, so he just ended up banishing him. But, and this is important for you, Sofia, he didn't banish him back to Karakorum. Instead, he merely shouted at him to stay away from his ordu on pain of death.

"I was aghast. I tried to suggest that he had done too much harm to you and others to allow him to remain on campaign at all, but Qacha turned on me and accused me of questioning his judgment. I'm sorry, Sofia."

"Good God, what should I do? Argamon thinks he knows everything, and he cuts me off every time I try to tell him more. It's hard to speak about anything with him now."

"Oh dear. I could try to tell Qacha again, but with the black mood he's in he's likely to turn against anyone. I'm afraid you must just stay on your guard." He sighed. "Qabul needn't have turned out this way. What a sad, misguided woman his mother was."

"What an evil woman, you mean," I countered, tears welling up in my eyes.

"No," said Dorje gently, "though what she did was terrible. We all grieve over Lady Q'ing-ling, but hating Har Nuteng won't bring her back, and it is best to mourn without befouling our minds with black emotions." He stood in kindly silence while I let my tears flow freely, grateful for a chance to cry.

Finally Dorje spoke again. "Alas, there is more. After Qabul left, Qacha began seeking out those who had helped the witch get the strips of fabric and the hair she used for her curses. He ordered Har Nuteng's favorite slave tortured, and she confessed that soon after she and her mistress first came to Qacha's ordu, she had bribed one of Q'ing-ling's slaves for a scrap of fabric from her gown.

"But most people will admit to anything under torture, and I know that she hated the woman she accused. Now both of them are dead, but not before Q'ing-ling's woman was tortured and made to confess terrible things. She even accused that old Chinese musician of evildoing because she held a grudge against *him!* I fear that before this is over, many innocent people may die. Who knows? If I offend Qacha again, I may be next. Be glad you and Argamon are here." Dorje had never looked so somber.

"Sofia, I worry about Qacha's mind. He still blames Argamon for sending Yulta Beki away. Some deep wickedness lingers on in the ordu, and not even the shaman can purify it. With Q'ing-ling gone, much is changing for the worse."

"Argamon blames himself, too. He's become like a wounded boar; he's ready to attack anyone blindly. He only feels rage, just like when Asetai was murdered. He hit Bourma yesterday for the first time in months. If I weep, he grows even angrier. We hardly speak to each other."

What I could not tell a monk was that the night before, Argamon had brought his anger to bed with him. The way he'd demanded submission from me—the recklessness and hardness—had thrust me back to the early days when he took me by force.

I could not hold back my tears any longer. "Q'ing-ling was my lodestone, Dorje. Where she was, that was *my* home. That's all gone now. Autumn is here, the next campaign starts soon, Argamon will be by Batu Khan's side, and I will have to question more captives. How many years will this war last? I feel such foreboding, and I feel so voiceless.

"Yulta Beki's prophecy was right. My presence did bring out what lay hidden in that family, all its terrible secrets, but at such a cost!" Dorje patted me on the shoulder, but there was little else he could do.

For a month Qacha was utterly consumed by rage. First *all* of Har Nuteng's slaves and servants were tortured and killed. And one of his concubines, a woman who had been close to Har Nuteng, was sacrificed to his fury. He was so maddened by his wife's murder that at one point he even began to suspect Temulun and Kamileh because of that scrap of fabric from my gown. Dorje rushed to Argamon with this news, and with Batu Khan's consent we raced to Qacha's ordu to plead for them.

Argamon approached his father and knelt before him while I waited fearfully just inside the ger's entrance. The noyan was drunk, his face meaner than ever. "Father," Argamon cried, "Kamileh worshipped Mother. She was her companion and friend, and she loved me like a son. She would kill herself before she would harm any of us. Please do not kill Mother's favorite slave. Temulun could never betray Mother, either. She almost worshipped her. If you must kill everyone you suspect, then kill me, too! I am ready to accept your blame."

Qacha was so frenzied that I thought he might take his son at his word. It took long argument before he agreed to spare the two women's lives, but

Argamon never gave up. In the end we took them back to Batu Khan's ordu, both of them beaten, starved, and marked by rope burns at wrists and ankles. Kamileh was out of her wits.

As we rode back, Argamon cradling her before him in the saddle, he said, "Seeing my father so grief-stricken and ruled by anger—I too have been the same."

"Master, may I speak?" He nodded. "We all grieve for your mother, you most of all. Yet you weren't blinded by your sorrow. You saw beyond it, and you saved Kamileh and Temulun. Your mother would have taken pride in you."

Argamon looked up at the sky. "I hope she has found her Heaven."

As the days passed, though, his spirits once again fell under a black spell. He flew into rages at small things, sat stonily through meals. I hid my tears and meekly bowed to his whims. Between trying to please him, overseeing his little household, and serving as scribe and interpreter for Batu Khan, there was little time to mourn Q'ing-ling's passing. A hollow ache followed me through the last warmth of summer and into dreary autumn.

AUTUMN TO WINTER, Anno Domini 1241-1242

The ordus moved to new pasturelands farther west. Late autumn storms swept brown leaves off the few trees still standing around the camps. The Mongols had begun chopping them down to build more wagons and siege engines, destroying the very beauty they admired. Whenever I heard the sound of the ax, I felt like begging the spirits of the woods not to curse us all. The Hungarian peasants had harvested the last crops and brought much grain to the camps to trade, along with vegetables and the soft bread that the Mongols now preferred to their flat, dirty hearth breads. Then they stopped coming. I supposed it was because the harvest was over and they had nothing more to sell.

But around then a shadow ate the sun yet again, turning earth and sky almost red, so I thought that might have scared the peasants away. Of course Batu Khan's shamans danced and chanted, and once again the sun returned. And again, the shamans agreed that it was a good omen for the Mongols.

Argamon had begun disappearing with his men for days. When they returned, he seemed worse tempered than ever. Once he brought back a pretty young girl, slung before him on his pony. He dumped her onto the ground, saying, "See to her," before riding off.

I brought her inside and wrapped a quilt around her, for she was shivering as if it was deep winter. Her dark hair and coarse garment were filthy and blood-stained, and she was tongue-tied with terror. I prayed that Argamon had rescued her from some disaster. Even coaxing her name from her took time: Anna.

For days whenever Argamon came near, she clutched at an amulet that she wore around her neck, and I had never seen anyone cross herself so often. At night she tossed and fretted and awoke screaming, just as I had. The first time, I went to her and comforted her until she could fall asleep again. When I returned to bed, Argamon was awake.

He seized my arm and twisted it. "Don't go to her again. You disturb my rest, and you stoop to menial tasks once again. She'll learn not to cry, just as you did."

He fell back asleep, but not I. His words hurt even more than twisting my arm had. To think I had believed I had civilized him! And why was he so harsh with Anna? Indeed, why had he brought her back? The poor girl could not be more than twelve. I refused to abandon her, though, no matter what my master said.

From then on I saw to it that the other women surrounded Anna with kindness, and when Argamon was away I paid particular attention to her. It made me glad that I knew her language.

Slowly her fear faded and her gentle nature revealed itself, though she seemed simple as an acorn. She followed me around ready to help with every task, and soon it felt as if she had always been part of our little household. In a way Anna became the child I thought I could never have. She was forever crossing herself while announcing some pagan belief she held dear—so like me at her age that I had to smile.

At first Dorje, or his robes, frightened her, and she would have nothing to do with him. But he gently won her trust with small gifts of food and a new length of wool for a garment. Even Wolf befriended her, as he had me when I was younger. Seeing the two of them together, her arm circling his neck, could briefly brighten my gloomy heart.

It was one of the few bright spots in my life. One chill morning, I was waiting outside Batu Khan's golden tent for Mahmud when Qabul appeared with a handful of men. I almost jumped back.

"You!" we both exclaimed.

"Bitch," he muttered as he reeled past me, reeking of liquor. But when he tried to enter the tent, Batu Khan's guards blocked his way.

"Move aside! I have business with my uncle!" he shouted.

"No one enters without the khan's consent. Wait while I pass on your request."

Qabul stood in surly silence, ignoring me. I stood with my arms wrapped around myself, wishing Mahmud would come out so I could get away from there.

Finally the guard returned. "The khan will see you." Qabul sneered at the man and grinned evilly at me. Throwing his bejeweled belt across his shoulder, he went in. I shivered with more than cold. A few times I heard Qabul shouting in there, but I could make out no words and Batu Khan spoke too softly to hear anything.

Finally Mahmud appeared at the entrance. "Oh, you are here, Sofia. The khan just sent me to find you. But before you go in, be warned: Qabul is there. He almost forced his way in, the first time since his witch mother died that he's dared come near the khan."

"Yes, he passed me on the way in."

"Then you know that he's drunk and raging. He threw himself at Batu's feet and swore that if his mother was a witch, he knew nothing of it. Perhaps, perhaps not, is all I say. But then he claimed that you are the real witch. And more. You will hear."

"What did Batu Khan say?"

"He smiled at him and told me to bring you in to answer his claims."

How could I answer anything Qabul cooked up against me? I had seen the venom of mistrust at work in Qacha already; what if Batu Khan were next? I almost crossed myself but stopped for fear Mahmud would mistake it for a curse.

I entered the tent and genuflected, feeling every eye on me, for several royal khans were present. All looked at me stonily. Qabul stood directly before them, his arms crossed, his body planted as if it had taken root. He turned and stared at me with such loathing that it was hard to believe he had ever felt anything else for me.

"Sofia, come forward," said Batu Khan, frowning. I crossed the tent, feeling as if stones were tied to my feet. "It seems it is now Qabul's turn to accuse you of wrongdoing. I think it only fair to let you answer his charge. He says you practiced witchcraft against him and that you are the cause of all his injuries and of a breach between him and his father. These are serious accusations, especially since Qacha seems half-mad these days."

I stared up at the khan. Batu seemed to believe Qabul. The memory of Har Nuteng, naked and bruised, sewn up to smother and drown, made my head swim. Batu waited while I fought my panic. If only Dorje or Argamon were there! I felt utterly alone.

"Well, what do you say?"

I stood there like a mute, praying for the right words to come. Finally I said, "How can I answer? I am only a slave, not just to Argamon but to the prophecy about me. I am no Child of Light whom everyone will believe. But when could I have ever done such witchery? Until I entered your service, I was always guarded because Argamon feared Qabul might try to steal or harm me. All I can propose is that you call my guard Temur or send for Argamon. Or I suppose the other slaves could bear witness for me."

"Common soldiers and slaves bear witness against a Child of Light? Ha!" Qabul looked as if he might jump at me and strike me.

Batu turned on Qabul and spoke with cold fury. "Do you forget that your father was once a common soldier, Qabul? I decide who can and cannot testify! What proofs do *you* offer?"

"My proof is the damage done to my body and the fact that my father has gone mad. He refuses to see me ever again. Everything went wrong after she came to us!"

"Hmm, I seem to recall that you once claimed she protected you from some accident—a falling bag of grain, wasn't it?" Berke Khan barked a laugh. Qabul turned red as a beet. "And as I understand the prophecy, Sofia was only supposed to protect the one who could possess her—clearly not you! Everyone else would be—what was the phrase Qacha once used—blown like leaves in the wind. That clearly was you. And correct me if I'm mistaken, but didn't *you* pursue *her* because you feared that very fate?

"Listen well, Qabul. We're at war, and you bring me such a stupid story? You have no proof against Sofia, only ill will. I know her, and while she is bewitching enough, she's no witch. Indeed it's only because of her that I allowed you to train new soldiers! You should be glad you're even allowed to lead them into battle. Be grateful I don't banish you altogether. Enough of this pettiness. Get back to your duties!" Qabul barely cupped his hands to his uncle and stormed out, nearly stumbling on the threshold.

Batu Khan turned to me, looking stern. "This foolishness must end. I don't need you today, and I don't need sons of witches around me at any time." Mahmud led me out, and as if to keep my mind off everything, he gave me more work than usual. Still, Qabul's claims tore at me all day along. I felt so helpless. What if Batu Khan *had* turned against me?

I worked so slowly and made so many mistakes that I had to stay almost until sunset when Toramun came to invite me for a round of airag. She stayed on to keep me company while I struggled to finish, drinking and making bad jests about my writing skills. Laughter and song spilled from Batu Khan's golden tent, which made it even harder to keep my mind on my tasks. I was the last to finish. I got up, stretched, and led my friend to the door.

But when I opened it, there was Qabul hovering near the entrance to the khan's tent. Was he waiting to go back inside? Or was he waiting for me? He looked over, and I retreated back inside and slammed the door.

"What is it?" asked Toramun.

"My master's brother. I think he saw me. He means me harm." And I told her all about Qabul's persecution. "You and Dorje are the only ones who know everything."

"I'll deal with the bastard!" She was halfway out the door before I could stop her.

"Please, if you'll just watch to see when he leaves and then walk with me to my ger, that will be enough. I want no more trouble, and he'll be gone tomorrow by Batu's order."

I waited in the gathering gloom while Toramun planted herself in the doorway, arms crossed. After the sun had set, she motioned to me and we walked together to my ger.

"You really should tell Batu Khan about all this," she said as we parted.

"No, he says he has had enough of such pettiness." She shrugged and left.

The next day I was translating for the khan, who even smiled kindly at me and dismissed me early. But when I returned to the ger, Kamileh was weeping, Kuchan was sobbing in his mother's arms, and everyone else was in utter panic.

"Qabul was just here ... He was looking for you ... He was drunk ... Temulun tried to keep him out ... He struck her and shouted at us all ... He tore down the hangings and knocked over the chests ... And he kicked the fire and overturned a brazier ... A carpet got burned ... It all happened too fast to call for help ... Then he stormed out!" I sank onto a cushion and held my head in my hands.

"There is more, Sofia. He says he'll return when you least expect it, and to watch your back or you'll find a knife in it," Tsetsegmaa said at last.

Like my long-ago nightmare! I picked up a ripped wall hanging. The carpet was ruined. If Argamon were there, I would tell him everything, but he was gone on some secret mission.

"Where did Qabul go?"

"He rode away," said Anna, clutching her amulet.

"I sent a man to follow him. He and his men left the ordu," added Bourma.

"Do you think he meant his threat?" Tsetsegmaa's arms were tight around Kuchan, who was crying and struggling to escape them.

"No, I do not," I tried to calm them all, though I had no faith in my own assurances. "Qabul must return to the ordu where he trains soldiers, wherever that is. The next campaign begins soon. All the armies will move deeper into new territories as soon as the rivers freeze hard, and then he'll be nowhere near us." Having written out Batu Khan's commands so often and learned what the armies did thereafter, I had worked out his codes for myself.

I told Argamon's male slaves to guard the ger closely from then on, but I had no idea what else to do. Finally, as much as I dreaded it, I asked for and was granted a free day and rode to Qacha's ordu with Temur to ask Dorje's advice. Luckily Qacha was away.

After hearing my story, the monk shook his head. "So Qabul is now your enemy."

"Why could he not simply give up instead of trying to turn Batu Khan against me? Haven't he and his mother already cooked up enough misery for anyone's appetite?"

"His mind and heart were both poisoned long ago. And when he finally realized he could never have you, he must have twisted blame for everything that's gone wrong for him until it fit you. Now I suppose he wants you to feel as much hurt as he does.

"This thrust at you through Batu Khan has missed its mark, though. Few believe anything Qabul says. He's an object of scorn among many of the Golden Kin."

"But what should I do about his threats?"

"You must tell Argamon everything when he returns. He'll protect you."

So I waited in an agony of hope and fear, pursued even in my dreams by an ever-changing Qabul—sometimes he was a snake slipping under the door of the ger, sometimes he was wolf-headed and waiting outside to spring on me.

But when Argamon returned a few days later, he was in a black temper. He spent the following days with Bayartou, singing war songs and drinking airag. Even when I begged to speak with him about Qabul he barked, "Shut up! My so-called brother is an adder and everyone knows it. I never want to hear his name again!" We women exchanged looks of grim despair. To cross Argamon would only lead to a beating.

That night after enduring the drunken assault that passed for lovemaking, I waited until Argamon's snores assured me he was deeply asleep. Slipping from his grip, I found my ikons, crossed myself and kissed them, and prayed for deliverance from Qabul, from Argamon's dark humors, and from the Mongols altogether.

But I could not stop there. I prayed for Kamileh and Temulun, Bourma and Tsetsegmaa, little Kuchan, and young Anna. Nor could I forget all the untold numbers of people brought to ruin by the Mongols. I prayed for everyone, not knowing whether anyone was listening.

Argamon's mysterious missions came to an end. Instead, as winter deepened he either served Batu Khan or sprawled in the ger drinking. One day he returned in a mood of wild joy. "The Danube River has frozen a spear length in depth. Once the khans consult their seers for a favorable date, we begin. Real action at last!"

The elaborate ceremonies that preceded any invasion were held on the next full moon. Argamon would go to the khan's great midnight divination with his shamans, but I was too unimportant to attend, though I went to the public ceremonies where the shamans chanted and made burnt offerings and so on before Batu's great tent.

Last of all, a procession of the other holy men passed before him, to bless him and the armies and pray for their victory. Mar Sauma, holding a cross aloft in one hand and carrying a lighted censer in the other, paced past the tent, singing in Syriac. Behind him an acolyte beat the wooden board. Father Kyril followed in just the same manner, intoning a blessing in his rich resonant voice. His ritual and Mar Sauma's seemed so alike; why must they hate each other?

A Muslim holy man passed, asking Allah to crush the infidel; a Jewish rabbi sang something doleful. Most surprising to me was the new Catholic priest, a Hungarian prisoner I had questioned some time ago. He too prayed for God's blessing, for a campaign against his own people! How could he do it? How could any of these holy men?

Last of all, the two saffron-and-purple-robed monks appeared carrying a portable shrine. On it rested a multi-armed black idol that reminded me of Yulta Beki's fierce mask. Like the Christians, they prayed, though in a peculiar chanting way, and lit incense and candles. But as their ritual ended, the idol actually rose up in midair! I was not the only one to gasp in horror and awe, for there was no way for them to hide strings and pulleys!

When it was over, I sought out Dorje. "Who are those men with the black idol? Are they Buddhists like you? What were they doing, and how did they get it to rise into the air? Was it a trick or black magic?"

"Slow down, my dear. One question at a time. Yes, they're Buddhist missionaries from Tibet, and what they did was neither trick nor black magic. The Mongols think religion and magic are the same, so these monks prove that Buddhism is more powerful than shamanism by performing such wonders.

"But they don't rely on black magic, only on the power of their spiritual practice. That is just a first step, though. Their real aim is to teach the Mongols the Holy Dharma, especially compassion."

"Well, it looked like devil worship to me!"

"Now, now, the Christians seek to perform wonders for the khan, too, yet they presume to call everyone else's works devil worship or magic. We Buddhists do not worship what you call devils, but neither do we fear dark energy. We know it can be tamed."

"But that idol looked evil and terrifying."

"Well, that statue—not an idol—is meant to look terrifying, partly because that is what a Mongol respects. But it is not a symbol of evil. It symbolizes protection from error, from being swallowed up by the frightening, hidden side of all things."

"I don't understand."

Dorje thought for awhile. "When a storm brings floods that destroy things, you call it an evil. But a deep riverbed will guide water and make it useful; you call that a good. But water is just water. Just so, when we don't look into what we don't understand, we flood the world with deluded feelings and deeds and even ideas. But when we have clear understanding, we can contain and direct ourselves like a riverbed. Our nature is the same either way, but with understanding, we can see clearly what benefits this world and choose that over deluded selfishness. *That* is what is at the root of what you call evil. And getting back to that statue: it simply pictures awakened mind conquering delusion."

I must have looked utterly confused.

"Well, Qabul is an example. He is bold in action, but lacking mercy or even reason, his boldness has turned him into a monster."

"All right, that makes sense. But I still cannot understand why those monks were praying for the Mongols to win wars."

"I was getting to that. What they truly pray for is for the Mongols to conquer their deluded minds. The deepest meaning of that statue is no: to wild mind, to greed and blindness, to outer *and* inner war!"

"Well, I don't see how that can happen without a miracle."

We walked in silence. Finally Dorje spoke. "There is another way to find inner guidance, a riverbed for 'no,' so to speak. The Buddha called it mindfulness, or the practice of peace. Just as a Mongol tames a pony, mindfulness allows us to gently rein ourselves in and cease to run wild. In time even what we thought was dark and untamable comes to light and becomes helpful."

I was beginning to feel overwhelmed.

"Hmm, I see I said too much. I know too little about Christianity to explain how your religion teaches the same thing, but surely it must. Every religion tries to express the same truth. It's a mistake to assume that only one possesses any and to claim that the others are all based on superstition or devil worship. And the Christians under Batu's control do admit that we Buddhists have tempered some of the Mongols' cruel ways.

"Well, enough said, yes? I wanted to ask after Kamileh. How is she?"

"Not well."

"I must find a way to visit her soon. Qacha keeps a tight rein on us all these days."

We spoke of other things then, but I felt at a loss. I wished I could talk with Father Kyril about what Dorje had said, because it made sense in some ways. But if the Father knew that Dorje was teaching me about his paganism, he would only order me to abandon my friendship. Yet Dorje's words kept haunting me, as if he had shot an arrow away from my understanding yet somehow hit my heart. It was so confusing that I never asked what "mind-fulness" was—some Buddhist way of casting spells, perhaps.

But there was no time for further ponderings. All the prayers and auguries over, certain that all the gods and spirits of this world and beyond were favoring them, Batu Khan sent out final orders to his noyans. In writing out one of the directives, I saw with relief that the tuman Qabul's jaghun had joined would be among the first to advance. I would have to leave my little household behind, too, though, something I dreaded.

On December 25, 1241, as I later learned, the tumans stormed across another great frozen river, the Danube. Indeed, it would seem their prayers for victory had been granted, for ordinarily the Danube doesn't freeze over—this I learned from the despairing prisoners I soon had to question. Winter tightened his grip, and city after city fell as the armies spread out toward western Hungary and the German principalities. After the Mongols' first onslaughts, I had thought there would be few Hungarians left, but I learned I was wrong when I was again forced to speak to new prisoners.

And then I began encountering captives who spoke an unfamiliar language called German. Although their land seemed much like Hungary, these people often had broad faces and fair hair instead of high cheekbones and dark hair. I had to ask one of our Hungarian translators to help me, not a happy solution, as there was little trust between the two peoples.

Yet from what little I could see, Germans peasants lived much as Hungarians or Rus' had. And the nobles held land under the arm of a prince or king, ruled their peasants for well or for ill, and worshipped the same God. All had fallen under the same Mongol yoke, were terrified, grief-stricken, angry—but still they clung to their old enmities.

Time passed in a bitter blur, full of tales of cruelty and loss. Although I no longer felt shaken in the same way, all I could offer these new captives were kindness and hopeless prayers.

Argamon was always at Batu Khan's side, never in action. And on the rare times when he was in camp, a gulf lay between us. When we lay together, he always hurt me. His mood was so black, perhaps he didn't even know. He took no joy in serving his khan, either, despite the honors heaped on him and his father, who seemed to regain his mind only when directing his men in battle. Qacha and he hardly ever saw each other anymore. All Argamon spoke of was war, all he did at rest was get drunk. He even hit me now and then. But he refused to admit to his grief.

Qabul's name came up only once. The ordus had rejoined the army, and my women were with me again, my only happiness. I was sewing while my master paced around our ger, drinking arki and muttering to himself about the generals' latest plans. He spoke as if I didn't already know them when I often wrote the dispatches myself. I glanced up. Temulun was trying to feed Kamileh, who had refused to eat so often that she had fallen ill and might die soon. But there was no question of letting her starve.

"Batu's cousin is already far to the south. Soon he'll find King Bela and your so-called Grand Prince Mikhail and kill them both. Father is in Bavaria, and so is that snake Qabul. All central Christendom will fall soon! These weakling kings and princes lie as helpless as wounded gazelles before us Mongol wolves. We're invincible!" His words swarmed around my head like angry bees. I felt so weary of it that I didn't even respond to the news about Prince Mikhail. "Yet here I am, following behind like an old woman, while Qabul wins renown. I only wish I could join them!" He glared at me.

Ungrateful wretch, I thought! "Perhaps you should," I blurted out.

He stared at me. "You'd like that, wouldn't you? And will you withhold your shield from me, too?" He stalked out of the ger, leaving me puzzled and uneasy.

Argamon soon returned in a mood of savage joy. "Batu Khan grants me my own thousand to lead. You have your wish, *Princess*. We'll see if you get all of it." His scowl warned me not to ask what he meant. Within two days he had left to replace a commander fallen in battle. I still prayed for his safety—if not for his sake, then for my own.

We awoke a few days later to find Kamileh lying stiff and cold. I grieved as though she had been my own grandmother. The women and I prepared her body for burial while Anna summoned Mar Sauma to pray for her. No one else cared, I thought, until Dorje arrived quite unexpectedly. I had never seen him so shocked nor had I ever seen him weep before, but he did, copiously. For the first time ever, *I* tried to comfort *him*.

Life continued in the same pattern: sometimes a scribe, sometimes a translator, sometimes forced to question prisoners. I began to wonder why I was still in Batu Khan's ordu when others knew these German dialects and I did not. When he summoned me to his golden tent to interpret for him, he often stared at me, his face a hard smiling mask.

Few people felt easy near such an important man, but I found too many reasons for his disquieting attentions. Was he thinking of all the troubles that

had erupted in Qacha's camp because of me, or of Qabul's accusations ...
or of Argamon's absence?

Each bitterly cold day brought messengers into the camp with more
news of victory. I hoped it meant the war would end soon, since Christian
armies were falling like wheat under the scythe. If so and the prophecy about
me was finally fulfilled, what would come next: serving in Argamon's bed for
endless years, enduring his pinches and slaps, his nightly rapes? It seemed
that the future could hold no promise for me or for Christendom.

SPRING TO AUTUMN, Anno Domini 1242

The days had begun to grow longer and warmer when the unimaginable happened. We were near the city of Vienna. English John had been sent to demand its surrender, and Batu Khan was holding court with some of his cousins and generals. Another interpreter and I were waiting to translate for some envoys who had come to surrender a nearby city—and unwittingly to entertain Batu with their pleas.

A clamor arose outside: men shouting, horses galloping much too fast for camp life, gear jingling. A sudden silence and a handful of filthy, weary-looking men entered and hastily genuflected before the khan. I caught the flash of a flat, oblong paize. It was gold, which meant that this token of free passage was from the court of the Great Khan himself.

"Well, what is it?" Batu Khan demanded.

"My lord, the Great Khan has gone to Tengri's embrace. You are summoned back to Karakorum for a kuriltai to elect his successor."

His words fell on every ear like an ax blow. Batu started up from his throne in shock and, waving to us lesser attendants to leave, turned to his closest advisors with hands spread in stunned surprise. Once outside, most men rushed off to spread the news while a few of us hovered aimlessly. Waves of noise rumbled through the ordu like thunder—shouting, wails, people rushing from their gers to gape or weep, but not from sorrow over losing their Khakan, for none of us knew him. We simply felt at a loss.

I stood at the edge of a group surrounding Mahmud. "The biggest question," he opined, "is whether Batu Khan will obey the summons when all of Western Christendom lies at his feet, or whether he will defy tradition and continue this invasion."

"Yes," said another man, "and remember his quarrel with Kuyuk Khan. As the Khakan's eldest son, he will likely succeed his father. Surely he holds it against Batu that he was disgraced!"

Mahmud nodded. "Exactly. I see nothing for our khan to gain by leaving and much to lose. His only friend in Karakorum is Mongke Khan." I wandered away at that point. In truth none of us knew the politics in Karakorum or what Batu Khan and his generals would decide, although as I returned to my ger, I heard plenty of men guessing.

The decision came quickly. Within days I was writing dispatches for Batu's arrow messengers to recall the armies. One message did divide me against myself. Not only were the armies in the Germanies recalled, but the pursuit of Hungary's King Bela was halted. So Western Christendom—and one king—were spared. But so was Prince Mikhail.

Ironically, long after I had stopped caring, I did learn Mikhail's fate. I think about three years ago, word reached us in Constantinople that he finally had come to Batu Khan to submit. To shame him, the khan ordered Prince Mikhail to bow to the golden ongghot of Chinggis Khan. When the prince and his men refused, the Mongols beat them to death. I don't think they even troubled with the usual royal carpet. And now it is rumored that the man who betrayed Kyiv will be sainted for standing firm against paganism!

For a day or two all was confusion, shouting, and hurried packing. Dorje, after some errand to Batu from Qacha, came to visit me and share his latest news. The other women were dismantling the ger, and I was directing little Kuchan, who was struggling to carry a small box. At first I only listened to the monk with half an ear.

"Qacha was at the council. Subodai had to argue Batu into leaving," he told me. "The khan didn't want to abandon the invasion, since it means he can conquer no more domains. I doubt he'll return to Karakorum, though. That proud and angry Prince Kuyuk is the likeliest man to become khakan.

"Batu has sent the messengers from Karakorum back with an agreement—not that he's happy about it—that Kuyuk's mother will be regent until the kuriltai assembles. She is the Khakan's main widow, and one of the messengers revealed that she's bribing all the nobles in Mongolia to ensure her son is elected. Ogedai wanted his grandson to succeed him, but the boy is too young and his supporters are bound to lose to Kuyuk's.

"Now scavengers eager for spoils are gathering, no doubt ready to attack and rend Batu to pieces at a sign from Kuyuk. But as long as Batu seems ready to go to the kuriltai, he'll draw no blame to himself."

These ugly politics boded ill, and I needed to think about their implications. Would Argamon return to Karakorum, since his wife was there? Would I have to travel all the way across Asia into an alien world to find Qabul's hatred awaiting me there, too?

I scarcely dared ask, "Will all the other troops go back to Karakorum?"

"No. Qacha won't go, if that's what you're wondering. He belongs to Batu's ordus, and he can expect to receive choice new yurts somewhere here in the west. I cannot guess about Argamon and Qabul. Qacha's sons have no reason to go east, though Argamon might send for his wife. And Batu will reward him richly—likely give him his own ordu. Who knows? You may be encamped near your old home soon."

I stiffened. Dorje meant well, but home was gone and nightmares still marred my rest from time to time. More important was what would happen when the Mongols were no longer at war and I was no longer needed. Would Argamon still want me then, or would I be a constant reminder of a painful past? And with Qabul ready to do me harm, my life would surely be full of fear. Dorje had heard me voice these concerns before, so there was no point in repeating them. Instead, I tried for a more cheerful subject.

"I hear that the armies took too many captives to travel quickly, so Batu has freed thousands of them. Are you not glad, Dorje? I've seen whole families I know on their way home, right on that trail over there." As I pointed, a group soldiers on horseback trotted past us and out that same path. Dorje looked and frowned. "I wonder where those soldiers are going."

I turned to answer a question. "No, put that over there, Anna."

Dorje suddenly leaned close to me. "They're playing a cruel trick on their prisoners," he whispered into my ear. "They go to cut them all down far from the ordu. They would never truly free them." I stopped for a moment and took a deep breath. I no longer reacted as strongly as I used to, but it still felt like someone had struck me in the stomach. It reminded me of Q'ingling. Had she felt this way, too?

"Oh, and more sorry news Sofia. English John is dead in Vienna. Batu Khan would have taken it next. I don't know whether the khan left him to his fate or if John's tongue finally failed him, but his head now sits on a stake on the battlement walls."

"God rest his soul," I said. "The first night I met him, he toasted to no tomorrows. Do you remember? How sad life is."

We bade each other farewell, but what Dorje had told me about the freed captives haunted me. I could only comfort myself with the thought that with the armies leaving, they would soon cease to plague these sad lands. I was mistaken.

Within days Batu's tumans had regrouped and we had left for unfamiliar territory. At first I thought we would pass through Hungary again and that we were merely following the Mongol custom of never taking the same path twice. But from the army dispatches I now had to write, I learned that we were moving southeast into Bulgaria. Noyan Subodai intended to crush more peoples on the way back to the steppes.

The days passed in a cold haze of hurry, first over dry terrain and great sandy hills, then across fertile plains and over snow-laden mountains. Nothing could cheer my heart: not the great dark forests or the well-watered valleys or pearly crocuses blooming in the melting snow, for the armies carved a highway of destruction. Thick, dirty walls of smoke often rose in the distance in all directions.

At least my household was allowed to stay with me. But things began to go wrong. Once a cart wheel suddenly fell off, and goods toppled everywhere. A week or so later, a huge gash mysteriously appeared in a tent panel overnight, all the ropes slashed through. And the mischief got more direct and more threatening. One morning I found a piece of meat in front of the ger with a black substance buried inside a slit cut in it. Was someone trying to poison Wolf? I could not forget Lu's agonized death throes.

Worse yet, I awoke one night thinking I heard a rustle. Little Kuchan sat up with a cry and Tsetsegmaa began whispering quietly to him, so I thought no more of it and went back to sleep. But in the morning, I found a knife lying on Argamon's side of the divan, pointed at me. Bourma had been missing it for days. She and Tsetsegmaa muttered together about witchcraft and set protective charms around the ger.

I wanted to blame these mishaps on Qabul, though there was no reason other than his hatred to connect him with them. But I could not forget that the night he'd tried to rape me, all the guards seemed to have disappeared. He could have allies in Batu Khan's ordu or Argamon's, or I could have secret enemies, someone jealous of our standing who could be bribed to do us mischief. From then on I made Temur sleep just inside the door.

One morning shortly thereafter, we opened the door to find a strip of stinking fabric lying across the threshold. It had been smeared with blood and offal, but I knew what it was: the same blue silk from my gown that Har Nuteng had used in preparing her fetishes. That *had* to be Qabul. I must brave Argamon's wrath and expose this madman!

I even told Toramun, who cried, "Let me get my hands on that dog!" She laughed at herself. "Well, I know it's not possible right now, but I can warn all the other translators and get them and their menials to look out for you."

To my relief, there were no more incidents after that.

Now that we were on the move, I saw Dorje only rarely, and I missed him far more than I missed Argamon. Once we met by chance, each of us on an errand to Batu Khan, and we spoke together afterward. I asked him how things were in Qacha's ordu. "Quiet. He's away as often as possible. He buries himself in war, and his men are often in the forefront of these new invasions. He leaves me behind mostly."

I sighed. "When will it end, Dorje? Spring has barely arrived, and already the armies sweep over new lands—Croatia? Serbia? They're like a plague. They burned a big city, too. I think it was called Belgrade. I saw the smoke."

"Yes, I remember it."

"I know they wipe out any Kipchaks who fled here after their khan's murder, but the dispatches I write command the armies to grind not only people but even the land itself to nothingness. Why? The Mongols will never return here; the river valleys are—or were—lush, but they're wedged between mountains, and they are useless for the Mongol way of life."

"It's another war plan," he answered. "Subodai has decided that the Carpathian Mountains will be the border of Batu's domain—so that is their use for mountains. As to the rest, it's the same as always: terrorize and cripple your enemy so he can never attack at your back. No one will dare cross this border. At least the Khan of the Bulgars has submitted to Batu, which hopefully will spare his people the worst blows."

"I sometimes think the fate of the world turns not on the great events that find their way into our histories but on hidden ones that few will remember," I mused. "Had the Kipchaks and Alani not rebelled, the Mongols would likely have taken Kyiv a year sooner, and all of Christendom would have been swallowed up before Khakan Ogedai's death."

"Yes, karma unfolds in strange ways," he answered. We walked in silence for several steps. "How are you these days? I hear that Argamon is rarely here."

"Yes. And things are not good." I told Dorje about all the mischief done to us.

"Were you ever able to tell him what Qabul did?"

"No, he refused to listen."

"If you wish, I'll speak for you when I next see him. Argamon can protect you, but for now you must be on your guard at all times. Keep Temur nearby, and never walk alone. I wish I could do more ... Would you like me to speak to Qacha?"

"No, I doubt it would help. He probably hates me enough for all the trouble I stirred up in his family. I'll wait and try again with Argamon."

I still wonder if it was foolish to reject Dorje's offer.

After crossing countless mountains, hills, valleys, and rivers, we turned northeast, halting on the flat flood plain where the Danube enters the Black Sea. There we stayed for the rest of the spring while the remaining armies and their ordus assembled. I was able to rest from my labors, as fewer secretaries and no translators were needed. I could have rejoiced in my surroundings, for this was a lush and beautiful land. A myriad of birds and waterfowl sang among lazy streams meandering to the sea, and the air was damp and sweet. But though there had been no more uncanny happenings, I still felt uneasy.

Argamon arrived to serve Batu Khan again, but his temper was still short. For several days I sought an opening in his mood so I could tell him about Qabul, but he was elsewhere in his mind when he wasn't angry. Too often he was drunk. When I tried to speak with him, he shouted at me to shut up. Yet he still used me to satisfy his lust, though he no longer tried to please me—indeed, he seemed to like hurting me.

And I had a new worry. Argamon began pulling Anna's dark hair, pinching her growing breasts, or seizing her from behind and fondling her privates. Her starts of terror made him laugh. My distress and her fear spurred him into ever-bolder lewdness toward her. The poor girl lacked any spirit, and if he were to supplant me with her, she would be the target of his growing cruelty. I'd have been lost but for Dorje and Q'ing-ling; must I now befriend—indeed guard—a rival? It felt like being trapped in thick mud.

Everything changed with a dream. In it I was alone on an empty morning. All around me stretched a clear green plain that went on forever, flat and desolate. Nothing moved on it except waving grasses. There was no sound but the sighs of the wind. At first the vast emptiness felt unbearable. Loneliness tore at my heart like a hooked lance. Then I realized I could hear my own breath coming in and out, that the sighing wind was the same as my breath, and that my aloneness was also my freedom. I awoke at dawn, surprised to find that I was smiling.

I decided to speak to Anna and reassure her when the other women were outside.

But the moment we were alone, Anna cried, "I must warn you: I had a bad dream last night. Argamon was chasing us, trying to bite us. Dreams about teeth mean bad luck."

Her words recalled to me Qabul's gleaming teeth, white as bones. "Anna, listen. I know Argamon frightens you, and I understand. He teases you because he wants to bed you. He isn't a bad man. He's just angry and confused. He means you no real harm."

Anna burst into tears. "Means me no harm? These monsters mean us nothing but harm. I don't know how you can stand that murderer's touch."

Tears started to my eyes as well. "It hasn't been easy, but I found friends who showed me how I could help Argamon at least to become less cruel and—"

"Less cruel? Since when? On his orders, his men killed my whole family before my eyes! Then he "bedded" me, as you call it, in front of their hacked and headless bodies! We should have stayed hiding in the woods! My father believed those demons—they promised we could come back and raise crops in peace—we thought we were safe, all lies. They just wanted us to reap the grain before they stole it and killed everyone and burned everything. When Argamon took me back to his camp, I saw fires and death everywhere!" Anna was sobbing too hard to say more. I took her in my arms and rocked her gently.

I waited outside all afternoon for Argamon. As soon as he arrived, I sent Anna and the other women inside while I stood before him, trembling like a birch tree in the wind. Indeed, a wind had begun to rise, chasing dark clouds before it.

I faced him boldly. "Argamon, when you were in Hungary last fall, did you and your men kill all the peasants and take their grain? Does Batu Khan know? And did you rape Anna after killing her parents?"

He frowned. "Of course we killed them—those were our orders. The khan decided we didn't need them anymore. But I didn't kill Anna's family. I found her cowering in a corner of their hut just before we set it on fire—but yes, I fucked her! And I brought her to you instead of burning her to death in her hut! What is it to you, anyway?"

But I was already running away. The world dimmed as tall thunderclouds rode in on the warm wind like sky warriors. I ran past tents and people and herds and onto the green plain, leaping little streams where birds flew from the grasses in alarm. Above, the massive clouds slowly shut off the sky.

Finally I fell at the top of a little rise, gasping raggedly, lost in misery. What a fool I was to believe I could civilize even one of these fiends from Hell! My life with Argamon was a web of lies, the Lady was dead, Dorje was another fool if he thought it would ever change. And I was nothing but a sad, lost whore.

I must have huddled there for some time, scarcely aware of the rising wind whistling through the grasses. But slowly, underneath my despair, something began to move within me, a deep kernel of my being that had lain fallow too long.

I lifted my head. I was not defeated, I was outraged! A cleansing wrath swelled within me and flowed through my entire being. I was not like these uncaring monsters, and I never would be. At that moment I felt a rush of strength: somehow, somewhere, I would flee this vicious, twisted Mongol world. I would seek out the good, and I would never look back.

I stood up just as lightning illuminated the darkening plains and clusters of ordus in blinding white and blue. In the distance, groups of horsemen were galloping for shelter.

Thunder assaulted my ears; huge raindrops struck the ground like arrows. The downpour drenched me, soaking my gown and sending my hair streaming past my knees like a river of blood. The angry sky, for once, mirrored my fury. I looked up, raised my arms, and shook my fists at the sky. "You, Tengri, you and your gods of cruelty, of storm and fire and flood, I defy you! You cannot take my heart from me! Strike me dead if you dare, but I will leave here, I will leave your power behind me! I will escape your grip!"

Lightning blinded me, thunder cracked the air, winds buffeted me in great gusts, rain fell in sheets, and a bolt shot between sky and ground. One group of horsemen scattered in panic. I almost laughed. I stood firm, glorying in the danger, my head thrown back to the sky, rain striking my face, until like a lightning raid the storm raced off, leaving a wedge of sky between cloud and earth to the west.

The setting sun appeared between them and cast brilliant rays over the countryside, transforming it into glowing gold and green. I turned and walked slowly back toward the ordu.

I was halfway there when Argamon came toward me in the gathering dusk. When his mare reached my side, he silently held his hand out to me to pull me up behind him. I shook my head and kept walking. Silence stretched between us.

Finally he spoke. "I was coming for you when the storm broke, but the lightning drove me back." I snorted my contempt. "I know what you did out there. You controlled the storm. You *are* a shamanka, aren't you? I should never have hurt you. All that time you could have destroyed me, but you did not.

"Sofia, I beg you to forgive me. Please."

I stopped and stared him in the eyes until his gaze faltered. "Why should I even answer that? Believe what you wish, Argamon, but do not expect me to care. You and your people are without soul or heart. Soon, somehow, I will leave you for good."

I strode straight back to our ger where I dumped out my lacquer chest, gathered up a few things, wrapped myself in Papa's precious cloak, and stalked past Argamon, standing with his mouth agape. I went to the tent of the other women translators; without a word they made room for me. After a silent meal and drinking more airag than usual to warm myself, I stripped off my damp clothing and fell asleep.

Early the next morning, a sharp pain in my side startled me awake. I sat up. Two of Batu Khan's men stood over me, scowling. The rest of the ger was empty. "Get up," snarled one of them. I scrambled up, bleary with sleep and too much airag, snatched my gown, and put one arm through a sleeve, but they seized me and almost dragged me out of the ger, still naked.

Now I came fully awake—fear gripped me as hard as the men's hands. People stopped and stared, but I scarcely saw them. The men dragged me along, shoved me into one of the khan's smaller gers, and thrust me onto my knees. It was warm and dim. A small fire burned in the hearth. Batu Khan was seated on a low divan with his sore foot on a stool, and Qacha, Argamon, and Yulta Beki stood around him frowning at me.

"Come here, Sofia," the khan ordered sternly. I felt like a doe putting her neck into the wolf's mouth as I slowly crawled forward, my heart pounding out of my chest. Hands cupped, partly to shield my breasts, I sank down before him. I had never felt—or been—so naked. I looked up at him and he stared down at me, but what he sought I could not guess.

"You were out in the thunderstorm yesterday. What were you doing there?"

"I was angry with Argamon and I ran away. I got caught in the storm."

"No, I mean what were you *doing* in the storm?"

I paused, thinking quickly. What *had* I done? "I was so miserable, I asked Tengri to strike me dead." Not quite the truth, but neither was it a complete lie.

The men stirred in surprise. "Why would you want to die, Sofia?" Batu asked. "You have everything: prosperity, a good master, a position of respect. Why?"

I hung my head. These men had no more understanding than the sad half-wit beggars who had once roamed the streets of Kyiv. "I was miserable. I can say no more."

"She was angry that we cleansed the earth of more filthy peasants before we left Hungary, my Khan," interrupted Argamon.

"I *was* angry, and sad, too!" I retorted, suddenly feeling outraged again. Courage welled up from nowhere. "Why keep hurting and killing innocent people, my Khan? I thought Argamon had begun to understand the need for—for—at least mercy, but I was wrong, and it hurt." I glared at Argamon, and to my surprise he flinched.

"Well, your quarrels with your master seem to be only the beginning," countered Batu. "What I want to know is whether you can call down thunderbolts!"

"No, I cannot, since I'm still alive," I muttered.

"Do not speak lightly, young woman," snapped the khan. "Would it surprise you to learn that Qabul was struck dead by lightning yesterday as he and his men tried to outrace that storm? He was clutching an amulet hanging from his neck, and red hair was wound around it. There are many questions here. Did you give your hair to Qabul in secret? You were once secret lovers, weren't you, and you feared he would betray you. Are you waiting to destroy Argamon next?" He leaned back, crossing his arms.

"Qabul? Dead?" The lightning that had hit the ground near those horsemen: it had struck him? The blood drained from my face. Then I fully understood. "You cannot believe Qabul and I were lovers, or any of this patchwork of lies!" All four men stared back at me; their manner said everything.

Realizing that my life depended on it, I tried to still my racing heart, tried to think of what to say. I did not want to die like Har Nuteng or her sorcerer. "I always feared Qabul. And why would I curse Argamon? I have been ever faithful to him—ask anyone who knows me, including him!"

"Not after what I saw last night—maybe you even meant to kill me then! You were angry enough, and you told me you cared nothing for me. I'm bound to be next."

"You misunderstood me, Argamon. You know why I said what I did, and it was because I abhor killing and cruelty. Would I then be capable of murdering Qabul?"

"Maybe your thunderbolt just found the wrong target," Argamon repeated, ignoring me. "Or you just began with killing him before moving on to me. Maybe he was about to betray your secret affair to me—he'd have loved that—and you stopped the bastard!"

"This grows more and more absurd," I cried. "I didn't know Qabul was out there yesterday. None of us has even seen him in months! Even if you overlook how I feared him, when am I supposed to have been unfaithful?"

"You've had plenty of chances to betray me, especially since coming to this ordu! That day we were to go to my mother, one of my servants saw you with Qabul. You said he waylaid you; a lover's quarrel, he said! Were you trying to get back your lock of hair?"

"One of your servants?" I too stunned to say more.

"Oh yes, he's told me other things, too, over the last while—"

"He lied, Argamon! And I think I know why. You should question him, for many strange and evil things have happened to me since I came to this ordu. And I will show you how Qabul got a lock of my hair—by ripping it from my head when he once tried to seize and rape me!" I leaned over and parted my hair to show the men my scar.

"I can think of more than one way *that* could have happened," countered Argamon.

"Then let me call my own witnesses! Rage and fear are blinding you into believing these lies about me, and not only about Qabul being my lover. Foremost, I am no witch! A powerful shaman like Yulta Beki would surely know. I have done foolish things since you enslaved me, but never have I practiced magic or sought anyone's harm. He knows this, for he has more than once read my heart." I looked straight into the old man's pale eyes, and doubt crept over his face.

I turned to Batu. "My khan, it's not in my nature to curse or destroy. That is why I fled Argamon yesterday and got caught in the storm." I paused, choosing my words carefully, reveling in having my voice back at last, as though a curse had been lifted from *it*.

"I believe Tengri himself punished Qabul." I looked up at Qacha and then Batu Khan. "I beg you: call Dorje and Toramun. You trust them. Ask them about Qabul. Or ask Temulun or Bourma or Tsetsegmaa. I know they're slaves, but any of them would gladly speak for me."

Batu Khan stroked his thin beard and reluctantly summoned his guards. "Find Qacha's monk Dorje, and bring him here, along with Toramun."

Qacha added, "I left him with my men-at-arms outside the khan's golden tent."

The men stared at me stonily the entire time we were waiting. I slowly slipped my gown on, though I doubt any of them cared whether I was naked or not.

The wait seemed endless, but finally the old monk arrived, looking both alarmed and curious. He probably only knew of Qabul's death or he'd have defended me to Qacha.

"Dorje, would you please tell Batu Khan why you asked to bring me to his ordu?"

"Of course, Sofia."

In a clear and quiet way that added power to his words, Dorje spoke of Qabul's attempted rape, including the hair he had torn from my head, and how I had fled in terror. At one point Argamon interrupted. "I remember that night," he said, looking a little shamefaced. "You were trembling like a leaf when you returned to the ger. I thought you'd seen a ghost."

Just then Toramun entered the ger and bowed, looking grimmer than I had ever seen her. The old monk was explaining why I had been afraid to tell anyone and how I'd been forced to leave Q'ing-ling behind against my will. Argamon's face crumpled with shame.

Toramun interrupted. "If you're speaking of that adder Qabul, there is more." And she launched into a colorful description of Qabul's harassment, his invasion of our ger and his threats, of the petty injuries I had endured since then, and of the protective circle she and the other translators had formed around me. She ended with, "You have a traitor among your servitors," and she named one of Argamon's minor grooms who never traveled with him. "Ask him who bribed him, and he'll fall apart as he did with me, the coward! He hasn't tried any more mischief because he knows what I'd do to him."

"He's the one who accused you, Sofia!" Argamon exclaimed. Toramun looked ready to march out and punish the man herself, but my master said, "Leave him to me."

"Well, you can see that Allah had ample reason to destroy Qabul," added Toramun.

Dorje said, "And Sofia has been trying to protect her master all this time, at great risk to herself. I feared to make more trouble, Noyan Qacha, when you were so burdened by grief. That is why I never spoke of Qabul's crimes to you after that dark day. Please forgive me if I was wrong." He bowed to Qacha with cupped hands.

I glanced up. The noyan had shrunken into himself and turned old. He had finally seen what a criminal his eldest son was, that Qabul might even have helped Har Nuteng perform her witchcraft—and that he had lied to his own father. For the first time I pitied the man, whose heedless behavior as a father had done so much damage. And to think that once I had wanted only to live long enough ruin him and Argamon.

Argamon took a deep, shaky breath and turned to Qacha, his hands cupped. "Father, I must add to what Dorje and Toramun say. Qabul often did evil things to me, including stealing Bolgana from me. But when you forbade me to take any revenge on him, I could never speak out against him. Now I must." We all stared at him in surprise.

"Qabul murdered Bolgana. He might as well have stabbed her to death. Demons never attacked her, unless he was one. When she was dying in labor, Bolgana told my wife what happened. Out of shame she made her sister promise silence. But it was too much for Doquz to bear, so she told me.

"After he married Bolgana, Qabul tried to turn her from loving me by boasting that he was the better man. But he turned vicious when he saw it won him no favor. When they lay together, he began hitting her and forcing himself on her. Even after she became pregnant he found reasons to hurt her, and he threatened to kill anyone who spoke of the beatings.

"Finally he forbade Bolgana's servants ever to sleep there again. An irony, is it not, Sofia?" He glanced over at me and my eyes widened. "The last time he beat her, she went into labor and lost both their baby and her life. He must have damaged his child while it lay in her womb. And one by one he killed all of her servants, too.

"He had almost a private prison in the east wing, Father, with his friends as guards. I think that's why he never returned to your central camp after you promoted him. Hearing this may pain you, but it lends power to these other claims."

A dead silence followed. That sad doomed girl and her baby—and her women, too.

Finally Batu Khan spoke. "There can be no doubt, then. Sofia is innocent, and Qabul was guilty of far more than we thought. He violated the sacredness of marriage!"

He looked down at me. "The Eternal Blue Sky has a special feeling for you, Sofia. He brought the felon to justice in his own way and his own time. You must mend this quarrel with your master and return to his ger. And Argamon."

"Yes, my Khan?"

"Treat your young princess well. She's a rare treasure. Were it not for her, you and Qacha might both be dead by now."

He turned to the old shaman. "Your prophecy has been amply fulfilled, yes?"

Yulta Beki nodded gravely. If it was possible, he looked whiter than ever and, for the first time, humble. "Yes, my Khan. Often I have read Sofia Begi's heart and found it innocent, even when events sometimes cast doubt on it, and now … I regret my error."

He looked at me. "Argamon sought me out after your quarrel last night, almost shaking with fear and certain you were a dark shamanka. And before dawn came word of Qabul's death. The amulet with your hair on it made suspicion fit upon you like a sheath upon a sword, for no one saw how Qabul could have gotten it. I began to doubt myself.

"Yet thinking back on my prophecy, it all fits: lightning from the sky *did* reveal what was hidden—more than anyone could guess. You were merely present." The shaman turned and bowed to Batu. "May I go, my khan?"

Batu nodded. "In fact, all of you but Qacha can go. We must speak together. There are still felons among Qabul's companions to bring to justice.

"And Sofia Begi, you can finish dressing." The khan barked a strange laugh. I pulled my gown closed, bowed, and followed Argamon out, struggling with the fastenings.

Outside, Dorje said, "I will wait here for Qacha." He smiled at me encouragingly.

I dragged my heels as my master strode to the translators' tent. People stared at my half-dressed state, but I was past shame. He stood by the door while I slowly pulled on the rest of my clothing and collected my belongings. Then I had to follow him back to our ger. The other slaves fled, Anna sobbing with fear.

Argamon took my arm and forced me to look at him. "Sofia, for over two years you have been with me. I see now that you are no witch and your heart is good. I caused you needless harm since Mother died. That bastard groom!

"But you do have power over me. I know you hate me now, but I want you to see: soon I can be fair-minded and—"

I looked away, mistrusting anything he said.

"Look at me! This time *you* must understand. All my life I strove to be a tiger of strength and fearlessness like Father or Qabul. It was hard, for I must constantly choose between Father's ways or Mother's. She always said that valor is more than crushing enemies. She was wise and kind, but her wisdom was like glass, too fragile for war. But I never forgot her counsel, nor was I blind to your kind ways. Soon there will be a time for all that. This war is over, and soon I'll be a clan leader in my own right. I promise you before Tengri that then I will be just to those under my boot heels. Chinggis Khan himself told us the same: be like a tiger in war and like a dove in peace. You will see."

I snorted. This was the domain of the tiger; there was no room for doves. "Look at your past! You not only hurt me, you hurt and killed so many others, like Anna's family! Even if your sword didn't touch them, it came to the same thing!"

Argamon flushed, loosened his grip on me, and looked down. "Yes, I ordered my men to kill everyone we found. Those were Batu Khan's orders. And yes, I raped her.

"When I took her, she looked up at me just as you did when I first seized you by your tent—remember? Madness seized me. I saw *you* under me, not her. Ever since Mother went to Tengri, I felt shame over dismissing Yulta Beki. And I blamed you for going to Batu Khan instead of staying with her—your powers might have saved her in the first place.

"As for Anna: I just wanted you to suffer after that serpent groom hissed lies into my ears about you and Qabul. I was crazed with doubt and anger! Yet I could not believe them, or you would be dead." I shuddered and he dropped my arm.

Turning away and crossing his arms, he added, "One more thing. We were at war. It's my duty as a warrior to kill, and I will never feel shame for that." He fell silent.

I thought carefully. "Argamon, I will pass over what you said about your mother and Anna and even about war. Just know that I cannot hate you after all we've shared. But also know this: I stay with you now because I have no choice. When you reap your rewards, I will not be there. You say you will be just when the time comes. Well, do so, not to please me or your mother, but because it is the right thing to do!"

Once Argamon might have struck me for my boldness, but instead he simply turned and stared at me in fearful awe. Now that I no longer desired it, I did have power over him.

"I must think about this. Will you stay here if I go riding alone?"

"Where else would I go? But may I look for Dorje while you are gone?"

"Of course." Argamon turned to go, but he paused at the threshold. "Yulta Beki's prophecy was wrong in one way: I have *never* known how to make you mine; nothing I tried ever worked. Instead, you made me yours."

For some time after he had left, I stood there, stunned. Made Argamon mine? What did he mean? Too much had just happened, and I felt swept in too many directions at once.

Finally I sat down by the hearth and began putting my belongings back into my lacquered chest. But my mind wouldn't stop. What *had* happened?

Well, I was free from Qabul at last. Had I somehow caused his death? No! Or any of the other troubles that had haunted Qacha's family? Again, no; they had merely been exposed. And did lightning striking Qabul just as I was defying Tengri to strike me mean that the Mongol gods were real after all? Had Tengri truly punished him, or had God? What was this unimaginable power that could take so many forms and could grip us and toss us about? Was this God the Father who had sent His Son as proof of His love?

Suddenly I stopped and looked at each item as if I had never seen it before: my two ikons, a faded linen towel, a jade bracelet Q'ing-ling had given me, a cup. Looking into the chest I found the box of jewelry from Khwarizm and an ivory comb Argamon had carved for me. I opened the vial of scented water from Selim and inhaled soft fragrance. Last, I took out a polished steel mirror and saw a face, as hazy as I was to myself: so serious for my fourteen years. I had learned to hide my feelings—not to cry—most of the time. Had my imagination, my curiosity, my sense of adventure fled, or were they just buried, as my outrage had been?

At that moment the dusky interior of the ger grew brighter, objects stood out in sharp color and detail, the smoke from the fire smelled stronger. Noises from outside sounded louder. A chorus of bird song burst from nowhere. And I was filled with love, as if *my* God had released His grip and effortlessly made me—and the world—whole again.

I turned at a noise, and there was Dorje standing at the door, his saffron and wine robes brilliant as if lit from within.

"May I come in? I saw Argamon ride off and came to ask how you are."

"I was just about to look for you," I smiled. "Is it not amazing to be alive?"

He smiled, too. "Yes, indeed." He sat down and peered closely at me. "You look radiant, especially for a girl who just had a brush with death. Or perhaps that's why."

I recalled Dorje's brush with death, but since I was not supposed to know, I replied, "I cannot imagine why, Dorje. I only know that suddenly I feel truly alive and at peace with the world and myself. Do you ever feel that way?"

He smiled. "Yes, my dear."

"Just a moment ago, I was thinking about that storm, how strange that both Qabul and I were out in it and that he, not I, was struck by lightning. He was so terrified of it." Dorje nodded. "The truth is, I was defying Tengri at that very instant. And it was as if *Qabul's* god answered me by killing him in that way. Utterly confusing.

"And then I was just sitting here, and the world opened up. I was no longer divided from it or myself or anyone else. Even from Qabul, though our link was twisted and sad." At that moment a great pity for that cruel, deluded man flowed through me.

"Why, I see! Whether we say Tengri or God, it's the same power and wisdom, and we all share in it." Dorje smiled and nodded.

"Still, some beliefs must be truer than others, so how do I know what to believe? I don't know what Father Kyril would say if I told him all this. I want to make sense of what I feel, to know what to believe. Do you see?"

Dorje stroked his cheeks. "Yes. But truth is always too big for any belief, Sofia. If we rely on fixed notions, including God, as a lodestar for our life, the idea too easily twists into an idol. Ideas are like arrows shot by children that always fall short of the mark.

"Sofia, trust your heart and your intelligence. We may need ideas to navigate the seas of life, but best to rely on experience first."

We sat together in amiable silence for a while. Finally I said, "You have always been such a good friend to me. I'll always remember you."

"Why, am I going to die soon or are you planning to?"

"No, but I won't be staying here much longer. I can feel it. Your place is among the Mongols, but mine will never be. When I can, I will escape and find my Uncle Vasily in Constantinople. He'll certainly be surprised." I laughed, but tears sprang to my eyes.

"Well, for now let's take a walk. It's a beautiful day, and I feel strangely cheerful."

"Yes, it is beautiful," the old monk agreed. "And as you say, cheerful and strange."

AUTUMN TO WINTER, Anno Domini 1242

On our way east, for over a month I could stop at any time and feel enveloped by love. It enabled me to be obedient and humble with Argamon, who seemed to have taken my words to heart. At least he no longer struck anyone—except his groom, whom he only beat senseless when I begged him not to kill him. He sent the man to Qacha for judgment, so I doubt the fellow lived much longer.

Still, Argamon seemed distant toward me. When he had returned that evening after my trial, he looked away from me, so I slept with the other women. As time passed, he began taking Tsetsegmaa or Bourma into his bed. Anna he never touched again.

I tried not to mind. If I had failed to truly civilize him, I did not poison my heart with bitterness over it. And at least I was following Father Kyril's counsel, little though it meant to me now. I had but one aim: to escape.

But as the days passed, just as Dorje had foretold, that bright wholeness dimmed into my idea of it. And doubts crept in. Who was I to think God had touched me? And how could I trust myself when I wouldn't trust His priest? I tried to push these worries away with prayer and patience, but I didn't know what else to do. I wished I could speak with Dorje again, but he was traveling with Qacha. Life shrank back into dull duty.

The one time I tried to speak about my experience with Toramun, she just snorted and offered me airag, saying, "You can get lovely visions from this, too!"

I was taken aback. "So you have no faith?"

She shrugged. "Certainly I do. I'm Muslim—although not a good one or I wouldn't drink. It's a beautiful religion, but nowadays I have no use for rituals, and the same with love. I've seen too many people abuse religion—*and* love! If they don't make you a better person, then what use are they? I keep my faith in my own way."

I had no answer to that, for I agreed with her about abuse; on the other hand, that moment of perfection was no false vision. It was more a feeling of connection to the world and to God through ... I had no words. I never spoke of religion with her again.

The ordus continued their eastward journey at a leisurely pace. We often stopped for days to rest among the long grasses beside some slow-moving creek or river that fed the Black Sea. Having pieced together remarks that Batu had made in my presence, I knew our goal was the mighty Volga River, which flows into the Caspian Sea and lies far to the east of the River Don. Batu Khan and his brothers had often wintered there with their father. The question clearly was not whether to return to Karakorum but how to create endless delays, thereby putting off Kuyuk's election as Khakan.

Batu had taken to summoning me on the pretext of interpreting for him. But I would often arrive to find no one there but him, his musicians, and a servant or two. Instead, he might show me a casket of pearls sent by someone seeking his favor, or he would be examining a sleek falcon on his wrist and would call me close to look at it. Once he showed me a new gift from India: a little hairy brown man-creature with a long tail, called a monkey. It ran up his arm to his shoulder, perching there and chattering like a demon. Once it jumped onto me, and I shrieked with alarm. It shrieked, too, and jumped off. Batu laughed until he almost fell from his divan.

Every time I went he would ask, "And how are you and Argamon faring with each other these days?" My answers were guarded, but the khan saw right through them. "Hmm, not so happy as we once were?" His smile would linger ominously.

And after every visit I paid to the khan, Argamon would behave like some bear afraid for his special hive. Once he had been ready to give me up rather than let me suffer harm, so I saw no reason for his jealousy now that he no longer came near me.

I returned from one of these summonses to find him pacing angrily in front of the ger. Batu had not sent for him for days. "What did he want from you? Why does he keep sending for you? Does he try to touch you?" He followed me into the ger. "Get out," he shouted at the other women. They fled.

"I don't know what he wants. I just seem to amuse him. And no, he never touches me, anymore than you do these days," I replied wearily.

"As if you'd let me! You're a stranger to me now, as cold as ice and as hard."

I stared in confusion. I thought I had been behaving meekly, that he was the distant one. "I don't understand. You are the master, and I obey your commands."

"You bitch, listen to you: that's exactly what I mean!"

Suddenly Argamon's arms wrapped around me like a serpent around its prey. He kissed me hard, picked me up and carried me to his divan, cursing at me in a frenzy, undressing me, flinging off his own clothes. It rekindled my passion. We united, almost weeping with intensity. I felt as if Argamon's body was my own, it was so familiar. How confusing it was to care for this mystery of a man, to need him even as I wanted to flee him.

For the rest of our journey, Argamon kept me by his side every night.

By midsummer the ordus had reached the Dnieper River. We rested on its banks for a few days, near some kind of encampment. When I asked Argamon about it, he said, "Merchants from the Italies. They take some of our spoils and slaves in trade for goods from Christendom. It relieves us of the burden of so many mouths to feed." He saw my expression. "Better than killing them, yes?"

I made no reply; I was thinking of my vow to escape.

Then we moved on. As big-wheeled wagons, herds, horses, flocks, and thousands of people forded the river, memories flooded over me. When I was a child, every spring the Dnieper and her many streams had overflowed and blessed our fields with new, fertile soil. We had honored their gift and poured water, milk, and flour into the fresh furrows of Mother Earth's fields to repay her. Doubtless the river still rose every spring, but who in Rus' was left to celebrate? My own home surely lay in ruins. Somewhere north of us along the riverbanks, the bones of my companions were one with the earth, while their souls wandered, lost.

And somewhere to the south lay the Crimea, where Selim al-Din had gone to trade. There was little hope of seeing him again. I looked back with an aching heart as we continued onward. Several merchant caravans laden with goods and slaves were just leaving toward the south.

That was when inspiration hit.

The cities there all traded with Constantinople. Perhaps I could find my way to one of them! Fantasies about escape blossomed effortlessly. What would Constantinople be like? When Uncle Vasily and I met, would he recognize me? I would have a real home again. No need for anyone to know about my shameful past, for I could tell them whatever I liked.

I began to lie awake at night, Argamon's arms around me, and come up with wild schemes. I would prevail on him to free me. Impossible. I would steal a horse and ride away into the night. To where? With no guide or protector, it would be simple-minded and dangerous. There was no way to leave on my own; I would have to wait and see.

My hopes flickered bright and dim. Some nights, under the spell of Argamon's embrace, I wondered if I even had the courage to escape. But then apart from a few chess games, we barely spoke, and he was so jealous of Batu Khan and me that I had to work hard to avoid quarrels. It was a strange time, as though the journey eastward mirrored some inner passage. Sometimes I felt as if I had already left and that my body need only follow.

In late autumn, the ordus reached the Volga River and settled into one huge tent city. Massive festivities followed, beginning with the ceremonial removal of the black yak tails hanging from Batu's Spirit Banner. I was watching with Toramun and the other translators while Argamon stood with the khan's close advisors. To my delight, Dorje appeared next to me. I rarely saw him anymore. As if continuing a conversation, he announced, "With the Mongols at peace, the Spirit Banner will fly white tails. Black is only for war." I had to smile; he was still as ready to instruct me as ever. With the standard newly adorned, a cheer spread throughout the entire encampment.

"I've missed you, Dorje."

"And I you, child. But I suppose we'll see even less of each other when Argamon receives his own ordu. I got special permission to stand with the other translators today just so I could see how you are doing."

I shrugged. "There is little to tell. My mood matches the autumn weather. Argamon is jealous of the khan's attentions to me."

"Don't worry about that. Batu will reward Argamon well, and when you're gone you'll be free of the khan," said Toramun. "I'll leave you two to gossip together."

As soon as she had left, Dorje leaned toward me and whispered, "And you'd be free if you escaped. Is that still your dream?"

"Always, Dorje."

"Come visit me; Qacha's ordu is close. If we think on it, we can find a way."

"I will."

"Here comes Argamon." Dorje bowed and smiled innocently at my master.

"Hello, old man. I think my father is looking for you."

"I bid you both farewell, then." Dorje melted away into the crowd.

"Come, Sofia. The celebration begins."

For the next week, people feasted, drank, competed, sang, danced, watched spectacles, gave gifts. Argamon distinguished himself in all Three Manly Sports and won a stallion and a camel. And after leading his team to victory in a polo match, he received more prizes, including lengths of wool, brocade, and silk, which he gave to me. Every evening the khan hosted a gigantic feast with a different wife by his side. I sat among the women of the court in his huge golden tent in view of two of his most honored guests: Argamon and Qacha. Nearby as if looking on in approval, the brocade-adorned golden idol of Chinggis Khan gleamed proudly among the lesser idols on Batu's shrine. The khan showered all of us guests with gifts, including fine brocade garments, a different color for each day. We were like living rainbows that stretched over time instead of over the earth.

The khan especially delighted in lavishing gifts on his favorites: fiery stallions from Fergana, home to the best horses in the world; superb riding mares; elegantly worked saddles and gear; jewels and gold; slaves of talent and beauty. And, with so much territory under their boot heels, many yurts. Batu confirmed his brother Berke's control over the lush country surrounding the Caucasus Mountains and his brother Orda's vast holdings to the east. A nephew, a fat, wily khan named Nogai, would guard the borders between Western Christendom and Batu's new empire. And, as though to make up for all they had lost, the khan showered special attention upon Qacha and Argamon. He even offered them drinks from his own cup, a signal honor.

The feasting lasted well into each night. Sometimes men were so carried away by music and drink that they joined the trained dancers in leaping wildly about. It was so like the long-ago feast when Argamon and Qabul had danced and Qabul had smiled at me. His smiles were gone forever and with them all his lies and evil influence. Indeed, it all felt like a dream that would soon pass.

The last feast began at midday. As always it started with an offering to the gods. By now the silk ongghon were saturated with liquor and stank of grease and blood. Batu's servant took the liquor offering outside while the khan poured a libation onto the floor of the ger. Musicians struck up a song as he took the first drink—no one would challenge his right this time. The toasts began; and after everyone was drunk, he offered choice meat around to his favorites. Now the serious eating and drinking began. Servants streamed in with heaped platters of food or flasks of many kinds of liquor. Each time Batu Khan reached for his cup, which was often, his musicians struck that special melodic flourish, and more drink was passed around to his guests.

At one point servants brought in a procession of the khan's animals: his cheetah, his long-tailed monkey, and his new bear, which was made to dance amidst howls of laughter. Then followed a procession of acrobats, jugglers, fire-eaters, puppeteers, and dancing men and girls. By evening few of the guests were able to stand unaided, and the tent reeked of wine, sweat, and vomit. But more food, drink, and music were to come. Bards took turns praising the khan's greatness in war and peace and then turned to praising his generals.

The highlight of the evening was the entire saga of Chinggis Khan, sung by all the minstrels in turn. I was surprised to hear him compared to Alexander the Great. I knew Alexander was the mightiest emperor in history, but I had not known that his fame had reached Mongol ears. Last, minstrels sang praises to Mongolia: its beauty, its mountains and valleys, its horses, its rivers, its women, anything they could think of. Even the men got quite tearful. Indeed, these songs enchanted me, too. I had finally conceded that Mongol poetry could equal the verse of my homeland.

The thought my old home brought me painfully back to my present state. What a contrast to those evenings at home in the Great Hall, when music had flowed from Matvei the Bard's kobza as he chanted about war and valor. Men's tears had fallen freely there, too.

I had once asked Matvei why there were rarely women in them and why he never sang love songs, and he'd just laughed at me. I had been almost a woman then, thinking I would soon marry, and I had wanted to be ready. To think I had once longed to have soft arms like Igor's lady in The Lay of Igor's Host, to welcome my husband home from some glorious quest. Now I had vermin-bitten arms and was a mere concubine to a foreign master, and I could no longer imagine any quest of war being glorious.

More gift-giving followed. Batu surprised Qacha with a new wife, a young Mongol noblewoman hardly older than I was. The noyan had grown old almost overnight, and the thought of the two of them together, like winter and spring, seemed a bit absurd. But that was not my concern. Argamon and I were now part of the khan's retinue.

It had grown dark outside by the time Batu seemed done dispensing largesse. Argamon caught my eye and motioned that he wanted to leave. I was ready. Having downed a last drink, he lurched up, barely able to stand. I too was about to rise when Batu called to him, smiling his widest.

"Do not go yet, my young friend. Sit down a moment. Tonight's feast ends our celebration, so it's my last chance to sing your praises. You bring such honor to your family, both as a warrior and as an advisor wise beyond your years. I've given much thought to how I should reward you, and I have decided to present you with your own ordu as my final gift. In addition to what your father gives you," he nodded to the flushed and smiling Qacha, who seemed to know the khan's plans already, "I grant you herds of horses and cattle, many camels, and flocks of sheep and goats. All the men who served under you in war will now do so in peace, along with their families and herds. I'm assigning you a choice yurt, well watered and green, which lies far west of the Volga. One of my lieutenants will guide you there. Your domain will also include the lands of several tribute peoples, so your days will be filled with prosperity, pleasure and ease. Oh, and of course I give you many slaves."

Around the tent men clapped and shouted their approval. The men near Argamon slapped him on the back.

"There is more," the khan continued. "I need trusty men like you to oversee my new empire. It's a sign of Mongol greatness that once we only thought to unite our tribal nations. Now we rule the many nations of the world!" More cheers and shouts followed, but Batu waved down the noise. "My men are already counting our subject peoples and assessing their wealth, and I want you, Argamon, to oversee the tax collectors in the Volodymyr-Suzdal area of Rus'. You will be my chief basqaq there. I know that you'll ably deal with the arrogant local princes: Prince Yaroslav and his sons, Alexei and Alexander Nevski."

In one stroke Argamon had become not only a clan leader but also staggeringly wealthy and powerful. He bowed and stammered, "My lord, your generosity exceeds all bounds. My heart overflows. How can I ever repay such generosity?"

Batu smiled graciously, basking not only in Argamon's gratitude but also in his courtiers' lavish praise. "Hmm, well, there is one little thing you can do. You can leave your red-haired princess with me. I've taken a liking to her, and she might still be of ... service ... to me." The laughter almost drowned out his words. "As a translator, perhaps."

While laughter and bawdy remarks crowded the air, Argamon stood up again, his face flushed but otherwise a mask. Batu beamed at him as he forced out the words, "Of course, my Khan. What is mine is yours."

At first I had felt gladness for Argamon, then a clutching at the heart—must I go back to a destroyed Rus'?—and now cold disbelief. I was to leave Argamon's bed for Batu Khan's? I knew that the khan desired me, yet he had never touched me, so I had chosen to believe it would stay that way. Now I understood: while he could have taken me from Argamon at any time, he had chosen to wait until this public display to buy my master's loyalty and cut off all room for complaint. Now Qacha and Argamon would leave with their own ordus, and Dorje would be far away! Only Toramun would remain.

Batu Khan added, "Everything is arranged. You may leave as early as tomorrow, though I wouldn't want you to feel you must rush away. Sofia can stay with you until then, as I know you'll want to say farewell. She has meant so much to you." I looked from one man to the other. Argamon's face was like rock, while Batu was still smiling.

"You may leave now. "Oh, I almost forgot. When Noyan Subodai leaves for Karakorum, he takes a message to your wife and son to join you in your new yurt. You can begin life again where you left it when you went to war."

Argamon cupped his hands, bowed deeply, and left without a word, Bayartou and another of his men behind him. I slid from my seat. "Ah, Sofia Begi," Batu called out, grinning. I had to stop and cup my hands to him while he kept me waiting. "One of my servants arranges new quarters for you. You will hear from me in a day or two." He paused for a small eternity while I stood there and he gloated. Finally he said, "You may go with my young hero now. I know you'll want to say your good-byes."

I bowed and retreated after Argamon, weaving in and out of the crowd of late-night revelers. A sudden panic descended on me. I did not want to be lost again. I was out of breath before I saw him staggering blindly ahead.

"Argamon! Please wait!"

He turned and glared at me, flickering torchlight distorting his angry features. "You knew! You planned your escape well, Sofia. It was only me you wanted to leave. Did you think I wouldn't mind as long as the khan bribed me well enough?"

I tried to take his arm, but he wrenched it away. People briefly stopped their drink and laughter to watch us; his men stared at me uneasily. I spoke intently, trying to keep pace with him. "Master, how can you even think such a thing? Batu Khan is almost old enough to be my grandfather. The idea of belonging to him disgusts me. This is as much a blow to me as it is to you. Think of all we've been through, how I've always served your interests. I would never sell myself to him—not for myself, not for you!"

He slowed his stride. "No, perhaps not." He still refused to look at me. We arrived at our empty ger; even the slaves were off celebrating. After waving his men away, he looked around aimlessly. "I cannot imagine life without you. You are in my blood. Now my own khan has cut my heart open. What will I do without you? What will I do?"

His back was still to me, and I stood uncertainly for a moment before shyly reaching out for his hand. He took it and turned to me and we clung together, weeping.

We made love until almost dawn, hardly speaking at all. By morning he already seemed to be making peace with his new life. He was an extremely important man now, and he seemed to find comfort in that. But I had none.

Bayartou reported to him early, and they went off together. None of us women knew what to do next, although we began to pack a few things. That took little time, and then there was just waiting.

In no hurry to find out Batu Khan's plans for me, I finally decided to visit Dorje. Who knew when I might see him again? He was likely in Qacha's ordu, and they would still be encamped nearby. I even had an excuse: I wanted to give him a gift. One of the prizes Argamon had given me was a length of yellow silk, an apt parting gift. And there was a length of wool that seemed like the right color of reddish purple.

Guided by one of Argamon's servants, I rode Little Liubyna through Batu Khan's vast new city, marveling at the variety of people who had made their way there. Riding beside the Volga, past many foreign boats plying the waters, brought me to Qacha's ordu, now regrouped into an informal arrangement. It was surprisingly empty. And there stood Dorje by Qacha's ger, looking as if he expected me, waving cheerily. I dismounted, we stood looking at each other, and a rush of love for my gossipy old friend swept over me.

"Come, let us get out of the wind and away from other ears," he finally said. I followed him to a great slab of rock jutting up near the riverbanks among trees and bracken. With our backs against the rock and out of the wind, we let the sun's faint autumnal warmth soak into us. The Volga murmured nearby, jackdaws soared and squawked to each other, and distant horsemen drove their cattle over the brown grasses, whooping and calling.

"So, Sofia, you have landed in quite an odd place," Dorje said.

"You already heard the news. A mixed blessing for Argamon and no blessing at all for me. I had to seek you out. You're my dearest friend, and soon you'll be gone."

"Won't you be sorry to lose Argamon, too?" The monk looked at me sharply.

"Yes, I will," I said, surprised by the surge of sadness that swept over me from nowhere. "I didn't realize it until just now. I spent so long hating and fearing him, then trying to understand him. I never will, but I can never forget him. What will my life be like without him? Worse, I feel I failed with him. Everything seems so heartbreaking."

"Sofia, I know you think Argamon hasn't changed, but he has—and because of you he may yet flower into a decent leader. Even without you beside him, I don't think he'll be as cruel or indifferent to his subject peoples as most tax collectors are, fomenting dissent to keep them weak and cutting them down if they try to band together."

I sighed. "Perhaps, perhaps not."

"And what if Har Nuteng had actually murdered Argamon? Qabul would have been Qacha's heir, and under her sway. You know what would have come next: she would have rid herself of her husband and then Yulta Beki."

"Yes, I suppose you're right." We sat together in silence.

"Dorje, do you remember right after Qabul died, when you found me in Argamon's ger?" He nodded. "We spoke then of a love, a wholeness that awoke in me."

"Yes."

"It lingered on for a while and gave me such strength, like you do, but it's only a precious memory now. And when you're gone I'll be left alone with nothing but questions. I know you think God is only an idea, but my search for Him has haunted me for so long."

"I know," Dorje nodded. "I have witnessed."

Suddenly, like draining a great wound, I poured out everything to him: both the loss and the love I had felt as a child, my ties to paganism and its view of a world in balance, my struggles with Father Kliment, and the questions I had never felt free to ask him. And about life after the disaster at the Dnieper.

"When Argamon captured me, love disappeared and all I saw was evildoers flourishing everywhere. Without you and Q'ing-ling, I'd have died of despair. I was both angry with God and afraid of Him, yet I was also terrified that He might not even exist. And when I spoke with Father Kyril about my doubts, he tried to be helpful, but he wanted to separate me from you and the Lady.

"Then on that day of grace I felt transformed, and both the world and I were one with—I don't know what to call it, for it was not like what I had ever thought of as God. Since I was very young, I had relied on my own comforting beliefs, but after the disaster at the Dnieper, living among Mongol barbarians with all their religious tolerance destroyed my faith. I met people like you or Selim, or even Yulta Beki, who aren't Christians but who have such good heart. Clearly your faiths possess truth, too, which still confuses me: heretics like Q'ing-ling and pagans like you behaving with more charity than many a Christian! But that day I thought I'd finally found what I was searching for … until so much self doubt crept in."

Dorje didn't answer right away. "Hmm. Yes, sorting out truth from falsity is the work of lifetimes, and it requires both heart and head. Without proper mind training, these times of true being—what you call grace—come and go in the flicker of an eye. They happen to us all, but if we catch and then seize on them as great revelations, we end up with more idea than truth. Worse is when someone then gets others to follow him blindly. I think this is what Chinggis Khan did when his vision from Tengri led to so much destruction."

He paused. "There are things you can do to steady your mind and heart, to be able to rest in such moments. Praying before your ikons might be one

way, but I can only guess. I only know what I was taught: mindfulness medi-
tation, the practice of peace."

"Isn't that what those monks did to get powers?" I asked. "How is that
peace?"

"Sofia, the only true power flows from a steady mind and compassionate heart. Those monks' rituals may seem alien to you, but what I speak of
is simply a way to open our hearts without fear or favor. That is true peace."

"You've told me this again and again. But I cannot see how to feel compassion for everyone in the same way, even though Christ did teach the same
thing."

"Sofia, you've done it much more than you realize. Unlike so many people, you have an open heart that never yields. You were even able to see
Qabul as merely human, with the same light and dark qualities we all have."

Dorje paused and seemed to decide something. "If you wish, I can
teach you a simple way to practice peace that won't part you from your
Christianity."

Having doubted my God and myself, I had to search my heart deeply
before accepting such an offer from a pagan, even a friend. Finally I decided
that Dorje's good heart had never failed me and that if he found this peace
practice helpful, then I could at least find out what it was. If I found it wanting, I need never do it again; and if it truly did not conflict with Christianity,
then I might freely use it.

"Yes, I will try it."

"Sit like this." He sat up, legs crossed and back straight, and I did the
same.

"Now, feel your breath go out and be present, very simply. Repeat that
for as long as you have time. If thoughts or strong feelings arise, neither fight
them nor follow them. They'll dissolve on their own like waves rising and
falling on a great sea. The more you do this, the less these waves will sweep
you away. Then you can gently join your mind with everything as it is, right
that moment. When you are done, just stay with your world each moment
and be grateful for it. And of course, be kind. Let us try that together."

We sat for what could have been a few heartbeats or much of the morning. Camp noises whispered in my ear, the chill breeze tickled my cheek with
wisps of my hair, the dry grass yielded a faint perfume, the rock cooled my
back, the sun warmed my face. Each moment felt full, each passed, all connected me to a deep stillness that felt familiar, gentle, and present.

A flock of geese passed honking above. We looked up at them at the same moment, turned to each other, smiled.

Suddenly I remembered both the passage of time and my gift. "Dorje, thank you. I must go, but I brought you a gift I hope you can use. I left it in my saddlebag."

"Your friendship is gift enough for me, my dear. Monks aren't supposed to have possessions." But he did look quite pleased.

"This may be the last time we ever see each other," I announced solemnly as we slowly walked back. "Once you and Argamon are gone, there is nothing to hold me here."

"You don't despair of escaping the Mongols, then?"

"No. The camps are no longer guarded closely, and I think I could escape easily if I found a way to travel after that, perhaps under someone's protection."

"A merchant. That's what you need, a trustworthy merchant with a caravan."

We both spoke at the same moment, "Selim al-Din?"

"He'll reappear one of these days, no doubt," said Dorje. "He'd gladly help you!"

"It might be a long wait—if he ever returns at all," I responded, thinking dismally of what it was going to be like as Batu Khan's concubine.

"Yes, but he's your best hope. He may be sly, but I know he would protect you. He intends to return if his Allah wills it." We neared my waiting guard. "Sofia, when you succeed, and I'm certain you will, do try to find a way to let me know."

"I promise." We reached the horses. I found my packet and handed it to him, saying, "I wish I had a better way to express how dear you are to me."

When he opened the packet, the golden silk glowed like a sunrise. "This is a lovely gift, Sofia, and one I can accept. I do need new robes! They will remind me of you, who have taught me so much about the nature of …" He paused and said shyly, "And I hope what you've learned from me will help you."

Another pause. "I have one last thing that I want to tell you. I hope you will remember it. You are never merely what you think you are." An odd thing to say, but it has haunted me.

We embraced for the last time. I mounted Little Liubyna, waved goodbye, and followed my guard out of the ordu. I looked back as long as I could to see him standing, waving occasionally, until he was out of sight.

When I returned to my ger, a messenger from Batu Khan was waiting. "After your old master has left, probably tomorrow, you move to new quarters. Follow me."

We rode to the quarters of the khan's concubines where a new ger stood, several wagons standing before it and a beautiful brown mare tethered nearby. Inside, two slave women were already arranging exquisite carpets and wall hangings, lovely chests, furs, and all the equipment and utensils I could need.

"The khan says you should decide where you want your menials to put things. You can find your own way back to your former master's ger if you need to bring anything back here. Your new master expects you to be settled in here by tomorrow." The man bowed coolly and left.

I stood looking at all the blood-bought finery. "You can decide where to put it all. I'll return tomorrow," I said to the women, and I rode straight back to Argamon's ger.

When evening arrived I dressed finely for our last night together, perfuming myself with Selim's rosewater while Anna combed my hair to a deep gleam and the sisters adorned me with the jewelry from Khwarizm. Finally I sent them all to their tent and then waited. And waited. Late into the night, I fell fast asleep on his divan.

It must have been near dawn when Argamon reeled across the threshold. It took a few heartbeats to come to full awareness. He was staring down at me and breathing heavily, his face distorted by anger and sorrow and too much liquor. His hand was on the knife at his waist. I froze in terror.

He looked at me for a small eternity. But finally he knelt down by me. "Sofia. I thought you would be gone."

"How could I go yet?" I reached out a trembling hand and stroked his cheek. Groaning with mingled pain and desire, he pulled me into his arms. We spent the rest of the brief night in each other's embrace. The last time we were ever together, it was as if my inner barriers melted away and I crossed over from simple lust into—how shall I say it—caring for the good in him. That night, briefly, we two became one. I feel no regret.

At daybreak he said, "I must see to my men and herds." He looked away. "Will you be here when I return?"

"Of course, Argamon. I am in no hurry."

"I'll return soon." I heard him make sun offerings before riding off.

Anna came in as I finished dressing, tears in her eyes. "Argamon is really leaving you behind?" I nodded. "Was this because of me, oh please don't let him take me away from you, I know he blames me and he can be so cruel. Oh, please." She began sobbing, and I had to hush and hold her like a baby.

"Anna, it had nothing to do with you. Batu Khan forced Argamon to give me up because he wants me as a concubine. He won't be cruel to you. I'll make him promise. Believe me, you're safer with him than you would be here."

But even as I spoke, I realized I had no idea how Argamon might treat Anna. He cared nothing for her. But how could I escape burdened by a helpless girl? And how could I leave her behind? Well, perhaps both of us *could* flee.

"Listen, Anna, I'll ask Argamon if you can stay here and serve me. If so, I'll try to protect you. But I warn you: you may be in much more danger."

"No, no, I want to be with you. I'll do whatever you say, just don't leave me!"

By the time Argamon returned, we had packed everything but the ger and had hitched the wagons and oxen in a line. I was still inside, holding Anna, who was weeping and refusing to move a finger's breadth from me until he sharply commanded her to go.

I rose unsteadily to say goodbye. "Argamon," I almost whispered.

He had been staring around the ger as if he'd forgotten something, but now he looked at me. "Sofia. I—" In an instant, he was enfolding me in his arms, covering my face with kisses. "How can I live without you? You're all that is beautiful and kind. I was never like that. I don't know how to be. Instead, you were my goodness. When I see you again, you'll belong to Batu Khan. That will tear out another piece of my heart."

"Argamon, I—I will miss you, too. My heart breaks, too. I hate going to the khan. But please, never despair. I see goodness in you every day. Whatever I've been to you, keep that in your own heart and keep me there, too. That is how you truly make me yours."

He held me and stroked my hair. Finally he said, "I want Anna to stay with you." So I never needed to ask. "She still reminds me of you when you were a child and I tried to make you my own. I have no wish for that memory." He laughed mirthlessly. "Not that you ever became mine as I had imagined. But you are right. You'll always be in my heart. I'm now a mighty warrior because of you, and because of you and my mother I will seek to govern justly."

We walked out into the chill morning. Behind us, slaves began dismantling the ger. It was almost as if our life together had left no outer trace.

Anna was hovering by the nearest wagon, hope and fear chasing each other across her face.

"Anna, stay here and serve Sofia well," said Argamon

The girl's face lit up with joy. "Yes, Master, gladly." She rushed to find her small bundle while Temulun, Bourma, Tsetsegmaa, and I embraced each other and exchanged farewell blessings. I lifted Kuchan for the last time; his little arms encircled my neck. Even Wolf seemed to know this was goodbye when I scratched his shaggy back.

Argamon mounted his horse. He reached down and I took his hand, held it against my cheek. "May blessings go with you everywhere, Argamon."

"And may Tengri's goodness follow you everywhere." He paused, struggling with something inside him. "Sofia, I want you to know. I never said this to any woman before. I want to tell you," he stammered, "that I—I love you." With that, he took away his hand and spurred his horse forward to meet Bayartou and his men.

Not once in our years together had we used that word with each other. My heart torn open, I watched them ride away along a row of gers until their small caravan met with the rest of the men, their families, and the herds and wagons that were now his. I stood watching until they disappeared. Argamon was gone from my life forever. He did not look back.

Anna spoke at my side. "Thank you for getting him to leave me here. I was afraid he'd keep me, just to be cruel."

I looked down at her. "It was his idea. He's not so much cruel as confused."

"I'll never think anything good of any Mongol!" she declared. I had to smile. Yes, in many ways she was like the girl I had been only a few years earlier.

"Well, Anna, we must go to our new life, and the best place to begin is at my new ger. Look, Argamon has left Little Liubyna all packed with my things, and this pony must be for you. See, he wishes us well—don't be so disbelieving."

When we arrived at the new ger, everything was in place. My new servants timidly presented themselves. One, Ruth, was a pale-haired Hungarian. The other, Judyta, was a dark, slender woman from Poland. I was surprised: in my mind, a Hungarian should have the dark hair. Both were beauties, both seemed ill at ease.

"This is Anna, who will also serve me. I'm a slave too. I won't be unkind to you."

The women broke into smiles, and Judyta blurted, "Mistress, Batu Khan's messenger was here looking for you. He was angry with us for not knowing where you were, and we thought that when you heard, you would be angry at us for not finding you."

I had to laugh. "Not at all. Let him be angry. At least for now, I'm in the khan's favor. He likes me not to behave as he expects. I see no reason to change my ways and beg forgiveness from a messenger. He will find me soon enough."

I looked around. "Tell me about all this."

Ruth spoke eagerly. "The khan provides you with meat and drink, and you may trade with any merchants who come to pay their respects." She opened a small casket. "All for you." Anna peeked over my shoulder and gasped at the gleaming pearls, coins, and gems heaped inside. "And for tonight, this gown." It was white and gold brocade, just like Batu's robes! I set it aside. He might wish to appear gracious, but he had been cruel to Argamon and me. I had yet to learn what good fortune he was handing me.

"We know your story, Mistress," Ruth broke in on my thoughts. "It seems quite sad." Judyta nodded her agreement. Presuming on my kindness, she added, "You already miss your old master, I expect. I hear he adored you."

"That is my business alone," I said. Judyta blushed.

"There is more," Ruth said, and they led me outside into the breezy day. Flocks of birds were heading south, and soggy-looking rain clouds loomed low. Now that the festivities were over, most of the other ordus had left and those remaining were preparing for winter. It seemed almost quiet around me.

Two men stepped forward and bowed respectfully. "We will guard you and do menial work," one said.

"Batu Khan displays generosity at every turn," I felt forced to say. "Now I suppose we must wait for him." I looked about at the camp filled with people and animals, all with their own place in the world, and felt a great emptiness. I had again lost my place in it.

Then I remembered the silks and brocades Argamon had recently given me. One length, blue as a robin's egg, with golden roundels of birds woven into it, would make an excellent robe for him—a gift of farewell. "I'll sew until then. You three can help. Now, where are my sewing basket and fabrics?"

Once again I found solace in creating something beautiful. We women spent a pleasant afternoon crafting Argamon's new robe and learning about each other. Outside, a soft rain began to fall, wafting in a wet earthy fragrance.

The khan's messenger found us in the late afternoon, lost in our work. He did look displeased. "I searched for you all over the camp! Expect a visit from Batu Khan tonight," he snarled. "Your women must prepare a proper feast for him. Do you have all you need?"

"We do," Ruth and Judyta answered, looking afraid.

He turned to me. "Wear the gown the khan sent you. And here is a maid to paint you." A small black-haired Persian woman entered, carrying a bundle of powders and paints. Kneeling down near the hearth, she began stirring a dark green, grassy-smelling paste she had brought in a shallow dish.

"If you will sit here near the light, and stay quite still," she said. Suppressing a sigh, I obeyed. She began painting lacy designs on my hands and upper feet.

Anna sat beside me, gaping. "It's a custom for special occasions like weddings, Anna. Lady Q'ing-ling told me the Mongols borrowed it from some faraway land. I saw it once before on a new bride, and it's lovely when it's done. Although this is no wedding!"

"But it's all green and ugly," Anna objected.

The maid eyed her disdainfully. "This is only the first step. The paste stains the skin a beautiful russet after awhile. It only lasts a few days, but meanwhile your lady will look like a meadow full of flowers, most enchanting. There, I am done. Now I will paint your face while we wait for the henna to dry: color for your eyelids, kohl from Egypt to outline your eyes, and fine red clay powder to brighten your cheeks. But I will not touch your brows; Mongol style will not suit you. You will look so beautiful when I finish."

I made no comment, thinking I would probably look like a painted camp whore. How ironic: in Rus', *pallor* was a sign of harlotry! Before some great prince arrived, I had always rubbed beet juice on my cheeks, not knowing what a harlot was but not wanting to be one. Now Sofia the harlot was to meet a prince, and painted with more than beet juice!

Ruth and Judyta started preparing the meal. "We both mastered the khan's favorite dishes. Judyta once cooked for a Polish lord and I wanted to make myself useful, if you take my meaning," Ruth said as she pulled out various foodstuffs from leather bags suspended on the ger sides. Take her meaning? Yes, no one wants to be used and then cast aside. Likely Batu Khan had used both her and Judyta as he would now use me.

Forced to sit still so that the drying henna paste would not crack and fall off too soon, I watched the women. Under Judyta's hands, dumplings appeared as if by magic. Meanwhile, Ruth had set a pot of soup to boil on a trivet over the hearth, adding rare spices. Royal fare was quite different from the rough food I had eaten most of the time. I looked down to see the designs dancing over my skin and wished briefly that I was about to marry Argamon instead of waiting to be bedded by a man I feared and despised.

Finally the woman scraped off the dried paste, bowed to me, and departed.

"Mistress, you do look like a beautiful meadow. And you have blue eyelids. Oh, may I help you dress?" as Judyta handed me Batu's brocade gown.

"Yes, and you can help me comb out my hair. I think I'll braid it now that Argamon isn't here to forbid me." My hair had grown well past my knees and it was easiest to keep it braided most of the time, but Argamon had always wanted it loose for him. He had also forbidden me to cut it, apparently thinking my power resided in it.

After dressing, Anna struggled with the comb and I realized something. "Anna, before the khan arrives, you must leave. Ruth and Judyta, do you sleep in a different ger? Can Anna stay with you?" Both women nodded. "In fact, I think it would be wise for her always to be out of his sight. He has an eye for pretty girls," at this, I caught a knowing look pass between the two women, "and she is safer with you two, yes?"

Both agreed heartily, which confirmed my suspicions about them.

Once attired and adorned by the Khwarizm jewelry, I had nothing to do but wait. Soon the meal was ready. Ruth set out wines and arki, along with golden platters and goblet, while Judyta pulled out coverlets and bedding for the low divan that waited by the wall.

Judyta spoke. "I'll stay here, Mistress, to serve you and the khan, but Ruth can take Anna back to our ger now." Anna looked ready to weep, and I had to assure her that I would be nearby. Would she be an impossible burden if—when!—I escaped?

The next few moments passed like hours. Judyta had lit several braziers, and I was putting a pinch of incense on each one to banish the smell of dung from the air when I heard Batu and his men. I knew how a doe with the hot breath of a wolf on her neck must feel just before its fangs sink in.

The door opened. I genuflected as Batu Khan limped in, an attendant behind him shaking rain off a parasol, followed by two retainers, a musician, and a woman carrying a tray of dried fruit. "You may rise, Sofia," he said, taking my hand and pulling me up. I looked up into his cat's eyes. He was barely taller than I was, but his grip was as strong as iron. I was sure he could feel my dread. "You look lovely. At last you're adorned as you should be. Look at what I bring, my dear: sweet honey cakes. I know women like them. And almonds, pistachios, dried figs, raisins, dates—even jujubes, my favorite." Seating himself on a silken cushion, he drew me down and scooped up a handful of dried fruit, tossing a few into his mouth. His servant poured him a huge goblet of arki.

"I believe you know the merchant who brought them to me as a gift today. He once rescued you from danger. Selim al-Din. You must remember him."

Blood rushed to my head and my heart threatened to leap out of my throat. Here? Now? What good angels were watching over me? "Yes, I do remember him, my Khan. He—" I suddenly thought better of letting Batu know how very well we knew each other, "once traveled with Noyan Qacha's ordu. He and the monk Dorje were good friends."

"Yes, that's him. Now, on to more interesting subjects: wine, music … and meat." His eyes glittered and he smiled slyly. This seemed to be a signal for the musician to play his horse-headed fiddle and sing a ballad, while the khan's retainer took the dishes of food that Judyta handed him and began serving Batu. He set to with hearty enjoyment. I barely touched my own food when I was served. It must have been delicious, but it sat on my tongue like straw. I tried to control my shaking hands as the khan himself handed me a goblet of wine. Hopefully he would think I was merely ill at ease and not recognize what I really felt. Selim here already! Praise and thanks to the Holy Family and all the saints!

I drank the wine down, and Batu ordered his servant to fill my goblet again. I downed it again, and he gestured for the man to keep pouring for me. He seemed amused that I was getting drunk so quickly—perhaps he thought I was preparing for what was to come. He could not know that it also hid my excitement. The meal finally over, Batu wiped his hands on a silk napkin and waved dismissal to the servants. They bowed out. We were alone. Despite having drunk so much, I remember almost every word that followed.

"At last, after all this time. I'm such a patient man," he smiled, stretching and leaning back onto the pillows heaped behind him. His arm rested behind me, barely touching. "How do you like your new lodgings? Is there anything else you might desire?" He spoke the last word with too much meaning. I shook my head, looking down. It felt heavy as an overfilled wine sack. "I suppose you miss your young lover. A good man, Argamon, and he'll be an excellent basqaq. He always knew this might happen someday."

Batu's words echoed in my head from a great distance. "I don't understand."

"Sofia, did you never wonder why Argamon didn't marry you?"

"Well, because I was a foreign concubine, unsuitable for marriage."

"No. I forbade him to marry you unless you gave him a child." I stared up at him in astonishment. Batu smiled gently and stroked my cheek. "I've wanted you ever since I first saw you. What a little jewel you were, so terrified and yet trying so hard to put up a brave front. Your childish threats were so charming. I knew even then that someday I'd find a way to take you for myself. But until the shaman's prophecy was fulfilled, there was no way to do that with honor.

Once that was done, I could have simply forced Argamon to give you up—and more than once I nearly did—but I saw how much you meant to him. So I let you stay with him a little longer. After all, I couldn't trespass upon the loyalty of such a promising young warrior ... and the waiting made my passion all the sweeter."

He laughed softly and began exploring my neck with his mouth. I tried not to shudder. "It's an irony," he breathed into my ear, "but it was Qabul who unwittingly showed me how I could take you one day without compromising my honor. It was when he tried to kidnap you at the victory feast after Kyiv fell." I sat bolt upright.

"Oh yes," Batu smiled, sitting back up and running a hand over my breasts, "I knew what he was up to. He was ever ready to take advantage of others for his own gain, a trait I admire up to a point. He just never understood when to stop. Do you remember what he said when Argamon asked for my judgment? That your failure to give Argamon a child was proof you didn't belong with him. I liked that argument."

So even now, Qabul's actions haunted my destiny.

Batu Khan's arm slowly encircled my waist, pulled me closer to him. "But when you never conceived, I knew it was a sign. You were meant for me someday. And a khan has his needs, too. Now, Sofia, it's finally my turn." I tried not to stiffen when he kissed me. "I do expect you to kiss me back. I won't hurt you," he said. "Here, have some more wine." He leaned around me to pick up my goblet and bring it to my lips. I drank deeply, hoping to go numb. "Now, let us try again." This time I resigned myself to kissing him.

He drew me over to the waiting divan and disrobed me and then himself. The wine must have been working because I could feel nothing beyond his hands on me, pulling me down and into his embrace. As he took his pleasure, Batu stared beyond me with his cat's eyes, locked into his own world. I felt like a whore, but this was the price I must pay for freedom. At least he expected little on my part. It seemed an eternity before he was finished and got up to pour himself some more wine. He seemed so old, probably forty!

He looked over and lifted his goblet in an offer. "No, my Khan, I've had quite enough." Suddenly I had to laugh. "So, was it worth the wait?"

He laughed, too. "Yes and no. It always takes time to find how to please another, and I expected little from you tonight. Next time you'll be better." He limped back over to the divan and lay down, drawing the silk quilt over us. "But yes, it was worth the wait. I've always thought that except for your nose, a little large by Mongol standards, and your small head, you are one of the most beautiful women I've ever beheld. Good night, Sofia."

"Good night, my Khan."

He fell asleep right away and began snoring like a saw, but I lay there fuming. 'Large nose? Small head? I do not have either! Mongols have big heads and hardly any noses at all!' Finally I too fell asleep, my head swimming like a crazed fish.

Sometime in the middle of the night, I was dreaming about Argamon when I felt a gentle touch. I drunkenly thought it was him and responded eagerly to Batu's kisses and embrace. It was not until I reached that peak of pleasure and heard him cry out that I awoke enough to realize who my lover really was. I had cause to regret my mistake.

"I see," Batu laughed. "The secret is to take you while you sleep. That was much better." He was soon asleep again, but I lay wide-awake, determined to give him no further chances to try. I stared into the darkness for an eternity, thinking about Selim al-Din.

When I awoke the next morning, Batu was dressing. "Hmm, I thought to bring you to my ger tonight, but instead I may return here—after you're asleep!" He laughed, summoned the servants waiting outside, and left without another word.

Ruth and Judyta bustled in, twittering like birds and followed by Anna. "We were only waiting until the khan was gone. Are you well? You look tired. Here, have some breakfast. There are some honey cakes left, much nicer than gruel, and look: some dates." They babbled on, determined to talk about anything at all, while I slowly dressed. My head felt like an ax was buried in it, but I was ready to set my escape plan into motion.

Preferring plain gruel to the khan's sticky sweets, I gave those to my fellow slaves. "I think I should have a gift ready for Batu Khan in case he returns tonight. Do you know where the merchants' district is? I want to find something there," I mused innocently.

Judyta offered to guide me to the market, but Ruth said she and Anna would clean up the ger. "Anna and I are becoming friends!" The girl nodded uncertainly.

The journey through the large encampment took some time. When we got to the market I was stunned by its size.

"What odd tricks fate plays, Mistress," Judyta said as I gaped at the crowds of people poking through seemingly endless numbers of stalls overflowing with goods. "Already merchants willing to trade with their old enemies make huge profits. When they arrive, they simply give Batu Khan everything they brought. Not to be outdone by a mere merchant, he heaps far more on them than he received. The merchants sell what they don't want to ordinary people and go home richer than ever!"

Had Papa lived, would he have traded with the enemy? Or would he have been too proud, too honorable? I only knew that *I* must compromise to survive. The previous night I could have overcome my scruples, slipped out of bed without waking the khan, and somehow tried to kill him. But even had I succeeded—not likely—what would I have gained? It would not return the dead to life or repair the damage done to the world. And another khan would replace Batu while I suffered a horrible death. No, I wanted my own life back. Until I could find Selim and a way to escape, I would seem to submit.

As I rode slowly through the crowded lanes, everything reminded me of Kyiv. Goods lay piled invitingly under canopies and in stalls: brocades, fine woolens, bejeweled golden cups, enameled caskets, tooled leather saddles, carpets. A Babel of languages and a mosaic of people: yellow-haired men who reminded me of English John, swarthy men wearing dulbands, now and then a black-skinned man in swirling robes, and men from faraway Cathay, all hawking their wares. And so many people pawing through the merchandise and haggling loudly.

No, I must not give in to any heart pangs now. Instead, I dismounted and searched for a gift for the khan, saw pepper, cinnamon, salt, dried fruit—Judyta's eyes devoured those, so I bought her some of each—as well as carved ivory chests, bright samite and brocades, Venetian glassware, chess sets, armor, ornate swords in embossed scabbards and other articles of war, all beautifully fashioned as if to hide their sharp purpose.

I hurried on, all the while seeking Selim or one of his men. Up one row of tents and down another. How had so many people found their way there? This could take days! Around a corner, and there stood a tall man in a dulband. I scarcely dared hope it could be Selim, but yes, it was he! My heart was racing, my mouth was dry as I turned to Judyta and spoke oh-so-innocently.

"I know what to buy for the khan. Look there. That merchant has songbirds for sale, as does this one. Our master likes strange animals, but he lacks birds. While I go there, you try this man. One of us may find something special enough."

Judyta eagerly obeyed, and I worked my way over to Selim. I hoped I looked at ease because I was torn between highest hope and deepest fear. Coming up behind him, I said, "Greetings, Selim. Please act as though you don't know me."

Selim turned around and, looking at the ground, responded, "Hello, Sofia. Am I behaving like a courteous stranger?"

I smiled. How little he had changed. "Please show me your birds while we talk. I truly do need to buy one or two for Batu Khan. Have you been here long? Have you seen Dorje?"

"I have a lovely pair inside, nightingales. In mating season the male's song calls you to Paradise," said Selim. "I've been here for several days, and yes, I rode out to pay my respects to Qacha yesterday and saw Dorje. He told me everything."

"Everything?"

"Everything." He closed his eyes and put his hand over his heart. "As always, I am ready, nay grateful, to help you in any way I can."

"I've given the matter some thought. Can we meet to discuss what I have in mind?"

"Come to me any time, Sofia. You can count on me."

I saw Judyta approaching and quickly changed the subject. "Perhaps you have other, more striking birds as well? He likes the strange and colorful."

"I suggest I send several to your ger, then. I have many more, though I keep most of them inside in this cold weather. Look into my tent. That one, for instance, is not only colorful; it's a true rarity, for it can speak. Since they're for Batu Khan himself, I can offer you a special price."

"What do you think, Judyta? Did you find any birds as fine as these?"

"No, Mistress, nor was the man as generous as this merchant. He didn't believe me when I said they were for our khan."

Soon one of Selim's men, a homely youth named Nasr, was following us back through the camp leading a pony laden with exotic birds, each cage carefully wrapped against the chill. After arranging them around the ger, he started to bow out.

"Wait," I ordered. "Now that I have them all, I don't want some of these birds. I'll write a list of what I'm keeping, and you can return the others."

I wrote a note, sealed it, and handed it to the young man.

"*You* can read and write? I cannot."

His averted eyes missed my wry look. So much the better! "Give it to your master. It contains my offer for the remaining birds. If the khan is pleased with them, I'll come back and pay for them myself." Nasr bowed and left with the extra birds.

Now I would have to wait, both hoping for and dreading Batu Khan's return. "I want to complete the robe for Argamon," I decided. "I must send it to him before his ordu moves too far from here. Anna and Judyta, you can help me while Ruth finds out the khan's plans for tonight. If he stays here again, we must be ready."

Batu Khan did return that night and was exceedingly pleased with the birds. "I thought you might be angry or sullen, Sofia, perhaps even harbor murderous thoughts. I hardly expected you to shower me with such charming gifts. I shall leave the nightingales with you, so that you'll have music next spring. Come here, sit next to me."

By night's end Batu Khan had taught me what selfish lust truly was. Even compared to Argamon, the man was a greedy pig. I was struck with regret: how little I had valued my master's attempts to win me. I had to remind myself that I had no reason to complain about the khan or even to care. I had always known he was selfish.

The next day I took Anna with me to meet Selim. He again played his role to perfection, looking at the ground or past our shoulders as if we were complete strangers. "Please sit under the protection of my tent, ladies, and enjoy some tea with me while we bargain." He went inside his tent and came back with a rolled up carpet and a pair of gorgeous silken pillows, which he arranged under the canopy before the entrance. As we sat down, Anna and I peered inside in wonder. It was beautifully decorated in Persian style with more pillows on the carpeted floor, a clean scent in the air, and a brazier burning near the bird cages. His servant Nasr produced a little plate of sweets, glasses, and a pot of hot tea.

"Please, enjoy. Here, let me pour you some tea." Selim lifted the pot high over the glasses and poured a stream of greenish liquid into the exact center of each. One waver and he'd have missed the cup entirely. At first I felt awe and then impatience, but it seemed rude to rush him. So I tried to settle into his quiet rhythm. Finally, when we had drunk some sweet mint tea and nibbled on dainties, Selim said, "So, how can I help you?"

"It's all so clean and pretty," Anna blurted, popping another date into her mouth.

"This humble tent is nothing. In Iran there are gardens that would melt a heart of stone, lovely pavilions, exquisite works of art. A beautiful and cultured world before the Mongols destroyed so much. Here, Anna, have some halvah. It contains honey and ground nuts." He turned toward me with a question in his eyes.

I said, "I must bring her with me. Whatever plans we make must work for us both.

"Anna," she looked up, halvah crumbs on her chin, "I brought you with me to meet my friend Selim. But now we will use his speech, to make it easier for me to talk with him."

To my surprise she said, "Mistress, do you plan to escape back to Argamon?"

"No, we are going to escape from the Mongols entirely. Selim will help us."

Instead of reacting with fear as I had dreaded, Anna's eyes grew huge. Then she nodded, smiled happily, and took another sweet.

In Farsi, Selim said, "So, Sofia, how can I be of service?"

"First, I deeply thank you, Selim. I will find a way to repay you one day." Rushing ahead, I added, "Can you take us to the Crimea? I surely can get to Constantinople from there."

But he put his hand on his heart, closed his eyes, and shook his head. "Sofia, I am honored to help you, and you must not think of repaying me. But I just arrived from there, and I must return to Iran before winter overtakes me. If I do not pass beyond the Caucasus Mountains before the snows begin, I'll be unable to get home until next spring.

"But if you agree to go to Iran with me first, I will take you wherever you want after that. I want to invite you to meet my master. He would be most interested in your story. If you'll do that and stay there as his guest, that would more than repay me as well. I know he'll welcome you. Otherwise you must wait until I come this way again."

My heart sank. I knew little about Iran, but I did know that it was nowhere near Constantinople. Yet to be caught much longer in Batu Khan's clutches would be unbearable. And as soon as the ice froze and his ordu could cross easily, he would settle on the east bank of the Volga for the winter, and I would be stuck. In spring he would move north into the grasslands, and he wouldn't be back until the following autumn. How could I keep Anna a secret from him for that long? No, I must flee now or give up hope.

"I agree; I must. When do you leave?"

"In a few days. But please tell me exactly what you had in mind, Sofia."

"What I wanted was to vanish mysteriously. I was thinking to follow the river south for several days and then to go west to join your caravan. That way even if the khan thought of you and pursued you when I went missing, he'd find nothing. But now ..."

"That is still a good plan," said Selim. "I know a route along the river. And your stratagem means I can return to Mongol territory and keep visiting Sarai." I must have looked blank. "This tent city: Batu Khan's new capital. From it he can control the trade route from here to the River Don and into the Black Sea. It is common knowledge that he never means to return to Mongolia, and his empire is no longer the Blue Ordu, as he once called it, but the Golden Ordu, perhaps after his Golden Family, or after the Kipchaks who once lived here and thought of their lands as golden. Or maybe his golden tent. But it seems fitting to me because of all the gold and treasure Batu has seized from others."

"Yes, it is fitting. But all the gold in the world could not keep *me* with him. And if you think my plan might still work, could you make a map or a list of landmarks for us?"

Selim nodded, but he was frowning. "Yes, but when I think on it, the khan's men will know the path, too. You must follow streambeds instead, and you'll need a horse or two to travel faster. And I think you will have to go all the way south to the Caspian Sea."

Feeling a little disheartened, I countered, "Could you wait a few days to leave? Meanwhile, you could send some trustworthy men down the river with extra horses to await us, just in case Anna and I must travel on foot." Selim looked doubtful, but he nodded.

"But I will try to buy at least one horse for the journey, and we'll join them as soon as we can. Then they can take us to you."

"Well, Sofia, if you are brave enough to attempt this, I will certainly do as you ask. I'll try to await your signal before leaving, though I cannot delay too much longer."

"How can I ever thank you enough, my friend? Please at least take this in exchange for the birds." I placed a little pouch before him, filled with pearls and gems worth far more than the birds were. "Again, thank you a thousand times."

After a few polite refusals on his part and insistences on mine, he accepted. "My joy is to serve you, princess." Selim closed his eyes and smiled, hand over his heart once again. He seemed deeply pleased.

"Anna," I said as I arose, "we go back now to plan our escape." How pleasant that would be, to *do* something!

"Yes, I'll help! I know things, too," she cried. Unlikely, I thought, but I said nothing.

On our way back to the ger I explained, "We must be ready to leave at a moment's notice. We can bring little with us, and only what will be useful. From now on whenever no one is near, take a little food from the storage bags and hide it in my chest. We need enough for several days. I only pray that the khan loses interest in me soon so we can slip away." I smiled to myself: my strategy was to be remote yet polite so that the khan would give up on me. I felt defiled by his every touch. How ironic that once I had feared that Argamon might tire of me, and now I feared that Batu would not.

"I'm so glad we're escaping, Mistress. I hope the khan won't be angry and find you and punish you!" Anna's trust in me was so childlike, much as my own had been in Papa. Realizing how daring it truly was to flee, a great weight fell on my heart.

But I only said, "Have no fear. Selim will help us." If we could leave soon enough; otherwise we would be trapped all winter, perhaps forever.

I spent the next two days terrified that Anna might let something slip. I kept going over my plan trying to find a way to include Judyta and Ruth, but four women could not disappear without giving rise to a huge search that would only end with our being caught. And what if they were happy there or tried to stop us? It seemed safer not to involve them.

Finally Selim's servant Nasr stopped at the ger to ask how the khan was enjoying his birds. "Winter hastens our journey. We must leave tomorrow. If you wish, my master could bring more rare animals to you on our next trip. He sends you this note," he said.

I tried to open it without looking too eager. It contained Selim's regrets for having to leave before I gave him notice. However, it also contained instructions, a map of the Volga, and a promise that men and extra horses would await me for several days.

"Wait, I must respond to his courteous offer." I wrote a reply, asking that my guides move slowly so I could catch up with them. I also asked that his men carry Persian clothing for us, men's if possible. After Nasr left, I hid Selim's map in my sewing basket.

And now I had to wait for a free night, since Batu Khan had been summoning me to his ger every evening. That at least meant that Anna was out of his sight. But I began to worry it might take too long before he left me alone. I see now that my remoteness was what fascinated the khan, just as it had Argamon, and that it was driving him wild.

After several more nights of my studied compliance, he finally grumbled, "You submit, you obey my every whim, yet you show nothing of yourself. Where is your fire, Sofia? Let me see it again, as you did on that first night. I want to know what you did with your young lover. I want you to do those things with me."

"But I do, my Khan, I assure you." I smiled sweetly at him. "I'm sincerely sorry for disappointing you. Perhaps you'd prefer one of your wives or other concubines. Perhaps you could use me as a translator again instead of—" I nodded toward the divan.

He burst out laughing. "No, but I leave tomorrow on the last battue before winter, which gives you time to think about how you could please me better."

It suddenly felt as if a door had opened into my future and the world was beckoning me to pass through it. I merely smiled and bowed to him.

The khan sent me back to my ger that night, and the next morning he was gone shortly after daybreak. Hearing distant bustle, the shouts of men, the clatter of horses, I almost shouted for joy. I could barely stay still all day. There was only one task that needed doing, and it took little time. Having finished the robe for Argamon, I wrote a simple farewell message for him, hoping he had some literate slave to read it to him. If only I knew a way to let Dorje know that I had found a way to escape. I called one of the men assigned to me and ordered him to take Argamon's gift to him. "Take a companion if you must, but don't return until you have put it in his hands!"

"Yes, Mistress." The man bowed and backed away. Now Argamon would receive a token of farewell, and one of my serving men would be gone. After that I paced about in the ger, wandered in and out repeatedly, and even lost my temper with Ruth, who kept begging me to rest. I finally remembered the practice of peace that Dorje had taught me.

I tried to sit still and feel the present moment, but this time it did not feel peaceful: I was quivering with hope and fear. Nonetheless, better to do this than to scold a blameless slave, so I sat and worked hard to watch my breath go out, while my mind wandered and babbled endlessly. Just as I gave up, for an instant I felt that stillness—and a tiny flash of conviction. 'Yes, this will work and you must do it,' it said. That was all, but it was enough.

In mid-afternoon I sent Judyta and Ruth and the other manservant away, each to visit friends: fellow slaves who lived in another part of the encampment. They thought me astoundingly kind. Now only Anna remained, eager to help. After we had packed—I could not bear to leave Mama's collar or Papa's coat behind, or the jewelry Argamon had once given me—I told her to put our bundles into the farthest cart just as if storing some things. She was almost quaking with excitement.

"If Ruth or Judyta come back, tell them I am already asleep, that I want you to stay with me. Can you do that?" Anna nodded gravely. "Now I'm going to leave you for a while to buy us a horse because we cannot ride away on *our* horses if we're to vanish like magic. I might not get back until well after dark. You must act as if everything is normal. But I will come back for you as soon as I can."

"I know you will, Mistress. You've always taken care of me."

"I found some old ragged clothing, and I'll smear dirty grease on my face. Help me hide my braid under this cap and jacket. With any luck, no one will know me."

I waited until no one was near and darted out of the ger. Walking briskly with head down, I made my way toward the merchants' section. Fears assailed me from all sides: had I allowed enough time? What if everyone closed for the night before I got there? Perhaps this whole plan was too simple-minded to work, and I was a half-wit even to try. Panic set my pace ever faster, until I remembered my moment of clarity. No, I decided, I would trust … though I could try walking faster!

It seemed forever before I arrived at the outskirts of the market. The crowds were thinning, but enough people lingered for me to pass unnoticed. One merchant was trying to rid himself of his last horse, a sturdy-looking creature but scarred as if it had been in a fire. "I leave tomorrow. A fine stallion for sale, bargain price. Don't lose your chance. If you don't want to ride him or put him to stud, you can eat him," he called out to a passerby.

"What you ask for horse?" I mimicked an Alan who knew little Mongol speech.

"What, do you speak of this fine steed, this select, high bred beauty? It's much too fine for a slave like you. Get along with you," he laughed.

"No, you say you sell it for meat. Is why I want it, for master's plate," I grinned. "I give you gold piece for scarred old thing. Master hungry for horse sausage. This gold two times what it ever worth, but master not caring. He rich. He eats half horse tonight and half next night. He love horse meat." The man's eyes lit with greed, and the horse was mine.

As I led it away, I said, "And you no come back next day, sorry I put it in pot!"

He laughed. "Next day? I'll be gone by dawn!" So he meant it; good! I looked around for another horse dealer but there was none nearby and the stalls were closing, so I turned back feeling lucky I had found the one. The sun was setting, the evening goddess there as always, spreading a blanket of gold for her mistress. Why had she and her sister of the morning never forsaken me? Alas, for once I was sorry to see her, for I would have to hasten back to the khan's quarters before it grew too dark to make anything out. As dusk thickened, I began to panic again. I struggled onto the horse and kicked him into moving faster. Then I began to worry that I was drawing too much attention to myself, so I hunched over, trying to look like a menial on her way home.

By the time night had fallen, I was on the edge of the khan's quarters. I dismounted and led the horse toward my ger, praying no one would pass by. A guard was coming my way, and I nearly fainted with dread that he might question my right to be there. Instead he ignored my humble bow and walked past. I was just another invisible slave, one of many hurrying to finish their tasks.

Finally I saw my own ger up ahead, a dim band of light seeping out under the door. Behind it, a glow came from the ger Judyta and Ruth shared with some other slaves. The sound of music and women's laughter spilled out of several nearby gers. I tethered the horse to the wagon where our bundles were stored, grateful that he was such a biddable creature. He began nosing the ground for shreds of withered grass. I threw a blanket over him before pulling out the bundles and awkwardly fastening them around his neck with ropes. I dared not take a single saddlebag or a saddle. Anna and I would have to ride bareback until we found Selim's men. I crept into the dim ger, its hearth burning low.

"Anna, are you there?" Even my whisper sounded like a shout to me.

"Yes, Mistress, I'm ready," Anna whispered back. "I did just as you told me. I'm sorry to leave Ruth and Judyta. They were kind to me."

"Yes, but I cannot take you all. They'll be as surprised as the khan, and they're such good cooks that hopefully he won't harm them. We must act quickly now. Find everything you can that might burn easily and bring it here." I pointed to the low divan.

I began by stacking dung on it, a perfect symbol of my disgust for that old dung heap Batu Khan. Anna caught my spirit and joined in gleefully. Next we piled on sheets of oily felt, fabrics, lacquered chests, even wooden bowls. I threw a small carpet on the stack, recalling how Qabul had once set fire to one in my ger. Perhaps this one would burn the entire tent down! Then I tore all the pages from the other book the khan had given me and crumpled them on the heap. I even seized his casket of riches and dumped it on the mess, sending a cascade of gems, pearls, and golden coins rolling in all directions.

"Mistress," Anna was aghast. "What are you doing? Let's take those and be rich!"

I smiled, feeling a fierce joy surge through my body. "Take them if you wish. I want none of them. They're a whore's payment! I have my own riches."

While she groped on the floor for gems, I set a circle of beeswax candles on top of the heap and lit them. They would take awhile to burn down, and hopefully at least one would set fire to that oily mess. I laughed to myself. Well, Batu had wanted to see my fire! It would look as if Anna and I had burned to death, but I almost hoped the pile would not catch, because if the candles didn't work I had another plan, a little warning note from his shamanka written on the Khan's own paper and placed on top of the heap. I hoped it would frighten him enough to keep him from searching for me.

I remember exactly what it said: 'Batu Khan, be warned! Tengri is watching you. Mend your ways, for this is what all worldly goods come to one day.' I signed it, 'Sofia, Tengri's emissary.'

How foolish I was, given how fragile our chances were for a clean escape.

The camp was growing quieter. I stared at the heap, at the burning candles. A fitting end to my life among the Mongols, who had burned and destroyed half the world! Then I remembered the nightingales. I was like a bird about to fly away myself and without a trace, too, if all went well, but they would not survive the cold if I freed them. I wrapped their cage carefully and set them inside one of the wagons where they would be both warm and easily found.

Last, I took the remaining book and writing tools Batu Khan had given me and packed them with Papa's book. I would finish my story and give it to someone who could benefit from it.

We slipped out of the ger. I so regretted leaving Little Liubyna, who had served me well, but I knew she at least wouldn't be mistreated. What might happen to Judyta and Ruth was more worrisome. And I was sorry I could not say goodbye to Toramun, who had been such a good friend to me. I had seen nothing of her since becoming Batu's concubine.

"Lead the horse, Anna. We walk for now, toward the southeast end of camp."

We silently crept through the camp, always heading south and east, until we could skirt the edge of the ordu. Whenever we came across a guard, we stopped and bowed humbly and were told to move on quickly. None questioned the presence of two lowly slave women and a burdened old horse. Batu had already killed all his enemies.

As camp noises gradually faded behind us and the darkness turned to pitch, Anna and I mounted our horse. It was too dark at first to see where we were headed, but the ground was level. As long as the ordu campfires were behind us and we could hear the river on our left, we would be going in the right direction. By morning we'd be far enough away that I could begin following the map Selim had left me. At first I looked back often, but soon the fires were hidden behind the grasses and the ordu became only a denser blackness against the dark horizon, a place where there were no stars.

I knew I was courting death fleeing like that, but a life serving Batu Khan seemed worse: perhaps ending up as just another slave, forced to serve some new favorite concubine; or sent back to the translators' ger to face years of loneliness. Or given away on the spur of the moment and left at the mercy of some other Mongol lord's lust until I was too old and only fit to become another painted whore. And as to danger, I also knew that life is always uncertain.

But we would never be far from the Volga, so there was little chance of getting lost. We were just like peddlers and other lone travelers wandering from one town to another. The distance might be greater for us, but the risks seemed the same.

Certainly that night was encouraging. The faint sound of the river to our east guided us until a crescent moon rose, allowing us to see a little better. And we soon found a shallow, south-flowing brook wide enough for our horse to use as a watery road. With luck we might leave little trace of our passage. All night we let the horse walk slowly, brushing through marsh grasses that grew stiff with frost and listening to the stream's icy skin crackling under his hooves. Selim's note and map had assured me that the great Caspian Sea lay but a few days' walk ahead. I imagined it, beckoning to us. Finally a dense night mist rose up from the river and spread a damp blanket over us. Thanks to the tuman, the "thick mist" of Rus', we would win free of Batu Khan's tumans!

Anna and I had to change streams twice that night when the watercourses we followed grew wider and deeper and boggier, forcing us to retrace our path. Yet I felt undaunted. Sunrise found us in a meadow filled with marsh reeds taller than a man's head. Despite the damp ground I decided we must stop and rest, as we were both chilled and weary.

"You lie down and rest for a while, Anna. I'll keep guard," I said. After a brief prayer, she lay down on an oiled felt blanket and curled up under the quilts I had brought. She was soon sound asleep. But while I kept watch, enclosed by reeds and unable to see around, worry assailed me. If my ger had not burned down, how easily the khan's men could find us. At least it might take time for Batu to learn I was gone; unlikely that someone would send him word. I was only a concubine, and my strange disappearance might frighten his servants into waiting until he returned. But now I regretted that childish note, not to mention that heap of dung and jewels! They might frighten the khan … but they might also anger him!

Good God, even if my ger had burned down, those songbirds I had saved would betray me! Wearying of endless inner babble, I decided to sit and practice peace as Dorje had taught me. At first I could only feel how foolish I had been, but slowly my thoughts settled into quiet murmurs. As the mists vanished and the sun rose into the sky, all was so still and serene. A deep stillness rose in me, and not only peace but a certainty that went beyond words: one day I would greet my uncle.

I didn't allow Anna to sleep long, having decided it was better to travel during daylight than to wander into any more bogs in the dark. We fled southwest across marshlands, never straying too far from the westernmost rib of the Volga. In its approach to the Caspian Sea, the huge river seemed to break into separate courses that spread out like the intertwining branches of a tree. Selim's map provided only a few landmarks: a huge rocky outcrop, a lightning-blasted tree. But often, fearing we would become mired in the mud, we had to circle around great stretches of sodden swamp. I never spoke of it to Anna, but whenever the guiding whisper of the river stopped, my heart scarcely beat for fear we might roam too far away and be lost. Our horse bore us steadily and without complaint. We called him Freedom. To spare him we took turns walking some of the time.

The first two days of our journey passed without problem, although one night I saw a rusalka's cold globe of light appear and disappear over a stretch of swamp near our camp. I crossed myself and prayed, and it never came near us. But on the third day, bitter autumn rain swept over us, chilling us to the core. "I'm so cold, Mistress," was Anna's endless refrain as she clung to my back and I clung to Freedom's mane.

"Rain is good, Anna. It's not as cold as snow, and it blots out signs of our passage. Hold tighter around my waist and keep your hood well over your head. Press against my back and use me as your shield," I told her, secretly wishing I had a shield of my own.

But that night I dared not light a fire, even though mists swirled around us, rain pelted us like tiny darts, and we were bitterly cold. Instead, we burrowed like rabbits under our felt quilts. When those failed to warm us, we huddled together, both for warmth and for comfort. Several times I startled awake, once when a fox trotted right by us through the reeds and once when a mouse shrieked as it was carried off by a night bird. But I took both events as good signs. When the natural world paid us no heed, surely not even a Mongol tracker would find us.

The next day, although we grew ever wearier as we struggled onward, I still felt hopeful. Freedom tramped tirelessly through the marshes and along trickling streams where tall reeds often cut off any view of where we were going. Sometimes when the rain and mist threatened to overwhelm us with despair and Anna would complain, I would say, "Remember, freedom lies only a little bit ahead, perhaps around the next bend of the river or just beyond this wall of grass." And attempting to lift her spirits, I once added, "We're riding Freedom to freedom!" She laughed a little, but *my* courage was beginning to fail.

Late one day, the rain turned to snow. Because we had been forced to avoid yet another marsh, we could no longer hear the Volga. When it got too dark to see, we gave up and stopped for the night. The next morning we awoke, wrapped in each other's arms and stiff with cold, to a world turned white. With snow blowing past us, we could see no more than a few feet in any direction. I could not tell which way was east.

Anna turned to me with that trusting look and said, "Well, we've washed our faces in the first snow, so now we'll be beautiful. Which way do we go?"

How did she come up with these things at such odd times? At least surprise helped keep fear from my voice. "We'll have to wait until the sun rises higher, Anna. Perhaps the snow will stop soon, and then I can decide. Meanwhile I think we should drink some arki to warm ourselves." We shared half a flask and ate some dried meat. But although the snow did stop, the light seemed to come from everywhere. Afraid to linger there and freeze to death, I decided that we would try to keep the wind at our backs. With a silent prayer, I pointed our horse toward what I hoped was south. For the first time, I truly saw how easily we might become lost and perish in that lonely wilderness. I felt sick at heart.

We drove our poor beast forward, constantly looking behind us to test if we were moving straight ahead. As the sun rose higher, the clouds slowly began to thin until I could see her through them, a disk as pale as the moon. Finally the Volga began to sing again to our left, muted but clear.

I breathed a prayer of thanks and half-turned toward Anna, exclaiming, "We are traveling in the right direction. I only wish we could find a new stream to guide us. Perhaps we should stop and rest Freedom—" when our mount plunged through thin ice up to his knees and both Anna and I tumbled shrieking into icy water! Our clothing, our bedding, even our food spilled after us. The water was so cold that it burned. We pulled ourselves out easily enough, but we were drenched and cold as ice, and so was poor Freedom, though we rubbed him down with the blanket we had been riding on—it hadn't gotten wet, at least. But we could not dry our clothes.

"We must light a fire or risk freezing to death," I decided. "If the Mongols catch us, so be it!" Anna looked frightened, but she helped me clear a small space and shake the snow off some brittle brush and dead grasses that might burn. I had brought a little tinderbox and several bundles of kindling sealed in watertight packets, but try as I might, I could start no more than a plume of smoke. Finally Anna gently took the tinderbox from me.

"Let me do it, mistress. My mother always told me I was the best fire builder in our family." After crossing herself and whispering a charm, she coaxed a little fire into being. She seemed to have some deep link with it, for I had never seen her so confident. At last she built a crackling blaze that gave us far too little comfort for the amount of telltale smoke it made. At least by constantly tending it, we warmed ourselves slightly and partly dried our coats and mittens, though we still felt as clammy as mud. We drank the rest of the arki and continued our journey. I at least felt utterly discouraged.

As the day drew on, the snow on the ground grew thinner and patchier until we had mostly left it behind. Late that afternoon the sun broke through the clouds, and near sunset we sighted another of the signs on our map. We were not lost, even if we were cold beyond belief. Yet the immensity of the challenge we faced pressed on me like a great unseen hand. Batu's trackers might be right behind us, or the elements could undo us. But it was far too late to turn back now.

By nightfall of the next day, we were both utterly worn out, although we had passed the last major sign on Selim's map. We scarcely had energy to set out our felt sheets and wrap ourselves in our damp quilts. "I must watch first tonight, Mistress," Anna insisted. "You always stay up longer than I do, and you need to sleep." I tried to protest, but she said, "No, you're chilled to the bone. If you fall ill or get lost because you didn't rest, we'll both die. You lie in my arms to keep warm." I nodded, sank into her arms, and fell asleep.

It seemed as if I had only slept a few moments when I startled awake to a night darker than pitch. A spill of stars beyond the scattered clouds gave the only light. Anna was nestled next to me asleep, but a noise had wakened me. I heard it again: Freedom snorting and tugging at his tether—I had tied his reins loosely to a tangle of reeds.

A nearby howl almost stopped my heart: a wolf. No, I realized, several wolves were calling to each other. Terror rolled over me like dark mist, and I lay unable to think or move. A few feet away, Freedom reared and whinnied in alarm. He would lead the wolves straight to us! Suddenly with a terrified bellow, he wrenched the reins free and galloped away. The cries of the wolves faded after him. I heard a distant horrible bray and then silence.

The wolves never knew we were there. Still, I spent the rest of the night stiff with fear, never knowing if they might come back and discover us. Just as dawn broke, a fatalistic peace stole over me. My destiny, whatever it might be, had never been in my hands. I must trust in God's mercy—had He not loosened His grip on me already?

As the sun rose over the misty plain, I woke Anna. "Visitors came last night and exchanged Freedom for our freedom. We must walk the rest of the way."

She stretched and sneezed. "What a strange bargain."

We had walked for half the morning before she awoke enough to wonder what kind of visitors could have visited in the middle of the night. "Spirits, Anna," I told her. "Good ones and bad ones. The good ones protected us from the bad ones, and they took our horse as payment. But tonight I keep watch first."

She fervently crossed herself and gripped her amulet. "I'm sorry I fell asleep."

"I am not. I'm very, very glad," I answered with complete truth. Had she awakened and cried out, she might have drawn the wolves to us before our horse ran away.

That night I scarcely slept, my fear of wolves was so deep. Yet as dawn spread glory across the sky, I laughed aloud. "Anna, wake up. We're almost there. I can feel it!"

Before the sun had reached her zenith, the faint melody of a flute drifted toward us. It seemed to defy the empty wilderness around us, to call us forward into hope. We followed it; it grew stronger and was joined by another sound as soft as wind, as gritty as sand, as rhythmic as breathing. Ahead stood a dead tree, surrounded by bracken, tiny streams, and low sand dunes. Beyond it lay the sea. Three men sat under it, two horses and three mules tethered nearby. As we approached, one of them stood and waved.

"Anna, there is Nasr, Selim's servant. We've done it!" We burst into tears and embraced each other, and then we fell on our knees to thank God. And my special prayer was thanks for the gift of Anna. Had I tried to flee by myself, I'd have turned back in despair on the first night. Needing to take care of her had given me the courage to go on. And in turn, this simple peasant girl had saved both our lives when I couldn't light a fire. She *did* know things. I have always held her in gratitude for that, even to naming my beloved daughter after her.

And our reward was hot food, hot water, and Nasr's friendly chatter, all balms to my soul. Although all three avoided looking directly at us, Nasr presented Anna and me to the others: a handsome young man named Ali and an older man, Da'ud, who was their leader.

Da'ud explained that they had parted from Selim al-Din's caravan on the main route some two weeks earlier and then turned east, following the shore of the Caspian to arrive here. After awaiting us for many days, they had thought to leave the next morning.

When Nasr asked about our escape, I gladly shared the whole story. The boys laughed so hard at my ger-and-fire ruse that I decided I had been brilliant after all. And they reacted with gratifying alarm to my tale of the spirit battle.

After our meal, Da'ud pointed out a bundle of clothing. "From my master, Selim al-Din."

"Many thanks." I eyed it, wondering how Anna and I were to change clothes in front of strange men. But at a sign from Da'ud, the three men gallantly wandered away into the marsh grasses to examine nothing in particular.

"Here, Anna. Put these on." We hastily transformed ourselves, we thought, into Persian boys, though our clumsy attempts to wind dulbands around our caps made us laugh. But then I felt rather shocked, for do not the Holy Fathers forbid wearing the garments of the opposite sex? I had once condemned the Mongols for that very thing, and now I was the offender. Well, in our present need, surely we could be forgiven.

We gathered up our oily Mongol clothing and fed it to the campfire. "I hope our ger caught fire as easily as these did," I said.

When they returned, Nasr raised his eyebrows in surprise at our garb. "Taqqiya?" he breathed to Ali, who nodded and gave a half-laugh. I had never heard that word before.

"Your dulbands are all wrong. We need not even look at you to see that! Here, watch how we do it." Learning how to wind a dulband, I forgot to ask what taqqiya meant.

It quickly became clear that unless Anna and I cut our hair, we would never be able to do it correctly. So while Nasr and Ali packed up their remaining belongings and Da'ud destroyed the traces of the campfire, she and I made our way to the narrow beach. We stared in awe at the great Caspian Sea, larger than anything I had ever imagined in my childhood, as wide as the steppes and, like them, reaching out until it met the dome of the sky. How huge, how magnificent the world was!

Da'ud approached, leading his horse and mine. "We must go, Lady. Today and tomorrow we ride below the tide line to cover our tracks; though if anyone pursues you, they'll first follow your horse's tracks until they disappear into the spirit world. We head west and then south, to my home."

Home. Someday I too would find home!

"First we must cut off our hair." I began slicing off Anna's with my eating knife, and while I worked I realized something else. I was not simply entering a new life, I was about to become an entirely new person. My future suddenly glowed with possibilities! I looked out at that endless bounty of water, and my heart swelled with wonder and gratitude. I felt as if a great well of vitality and purpose had always been there that I might always draw upon. God no longer gripped me; I was resting in His hand.

I gave Anna the knife and she sawed steadily until my braid fell off and lay in her grip like a dead snake. My head felt light enough to float away. I hadn't realized that it had been hurting dully for years. She handed the heavy, greasy braid to me, and I stared at that symbol of sorrow and oppression for a moment. Coiling it around a rock as large as a man's fist, I flung it as far as I could into the lapping waves of the Caspian Sea and watched it sink out of sight.

"With this, I vow to begin a new life," I said. And that vow I kept—or it kept me.

Look for Volume Two of The Tiger and the Dove

SOLOMON'S BRIDE

In light of what came later, I sometimes wondered if escaping Batu Khan was such a miracle after all, although it seemed so after that dangerous flight across an unknown wilderness. Thinking I was free from the Mongols forever, I felt such joy that I almost cried my thanks aloud. But how could mere words express my gratitude to this God-beyond-idea, my awe at the wondrous new world of possibilities that lay before me, my hopes for a speedy reunion with my uncle? Everything seemed to have fallen into place, from my having taken my fellow slave Anna with me to our having met up with our guides before they gave up and left without us. Without Anna, I would never have succeeded. Her trust in me had driven me onward. Without her, too, I'd have perished in the wilderness, for she could light a fire when I could not.

And now here we were, all the way to the Caspian Sea and among friends, or at least trustworthy guides.

How naïve I was. We were plunging into an alien world led by three strange men of a different faith! And I was a little taken aback when we stopped after only a few miles of travel. It was beside a stream flowing into the Caspian, so at first I thought that our guides wanted to water the horses and mules.

But after briefly seeing to the animals, they proceeded to their real business. Having washed their faces, hands, forearms and feet in icy water, spread out small carpets in the same direction, and placed some kind of packet at one end, they began to chant softly, each before his carpet, and to bow, kneel, prostrate, and touch his head on the packet three times. Anna and I stared in shock.

"Do they worship demons?" She was clutching her amulet tightly.

"No, I understand their words," I said after listening carefully. "They submit and offer thanks to our shared God."

"But it looks like they're worshiping demons or something."

I smiled. "It's just a different way of praying."

"Well, it's not Christian!"

"Hmm. But you are a Christian and you don't pray to demons when you rely on your amulet, do you?" Her eyes widened and she shook her head no.

Yet I too felt uneasy, for they had entered their world of worship and closed an invisible door behind them without a word to us. I could only assure myself that my good friend Selim al-Din, merchant and fellow-conspirator, had chosen them to take me into Persia and that I already slightly knew Nasr, who had brought Selim's map to me back in Batu's ordu. I had no choice but to trust them now, anyway.

The rest of the day passed mostly in silence, except for two more stops for prayers. I soon recovered my happy mood. A guardian angel was surely watching over us, for the Mongols had not found me! Of course my escape might have pricked Batu Khan's pride, and his warriors might still be searching for me, but he did have so many slave concubines that he might not care if I disappeared.

So when the sun lifted her veil of clouds, tinting the Caspian a deeper blue than the sky itself, my heart soared. I had always wanted to visit a real sea and there it was, vaster and more vivid than I had ever imagined, with waves rippling as gracefully as steppe grasses. Once when a bird glided past us and skimmed over the sea's sparkling surface, the fellow named Ali began a rather flowery poem. But Nasr quickly threw in a silly line that made Ali and me laugh. Our leader Da'ud, however, pointedly did not, and the boys quieted down straightaway.

That evening I studied them while they set up camp in the creeping gloom. Nasr and Ali were clearly bosom friends. Both were perhaps eighteen, dark-eyed and dark-haired. But while Ali's sad eyes and noble profile were beautiful, Nasr's single heavy slash of eyebrow, flat nose, and too-full lips made for mere homeliness. Da'ud was a mountain of a man. Only his gray hair and stern dignity betrayed his age. His nature was like a mountain, too, as I was soon to discover: his surface might change in sunlight or rain, but not his solid core.

I was warming my hands at the fire when he sat down near me after their final prayers. Looking into it, he said, "I am a man of few graces, Lady Sofia, so I speak bluntly. We obey Master Selim al-Din without question. I am your father on this journey, and I protect you with my life. But like all good fathers, I expect you and your servant to obey me without question."

Recalling Captain Oleg and my other lost companions, and how much harm I had caused by insisting on my superior status as his princess, I nodded. Nor could I reasonably take offense that he merely called me 'Lady' since I had not truly been a princess for years. Lady would be a good title for me now. But when Da'ud would not look toward me, and I had to add, "Yes," my pride was pricked further, so I decided to seize the moment. "But may I ask you something?"

He did not look pleased, but he nodded.

"I am unfamiliar with your religion. Will you tell me about your way of praying?"

My question seemed to surprise him. "The Prophet, Allah's Peace upon him, taught us to rely on five great pillars of faith. One of them is to submit body and heart in prayer to Allah the All-Compassionate five times a day when we can. Today we also thanked Him for liberating you from those heathen idol-worshippers. You should offer prayers of gratitude to Him, too."

I tried not to heed the prick of judgment in Da'ud's voice. I had been giving silent thanks all day! I thanked him politely.

"And *I* have more to say," he added sternly. "We will follow the Caspian shore for many days, since few merchants come this way; remote fishing hamlets do not interest them. But if we do meet anyone, your clothing masks you poorly. You two must behave more like boys and look less like women. In the morning you must wrap your—upper bodies—with lengths of cloth to make you look more boyish. And Master Selim says your servant must act as a mute, as she speaks no Farsi. Go tell her now." He rose and left.

Though I did not like his curtness, I did as I was bidden. Happily, Anna was only too glad to agree when I explained that her disguise would protect us further. "I have nothing to say to infidel strangers, anyway," she shrugged.

"Well, speaking of differing faiths," I answered a little tartly, "we are in their world now. You can pray silently, but you must never cross yourself or touch your amulet, or you will betray yourself. In fact I think I should tie it around your arm right now."

She gripped her amulet fearfully, but seeing my frown, she nodded. "If I must." And while I was tying it for her, "Mistress, why don't they pray the right way, like we do? They must be mad." I shrugged and said nothing; she was, after all, only thirteen at most and but a simple peasant. Then I had to laugh at myself. I was how old now—fifteen? Well, that made all the difference. I was a woman now, while she was still a girl, at least to me.

That night she and I huddled together for comfort in a small tent. At one point I started awake from a deep sleep. Anna was sitting up and coughing. She assured me it was nothing, and I fell back to sleep.

I awoke early the next morning to what I thought at first was the whistling of a Mongol arrow. I sat up, terrified, and realized it was only the wind shrilling through the tent ropes. A storm was blowing in from the sea, and by the time we broke camp, fat dark clouds were dumping sleet on us. But I was determined to believe in my happy fate, and surely bad weather was a blessing sent to cover any trace of our flight.

Over the next two days, we pushed south against rain, sleet, and fog. Once we had to ride inland to avoid a fishing village, but mostly we simply followed the shore so that our tracks would wash away. Our guides were courteous enough, but they clearly thought of us less as people than as valuable merchandise to be handled carefully and delivered in good condition. I think they knew no more how to act toward us than we did toward them.

It was partly because we dressed as men. That was also why Nasr and Ali thought we were practicing taqqiya, which I later learned means to avoid religious persecution by dissembling in some way. Since I was somehow serving their cause, wearing men's attire was permitted.

Yet—I pieced all this together later—many Muslims welcome what they call martyrdom when they choose the time and place.

Over the next day or so, though the men rarely talked with Anna and me, Nasr was full of jests that Ali and I delighted in, but which Da'ud seemed to scorn and Anna could not understand. At night with the weather so bad, we ate quickly in silence before she and I curled up together in our tent and they went in theirs.

Her cough was no better, but she was as warming as a little fire. I often awoke during the night, partly from her coughing and partly from unease, and cradling her in my arms kept me from falling into some pit of anxiety. I must keep up my spirit in order to keep up hers. She deserved that.

We'd have maintained our rapid pace, but one morning Anna coughed so hard that she almost fell from her saddle. We reined in at once. The two boys awkwardly helped her off her horse and laid her on a saddle blanket on the ground. I hastily wrapped her in my own cape. Her eyes were too bright and her skin too pale, and when I felt her forehead it was on fire. With none of my familiar remedies at hand, panic stole my very breath.

But Da'ud was already sending Nasr to find wormwood among the bracken and Ali to bring him water from a nearby stream. After giving me some more blankets and saying, "Put your cloak back on or you will freeze," he built a small fire and pulled out his cooking pot, as well as a piece of dried willow bark from his pack. When the boys returned with water and wormwood, he boiled the water and made a tea.

Meanwhile, all I could think to do was to chafe Anna's hands. At one point, I cried, "I should have seen … we should have stopped for you…"

"No, no, I didn't want to slow you down, Mistress. I thought I would get better. But now I hurt everywhere—oh, please don't let me die!" She burst into tears.

"You'll not die, Anna. I will take care of you," I said. But it took almost all my powers of command even to coax her into slowly drinking Da'ud's bitter brew. And in truth, I was afraid for us all.

Da'ud and the boys, meanwhile, had been standing apart and speaking in low tones. Now he came and knelt beside me. "Come aside; I must talk to you." He led me away from Anna and spoke softly, "There is a fishing village a little further on from here. I meant to pass it by, but your servant will die if we do not take shelter. I know someone there who will take us in. He is one of us. Nasr, if you permit him, can carry her before him while Ali takes her mule."

"Yes, please!" I could not hold back my tears. I turned away so no one would see.

We were soon on our way again, Anna so wrapped in blankets that only her face showed, her head bobbing against Nasr's chest. He had wrapped a white scarf around his nose and mouth, making him look like some ghost carrying her off into death. And having been without my cloak, even for that short time, I was chilled to my bones. After an endless struggle against walls of sleet, we finally came upon a huddle of tiny dwellings, a decrepit pile of fishing tackle, and a few boats turned upside down on the shore.

Da'ud stopped at one of the hovels and pounded on its door; when it did not open at once, he beat on it again. Finally a man as worn and gray as old wood opened it. Scarcely raising his eyebrows, he motioned us into a small, dark, bare room. A fire in a round central hearth provided warmth and smoke in equal amounts. A few threadbare carpets on the dirt floor kept it from total desolation. Two boys sat together on one side of the fire mending fishing nets. A woman on the other side quickly drew a veil before her face. She looked far too old to be bearing children, yet a thin-cheeked baby pulled from her nipple to stare at us with hollow eyes. A girl of perhaps ten was spinning beside her, and a loom in one corner held a partly-finished carpet.

Da'ud spoke in an unfamiliar language, perhaps explaining our needs, for when Nasr set Anna down near the young-old mother, she signed to her daughter, who dropped her spindle and distaff and took the tiny burden from her mother. It began to cry feebly. Da'ud vanished outside with the boys, saying they would tend our animals.

When I sat down beside Anna and began removing her dulband and cloak, the woman gently motioned me aside, felt my servant's forehead, and shook her head in dismay. After handing me a bowl of cold water and a worn rag for bathing Anna's face, she silently prepared a meager repast of hot water, flat bread, and dried salted fish. The girl stared at us and bounced the fretful baby.

When the men returned, Nasr and Ali brought in not only Da'ud's medicines but also, to my relief, some of our food. I'd have felt like a thief taking bread from the mouths of such poor people! While Da'ud sat near the fire and talked, the old man went back to mending his fishing net. It seemed to hold all his interest. Indeed, none of these weather-beaten folk seemed to feel much curiosity. If the man now knew we were fleeing the Mongols, then I hoped he truly was "one of us" and could also hold his tongue if they came looking for us.

We spent the rest of the day in semi-darkness and silence but for the rustling nets or crackling fire, or cries from the baby and Anna. Though I kept bathing her face and hands and feeding her the broth, she seemed on fire. I held her hand when she would let me. When dark came, the men set up a dividing curtain—so like the Mongols!—and those who could went to sleep. I stayed up with Anna, dozing in fits.

I awoke the next morning with a huge sneeze, feeling as if a cat had scratched my throat. But Anna needed me. She groaned and tossed endlessly, thrusting off the blankets crying she was too hot or wailing that she was freezing and wanting them back. The fisher family had gone back to their silent tasks as if we were not there. Da'ud and his boys came in and out but mostly sat staring at the fire. Only prayers and meals broke the tedium.

By nightfall Anna no longer knew who I was. When I tried to help, she pushed me away. Again and again she croaked, "No, no! Please stop! Let go! It hurts so!"

Another night passed. Anna thrashed about and wept, and I prayed. I began to cough, too. My throat felt as raw as if scraped by a file, while some invisible brute had crept inside my skull and was battering it with an iron bar. My whole body began to ache. When I tried to stand the next morning and nearly fell, I finally had to admit that I was ill, too. Da'ud and his boys started up in alarm. He spoke, and the old-young mother came over, almost pushed me down next to Anna, felt my forehead, and gave me some willow and wormwood broth.

"Don't come near," I cried, "the fever might spread to you or your baby!" But she simply covered me with my camping blankets.

"Lady, you must rest," Da'ud ordered me. "Stop fighting her." I gave up and drifted off to sleep, but coughing fits kept waking me. By the next morning I was unable to rise, and by afternoon I had fallen into a nightmare that repeated itself endlessly: howling Mongol wolf-demons pursued me through icy rivers, between fiery piles of beheaded bodies, thrusting spears into my throat or beating my head with clubs while the cries of living corpses rang in my ears. I looked back and there was Batu Khan, a wolf grin on his face and fiery rage crackling in his eyes.

Once I thought I heard Da'ud say, "She is dead. There was nothing anyone could do. May All-Merciful Allah take her to his bosom and grant her eternal peace."

"Who died? Anna? The mother? Me?" I thought I spoke aloud, but no one answered and I sank back into painful dreams.

When I finally truly awoke, it still seemed to be dusk. Anna was sitting next to me, drinking a fishy smelling broth and looking wan and afraid, but when she saw me open my eyes, she smiled in delight. I was so happy to see her alive!

"Praise God," she said. "I thought you lost." And she burst into tears.

That seemed strange. I surely hadn't been asleep for long if it was still afternoon. Da'ud rose from beside the fire and came to my side, the usual looking ban forgotten in his joy. "Praise Allah's unfailing Mercy! Fever stole your mind for three days!"

"I thought it was still the same day," I croaked. I tried to sit up but could not. The mother appeared by my side, looking even older than I remembered, with a steaming bowl of fish broth. She helped me drink it. My throat still hurt, but I could swallow.

Anna said, "I was ill, too. I fell into a dark pit of dreams. Dogs were howling and trying to bite me, sure signs of bad luck and death. I awoke last night, and you were out of your head. Where are we, Mistress? And who are these people? I don't understand their speech."

"We're in a fishing village, and they are friends. You were very ill and they took care of you. I'm glad you're alive, too." I was too weary to say more.

Da'ud spoke from far away. "You both must rest now. You'll be better soon."

I fell back into uneasy dreams. The next morning, I awoke to sunshine and bitter cold—someone had opened the door—but I felt much better. Blinding bright snow blanketed the world outside, and the sky was brilliant blue. The door shut again and Da'ud was crouched next to me on one side, Anna on the other; the daughter was sweeping the room while her mother sat at the loom. The other men and the little boys were gone.

"How do you feel?" he asked. "Can you sit?"

"I think so. I feel much better," I smiled.

Anna helped me up, her face lit with joy. How thin she was! "I am so glad, Mistress! Here is some bread and tea. They help."

As I slowly ate, I looked around the room. "Where is the baby?"

"Da'ud said, "With Merciful Allah. She was already sickly, and she caught the fever."

"Dear God, we killed her baby!" Tears sprang to my eyes.

Da'ud eyed me with alarm. "Lady, we were only fulfilling the plans of Allah the All-seeing. Our fates are subject to His will. Death took the child quickly."

That was no comfort whatever.

Rebecca Hazell is both author and artist. Her award-winning non-fiction books for older children have been purchased for distribution by Mercy-Corps and Scholastic Inc., and been published in Greek and Korean. She is passionate about history, both for its romance and for its value in understanding how we are always connected to and driven by the past. She has also written educational materials for high schools on such far-flung topics as Islam and Russian serfdom, produced award winning needlepoint designs, created science kits for children, and was a tailor and dressmaker/clothing designer in her youth. As well, she is a senior teacher in Shambhala International, a worldwide Buddhist organization. She has been married for forty years and has two grown children. For more information on Rebecca and her other works, both literary and artistic, please go to http://www.rebeccahazell.com.

42240157R00226

Made in the USA
Middletown, DE
05 April 2017